"Up-and-coming romance author Rebekah Millet shines in this delightful second-chance story. When an old flame re-enters a widow's life, she guards the heart he once shattered. But his charm and persistence soon have her grappling with forgiveness—and the chemistry that still sizzles between them. *Julia Monroe Begins Again* is a warm and witty tale that will grab you by the heart!"

—Denise Hunter, bestselling author of the
RIVERBEND ROMANCE series

"Smiles on every page! I loved that both characters were older than most heroes and heroines, loved Rebekah's kind and funny writer's voice, and loved taking a getaway to distinctive New Orleans via this novel. Ideal for Christian fiction readers who enjoy rom-coms!"

—Becky Wade, author of *Turn to Me*

"This is one of the most adorable debuts I've read in a long time. Millet has written an achingly sweet story about second chances and the beauty of how forgiveness creates freedom . . . and joy."

—Pepper Basham, award-winning author of
Authentically, Izzy

JULIA MONROE
BEGINS AGAIN

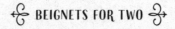

BEIGNETS FOR TWO

JULIA MONROE BEGINS AGAIN

REBEKAH MILLET

BETHANYHOUSE

a division of Baker Publishing Group
Minneapolis, Minnesota

Published by Bethany House Publishers
Minneapolis, Minnesota
www.bethanyhouse.com

Bethany House Publishers is a division of
Baker Publishing Group, Grand Rapids, Michigan

Printed in the United States of America

Library of Congress Cataloging-in-Publication Data
Names: Millet, Rebekah, author.
Title: Julia Monroe begins again / Rebekah Millet.
Description: Minneapolis : Bethany House Publishers, a division of Baker
    Publishing Group, [2023] | Series: Beignets for two
Identifiers: LCCN 2023012883 | ISBN 9780764240959 (paperback) | ISBN
    9780764242182 (casebound) | ISBN 9781493443703 (ebook)
Subjects: LCSH: Widows—Fiction. | New Orleans (La.)—Fiction. | LCGFT:
Romance fiction. | Novels.
Classification: LCC PS3613.I56265 J85 2023 | DDC 813/.6—dc23/eng/20230327
LC record available at https://lccn.loc.gov/2023012883

Author is represented by The Steve Laube Agency.

Baker Publishing Group publications use paper produced from sustainable forestry
practices and post-consumer waste whenever possible.

23 24 25 26 27 28 29   7 6 5 4 3 2 1

JESUS, THANK YOU FOR PLANTING THIS STORY
IN MY HEART AND KEEPING IT THERE,
EVEN WHEN IT WAS AGAINST THE ODDS.

1

IN HINDSIGHT, SCHEDULING MY FIRST routine mammogram on my fortieth birthday may not have been a wise choice.

I sat in the empty waiting room of the New Orleans Women's Clinic, clipboard on my lap and pen in my hand. A fountain wall dribbled to my left, trying to emit calmness and having the opposite effect on my bladder.

I sailed through the beginning of the patient form: name, birth date, address, The next section, though . . . My pulse slowed as I read the question of my relationship status. *Single* and *married* were the only options. Where was the *widowed* box? And why did they need to know this information? Did my marital situation really impact my breasts? Well, maybe it did. Today would be the first day in ten years my North American regions had seen this much action.

With the paperwork completed, my gaze swept the pamphlets on the end table. Colonoscopies and mammograms and colorectal screenings, oh my! Didn't they want women to willingly return to this place? There should be *People* magazines, a coffee bar, and one of those mall masseuses set up in the corner.

The fountain continued calling to my bladder as though it were the Pied Piper. I'd already scoped the reception area for a bathroom and had come up empty. Curse that café au lait I'd had on the drive here. Of course, that was what having two babies did to you.

My boys. The urge to text them distracted me from the call of nature and the impending doom of being squeezed like an orange in a juicer. My youngest had started his first year of college in North Carolina at the same university where my oldest was now a sophomore. They had each other and my in-laws, who lived fifteen minutes from the campus. Those two reasons, and the fact that they had full scholarships, made the distance between us somewhat bearable.

"Julia Monroe?" A nurse in pink scrubs stood next to the back door, a folder in her hands.

I pushed my self-dyed brown hair from my shoulder and grasped my purse.

"Are you a healthcare worker too?" She motioned to my black scrubs, ironically appropriate for today.

"Oh. No, I'm a maid."

She nodded. "I bet the last thing you want to do when you get home is clean."

If I had a dollar . . . A forced chuckle matched my smile.

⚬—⚬

"I can't believe you put Harry in mourning clothes." I shook my head at the life-sized Harry Connick Jr. cardboard cutout and my friend Kate Landry, who owned Beignets & Books. The eatery operated within a historic house handed down through her family. The tourist and local hotspot nestled on the edge of the neighborhood known as the Garden District. Each room on the first floor held dining tables and shelves brimming with well-loved books ready for perusal on everything New Orleans.

Kate, also dressed in black, took a seat across from me at the round table for three. "Since you wouldn't let me throw an official over-the-hill party, I had to make do." She set a plate of fresh beignets on the black tablecloth spread before us. Powdered sugar drifted from the dish, dotting the fabric. Matching streamers mummified our chairs.

"I'll be sure to return the favor when you hit forty."

"I plan to stay in my thirties forever." Kate rubbed her index finger between her brows, smoothing a crease she'd recently become obsessed with.

The rest of the establishment was empty of customers, Kate's business having closed half an hour ago. The murmur of voices, laughter, and dishes clattering drifted from the kitchen at the back. Smooth jazz music piped in through the speakers.

We were breaking the cardinal rule of not wearing black while eating these confectionary treats, but considering the occasion, spilled powdered-sugar stains could be overlooked. I sank my teeth into a puffy square-shaped pastry. Soft sugar dusted the crispy outside, giving way to a melt-in-your-mouth tender middle. This week's food cheat had been worth the wait.

Kate's sideswept auburn bangs cascaded over one eye. "Do you know what I realized today?"

"That you need to get Harry a kilt for when St. Patrick's Day rolls around?"

A smile unfurled, bringing a sparkle to her blue eyes. Grabbing a packet of raw cane sugar, she ripped the paper and added the crystals to her mug. "Other than that."

"What?"

"With the boys gone, it's like you're really single again."

"I've been single for a decade." I placed the last bite of beignet into my mouth and sagged back in my chair in ecstasy.

"I know that." She poured decaf coffee from a French press, stirred her brew, and rested the spoon on her saucer. "But now you don't have the boys to take care of or to keep you from going out. Have you thought about dating again?"

"Have you?" I boomeranged the question, raising my brows for good measure.

Kate tucked her bobbed hair behind her ear. "What about Hayley?" She had adopted her niece when her sister had died around the same time as my husband.

"She's eleven with internet access. I think she knows adults date. Where is she anyway?"

"Spending the weekend with my parents. And nice try, but I know you're *stal-ling*." Kate sang the last word.

Grumble, grumble. My attention wandered past Harry's soulful eyes and beyond the front windows. Lampposts dimly lit the neutral ground of St. Charles Avenue, and a streetcar stuffed with passengers glided along its tracks. "Why would I want to pretend I don't belch or pass gas? Or worry about shaving my legs?"

"You shave your legs."

"Only for church and not in the winter." I raised my mug, eyes lifting to the ceiling. "Thank You, Lord, for knee-high boots."

"I'll toast to that." Kate lifted her cup too. "But I've read that people who had great marriages have a higher likelihood of happily remarrying." Her head tilted. "Is it because of Mark?"

"No." A feeling of sorrow descended, having nothing to do with the mentioning of my departed husband's name. Time, counseling, and God had shepherded me and my boys through our abrupt loss via a car accident. "Mark would've wanted me to move on."

I busied myself with pouring coffee I had no interest in drinking. If there was one thing life had taught me, it was that if you loved someone—one way or another—they could be taken from you, and I didn't have the strength to go through that kind of pain again.

2

"I THINK HENRY CAVILL JUST GOT SAVED or joined our church."

Kate's whispered words jarred me from my prayers during the invitational part of our service. She inclined her head to the altar of the large sanctuary while the congregation sang "I Have Decided to Follow Jesus."

My gaze channeled on the back of a tall, broad-shouldered man. Recognition feathered my brain. Was he a former client? No, I'd remember a stature like that. And it wasn't only his physique that stole my admiration but how he carried himself. He oozed military. A thin leather strap ran along his shortly clipped brown hair. If this man was half as appealing from the front—*Ack!* I screwed my eyes shut. What was I doing? This was exactly why hot men should not be allowed in church, and unquestionably not in a pastoral role of any kind.

The guy turned, confirming the eye patch pulled flush against his face, and my feeling of recognition crystallized.

Samuel Reed.

One of my ankles caved, my heel slipping out from under me. I seized the seat-back before me, righting myself.

No. No way.

My instinct to haul butt was stopped by Samuel heading in the other direction through a side door with the pastor. They exited, all buddy-buddy, and my stomach dropped. Why was he in my church? How had he lost his eye? Had he seen me?

Kate nudged my arm. "Are you okay?"

I managed a nod. Intense warmth rushed my neck and face. Was I having my first hot flash? The blood thrashing in my ears muted the congregation's singing of the hymn's last verse.

The service concluded, and we poured into the modern welcome center, where members made their way to leave or stood in line for one of the coffee carts. My floral-print dress swished around my legs as I beelined for the exit. I faked smiles and good mornings to people, and prayed I wouldn't run into Samuel.

Maybe he was only traveling through town and wanted to ask the pastor to pray for him. Or douse him with holy water. Goodness knew he needed it.

I winced. Oh, how easy it was to slip into old judgmental ways.

Kate kept pace, which was a good thing since we'd driven together. "Why are you rushing out of here? Do you know the sexy pirate?"

I pushed through the glass doors, September's humidity drooping my hair. "Yes." I lowered my voice, the noonday sun beaming a spotlight on me. "I dated him before Mark."

"Whoa." Kate's steps slackened. She recovered, catching up quickly in her cute flats. "I thought I knew pretty much everything about you."

"You do." My throat constricted. "Mostly." Ten years ago, Kate and I had met and bonded at Grief Share, a group counseling program through our church. We'd been inseparable since. She certainly knew all my clean and dirty laundry from my marriage on—but before that, not so much.

"'Mostly' should include me knowing you went out with a Superman look-alike." Sass tinged her tone. "How long were y'all together?"

I rummaged through my purse as though a serial killer were

approaching. *Keys, keys, keys.* "Two years." My fingers stilled over my pepper spray. I paused. Glanced back at the building. *No.* It would definitely be frowned upon to assault someone at church. Even if they deserved it.

"Here." Kate handed me her Bible and took my handbag. "I don't think you should be driving." She swiftly located my keys and advanced on to the parking lot, she toting two purses, me carrying two Bibles and a crawfish sack of emotional baggage.

We slid into my old-but-trusty Toyota Highlander.

She fastened her seat belt and cranked the ignition. "I take it things didn't end well with the pirate."

I reached for the A/C, rotating the knob to full blast. "That would be correct. And his name is Samuel."

"Did he have both eyes when y'all were together?"

I clicked my seat belt into place. "Why would that matter?"

"It doesn't." Her voice pitched guiltily. "I'm just curious."

"Yes, he had both eyes." I grabbed my sunglasses, using them as a barrier from the sunshine and a shield in case Samuel happened to be leaving too.

The flawless azure sky stretched outside, contradictory to the storm clouds I imagined invading my soul. One glimpse of that man had thrown open a door to a past I had kept sealed for over twenty years. My head pounded with each heartbeat. I peered at Kate.

Her softening features displayed everything I needed to know. Her steady eye contact conveyed comfort and no intent to be intrusive. Even after our time in Grief Share had ended, we still clung to the cardinal rule of not pushing the other to talk about things we weren't ready to. But counseling had also taught me that sharing what I could helped lessen the anxiety load.

My breaths calmed. "We met my senior year of high school. I was working at Blockbuster, and he was a barista at a coffeehouse." I rotated my neck, easing the tension forming. "Or is it a baristo if it's a guy?"

She reversed from the parking space. "How old was he?"

"Twenty. He was attending Tulane, gorgeous, and had his own apartment. I was young and foolish, and fell for him hard."

Kate pulled from the lot, departing the church campus situated on the outskirts of the city. "What was your relationship like?"

Within seconds we accelerated onto the interstate. Vehicles zipped past us, but not even their speed rivaled my racing thoughts. Samuel was back. It seemed unfair to be blindsided. And in church no less. Shouldn't there be a commandment about that? Thou shalt not step foot inside thy ex's place of worship.

"Being with him was . . ." A cocktail of nostalgia and devastation swirled through me. My stare coasted from my beige heels to the Bibles on my lap. I flattened my hand on my leather-bound guidebook from God, as though I were being sworn in to testify. The truth, the whole truth, and nothing but the truth. "Being with him was exhilarating. Confusing. He had this wry sense of humor." My reflection in the side-view mirror revealed a small, traitorous smile had snuck into place. I sobered to a scowl. *Don't think of the good times.*

Kate flipped on the blinker and switched lanes. "Was he your first boyfriend?" Skyscrapers glinted in the sun to our left, the white, curved roof of the Superdome emerging. How could everything look so normal while a tornado spun in my mind, wreaking havoc?

"I'd gone on group dates or to school dances with other guys, but they weren't anything special." I bullied my cuticles with my thumbnail. "Looking back, the red flags were everywhere with Samuel. For a long time, I hid him from my mom and dad. But after I'd turned eighteen and things became . . ." I licked my dry lips, wishing for a sip of water and searching for the right PG-13 words to use. "After things became intimate between us, I told my parents about him. When it was all said and done, he had only come to my house once in the two years we were together. My parents were not fans."

Kate cringed.

I held up my hand. "Young and foolish."

We passed the millionth billboard for a personal injury attorney and took an off-ramp.

"A couple of months before I graduated, he told me he wasn't ready for a commitment."

"Oh no." Kate readjusted her grip on the steering wheel.

"Oh yes. He stopped calling and stopping by Blockbuster. I was miserable."

We made the familiar turn onto St. Charles Avenue. Old and new architecture surrounded us. Condo buildings, store strips boasting services from tattoos to pizza, and several boutique hotels.

"The summer after graduation, he randomly showed up at Blockbuster. He offered to show me around Tulane, where I'd be starting in the fall. For the first time, he said that he loved and missed me. I was ecstatic. The funk I'd been wallowing in vanished. I dove right back into it with him."

The smattering of live oak trees along the sidewalks grew thicker the closer we came to the Garden District and its beautifully kept historic homes. Kate swerved, avoiding one of the many potholes plaguing the city.

I clutched the bar above my door. "Every now and then, he'd say he wasn't ready to settle down." And every time it had been a bullet to the middle of my chest. "He'd pull away for a week or so."

"I don't know if this makes it easier, but his ring finger was bare."

"You noticed?"

"It's the first thing I look for on a guy." Kate's freckled nose wrinkled, and she continued on to Beignets & Books, which sat majestically with its white two-story columns and wraparound porches. It occupied a corner lot, enclosed by elegant iron rail-ings. She pulled down the side street and parked in the driveway at the back of the house and the private entrance to her residence on the second floor. "Did he say he was seeing other people?"

"No." I unbuckled, letting the seat belt sling back into place. "And I was so desperate, so sure he'd realize how great we were together, that I rolled with his not being ready, thinking I just had to be patient." My sight blurred on the gate to Kate's courtyard. Like the many naïve women before me, and all those who would come after, I had thought I could change a man. "Then out of nowhere, he dumped me." My ribs tightened, a shudder rolling through me. I couldn't permit myself to think about the details of that day, or the dark time that had followed, let alone reveal them to Kate. Not now.

She turned the A/C down and aimed the vents she could reach away from me. "Was that the last time you saw him?"

"Yes. Until today." I leaned against the door. My eyes burned with the tears I wouldn't allow to shed. "I hate who I was with him. How much of a doormat I was and how I left my relation-ship with the Lord behind during that time."

"You were young." Kate's cool hand rested on my shoulder. "And you returned to God."

She eased away, a crease between her brows and her teeth scraping at the red lipstick on her bottom lip. "Considering your reaction today, I think you may have some unresolved issues with him, which makes sense since he was your first great love."

"A great love? No." I reached for my door handle. "He was my worst love."

3

"*THAT OLD CRANK DOWN THE STREET* stole my newspaper again."
Mama's three-pack-a-day voice greeted me. Still in her bathrobe, she scowled out the front window of her house as I entered from the kitchen's side door. The air was thick with her
ire and Glade plug-ins that did nothing to mask the smell of
her addiction.

The fifteen-minute drive from Kate's had done little to dispel
the sensation that my world had been tipped slightly off its axis.
Hopefully this pit stop would return some normalcy.

"You brought my bulletin?" Mama's short gray hair poked
and swooshed in different directions, revealing she hadn't gotten
far in welcoming the day. If only I had adopted her example and
smacked my snooze button this morning. I could have avoided
all this—whatever it was—eroding my insides like I'd guzzled
a bottle of Tabasco.

"Well, hello to you too." I locked the screen door and opened
the kitchen door wide.

Her glare shifted to me. "My air conditioning!"

"My lungs!"

Mama's slim lips squished. The coffeemaker beeped, notifying us it had completed its job and calling an end to round one

of our match. She gave up her post at the window, the curtains falling back into place with her retreat. "That man's going on the list."

The list, a.k.a. a sheet of paper held to the refrigerator by an NRA magnet, listed her enemies. Enemy number one was Lillian Sherman, who had supposedly stepped on Mama's fingers during a Mardi Gras parade when she'd been reaching for a doubloon. When they were ten. Enemy number two was Benedict Arnold.

"You know, you could come to church." I hung my purse on the back of a dining chair at the small table in the breakfast nook.

She grunted. "It's too hard getting up in the morning."

"It wouldn't be if you weren't up all night watching the History Channel." I arched a brow at the remote sticking out of her pocket.

She shrugged a bony shoulder. "I can't help it." Moving past me, she headed for the kitchen. "Those documentaries suck me in."

My eyes itched to roll in their sockets. Seriously, how many times could one watch the life story of George Washington? I placed the handout on the peninsula counter between us. Although Mama had stopped attending after Daddy's death ages ago, she gobbled up the bulletin each week as though it were a tabloid. "Since you're not a morning person, there's a service on Saturday evenings." Which was something I'd have to consider for next weekend to avoid Samuel. Or totally chickening out and watching online. I could schlep on a robe like Mama and—*Oh wow.* Nope. I wasn't about to turn into my mother.

"Church on a Saturday would feel weird. Besides, they changed too much when they moved to that bigger location. It's too modern." She lifted the carafe toward me, silently offering.

I shook my head. "The early service is traditional. All the old hymns you love."

"The keyword there is *early*." She filled her *Blue Bloods* mug, the chicory scent drifting, then added sugar.

At some point our roles had reversed in getting the other to be more active faith-wise. I sighed, resting my elbows on the counter, kneading the back of my neck.

"You look a little anxious." Mama's gaze narrowed, those tiny slits of brown zeroing in on me. At once I was a teenager again and averting my eyes. Only this time I wasn't hiding the fact that I wasn't actually spending the night at my friend's house. "Everything okay? The boys?"

I straightened and turned. *Be cool. She doesn't need to know about Samuel.* "Conner and Mason are fine." I retrieved my phone and found the screen empty of any missed texts or calls from them. *Shocker.* "I talked to them last night." And that would be good enough for them for at least a week. *Those turkeys.*

Mama stirred her coffee and dropped the spoon in the sink with a clang. "I still don't like them being in a strange place so far away."

"It's not strange to them. They grew up with us enjoying summers in North Carolina. They've always loved it there."

"Your in-laws brainwashed them." She set her cup down, slid the bulletin closer, and reached into her non-remote robe pocket. Out came a once-white handkerchief and her glasses. I shuddered at the hankie that was probably older than me. She perched the glasses on the tip of her nose and began reading.

My attention wafted to my cellphone and the tracking app I'd become obsessed with. Ever since driving away from the boys at college last month, I'd inherited a heaviness that had settled on my rib cage, burrowing deeper each day. They knew about the app. It was a condition of me paying half of their phone bills. But if they knew how much time I spent zooming in on their pulsing points and seeing where they were, they'd be horrified. Our daily check-ins, initiated by me, had waned—begrudgingly on my side—to every other night once school had started. They were growing up and needed independence. This was a part of life. A very hard part for me that required baby steps. This app, I reasoned, was like a patch for smokers. Though that wasn't the best analogy in view of Mama's failed attempts with them. Of course, she never sincerely wanted to quit.

Mama scoffed. "Rita Johnson remarried." She shook her head. "People my age getting remarried is ridiculous."

"I think it's sweet."

She pulled a face and kept reading.

"There's nothing wrong with Mrs. Rita finding love again. Perhaps she's been lonely. Don't you ever get lonely?"

"Heck no. I enjoy my freedom." Mama tilted her face to the popcorn-textured ceiling. "And I'm still clinging to Matthew 22:30, that I won't be married in heaven."

A withered sigh escaped me. That hadn't been the first time Mama had made that declaration to God in my presence. I don't think she ever truly loved my dad. Marriage had been something she'd been expected to do in her day. Get married, have children, go to church every Sunday, eat black-eyed peas and cabbage every New Year's Day, and die wearing clean underwear.

I, on the other hand, had loved being married. Having a partner in the ups and downs, the security, not being the sole bearer of decisions and responsibilities . . . the intimacy.

"Hmpf." Mama continued her perusal of the church info. "Looks like some people got saved last week. A few new members too."

"Poop on a shoe sole," I muttered.

"Why are you cleaning-lady cursing?"

Crud. "No reason." Would Samuel be in next week's bulletin? Mama would have a stroke. Maybe he really had just gone up to ask for special prayer. People were always doing that. But what if that wasn't it? Had he publicly professed his faith in Jesus today? Goodness knew all things were possible with God.

"You're cracking your knuckles."

I froze.

Mama's head deliberately lowered, her gaze rising above her cheaters. "You sure nothing's happened?"

I think the man you hate, the man who broke my heart, stepped back into my world today. "Everything's fine."

⚶

The next week dragged by. Especially the quiet nights at home. With two teenagers and their friends, someone had always been coming and going. Not anymore. The heaviness weighing on my chest grew, and so did the data usage on my phone plan with checking the kids' locations. Thankfully, work consumed each day, and I clung to the routine of it. In the first year after Mark's death, I'd welcomed a job that hadn't necessitated a lot of concentration or interacting with people, since my clients were usually absent when I cleaned their homes.

But this past week, my mind had kept wandering to Samuel. Questions about his reappearance buzzed in my brain like a hive. Even my dreams included him. I would've much preferred the ones where I was trying to use the bathroom unsuccessfully. Or my teeth were crumbling from my mouth. No such luck.

I'd considered internet stalking him to relieve the relentless inquiries pestering me, but I'd been afraid if I searched him, he'd find out. Facebook would somehow tattle on me, and I wouldn't give him the satisfaction of knowing that I was thinking about him in any capacity.

Sunday morning I entered the church building on full alert,

as though I were Black Widow in an Avengers movie. Although in place of a leather bodysuit and kick-butt boots, I donned a feminine yellow sundress that ended midcalf with heeled sandals.

I had planned to stream the service while Kate attended in person to see if Samuel showed his irksome handsome face. But then Kate had called with the news that Hayley would be singing for the first time with the praise team during our service. I hadn't missed a single big moment for Hayley since she and Kate had come into my life, and I wasn't going to start now.

The ding of a new text sounded from my phone.

KATE
I'm already seated inside. No sign of him.

My shoulders eased. *Thank You, Lord.* I switched my cell to vibrate as another message hit.

KATE
But his name is listed in the bulletin. He joined
last week.

My steps fumbled to a halt, my stomach hardening as though I'd ingested a bowl of concrete for breakfast instead of oatmeal. *Think rationally.* This was a large church. My dental hygienist was a member, and I'd never seen her here. Samuel could be the same way. But the sense of foreboding persisted. I turned, scanning the area.

And there was Samuel, entering the building, his attention on his phone. He hadn't seen me.

Not yet.

I turned again. *Breathe.* Why couldn't I breathe? My gaze pinged everywhere for an escape. My options dwindled to three choices: a half-dead potted plant, the private room reserved for nursing mothers, or the sanctuary. I didn't think God would instantly grant me the miracle of being a wet nurse, so I hustled forward, accepted a bulletin from a deacon, and walked through the doors to the worship center. I took my normal seat next to Kate, feeling anything but.

From Kate's reaction to my face, I knew I needed to pull it together.

I tried for a calming breath, still finding my lungs out of order. "I saw him. In the foyer."

"Did he see you?"

"I don't think so."

She skimmed my locks from my roots to past my shoulder. "You flat ironed your hair." It wasn't a question, but her expression almost came off that way.

I had indeed flat ironed my hair. Samuel had always favored it naturally wavy. On the off chance he did show today, I wanted to send a silent message. I was different now. Was it a hassle fixing it this way? Absolutely. But every clamp and slide over each section of hair had felt like a jab at him. *Take that, Samuel!*

The praise team took the stage with a bright-eyed Hayley flanking them. *Oh, to be a preteen again without these complications.* She scanned the audience, her smile widening when she found us. We waved and shot her thumbs-ups. The orchestra began playing. Thankfully my legs still worked, and I stood with the rest of the congregation.

Pretending everything was fine was much harder once the singing was over and I didn't have Hayley to focus on. I couldn't shake the vibe that Samuel was watching me. *Absurd.* In the next hour, my panic morphed into irritation. I had never stewed in church before. But that's what I was doing. How dare Samuel join my place of worship! I mean, I was happy he'd been saved at some point, but why did he have to pick my church? This was my turf.

As the service concluded, my irritation edged back to panic

and the crushing need to flee. Once we were dismissed, I turned to Kate. "Tell Hayley I said she did amazing. I'll call you later."

I exited into the aisle and kept to a natural pace, reaching into my purse for my phone to use as a deterrent so no one would stop me to chitchat. I moved through the doors into the welcome center, and there, standing against the opposite wall, was Samuel.

His stare was already on me.

4

THIS MOMENT WAS AKIN to the time I'd been in white jeans, stuck on a broken-down streetcar, and my period had decided to start right then and there. My body stiffened, my mind reeling on adrenaline. Wrapping a cardigan around my hips wouldn't save me this time. The fire alarm on the wall to my left caught my attention, becoming a rational option with each pounding heartbeat. But I'd probably have a witness. I glimpsed back and sure enough, Samuel still watched me.

He wore a light blue oxford with gray slacks and an expression I'd never seen on him before. Uncertainty.

A single flutter released in my belly, and I instantly squashed it.

People filtered past me as though everything was fine and my world wasn't wobbling. I should've asked the infallible question, What would Jesus do? Instead, I substituted Black Widow. She'd whip out a dagger from her thigh sheath and hurl it at Samuel's chest. Considering I was dagger free, I started moving for the exit.

Samuel pushed from the wall, apparently not content with my decision of evasion.

I stilled. It seemed my legs had received a memo from my lungs and they were joining forces in a strike.

He stopped a respectable two feet before me, "Hi." The low rough timbre of his voice was like hearing a song for the first time in forever, releasing a flood of wistful memories.

My gaze lifted up, up, up, and settled on a face so familiar and yet different. Other than the patch, time had graced him with creases at his eye and mouth that only made him more attractive. So unfair. How was it that men grew more distinguished with age? No one ever mentioned how stunning women's eye wrinkles were. I swallowed around the lump in my throat. "Hi."

He glanced at his dress shoes and back to my face. "How've you been?"

"Fine." *Other than this panic attack raging through me.* "And you?"

"Good."

We are the poster children for proper etiquette. Miss Manners would adopt us.

"I saw you last week."

"Oh?" I acted the part of innocent and breezy, but on that one-word delivery, I'd kissed my Oscar good-bye.

"I thought you'd seen me too and were avoiding me. I wondered if it was because of me or . . ." He subtly motioned to his black leather patch. It covered the area around his eye and part of his brow. "For most people who knew me before, it makes them feel awkward."

"It doesn't bother me." And it was the truth. My grandma had had a lazy eye. I'd grown up knowing where not to look.

For a long moment, he studied me with pure intensity.

I shifted my Bible and cracked my thumb knuckle.

"I believe you." The stiff set of his posture eased. "I wasn't sure." He shrugged a muscular shoulder, and a hint of teasing played in his features. "I don't think anyone's ever run from a church like that, except the devil."

The nerve! "I didn't run out of here." *Come on, Kate. Where are you?* I scanned the crowd and only found disappointment

28

and that fire alarm again. Could I pretend to trip and accidently pull it in an attempt to keep myself upright?

"No?" His brow quirked, right along with his mouth. Gone was his initial uncertainty. This was the Samuel I knew.

And I was not the doormat he once knew. "No." I straightened, a true understanding of what *girding the loins* meant becoming clear. Never had I ever thought it'd happen in one of God's houses. I hiked my chin and purse strap higher. "Why are you here? From what I remember, you prefer occupying your Sundays in a duck blind or on a fishing boat."

A playful twinkle lit his eye, but like a shooting star, it dimmed. His Adam's apple bobbed. "There's a lot of things I got wrong back then." His tone dropped to absolute seriousness, matching his expression.

Sweet sunshine. Sweat beaded behind my knees, my breaths quickening, and I clutched my Bible. The need to look away increased with each pulse thrashing in my ears, but I was held captive by his searing stare.

Our pastor, Brother Buford, approached, clasping his hand on Samuel's shoulder, rescuing me. "I see you've met Samuel."

A wild urge surged within to snitch on all Samuel had done. But then, I'd been equally guilty of some of the same offenses. "Yes," I said, and silently vowed never to make eye contact with Samuel Reed again. "We knew each other in college." *When he ripped out my heart and used it as a punching bag.*

"Ah." Brother Buford nodded, his bald, dark-skinned head gleaming in the light. He slid his hands into his trouser pockets. "Before his Green Beret days."

Green Beret? So he'd joined the army after all. Guess he'd given in to the pressure his dad and brother had put on him. Had he lost his eye in service? The flutter in my stomach I'd crushed earlier mounted a comeback.

Brother Buford continued. "He's been surveilling our services to recommend some security changes." If Brother Buford were an emoji, he'd be the smiley face with heart eyes. Bromance was in the air.

Samuel, on the other hand, appeared almost embarrassed by the praise, his hard jaw dipping.

Brother Buford turned his heart emoji eyes to me. "Julia started a ministry here for members who need help with household cleaning and minor home repairs."

How about fifteen years ago I began that ministry. Fifteen years, Samuel! Ergo, this is my church. We're basically common-law married. Get your own place of worship!

Brother Buford inclined his head to a man entering the building. "Samuel, there's someone I want you to meet." He nodded his farewell to me and walked off.

Samuel's attention ping-ponged between the retreating pastor and me, his lips pinching.

I jumped on my chance to escape, lilting a goodbye loud enough to include the pastor and dismiss Samuel. Moving away, I spotted Kate and wheezed in my first full breath. She wouldn't abandon me for anything in the world. I'd stroll with her past Samuel, pretending everything was fine. That Oscar could still be mine.

Kate's steps aimed for me, but her stare followed Samuel, her eyes round and mouth slightly ajar. Keeping the required preteen distance away from her was Hayley, excitement rolling off her while she chatted with a friend.

As Kate reached me, so did Emily Miller, one of the volunteers for my ministry. Emily was in her late twenties, adorably kind, and best of all, dependable.

Emily nodded hello to Kate and spoke to me. "When I was helping at Miss Marlene's house the other weekend, she told me about the cleaners you make. The nontoxic ones. I'd love to buy some from you."

Oh, how I wished Kate hadn't been here for that. A smug *I told you so* face emerged from her.

I offered Emily an apologetic smile. "I don't sell them. It's just something I concocted since I use cleaning products every day with my job."

Emily's angelic face fell.

"But I'd be happy to email you the formula." I reached into my purse, searching out my phone. "It's easy to make with simple ingredients you can get from the grocery."

Emily winced, fidgeting with a lock of her blond hair. "I can barely make a boxed cake, much less something like that. It'd be easier to pay you to do all the science stuff."

My vision snagged on Samuel, across the way. He was still with the pastor, but his focus trained on me, his lips pressed together in concentration, like he was trying to read my mind.

Take your smoldering hotness and go suck an egg. I returned my attention to Emily. "If you bring me some clean, empty spray bottles, I'll give you some."

"Oh no, I insist on paying."

"It hardly costs anything to make, and with how helpful you are, it'd make me happy to give it to you."

"Well, okay." Emily's dimples popped. "Thank you. I've gotta scoot. The singles group is having a lunch date today with another church." She held up crossed fingers and took off. I couldn't help but smile at her hopefulness.

Kate shook her head, her auburn hair untucking from her ears. "That's the umpteenth person I know of who wanted to purchase your products."

"We've already talked about this."

"No, I talked, and you tuned me out."

"I'm a college dropout—"

"I hate when you say that." She rolled her eyes with a sigh.

"It's true. And I don't have the time or money to sink into starting a business. Merely thinking about all the red tape and laws and rules makes my head hurt. This isn't like a bake sale where I whip up a batch of cookies and sell them. With cleaning products, there are all sorts of federal requirements. And liabilities of every kind with legal consequences. Besides, with the boys gone, I can put the time I'd spent with them on the weekends toward gaining another client."

Kate seemed to be tuning *me* out, her attention fixated elsewhere.

I trailed her line of sight and found Samuel at the other end. *Of course.* And he was headed our way. *Seriously?*

"I'm pretty sure I saw sparks flying between y'all." A distinct meddlesome tone entered Kate's voice.

I narrowed my eyes at her. "That was me trying to telepathically burn him alive."

"I've never seen you this riled." Kate tilted her head and elbowed me. "You're actually blushing. Plus, you obsessed over him all week."

"Shush," I growled.

Samuel and Kate introduced themselves with handshakes while I stood mute on the sidelines. My best friend and my enemy making small talk. What was Kate contemplating behind her Clinique smile? Was she envisioning Samuel's demise? Concocting a recipe for beignets laced with Ex-Lax? Or maybe—

"Well, I need to be going," Kate said.

What now?

She held up a folder containing flyers for an event she'd been planning. "I'm dropping these off at the church office for them to distribute."

"I'll go with you." I shifted away.

She grimaced. "Afterward I'm counting the offering."

Of all the Sundays. "What about Hayley?" My sight darted to her. "I can bring her home so she doesn't have to wait for you." My hopes of survival now rested on an eleven-year-old with a Korean boy band obsession and an alpaca-themed purse.

Kate waved at Hayley. "She's spending the afternoon with a friend."

Hayley returned the gesture and set off with her friend and their parents. A dull thud of defeat echoed from my heart.

"If you're interested . . ." Kate removed a flyer and handed it to Samuel.

My mouth opened, but my tongue had shriveled. *Benedict Arnold!*

"I'm on a committee that supports small local companies that rely on the public. We're having a business crawl Friday. This lists all the places participating."

"Thank you." Samuel skimmed the paper.

I fought the impulse to rip it from his grasp. Beignets & Books was one of those stops. What if Samuel showed up? Then again, would he really go to a quaint café? He'd probably stick to the restaurants and sporting goods stores. Scratch that. He'd spend the entire time in the sporting goods stores.

"I'll walk you to your car." Samuel folded the sheet and tucked it into his pocket.

I stopped grinding my molars. "I've been walking just fine on my own for thirty-nine years."

Undeterred, he swept his arm toward the exit.

Kate came across a trace too pleased with what was happening.

I gave her a hug goodbye and whispered, "You're dead to me."

Outside, the overcast skies and softly rumbling thunder quickened the pace of those making their way through the parking lot. My steps hastened for a different reason. One that was over six feet and had devastating charisma. Several vehicles away from my SUV, I pressed the unlock button on my key fob.

"Would you please hold up a second?" Samuel's voice remained low behind me.

I kept my back to him as though he were Medusa.

A family hurried to their sedan parked on the driver's side

of my vehicle and left. We exchanged waves and smiles. Nothing to see here, folks. Just a woman avoiding the sins of her past.

"Julia?"

I eyed the distance to freedom. Three steps.

"I was hoping we could talk."

A warm breeze whirled around me, tugging my dress and whipping my hair. If only it were strong enough to pluck me from this moment. If only I were wearing ruby slippers. I reached for my door handle. "I have nothing to say."

"I do. I want to apologize."

My rib cage squeezed. I turned, asphalt grit crunching beneath my wedge sandals, and stared up at him. Okay, I'd lied. There were a few things I wanted to say. Like how he could shove his apology where the sun didn't shine. That I didn't want his remorse.

My heart shirked as though it'd been nudged. I'd been through enough situations to know it was the poking finger of truth. And it was annoying and futile to fight. I *did* want an apology. I needed to know what he'd done to me so long ago had affected him. That I hadn't been the only one who'd come away wounded and with regrets.

Four rows over, a kid used one of the yellow parking blocks like a balance beam while his mom spoke to another woman.

Samuel glanced around. "Can we go someplace else? Somewhere private?"

I slowly shook my head.

He took a deep breath that came across as more resigned than annoyed. Scanning our surroundings again, he neared. The scent of mint and seawater drifted with his proximity, digging at memories I'd long buried. "I'm sorry for how I treated you back then."

My breath constricted in my lungs.

"I knew you wanted more . . . But I couldn't . . ." His mouth turned down, and he shoved his hands into his pockets. "I did love you."

My chin quivered. No, he hadn't. I'd known what real love was. My life after Samuel had been filled with it from a man who hadn't been afraid of commitment. Mark hadn't played games with my heart. He'd loved me the way I knew I deserved. The kind of love that had swept me off my feet with its total rightness. A 1 Corinthians love.

A crease formed between Samuel's brows. "I never meant to hurt you, but I know I did. I've always regretted it."

Those words. I wanted to hear them and yet hated them at the same time. His authenticity seemed real, but then again, he'd always been so smooth and convincing. A small ache throbbed at my temples.

His head angled down, his gaze sliding north, meeting mine. In the outdoor light, a shadow under his eye became visible. Because he'd been up late having a good time, or because he'd been unable to sleep knowing he would seek me out today for this conversation?

The Samuel Reed I knew never owned up to his behavior. Was God genuinely moving in his life? What did he expect from me? That we'd become friends? That I'd pick up his mail when he was out of town? Be his driver for a colonoscopy? Or was this typical Samuel, his two-week breakup extended to nearly two decades? Did he assume I'd walk right into his arms like all the other times I'd been so stupid? My vision blurred, the throbbing in my head turning to full-on pounding. I blinked the tears away, hating that one had escaped.

He gently lifted his hand toward my face.

I backed into my vehicle and swiped the renegade tear.

His hand dropped to his side. "I've thought so many times about this moment, and I'm getting it all wrong." He palmed the back of his neck. A raindrop pelted his shirt. "Are you sure we can't go somewhere?"

"I can't." The words croaked from my burning throat. I slipped into my SUV and managed to insert the key in the ignition despite my shaking hands. A steady drizzle cascaded onto my windshield as I reversed and drove away. In the rearview mirror, Samuel stood, his robust shoulders slumped, still watching me.

Regardless of the distance and the moment being over, the trembling intensified, hitting every muscle, including my heart. I kept to the slowpoke lane on the interstate, trying to avoid the truth that had me so rattled. He'd seemed genuine. And vulnerable.

And I'd wanted to stay and hear him out.

Ugh. This wasn't happening! Was I a masochist? I'd learned my lesson. Had been so careful to make wise choices since him. Maybe Samuel had some sort of brain-blocking ingredient in his cologne. Well, if there was one way to squelch any lingering, sympathetic feelings for that man, I knew exactly what it was.

Tell Mama.

⁂—⁂

The church bulletin felt as though it were a ticking time bomb. Entering Mama's house, I rethought my decision. I could stuff the handout in my purse and say I'd forgotten it, but she had just enough tech savvy to find the electronic version on the church website.

Mama sat at her kitchen table, the newspaper spread before her, a coffee mug sitting atop someone's obituary photo. "Did you see my Facebook post?" She also had enough tech savvy to be a nuisance on Facebook. From sharing political rants to questionable jokes, Mama was like social media Russian roulette. There was a reason I hadn't linked us as relatives on the site.

"No, I didn't." I hooked my handbag strap on the back of the chair closest to the door in case I needed to make a hasty exit.

She sipped her brew. "I put your name in it."

"You have to tag my name for it to notify me. Just typing my name won't do it."

"Hmpf." She licked her thumb and folded the newspaper to the next page.

Stomach churning, I gazed out her kitchen window to the distant storm clouds that hadn't reached here yet. *Come on. Get it over with. Like when you tried that at-home Australian hair wax.* I turned toward Mama, who was captivated once again by someone's death notice. "I need to tell you something."

Mama's face tipped up, her dark eyes magnified behind her reading glasses.

Lord, give me strength. "Samuel Reed joined our church."

Mama stilled. Slowly, her lips screwed together, the lines around her mouth from a lifetime of smoking resembling a metal bottle cap.

Sweat gathered across my back, and I fought the urge to shift my shoulders.

She scrutinized my face, her flinty stare skimming down to the bulletin in my grasp. She whipped out her hand, received the pamphlet, and flipped it open. Her scowl grew deeper with each passing second, the vein at her temple becoming engorged.

Another go with that Aussie wax wasn't looking so bad in comparison. I cleared my throat as soundlessly as possible. "It's not a big deal." My reedy voice snitched on the lie.

Mama smacked the bulletin on the table. "Have you actually seen him?"

"Yes."

"Last Sunday?"

Clogged toilets. "Yes."

"I knew something happened." She patted her robe pockets, retrieving a smooshed package of cigarettes. "Has he seen you?"

"We spoke today." I crossed my arms and raised my chin, trying for the appearance of a woman who had everything under control.

She stood and moved for the counter, reaching for her lighter. "And what did you talk about?"

My arms went limp at my sides. "He . . . apologized . . . for everything."

"Ha!" Mama's head reared back. "Did he now? And does he know *everything*? *All* of the pain he caused? The mess he left behind?"

"I don't want to talk about this." The tremor in my voice matched my nerves. "I only mentioned him because I didn't want you to be surprised when—"

"When I saw it in the bulletin." She narrowed her eyes and pinched a cigarette from the pack, pointing it at me as though it were a sixth finger. "Were you going to tell me?"

"Probably not. I knew you'd make a fuss."

Mama scoffed. "Just remember how miserable you were with him, and in the months that followed."

Tears welled. I held up a hand, regret and shame twisting my insides. "I don't want to go there."

"The last thing you need is to be mixed up with that man. Or any man. Your priority is your boys, not romance. And especially not getting tied up with a no-good—"

"All right."

"I'll say it again. Your boys are your priority. Like you were always mine." Mama shoved through the screen door to the carport, where she smoked when I or the boys visited. The thwack of the door closing punctuated her anger.

Oh, how I knew I'd been her priority, though I'd felt more of a burden to Mama than a joy. It was why I'd never complained about my job or life in front of Conner or Mason. I'd worked quietly, lived frugally, and saved like Scrooge McDuck. Mark's life insurance had paid for his funeral and little else. The fear of providing for my boys had burned to my core. If something happened to me, where would that leave them?

Dating or taking a chance on selling my cleaning products wasn't a risk I could afford. Adding to my client list by gaining weekend work solved both issues. It was guaranteed money in the bank for the boys' future, and it kept me busy and my heart safe.

5

FRIDAY EVENING, I ARRIVED EARLY at Beignets & Books in case Kate needed help with last minute preparations for the business crawl. According to the schedule, the event would move to her place next. Everything in the courtyard had already been arranged. Round cocktail tables, draped in cream material, scattered the area running the length of the house. Black satin sashes gathered the cloths in tight twists midway down the bases. Candles in hurricane glasses flickered atop them. Brochures describing the history of the building and detailing how to book special events graced each table as well.

The year-round lush vegetation provided a buffer from the tall brick walls lining the back of the space. My heels clacked across the pavers, my sight casting up, admiring the lights strung in the sprawling live oak tree. Louis Armstrong's voice sang through the sound system, adding a layer of smooth energy to the air.

My heart squeezed at the feeling of romance this setting evoked. Had Mark been here, he would've asked me to dance. Right on the spot. Mama would've balked. And she would certainly chastise me for seeing this moment as anything other than an opportunity to make more money. *"Your priority is your boys, not romance."* I bit back a sigh. She was right.

At the bottom of the outdoor stairs, I unhooked the *Private* sign roping off the way to Kate and Hayley's residence. In one hand, I held a canvas bag containing the clothes I'd switch into later for when I helped clean up. In the other, I grasped my black clutch stuffed with business cards, dreading the evening that loomed. I hated schmoozing, but at least I was at a place where I felt comfortable. And everyone attending did so to support local businesses.

I reached their covered balcony and knocked on the door. Within seconds, Hayley swiped the curtain back from the glass pane, a fleeting smile cresting her face. The sound of two locks unbolting followed.

"Hey, girl." I stepped into the open room and what seemed like another universe from what I'd walked through downstairs. The TV played a music video of one of her favorite K-pop boy bands. The guys danced in Western shirts complete with dangling fringe. On the couch, Hayley's laptop lay open with an online gaming world on the screen. Her avatar's shirt had an alpaca on it.

"She's getting dressed." Hayley returned to the living room portion of the dwelling. Baskets of laundry convalesced on the coffee table. No doubt put there on purpose by Kate to encourage Hayley to fold them.

I stopped at the dining table and set my bag down. "What are you up to tonight?"

"Nothing." She collapsed on their sofa with an air of desperation only a tween could pull off.

Kate entered, carrying her stilettos and wearing a Kelly-green cocktail dress that complemented her light auburn hair and creamy skin. "Look at you." She waggled her brows at me.

"Look at *you*. That color is perfect." I fidgeted with my V neckline. "I think I should have worn my black dress." This red frock hadn't left my closet since I'd chaperoned a Valentine's

Day dance at the boys' junior high school. The empire waist performed a miracle for my unshakable muffin top, allowing me to go Spanx-free and be able to breathe.

"No, you chose correctly." She slipped on her shoes and turned to her niece. "How do we look?"

Hayley paused the TV, her attention shifting between us. A sliver of a smile formed. "Like Christmas."

Me in red, and Kate in green. Ha-ha. Had she drawn any similarities between me and Mrs. Claus, I'd be on my way home to change.

"And with that, we should get moving." Kate grabbed her keys. "People are bound to arrive early. I want to ensure the extra waiters are ready." We stepped out the door, Kate locking it behind us. "Inside will carry on as usual for regular customers, while the courtyard will cater to the business crawl."

The skies had darkened to a beautiful navy. The landscape lighting softened the ambiance. A small wedding back here would be idyllic. Quaint and romantic. I blinked. *Goodness. Pull it together.*

Voices drifted up from below, and several folks entered the courtyard.

I pressed my purse to my stomach, jittering with nerves at the prospect of networking. "Are you sure they don't need help inside? Like directing people back here?"

"I'm sure." Kate smoothed her dress at her hips. "The hostess will take care of that." She jutted a thumb. "No dillydallying. It's time to get down there and sell yourself."

"This is sounding a little too much like *Pretty Woman*."

"I'd like to point out that if you concentrated on your cleaning products, you wouldn't have to do this."

"Uh, yes, I would. I'd just be selling a product."

"Those products would sell themselves through word of mouth alone."

"Cleaning houses I know how to do." I checked my shoulders, ensuring my bra straps weren't showing. "Starting a business? No way."

Kate scoffed. "I hope you realize you *do* in fact run a business."

"It's not like what you do. Employees and payroll and complicated taxes. Things I can't even imagine. That's all too much."

"But I could help you. I want to."

"Thank you." I gave her an appreciative smile. "Truly. But it's not something I can do." I turned for the stairs and descended. The time had come to channel my inner Mary Kay and become a saleswoman. My posture wilted.

Over the past hour, people had steadily filled the courtyard and feasted on the wide array of sweet and savory beignets Kate's establishment offered. I'd managed to make small talk and unload most of my business cards.

Scanning the party, I wondered if I'd interacted enough for the evening and could grab an order of crawfish beignets with remoulade sauce and head upstairs to kick off my heels and keep Hayley company until everyone left. My gaze flitted past, stopped, and reversed onto a familiar face.

Samuel.

Surprise struck, my body tensing, my mind racing.

How long had he been here? He stood in the back corner by the massive oak tree. His gray suit, sans a tie, was perfectly tailored to his athletic physique. He'd always been one to work out. When we'd dated, we'd regularly run or gone to the gym together. Either he'd recently gotten out of the military, or he maintained a healthy lifestyle. Well, he hadn't been the only one striving for fitness. Although my reason had been for my boys and not vanity.

Enough distance and people milled between us for me to easily slip away. Escaping to the second floor would bring me closer to Samuel, so that was a no-go. But I could sneak indoors and hide in the space where the least amount of foot traffic flowed: the sports room. Peyton and Eli Manning's cardboard cutouts could be my companions. Maybe I'd even position them to conceal me.

Samuel lifted a hand in greeting.

Stained sheets.

Had I been staring at him this entire time? How long had he been watching me watch him? If I fled—again—I'd lose face. And I'd lost enough to Samuel Reed to last a lifetime.

I made my way to him, stopping ever so casually to nab an iced tea from a passing waiter. Focusing on the cold glass in my grasp, I tried reining in the annoyance streaming through me. "What are you doing here?" *Tried and failed.*

A shine lit in his hazel eye. "Supporting a small business."

"Isn't this a bit of a namby-pamby place for you to be seen? Will you have to turn in your green beret?"

His mouth quirked. "I've been in worse situations. Maybe not as hostile as you when you're wound up."

"I'm not wound up." I lowered my voice and strove for calm and unaffected. "Just surprised. Unless you're here with some-one." The mint sprig in my drink clung to the rim, much like my hopes that I wouldn't have to face Samuel *and* a girlfriend.

"I am not."

I sipped my tea, consuming the perfect combination of sugar and relief. "Then perhaps you're interested in . . ." I surveyed the crowd. Even with one eye he'd see the much younger and prettier women here. Women who'd yet to experience pluck-ing a chin hair or hiding stretch marks. What a crock cocoa butter had been.

"There's only one woman here I'm interested in." His eye contact leveled on me, sending a shiver down my spine that had nothing to do with the cold beverage in my hand.

Was Kate pumping some sort of love potion into the air?

Warmth spread across my face. His directness had thrown me, my thoughts tumbling, scrambling to grab hold. *You hate this man. He broke your heart. And worst of all, he cheated on you.* That did it. I straightened. "Only one woman this time? That'll be different for you. I hope you find her."

Samuel's mouth turned down, his head lowering a fraction. I stepped away.

"Wait."

What would he want now? To defend himself against my jab? His apology this past Sunday hadn't included an excuse. Was that why he'd shown up tonight? What justification would he give for why our relationship ended? *I was drunk, possessed by aliens, sleep-cheating.*

He reached for a cocktail napkin on a nearby table and held it out. "Your drink's sweating on you."

There's a lot of other things sweating on me too. I accepted the napkin, wrapping it around my glass, and walked off.

"Julia," he called, his voice soft.

I turned, but only halfway.

"You look beautiful."

Another blush swept through me, sending tingles along my skin. What was I supposed to do with that? I moved away, unable to make sense of this version of Samuel Reed. Not defending himself, being attentive with a napkin, and paying me compliments? Maybe the Green Berets had a secret course on etiquette they made all soldiers go through.

In a haze, I took the steps up to the back porch of Beignets & Books.

Kate caught me as I entered through the French doors that led to the front of the café. "You look like you're trying to solve an algebraic equation."

"Samuel's here."

Her blue eyes glittered. "I know."

"Traitor!" I gasped. Without a doubt, my reaction could be made into a meme and go viral. "Why didn't you tell me?"

Kate smiled calmly at a couple walking past and inclined her head for me to follow. She ushered me to her small office off the hallway, flipping on the light and closing the door behind us. "I've been greeting people inside as they arrive and spoke to Samuel when he showed up." An antique desk, bookcase, and several metal filing cabinets occupied the space, along with a large window overlooking the courtyard. *Perfect!*

"Hit the switch," I hissed.

She complied, returning the room to shadows. "Why?"

Light from outside filtered through the window, making navigating the office possible. I skirted her impeccably organized desk. "So no one sees us spying."

"So *Samuel* doesn't see *you* spying."

"Oh, shush."

He stood in the same spot, some young thing talking to him. At most the woman was in her late twenties. Petite in stature, she wore a chic strapless dress. I'd given up on strapless dresses long ago. *Just wait, little miss, until you pop out some kids and gravity takes over.*

Samuel was so incredible looking that even with an eye patch, he was still devastatingly handsome. Maybe more so because of it. He oozed danger, a man not to be messed with. And as a Green Beret, he *wasn't* a man to be messed with. From what I could tell, his body looked better than it had twenty years ago. His leanness had given way to a sturdier build. I, on the other hand, had been left with stretch marks and the superpower of peeing a little when I sneezed.

The lady said something, and he smiled. A small burn ignited in my stomach, as though a charcoal briquette had been struck with a match. The creases at the corner of his eye only made him more attractive, gave an air of maturity. Life was not fair.

Kate moved, flanking the other side of the window.

Gracious. I'd forgotten she was here.

"Samuel is very nice," she said. "Turns out he did lose his eye in service."

"Hmph. I assumed he crossed the wrong woman, and she stabbed him in the eye with a fork."

"Julia!"

I shrugged, a pinch of guilt nipping at me. The man had, after all, sacrificed for my country.

Samuel excused himself from the woman and disappeared from view. I turned my attention to Kate. "Earlier this evening, a woman asked about buying my cleaning products. You wouldn't know anything about that, would you?"

"Hmm?"

"Don't *hmm* me." The air conditioning clicked on, the cool draft tickling my bare arms.

"I overheard you talking up Beignets & Books several times. So it's okay for you to help my business but not the other way around?"

"It's different, and you know it." I motioned for the door. "You should get back out there."

She obliged but paused with her hand on the knob. "I could have the woman who maintains my website give you a quote. Your products could be sold online."

Something I'd thought of and nixed. I was one person, concocting mixtures in my garage as needed. What if a ton of orders came in? And if they didn't, I'd be paying website fees for nothing. "Your mouth is moving, but all I hear is my bank account flushing down the toilet."

A sigh escaped from Kate as she opened the door. I moved past her into the hallway.

Outside, near the doors to the courtyard, stood Samuel, flanked by two women.

The briquette in my gut flared. "Look at them. Like two roaches on a bacon bit."

Kate chuckled. "I've never seen you jealous."

"And you're not seeing it now." Turning for the front of the restaurant, I gestured to my face. "This is aggravation. He shouldn't have come." I looped my arm through Kate's, and we walked toward the scent of fresh beignets. Unlike men, beignets never hurt anything. Well, except cholesterol levels. And my recent bloodwork had agreed I could splurge in that department. Plus, I hadn't celebrated the fabulous results of my mammogram. Beignets were a must.

Despite Peyton and Eli Manning's company, an order of beignets for one sat before me. I had followed through on my original plan of hiding in the sports room. Thankfully the other three tables in this section remained vacant. The Manning boys were placed strategically. If anyone walked past the cased opening, I should go unnoticed.

To help pass the time until I could be useful to Kate, I perused one of the books from the shelves. Since Eli and Peyton were my dates, I'd decided to be faithful and skim a book on their daddy.

"Well, that's something." Samuel's voice penetrated my fortress of solitude.

Curses!

He stood inside the room, his discarded jacket slung over his arm, and motioned to the cardboard props. "Never thought I'd see them play offensive linemen."

So true. I dabbed my mouth with a cloth napkin, concealing my pleasure at his joke. "I'm certain it's a sin for any New Orleanian to speak ill of the Manning family."

He slightly bowed to the cutouts, pressing a hand to his chest. "My apologies."

I returned the napkin to my lap and my focus to the open book on the table, wishing he'd take the hint at being dismissed.

"Can I join you?"

"Samuel." I exhaled his name. "We're not going to be friends."

Regardless of my declaration, a twinkle brightened his eye. "I know. And I'd like to talk about that." He moved Peyton to one of the corners, giving the appearance that he was being punished, and then claimed the wooden chair across from me, draping his jacket on the back.

The area was much too cramped with Samuel, tension, and our tumultuous past. My fight-or-flight instinct took root. I looked everywhere but at him. The ornate crown molding, cream-colored walls, the framed historical picture of City Park's golf course.

"I don't want to be friends with you either."

"Enemies it is. Great!" I closed the book with a little too much gusto and scooted my chair back.

"Julia, please."

Oh. He spoke in his gentle tone. I glanced at Eli, who stood there, seeming to enjoy my predicament. *Careful, Eli. I have a pen in my purse. You wouldn't look so smug with a handlebar mustache and Civil War sideburns.*

Samuel's features softened. "I heard about your husband's passing." Sincerity coated his words. "I'm sorry."

I cleared my throat. Talk about being thrown a curveball. My grip on the armrests loosened. "Thank you."

"How long ago was it?"

"Ten years."

"And you have kids, right? Kate mentioned that earlier."

"Two boys." It was like Samuel had known my kryptonite. Or perhaps Kate had given him a cheat sheet on how to appease me. I released my hold on the armrests altogether. "They're both at college now."

"In-state?"

"North Carolina."

His brows rose.

"They received full scholarships, and my in-laws live close to their campus. The boys grew up spending summers there and love it." My shoulders relaxed with the truth of that, my mind calming further. I smoothed the napkin on my lap. "I think all the memories here with their dad made the decision to leave easier on them." Oh, why had I said that?

He nodded thoughtfully. "North Carolina is a beautiful state. Are they at UNC?"

"They are."

"That's about an hour from where I did my training."

"Did you ever marry?"

He shifted in his chair. "No."

"I guess you never got over that commitment issue."

His lips twitched. "You didn't used to be this sassy."

"Yes, well, along with having two babies, I grew boobs and a spine." *Gah! What is it about this man that renders me filterless?*

"I noticed." A rascal smile formed.

Heat flooded my neck. I pulled my hair forward, hoping to cover the red splotches sure to be forming.

"That is . . ." He rubbed the edge of his jaw, teasing clear in his expression. "I noticed your spine."

I narrowed my eyes at him.

"What?" He feigned innocence. "You're the one who brought up lady parts."

I snorted. "Lady parts? Is that something the Green Berets taught you? To be more respectful of women?"

"No." His playfulness fell away. "Having a daughter did. She's in college too."

That stung. He hadn't wasted time moving on to someone else. Of course, neither had I. Six months after we'd split, I'd met Mark. A few months of dating Mark sprang into a brief engagement, marriage, nine months later followed by Conner's birth, and the next year, Mason's.

"She's a sophomore at LSU."

Avoiding eye contact, I nodded, nudged my plate aside, and hoped he wouldn't want to show pictures of her. I certainly didn't want to share photos of Conner and Mason. Didn't want to invite him any further into my world than he'd already intruded.

"Julia, I'm sorry for how I treated you. I was young and foolish, and my moral compass was severely skewed."

A kaleidoscope of feelings swirled and twisted within. The other week I'd described myself as young and foolish during that time. Wouldn't it hold true that Samuel could feel the same way? *What do I do here, Lord?*

He edged forward, his chair creaking, garnering my attention. The stubble on his jawline held flecks of gray, the overhead lights washing out his eye color but not the determination in them. "I want another chance."

An odd mental numbness splayed, as though I'd had Novocain injected into my brain. My eyes drifted to his shoulder, down his arm, and to his wrist. His sleeve had been rolled back, revealing tanned skin and brown hair on his forearm. The jazz music faded. How had my world been altered so much in, what? Two weeks?

He eased to standing. "I'm guessing you're still an overthinker and need time to process things." He tucked his chair against the table and grasped the back. One side of his mouth inched up. "While eating M&Ms and pretzels."

My lips pursed, the numbness wearing off. I hated how well he knew me.

"I just wanted to make my intentions known." And with that, he grabbed his jacket and left.

Elbows on the table, I massaged my temples. *This isn't happening. You don't need this type of drama in your life. This type of distraction. Or heartbreak.*

I pulled myself upright and nodded at Eli, who I swear nodded back. I didn't need time to overthink. My box would stay checked at *single*, thank you very much. Tonight had been a success in making business connections *and* being reminded of the pitfalls of relationships. Earning extra money with a new client wouldn't hurt anything. And another order of beignets wouldn't hurt either.

6

YOGA PANTS AND TENNIS SHOES HAD NEVER FELT SO GOOD.

Beignets & Books had closed an hour ago, taking with it the last of the business crawl guests. The once bustling courtyard now lay vacant save for me and one of the waitresses. The outside music had been turned off for the sake of keeping Kate's neighbors happy. The romantic lighting had given way to floodlights, making the cleanup easier.

The waitress lumbered inside with an armful of tablecloths, passing Kate as she made her way out.

Kate had also wasted no time changing into practical clothing of shorts and a T-shirt. "Thanks again for helping."

"I'm happy to." I wiped sweat from my forehead and started disassembling the last cocktail table, removing the top first.

Kate wheeled the almost full storage cart closer. "I think tonight was a success. There's interest for several special events, and I booked an anniversary party." Shadows from the floodlights hid her face, but her tone was bright. Kate had sunk a lot of money and effort into remodeling the courtyard. A necessity for her vision of expanding into a special event venue. Her dream, thankfully, was now reality.

"That's great." And I meant it. Kate had pressed in to making her dreams happen, not shrinking away from them like I had.

"How'd you make out?" She took the round top from me and slid it into its slat in the center of the cart.

I removed the support pole from the metal base. "I think I found a weekend client. I met the owner of Breaux Insurance."

She stilled. "Robert Breaux?"

"Yeah." I passed her the pole, more than a little curious about her reaction to the mentioning of the handsome man. "Do you know him?"

Kate briefly made eye contact, then positioned the pole into its holder on the cart. "He's my insurance agent."

"Is he now?" I teased. "Has he insured your heart?"

"You know I'm not dating until Hayley's in college."

"Does Robert Breaux know that? Because I saw him sneaking looks at you."

"Moving on." She huffed her bangs. "He needs janitorial services?"

I hoisted the metal base onto the cart. "He said he has an office of about fifteen employees. I'm supposed to follow up with him about seeing the space and giving a quote. Maybe you could come with me." I gave her an impish grin.

Kate rolled her gaze skyward.

We maneuvered the cart, which now held ten disassembled tables, over the uneven brick pavers. On the other side of the house, the small storage shed hidden by a trellis of English ivy came into sight.

Kate opened the shed door, unleashing the smell of fertilizer and rusted garden tools. She stepped in and reached for the pull chain connected to the sole light, illuminating the space. "Any other interest?"

Unbidden, Samuel came to mind. I channeled my frustration with him into force, thrusting the cart over the shed's threshold, rendering Kate useless. The metal table parts clanked against each other like demon wind chimes.

"Are you going to hike up your pants and spit now?" Kate shook her head, wheeling the cart the rest of the way to its spot next to some old paint cans. "I'm guessing something happened after you went into hiding in the sports room. And I'm guessing that something has to do with Samuel."

I dusted my hands on my thighs and returned to the fresh air. The need to tell Kate everything warred with my past and what it would bring. The memories. The shame. Only two other people knew the entire truth. Mama and Mark.

Kate locked the shed, and we silently headed back to the courtyard, each step building pressure within. Kate had become my soul sister, a true gift from God I hadn't known I'd needed. My next words would inevitably lead to the full story's revelation, because I knew what her response would be. Especially based on her practically inviting Samuel to attend tonight.

All that remained in the courtyard was an extra-long ice chest that had been concealed behind the beverage table during the party. Kate raised the lid and grabbed two bottled waters, handing me one. As though showing me she had all the time in the world to talk, she lowered herself onto one end of the cooler.

Resignation won, and I dropped my butt onto the other side of the ice chest. "Samuel told me he wants another chance."

Her head whipped in my direction. "He told you just like that?"

Nodding, I twisted the cap from my bottle and drank, my uneasy stomach unable to handle more than one sip. My carefully constructed life had become a soap opera, each moment with Samuel ending in a cliffhanger.

An encouraging smile with a dash of meddling appeared on Kate's face.

"It's not going to happen." I drew my shoulders back. *Just get it all out there.* "I told you things didn't end well with him."

"Yes."

"A few months before we broke up, I found a picture of his coworker in a bikini."

Kate's eyes widened, rivaling one of her coffee cup saucers.

"On the back of the photo was handwritten 'FYI' with three dots. The dots were heart shaped."

"Ew!"

"I know!" erupted from me in true Monica Gellar style. "He said it was a one-way crush on her part and threw the photo away." I shook my head at my gullibility. "When he dumped me, he admitted he'd cheated."

Kate's exhale bordered on a gasp. "With the bikini tramp?"

I lifted a shoulder. "He wouldn't say." My heartbeat thumped in my throat, constricting with each pulse. "Two weeks later . . ." My eyes grew hot, a painful burn joining until my vision blurred. "I discovered I was pregnant." I could still remember that faint purple line on the drugstore pregnancy test. The conflicting emotions of a life growing in me, a tiny heart pulsing so very near my shattered one. "I tried calling Samuel several times, but he never answered." Each ignored ring on the phone line had twisted my hope to despair, and then anger.

Kate touched the base of her neck, her mouth parting.

"Seven weeks later, I miscarried." I swiped a tear trailing my cheek. Had it been my grief over Samuel, my body so racked with emotional pain, that had destroyed our child? The doctor had assured me it hadn't been my fault. But the loss, disgrace, and guilt had been suffocating. I glanced at Kate, hesitant of what I would find in her eyes. The compassion made my own water again. "Samuel doesn't know." My voice shook with the admission, the trembling traveling to my hands. I set my water on the ground at my feet. Though I'd sought and received God's forgiveness for intimacy outside of marriage, I hadn't been able to escape the consequences of my actions. Even all these years later, the effects lingered.

"Oh, Julia." Kate wrapped her arm around me. "I'm sorry you had to go through that."

I tipped my face to the night sky, catching the moon peeking through the majestic oak's branches. As a child, I'd imagined the moon as God's night-light for me. Always there, calming my fears, reassuring. I inhaled deeply, breathing in His peace. "What's surprising is that it all brought me back to the Lord. Those dark months that followed the miscarriage had me yearning to return to church. To that joy I'd had before."

"And that's when you met Mark."

The tension that had built gave way, a fond smile forming. "Yes."

Kate's reaction mirrored mine.

"I'm sorry I never told you. It's just . . . I feel like I've had two lives. One before and one after Mark's death. And you came after."

"You don't have to explain. I feel like everything in my life is categorized as either before or after Claire died."

Her sister. I draped my arm at her waist. "I wish I could've known her."

"Me too." She leaned her head against mine.

The rumble and clack of a streetcar running along the rails on St. Charles Avenue carried over the house and faded with its distance.

Straightening, Kate opened her water, taking a drink. "Maybe you and Samuel can just be friends."

"No." I rested my elbows on my knees. "There's too much history. Too much to overcome." I pushed to standing. "Earlier tonight, he told me he has a daughter in college. I hoped he wouldn't show a photo because I didn't want to see her." Vulnerability's grip took hold of my chest. "I know that sounds awful." I fiddled with the hem of my T-shirt. "But I knew if he showed me a photo of what could have been if I hadn't miscarried . . ." I shook my head. "I'm not sure how I would've reacted."

Kate stared across the courtyard as though in thought, her mouth pulling to one side. Maybe now she'd see reason and stop envisioning me and Samuel together.

I squatted next to the cooler and pulled the plug, letting the melted ice run into the cracks of the bricks.

Kate picked at the label on her bottle. "You've mentioned how much you hated who you were when you were with him." She paused her peeling and looked at me. "Maybe he feels the same way. If he's in Christ now, has a genuine relationship with God, and has a daughter, I'm betting he regrets a lot of his past actions too."

I groaned and stepped away. "You're not making it easy for me to hate him." Samuel was the Thanos to my Black Widow. The Newman to my Seinfeld. I'd kept him in the villain category for two decades, and Kate was recasting him into the hero role.

"Then you're not going to like what I say next."

I closed my eyes, wishing I could close my ears just as easily.

"I think you may find healing if you tell him about the miscarriage. It was his baby too."

7

THE NEXT MORNING ARRIVED TOO REMINISCENT of my college days spent with little sleep because of fretting over Samuel. Kate's advice had struck a chord, reverberating until the wee hours of the morning.

At nine sharp, I pulled up to the public library. This institution was a single mom's best friend. Free books and movies? Yes, please. I returned the inspirational romance novel I'd checked out several weeks ago and headed to locate the second book in the series. My steps slowed as my attention caught on a sign hanging from the ceiling, declaring the nonfiction section.

It had been five years since I'd braved *that* area. With stars in my eyes and hopes for my cleaning products, I'd searched out *Starting a Business for Dummies*. I'd stood in the aisle, reading the opening pages, heart crumbling as I realized I was too much of a dummy to grasp the information laid out in basic terms. I'd slid the black-and-yellow paperback to its spot on the shelf and vowed never to return to this neck of the woods.

But today, curiosity needled. I glanced at the clock on the wall. There was plenty of time before I had to be at Miss Marlene's for today's volunteer work. I moseyed up to one of the computers for searching books within the building and typed two words: *Green Beret.* A scandalous sensation trickled through me. *Get a grip. It's not like you're looking for* Fifty Shades of Grey. Using the notepad and pen at the kiosk, I jotted down the call number on the first book that came up, cleared my search, and set off. Perhaps the nonfiction shelves would redeem themselves today. Maybe they would hold something to make sense of this new Samuel Reed.

⸙

Miss Marlene's house sat on the edge of my neighborhood. It was typical in style to mine, being an old, one-story ranch. I parked in her driveway and exited, making my way to the back of my SUV. Normally Earl, who handled the handiwork side of things, would've been here by now, sitting on his truck's rusting tailgate and scarfing his third doughnut while complaining about his wife's recent retirement.

A massive black pickup truck stopped alongside the curb. Tinted windows, black rims and grill. Definitely not Earl. The driver of that monster had to be going to one of Miss Marlene's neighbors. I opened the rear hatch to my Highlander and assessed what supplies I'd bring in.

"Good morning," a masculine voice called.

I stiffened. *You've got to be kidding me.* I turned, and sure enough Samuel approached, pocketing his keys. He wore work boots, jeans, and a T-shirt formfitting enough to show off his muscular physique but not so tight to say he was trying to flaunt it. I'd schlepped on navy scrubs and wrangled my hair into a haphazard ponytail. A deep grumble radiated from my core.

Humor touched his features. "Did you just growl at me?"

"What are you doing here?"

He stopped several feet away, straddling a crack in the driveway, and crossed his arms. The motion only made his pectorals and biceps look that much better. Things would've been so much easier if he had a dad bod.

I stared at the crevice beneath him, silently imploring the fissure to open up and gobble him whole. With the boys gone, these Saturday volunteer times were all I had to look forward to. Other than my Friday nights with Kate.

"Last night and now this morning." His head tilted in that irritating, easy way of his. "Is that how you're going to greet me from now on?"

"If you keep showing up where you shouldn't be."

"I'm certain I should be here. Got a call last night from church asking me to come. The regular handyman—"

"Earl."

"Yes, Earl. He had emergency gallbladder surgery."

"Is he okay?"

"He is. But he'll be out of commission for a while."

My shoulders wilted. *Poor Earl.* At least he had his wife to take care of him.

Samuel's forehead creased. "I figured you'd know all this since you run the ministry."

"I don't run it anymore." I turned to my trunk, needing to avoid Samuel's questioning stare. I reached for the pole of my Swiffer Sweeper, wishing I could sweep away my longing for the days when I had run the ministry and volunteered full-time. When I'd been making a real difference. "Earl being out still doesn't explain why you're here. Is there some new twelve-step program for joining the church you have to complete? Seeking forgiveness from me and everyone else you've wronged?"

"I'm here because I offered to Brother Buford to be helpful in any way." He reached for my cleaning caddy.

I thrust an elbow. "I've got it."

"Anything inside you need me to grab?" He jerked his chin to the front of the vehicle and took a step in that direction.

My stomach plummeted. The Green Beret book sat very

plainly in view on the passenger seat. "Take this." I thrust the dust-mop pole at him.

He arched a brow.

"And this." I practically shoved the cleaning caddy into his firm gut, closed the trunk, and rounded the SUV. "I'll be right behind you." I made a shooing gesture with my hands and exhaled at the sight of his retreating form toward Miss Marlene's front porch. I quickly opened the passenger door, grabbed my purse, and stuck the book in the glove compartment. I joined Samuel at the front door and rang the bell, pressing the button with a little too much force.

Samuel shifted to face me. "Maybe this is a sign from God that He wants us together."

"Or it's a sign that Earl should've laid off red meat and doughnuts." I took the dust mop from him.

With one of his hands now free, he perused the contents of my caddy. His fingers brushed past the duster, disposable cleaning gloves, and paused on the spray bottle labeled with an S for *surfaces*. He held the container to his nose and sniffed the sprayer's end. "You finally mastered your nontoxic cleaners?"

"Maybe." I couldn't help the swell of accomplishment rising. If anyone knew the troubles I'd had with creating my cleaning concoctions, it was Samuel. What had started as a class science project had morphed into a desire to craft something of worth.

He returned the product to the caddy. "I'll never forget the time you had my apartment smelling like rotten Easter eggs for days."

Against my will, I snickered. His apartment had stunk to high heaven. One of my attempts had been knocked over on the counter separating the kitchen from his living room. The liquid had cascaded across the Formica, down the wall, and into the carpet. Samuel hadn't gotten mad about the mess or smell. Of course, it'd been his fault in the first place. He'd snuck up behind me and begun trailing kisses up my neck.

Stop. Don't go there.

I took a slow breath in, redirecting my thoughts. Mama had forbidden me from working on my cleaning recipes at home, citing them as a waste of time and money. She could never see the big picture of what I'd hoped to do. But Samuel always had, even letting me use his place to store everything.

"Thinking about how you spilled that batch?" Samuel's dirty dog voice cut into my thoughts.

"No," I scoffed. "No, I'm not. And let's get one thing clear." I jutted the Swiffer pole between us. "There will be no reminiscing. None."

"None?" He drew himself up to his full height, a smirk on his lips. His hand covered mine on the mop handle.

Warmth and electricity glinted, thinning the air. I stared at our hands, wondered at the sensations zinging through me. It had been so long since anyone had touched me in a purposeful, intimate way. *Pull away, pull away.* My brain's instructions lost their way to my body. I couldn't move. I could only feel. My gaze rose to his face and found a fierce intensity there. *Mercy.* If there had been any doubts about our past attraction having fizzled, that theory had been squashed.

The door creaked open.

I startled, snapping to my senses, jolting from his touch. Stupid hormones. I expected to have hot *flashes*, not *the hots* for someone. Especially not Samuel. I nailed him with a glare.

He had the audacity to seem pleased.

The door opened farther, and Miss Marlene appeared, offering a smile. "Morning, Julia." Her short, stark-white hair contrasted against her dark, leathery skin. Miss Marlene had spent most of her life traveling and competing in swimsuit contests. Right up until the age of forty when she met and fell in love with a missionary in Mexico. Although that relationship hadn't lasted, her one with the Lord had.

"Good morning," I said.

Miss Marlene maneuvered her walker, opening the door all the way. Her eyes swept to Samuel, and a sparkle lit, as though reflecting the sky during a fireworks show. "Well, you're not Earl."

"No, ma'am. I'm Samuel Reed."

She held out her gnarled hand for him, releasing her walker faster than I'd ever witnessed. Not even when her favorite coffee mug had teetered on the edge of her kitchen table. "Marlene Richards. I'm ninety-three and single."

Samuel muffled a chuckle.

Gracious. If the old woman flirted shamelessly with Earl, then today would be a doozy. Until Marlene, I'd never met a flirt bigger than Samuel. And age had never mattered to him, just that it was a woman with breath in her lungs. When we'd been dating, his behavior had felt disrespectful and peeved me to no end.

"It's nice to meet you." Samuel carefully released her hand.

I waited for the charm to ooze from him. The heavy-handed compliments.

He adjusted his hold on my caddy and motioned to the front of the house. "You have a nice home here."

Slowly, I turned to him, bewilderment silencing me. Marlene had lobbed him a cabbage ball, and he hadn't swung for the fences?

"And you have a nice smile." Marlene reverse shuffled, moving her walker with her, the tennis balls on the bottom of the posts sliding across the parquet floor.

Samuel gave a slight nod. "Thank you."

I glanced around and pinched myself for good measure. Had I slipped into an alternate universe? Was he only behaving because he presumed that'd help win me over? I thought back to last night, when I'd been spying from Kate's office. He hadn't seemed flirty with the women I'd seen him with. If anything, he'd excused himself from the hottest lady there.

We entered Marlene's home, which deposited us in the center of her dwelling, the living room. A mustiness that hadn't existed when I cleaned this home every week hung in the air. With the ministry cutbacks, now Marlene was lucky if her place got cleaned once a month. *And it's all your fault.*

I swallowed the percolating guilt and took the caddy from Samuel, setting my supplies next to the front door. "I'll get started while you tell Samuel what he needs to do." In Marlene's bedroom, I pulled the sheets and pillowcases from her bed, bundling them atop the full hamper of dirty laundry in her bathroom.

I rolled the hamper through the living room, catching the tail end of Marlene showing Samuel her antique china cabinet. Instead of delicate dishes on display, framed photos from Marlene's competition days adorned the shelves.

"This one," Marlene pointed, "was from my last competition fifty-four years ago."

"Is that so?" Samuel spoke to Marlene, but his stare pinned on me. His expression was almost accusatory, as if to say *You knew this would happen, didn't you?*

I responded with a sickly-sweet smile and continued pushing the soiled laundry through the kitchen and out the side door to the carport where the washer and dryer were.

Every new person who stepped foot in this house was regaled with Marlene's history. Black-and-white images from the '40s through the '60s documented her wearing bathing suits, sashes, and crowns.

With the first load of laundry going, I returned inside and found Samuel still in the clutches of Miss Hawaiian Tropics.

"I had a lot of admirers back in my day." Marlene unleashed a wistful sigh.

"I'm sure you did, ma'am." Samuel clasped his hands behind his back. "Can I ask, what was the first task you wanted me to tackle today?"

She straightened as much as her hunched spine allowed. "I like a man who likes to get to it." Despite the wrinkles, one couldn't deny the mischievous set of Marlene's lips. "I need help in the bedroom."

Samuel and I locked glances. His pleading, mine on the cusp of laughter.

Marlene tossed me a quick wink. Poor Samuel. She was pouring it on thick for him.

"Um, pardon?" He rubbed the back of his neck.

"I need help in the bedroom. Come along now," she called, shuffling for the hallway.

Samuel signaled for me to follow.

I shook my head, biting my lower lip, the laughter begging to let loose. Oh, how I'd miss Marlene once I was working weekends.

⚬—⚬

I opened Marlene's dishwasher, my last task at her house. A fulfilling tiredness spread through me. I'd sleep better tonight, knowing Marlene would too. Fresh sheets covered her bed, her clothes clean and put away. Everything had been dusted, vacuumed, and mopped. Her bathroom and kitchen gleamed, the faint scent of lemon lingering.

Marlene dozed in her recliner in the living room, her soft snores carrying into the outdated, narrow kitchen. She'd worn herself out following me and Samuel (mostly Samuel) around, talking as we'd worked.

Samuel entered the kitchen, carefully setting his toolbox on the linoleum floor next to the breakfast table. Instead of lowering onto one of the chairs there, he moved to my side of the space, leaning his hip against the counter. "You want to talk about our moment outside?" He'd pitched his voice low, no doubt not wanting to rouse Marlene.

"There was no moment." I kept my voice normal, needing Marlene to wake and be a buffer. I purposefully clattered two coffee mugs together.

The snores stopped.

Samuel shot me an incredulous look.

I raised a brow in challenge. "I don't think Marlene told you about the time she competed for Miss California."

The snores started again.

Samuel visibly relaxed.

"If you're done, you can leave." I hung the coffee mugs from their handles on hooks fastened beneath the upper cabinets.

"I don't have anywhere else to be." He brushed past me to the sink and washed his hands.

This kitchen was too small for us. Shoot, this house—this planet—was too small for us. All it had taken was his hand on mine earlier. One touch.

He dried his hands and moved past me again, taking up residence on the other side of the open dishwasher. He reached for a glass from the top rack. "I'm curious about this ministry. How does it work?"

I pointed to the cabinet where the glasses were stored. "Church members who need help request to be put on the list. Sometimes it's temporary, like if they're recovering from surgery. Other times it's permanent."

He opened the cabinet I'd indicated and put the glass away. "Like with Miss Marlene."

"Exactly." I lifted a cereal bowl from the lower rack and placed it in an upper cabinet. Paisley-printed shelf liner peeled and curled from the edges of the ledge.

He put another glass away. "How many volunteers are there?"

"Earl is the only handyman and works when requested by the church member."

"Like today with changing the lightbulbs and fixing her bedroom window blinds."

"Exactly." My gaze darted to him and returned to the dish-washer, amusement bubbling. I reached for a plate. "I bet old Marlene will be thrilled to tell her friends how helpful you were in her bedroom."

He narrowed his eye at me. "Don't think for a second I'm letting you get away with that."

I flaunted a smug grin and set the dish on the tiled counter.

"Other than you and Earl, how many people are a part of this group?" He handed me the next two plates.

I made certain to avoid his touch. "I rotate Saturdays with three other volunteers." Although I was covering next Saturday too. Hopefully it wouldn't involve Samuel's assistance.

"So it's one church member a week that gets help?" He passed me the last dish.

"Yes." Too much heaviness weighed in that one word. I added the final plate to the stack and set them in the same cabinet as the bowls. "It used to be seven to eight members a week, at least, for the cleaning side of it."

"Eight?"

I nodded. "Back when I'd started it." My attention wandered through the window above the sink. In the late afternoon sun, a sparrow landed on the branch of a magnolia tree in Marlene's front yard. My breaths slowed and deepened, thinking back to when life had been simple. "Once my boys were in school full-time, I'd clean nearly every day, Monday through Friday." Oh, the satisfaction that had filled those days. I'd not only been keeping the elderly in a clean environment, but I'd also been company to them. Grown close to them. "Sometimes two houses a day, based on the shape they were in. But then . . ." My wistful smile collapsed, like my life had in a single moment. "My husband died."

The sparrow hopped along the limb and took flight, moving on. Just like I'd had to.

Samuel faced me, resting his palm on the counter. "And you began cleaning houses for money."

"Yes." I cleared my throat and pushed my ponytail from my shoulder. "We restructured the ministry to only Saturdays and found a few more volunteers so I could be home more. The church secretary handles the schedule now."

He tilted his head. "You always did have a soft spot for old people."

That was true. A tender smile blossomed within, one I refused to share with him.

"So this is how you spend one Saturday a month?"

"For now."

"For now?"

"I'm looking into taking on a Saturday client."

His eye squinted. "You need the money?"

"Nosey," I scoffed.

"I seem to remember you liking my nose." One corner of his mouth lifted. He slid the empty racks into the dishwasher, then closed the door with a click, removing our barrier. "Especially when I—"

"Stop that!" I grabbed a dish towel and took two steps back, my rear bumping into the opposite counter. "There will be no reminiscing!"

"Then answer my question." He eased his fingertips into the front pockets of his jeans.

Strangling the towel, I sighed. "Any extra money I can bring in for my boys makes me feel better."

He straightened, opened his mouth to speak, and paused, as though collecting his thoughts.

I wasn't about to wait for his opinions or drag out our time together. "Well, I'm done here." I looped the towel through the oven handle.

"Aren't you going to wake Marlene?"

"No, I just lock up on my way out."

He nodded his approval of my escape plan and gathered his toolbox.

I scooped up my supplies, gave Marlene one last fond glance, and trailed Samuel out the door, ensuring it was locked.

He opened the back of my SUV with his free hand. "Do you think your boys would agree with you working Saturdays? Or would they rather you be enjoying yourself?"

I knew the answer, which was why I hadn't planned on telling Conner and Mason. I loaded my supplies, shut the door, and rounded the bumper for the driver's side.

"If there's one thing I know about you, it's that money has never been a motivator." His voice neared as he followed. "Being helpful has."

I opened the door and turned on him. "Did you only join our church to torture me?"

He readjusted his grip on the toolbox, the tendons in his forearm flexing. "If you didn't have any feelings for me, then why would my presence rattle you so much?"

"I . . ." The snappy retort I'd had ready to fire fizzled. I studied my worn tennis shoes, where the rubber sole unglued from the tip.

"It seems my power to leave you speechless is still strong."

I bristled and climbed into the driver's seat, shutting the door on his smirking face.

8

THERE WAS NOTHING LIKE A ROOM full of extroverted tween girls hopped up on sugar to make me appreciate my low-key boys. That evening, I found myself at Boogie Brushes, a place where people with zero artistic abilities were plopped before a blank canvas and paints and followed a professional artist's step-by-step instructions. Everyone attempted to re-create the same prechosen painting while boogying in their seats to piped-in music. This place, with its psychedelic-colored walls and groovy logo, came across as a set cast aside from *That '70s Show*. If only Ashton Kutcher had been included.

Since we were celebrating Hayley's twelfth birthday, she had chosen the painting. A white alpaca with long pink eyelashes, a regal tilt to its chin, intensely gazing straight out. Its neck hair dramatically swirled in different directions, as though a heaven-sent wind caressed the creature. Oh, and a crown of flowers gracefully donned its head.

The things I did for love.

After a hug hello, Hayley banished me to the back-row table of the studio, where Kate had already been excommunicated to. She and her friends took up camp as far away from us as possible, as though we were biblical lepers. In between directions from the teacher, the sound system pumped up the volume, filling the air with Hayley's choice of music: K-pop. It may as well have been called K-lollipop for the amount of sweetness oozing from the speakers. Now I knew why Mama had cringed all the times I'd blared Tiffany or New Kids on the Block.

The highlights of the night so far? Breaks for pizza, cake, and knowing they'd kick us out at seven o'clock.

The music lowered, alerting us that the teacher, who stood on a platform with her canvas on a full-length easel, was going to give the next round of instructions. "Mix a touch of your gray and white paint, and add some texture to the chest hair."

Giggles erupted from the girls. Even Kate and I snickered. The teacher swooped her wrist, showing the technique.

"I never thought I'd be painting chest hair." Kate dipped the tip of her brush in one color and then the other, the scent of paint drifting.

Her alpaca looked almost identical to the teacher's painting, unlike mine that looked . . . drunk. One eye was partially closed, the neck bent as though it couldn't hold itself up, and one ear flopped.

"You've been quiet," Kate said. "Everything okay?"

I pulled my brush from the mason jar filled with water used to wash our brushes between colors. The once-clear vessel now sat murky like my thoughts. "Earl had emergency gallbladder surgery."

"Oh." Her eyebrows drew together.

"And Samuel showed up this morning as his replacement."

"Oh!" Her brows arched simultaneously with the corners of her mouth.

Several girls turned in our direction, Hayley shooting us the mom-warning glare. The music notched up again, and the girls resumed their painting.

Kate set her brush on her paper-plate palette. "Earl's okay, right?"

"Yes."

"And Samuel?"

Grabbing the paper towel roll we shared, I tore a sheet free. "He's got me rattled."

"Rattled in a you're-thinking-of-being-his-friend-or-dating-him kind of way?"

I wrapped the edge of the brush with the paper sheet, pinching the bristles to squeeze out the water. "Absolutely not." *Squeeze, squeeze, squeeze.*

Kate pulled the paper towel from my grasp, setting it on the table. Splatters of paint in varying shades covered the surface from previous sessions.

I ran my fingers over the brush's smooth spindle. "But let's say I can admit there's a spark with someone."

"An eye-patch-and-green-beret-wearing someone?"

I dabbed my brush in purple paint and raised it toward her in warning.

Kate's lips twitched, and she lifted her hand in surrender.

"And let's suppose I don't loathe the idea of shaving my legs year-round as I previously had." I diverted my gaze to my painting. *Good grief.* I was talking about my hormones in front of a drunk alpaca at a tween party. "But what about the boys?"

"What about them?"

"The last time a man showed interest, they didn't react well."

Creases marred her forehead.

"When I chaperoned their junior high Valentine's Day dance."

"Ugh." Her shoulders wilted. "I'd forgotten about that."

"I haven't." Their English teacher had asked me to slow dance, which we had done, keeping a respectable distance. Afterward, the man had walked us to my SUV and asked for my number, which I'd declined to give. The boys had acted out. At home and in English class. And that was with me having zero interest in the guy.

"That was a long time ago."

"Tell that to my brain, where the looks of betrayal Conner and Mason lobbed at me the rest of that school year are forever etched."

"Didn't they also draw some not-so-nice things on that teacher's picture in their yearbook?"

"They did."

She pursed her lips. "So for you to consider dating again, Samuel must've looked good in his tool belt today."

"He did," I begrudgingly admitted. "And there was a definite attraction. Which is odd after all these years of nothing zinging in that department. And I guess the first step is to acknowledge it, right? Rationally take control of these feelings . . . that lure. Then they'll go away. Like finding that gray hair in my eyebrow last month. I acknowledged it, took control and plucked it, and now it's gone."

"I've never heard of anyone metaphorically plucking physical attraction away. I'm no expert, but I don't think it works like that."

I rubbed at a spot of baby-pink paint on my arm, the background color of Princess Tipsy's portrait. The blob of pink had tightened my skin as it dried. *Hmm.* What if I smeared it under my eyes? Or on my stomach? I regarded the wall with shelves of different colored paint tubes. Maybe one was close to my flesh tone. Or we could concoct one.

"Julia, I wouldn't be your friend if I didn't point out something."

"What?" Even I heard the leeriness in my voice.

"For years now, you've turned a blind eye to the men who've shown interest."

I flinched. "What men? There's only been the English teacher."

Kate scoffed. "Ryan Bailey, James Broussard, Sean Crawford."

"You're imagining it."

"And your heart has been a citadel."

"Oh my word," I said on an exhale, my eyes sliding shut. "You've been reading the Old Testament too much."

"Well, it has. And Samuel has been the only one to get past your walls. To give you that zing. That in itself is a miracle in my book." And with that, she retrieved her brush and resumed painting chest hair.

Later that night, I crawled into bed wishing for sleep to end this outrageous day. The alarm clock read after nine. The ceiling fan whirred above me, sending a constant, cool breeze kissing my skin. A rerun of *Pit Bulls and Parolees* played on the TV sitting atop my dresser. Flickers of light from the show illuminated the room. My stare shifted to the window blinds, bringing Samuel to mind and how he'd fixed Marlene's blinds today. I couldn't help the smile that followed. His face had been horrified as he'd trailed her into her bedroom.

My glee faded at remembering his words on Marlene's driveway. *"Money's never been a motivator." Hmpf.* He didn't know me. I was a different person now. My rose-colored glasses had been ripped off and stomped on. First by Samuel and then by Mark's death. Providing for my kids was expected. I was adulting!

Once the boys were out of college and officially on their feet, maybe then I could slack off. Return to volunteering every Saturday or take a vacation. Ha! Mama would die. Money spent on anything frivolous, including pets, was a sin to her.

I glanced at Chewie, a poodle mix we'd rescued shortly after Mark's death. His head rested on the pillow next to mine, the fan's draft catching his wavy white ear hair. If it weren't for Chewie, I wouldn't be able to handle this quiet house. His fur had been soaked with my tears with Mark's loss, and more recently, tears over missing the boys.

My phone dinged with a text. A tight grip seized my chest, and I jolted up, the covers puddling around my waist. Chewie sprang to his feet with a woof. It wasn't Mama, she'd refused to learn how to text. Kate went to bed every night at grandma o'clock, so it wouldn't be her. My heart rate skyrocketed, and I turned on the bedside lamp. *Oh my goodness.* That only left the boys, and they never texted this late. Was one of them sick? Injured? I'd checked their pulsing dots an hour ago, and they'd both been in their dorm rooms. Or at least, their phones had. I reached for my cell on the nightstand.

Glancing at the screen, my pounding heart slowed.

UNKNOWN NUMBER
It was nice working with you today.

"Samuel." I said his name as though it were a curse. *Of all the . . .* How had he gotten my number? The backs of my knees began sweating. I kicked the sheets completely off my legs, reminiscent of a toddler throwing a fit. Chewie still stood at full alert, ready to slay any enemies despite his twelve-pound frame. "It's okay, boy." I soothed his velvety ear, and he leaned into my touch.

Staring at my phone, it grew hot in my hand. Should I block his number? Delete the message and pretend I'd never received it? If I did either of those, he'd be sure to ask me about it the next time he saw me. *Oh, gracious.* If his tenacity still held true after all these years, he'd make sure there'd be a next time. All those carbs I'd devoured at the party gurgled in my belly.

Replying could prevent his seeking me out about ignoring his text. But then again, it could open a can of worms. Letting him in. Granting him access to me twenty-four-seven. It was like Marie Kondo sat on one shoulder and Mama the other. I knew what my mother would advise, well, dictate. But shouldn't I give Marie a say? Would responding to Samuel's text spark joy? I dragged in a deep breath, expanding my lungs as far as they could, and slowly exhaled. It wouldn't *not* bring me joy. "Lord," I whispered. "Please guide my fingers."

> **ME**
> How'd you get my number?

Within seconds, three blinking dots appeared on the screen, indicating he was typing.

> **SAMUEL**
> I have my ways.

> **ME**
> Did you Green Beret your way into the church office?

> **SAMUEL**
> No comment.

I shook my head. What a scoundrel.

> **SAMUEL**
> Just wanted to see if you'd changed your mind and would go out with me.

My jaw unhinged. It was like he'd been privy to my conversation with Kate. Had he used his Green Beret skills and bugged Boogie Brushes? I typed *NO* in all caps, like I'd joined the ranks of the tweens, and hit send.

> **SAMUEL**
> You sure?

> **ME**
> Absolutely. I happen to be in bed with someone right now. And he's very territorial.

Three blinking dots started and disappeared. Twice. I chuckled.

SAMUEL
Please tell me you have some sort of pet.

ME
He's hairy and a wet kisser.

SAMUEL
You almost gave me a coronary. I'll see you at
church tomorrow.

Ha. *That's what you think.* My smile lingered as I set my
phone aside and snuggled back into bed with Chewie.

9

SUNDAY MORNING I SLIPPED INTO MY USUAL ROW at church, an hour and a half earlier than normal. Today, I'd be attending the early service. *Take that, Samuel!* The tracking app on Conner and Mason's phones revealed their pulsing dots to be alive and well at a Cracker Barrel off Interstate 40 in Raleigh. Our exchange of texts this morning corroborated their location, and hopefully, they'd be meeting up with my in-laws at their church after indulging in pancakes slathered in warm syrup.

"Were you intending to give me the slip today?" Samuel's voice floated over my shoulder.

Sofa-crack crud.

In my mind, Mama and Marie Kondo slid on boxing gloves, getting ready to rumble. A smidge of joy tingled from somewhere deep inside my core. I stiffened. *Nope. Sorry, Marie, I gave in to you last night.* It wasn't happening again. I shoved my phone into my purse and cast my attention straight ahead to the stage where the orchestra warmed up.

He chuckled, standing in the aisle. "You were. I must be getting under your skin."

I turned, tipping my head up, finally acknowledging him. A pang of admiration struck. Goodness. He was handsome.

Stubble from not shaving graced his strong jaw. His hunter-green polo enhanced his tanned skin and the hazel hues in his eye. "Why are you at this service?" For the sake of the other church members walking past and hearing us, I'd kept my tone cordial. My searing glare not so much.

"I'm helping with security." His attention lingered on me. Heavy. Purposeful.

My leg jittered beneath my cranberry A-line skirt. I shifted my Bible to my lap to cover it. "Then go." I widened my eyes for emphasis.

A soft snicker proceeded his departing steps.

I exhaled, my shoulders drooping, and adjusted my beige top. *Lord, this can't be good for my concentrating on You while I'm here. Can't You work Your stuff and take him to another church? Just poof him away?*

Once the sermon started, Samuel returned with his Bible and took the seat right next to me. Right. Next. To. Me. And it wasn't like I could protest at this point in the service. It would cause a scene.

I opened my Bible to the passage Brother Buford read from, striving for the impression of paying attention. But the only thing I noticed was the oddity of sitting in church next to a man. That hadn't happened since Mark's passing. It'd always been one of the boys at my side or Kate. Or no one.

Samuel opened his Bible too. A Post-it Note marked a spot in the New Testament. *Interesting.* One thing was for certain: unlike Kate or the boys, Samuel took up his entire seat, his elbow brushing mine. In response, the nerve endings in my arm seemed to reach for him, like those old Wooly Willy toys where you covered the hairless-faced man any way you wanted. He was the magnetic wand, and the metal filings were under my skin. I scooched away from him, breaking the connection.

Lord, please direct my thoughts.

I focused on Brother Buford, his dark, bald head gleaming

under the lights. "Now, we all know Jesus's stance on forgiveness." His wise eyes scanned the congregation.

Really, Lord? I fought the urge to squirm.

Brother Buford returned his attention to his Bible resting on the pulpit. "Forgiveness is not an easy thing to give. But you will be blessed by living in God's commands."

The rest of the sermon hit too close. It felt as though the spotlight normally used to highlight a choir member solo had been pointed at me. Wrestling with God's desires wasn't easy. And by the end of church, I was exhausted. In a fog.

I'd barely noticed Samuel walking me to my vehicle. Mama's lifelong caution of being careful what you asked for rang true. God had redirected my mind, just not where I'd wanted it to go.

A child screamed to my right, yanking me from my haze. A little girl had dropped her sucker in the parking lot, plump tears tumbling down her cheeks. The man with her retrieved the dirty candy and the child, toting them off, promising her ice cream after lunch.

I pulled my keys from my purse and pressed the remote, a beep following. "Did you arrange for Brother Buford to preach on that topic?"

"No." Samuel reached for my door handle, opening it before I could. "But since he did, maybe that's another sign from God for us."

I stepped back, adding much-needed space from him. "There is no us."

"There could be." He angled that penetrating gaze on me, as though measuring. His lower lip rolled in, one of his nervous tells.

Mercy. The earnestness in his expression sent my heart fluttering. I ignored it, hiking my purse strap higher and inserting irritation into my voice. "No, there couldn't." I moved past him and climbed into my SUV, closing the door before he could respond.

Two days later, I left my least favorite of my clients, the Holdens. Not because of them or the cleanliness of their house, although one of their teenage boys had some questionable magazines hidden under his bed I'd have to snitch on. No, it was their neighbor. Their creepy neighbor. He was midthirties and stocky. Not muscular per se but solid. Like a can of Spam. His appearance? Sloppy. His attitude? Arrogant and pushy.

I'd been cleaning the Holdens' house for several years with no issues. Like my other clients, they weren't home when I cleaned. A huge bonus. With a key and personal code to the homes with alarm systems, I could get in and move around and get my job done. No working around napping babies or Chatty Cathys.

Mr. and Mrs. Holden were at work when I came. And during the summers, their kids were away at camp. Their house was an enormous two-story with five people living in it, which meant more money for me. Sometimes they forgot to leave their payment, and I'd have to remind them. But other than that, they were good customers.

Until three months ago.

When *he* showed up.

His name was Pete, and his offbeat behavior had slowly but steadily escalated. What had started out as waving at me when I loaded my SUV and left had moved on to him coming closer each week and trying to engage me in conversation. First from his run-down Saturn parked outside his garage, then from the sliver of grass that separated his driveway from the Holdens' driveway. *"Where do you live? What's your favorite dessert? Mine is anything with whipped cream."* Wink. *"Do you know how to fix a vacuum cleaner? Mine's not working right, and I was wondering if you could come inside and take a look."*

My answers had been clipped, and I hadn't asked him anything in return. As far as he knew, my name was Juanita, I lived in Baton Rouge with five pit bulls, all desserts gave me violent diarrhea, and I knew nothing about fixing anything. I'd even gone so far as to wear my tucked-away wedding band on Tuesdays as a deterrent. One time, as I'd dusted the upstairs master suite, I'd spied him looking in the windows of my vehicle. Every single window. His fingers had cupped the sides of his eyes, pressing right up against the glass.

When I'd left the Holdens' that day, he'd brazenly strode— well, flip-flopped—his way over, placing his meaty hand on the hatch of my SUV, way too near my own. It'd been like four and a half jumbo hot dogs, sliding toward my fingers. His breath had reeked of beer. I'd slammed the door and left wordlessly. That had been a week ago, and the last time I'd seen him.

I'd asked the Holdens about Pervy Pete, and they'd basically blown off my concerns. Said he'd moved in with his elderly mom to care for her. The only thing I suspected he nursed was a six-pack. Today I'd parked in the driveway space closest to the front door and made one trip when leaving with my supplies. Thankfully he hadn't been waiting for me. Maybe he'd found someone else to give the heebie-jeebies to.

I turned off their street and peered in the rearview mirror, ensuring he wasn't following. Overkill? Maybe. But I was a woman in New Orleans. We were raised looking over our shoulders with our car keys poised between our knuckles, ready to use as a weapon. And we knew where to go and where to avoid. Especially at night and during Mardi Gras.

My phone rang, connecting to the Bluetooth in my vehicle. I pressed the button on my steering wheel, accepting the call.

"Was Pervy Pete there?" Kate's voice mixed with concern and the racket of Beignets & Books' kitchen.

"No, thank the Lord." I eased to a stop for a red light.

"I've been praying."

"Thank you for that."

Dishes clattered in Kate's background. "I wish you'd drop that client."

"We've been through this. I can't without having a replacement."

"Then I'll be your replacement."

"Kate," I sighed.

"Julia."

The light turned green, and I accelerated through the intersection. "If it helps, I'm meeting with Robert Breaux Saturday morning to view his offices."

"Yay! Maybe you can clean his place on Tuesdays and bid good riddance to the Holdens."

"He specifically wants his offices cleaned on Saturdays." I slowed for another red light. *Ugh.* I'd hit them at the wrong timing today. Two seconds earlier and I'd have been cruising through each of them. "Do you want to come with me to meet him?"

"No."

"Why not?"

"Because I don't need you insinuating things." Her background had grown quiet, and a door closed, no doubt to her office.

"I can't help it if he was openly staring at you at the business crawl."

"Well, I wasn't staring back."

"You're really not interested in him?"

"No. But I am flattered."

Hmm . . . Her *no* sounded iffy. "Maybe I want you there for protection. He could be a serial killer." I glanced in my rearview again, thinking of Pete.

"If this is for safety reasons, I know someone you *should* take."

I gasped. "Don't you dare say his name."

"I won't. But it rhymes with *spaniel*."

84

The mental image of Samuel in protector mode, shoulders squared and muscles bunching, flushed my skin. I aimed the air-conditioning vents on both sides of my wheel to pelt my face. "I'm hanging up now."

"Wait! I thought you were volunteering this Saturday, covering for someone else."

"I was, but now I'm meeting with Robert Breaux." The light turned green, and I pushed my gas pedal with more gusto, trying to clear the next intersection.

"Does this have something to do with Spaniel helping until Earl returns?"

Yes. "No."

"Who did you get to fill in for you?"

This, I knew, was a test. And one I would fail. "Norma."

"Ha! If you didn't care about Spaniel's dating life, you would've asked Emily. She's sweet and single."

I bit the inside of my cheek, hating her correctness. Emily would have been the right one to ask, but . . . Norma had a unibrow and was anti-deodorant.

"All right. All right," Kate acquiesced. "Will you be home Saturday afternoon? Around three?"

"Yes. Why?"

"You'll see." She disconnected.

10

ROBERT BREAUX WAS A TIGHTWAD. I'd toured his insurance offices that morning and counted on all ten fingers and toes his references to saving money. He'd even asked if corners could be cut. Like having his employees haul their own trash to the dumpster. This from a man who wore designer jeans, Cartier sunglasses, and departed the parking lot in a brand-new Mercedes. His personal office had been upscale and sharp. His employees' cubicles—which were out of sight from visitors—were shabby. I did not have high hopes for him agreeing to the quote I worked on.

I sat at my circular dining table for four, my laptop before me. Long ago, Kate had created a spreadsheet to calculate estimates for cleaning jobs. My hourly rate, costs for products and supplies, and consideration for distance to the client's location were all accounted for. Her ingenuity made this process so much easier.

The doorbell rang, alerting my second doorbell, Chewie. His yapping shadowed me as I walked through the living room. The palest of grays coated my walls, bordered by white trim. The large picture window overlooking part of the front lawn and street showed Kate's car parked at the curb.

"It's just Kate." I shushed my overprotective dog, picking him up and holding him with one arm against my side. I opened the door and found Kate standing on my front stoop. With Samuel.

My mind blanked.

Chewie's growls vibrated his tiny body. I rubbed his head, searching for the right words to gouge into my former best friend.

Samuel wore an outfit similar to last week. Jeans, a plain T-shirt, and work boots. He flicked his gaze to Kate. "Is that her or the dog growling?"

Kate had the audacity to grin. "I'm not sure."

"Both." I nailed Kate with a glare.

She held up a watermelon-pink envelope that looked like a greeting card. "Can we come in?"

"Do you want me to turn my back to you first, Brutus, so you can thrust your knife into it?"

"I come bearing a delayed birthday gift."

I motioned to Samuel. "I've had that gift—and returned it."

Kate didn't bat an eye. "Samuel's been hired to screen in your back patio."

I blinked. "What?"

"I'd originally planned to hire Earl, but with him being out of commission, and honestly, he was a tad too old for this job—"

"No—"

"And I don't want some untrustworthy stranger working at your house."

I pointed at Samuel. "He *is* untrustworthy."

"Um." Samuel raised his hand. "I'm right here."

"He's only untrustworthy with your heart," Kate said. "He can handle carpentry work. He has a lot of experience from his military training."

Samuel sighed and turned, eyeing the cream-colored bricks that made up my house, the robin's-egg-blue shutters. He probably thought it a feminine-looking home. Good.

Chewie released a yelp.

I hushed him and redirected my agitation to Kate. "I don't care if Chip Gaines vouches for him."

She shoved the card at me, my attention snagging on the word *Mom* handwritten on the front. My heart squeezed. It was Conner's neat penmanship. I stepped back, allowing them in. Samuel closed the door, and I set Chewie down. He moseyed to Kate, his nails clicking on the wood floors, and sniffed her shoes.

I peeled open the envelope and found a card with a ninja on it. The preprinted message inside relayed belated birthday sentiments. I skimmed over it to my son's handwritten words.

Mom,

We've been saving up the past few years to get the back patio screened in. We want it to be your spot to enjoy outside without the bugs that creep you out. Miss Kate is finding the right person for the job. We're looking forward to seeing it all done and you relaxing in it when we come home for Thanksgiving break.

P.S. We'd planned to give you this gift for your next birthday, but when we told Grandma and Grandpa about it last week, they wanted to match what we'd saved.

Both boys had signed their love and names. I laid a hand to my heart. *Lord, what good children You blessed me with. And dear in-laws.*

I glanced at Kate, whose eyes slightly misted. Behind her, Samuel came into focus. *Ugh.* My shoulders sank. Kate hadn't just given me a birthday card, it'd been her golden ticket to my assenting to this ridiculousness. Because if I didn't go along with the gift, Conner and Mason would be disappointed.

It would be like the time they'd saved their money and bought me an elliptical machine. It had been way too expensive for them. My knee-jerk reaction of wanting to return it wasn't what it should've been. I'd spoiled the gift. Taken away their desire to be a blessing. And I'd vowed never to do that again. All of which Kate had had a front row to because they'd gone to her for help with orchestrating the purchase and delivery.

"Now that everything's settled . . ." Kate pulled her phone from her purse and glanced at it. "I need to get back to the café."

My stomach bottomed out, as though I'd gone over the precipice of a roller coaster. "You can't leave."

"I can, and I am." She reached for the door.

"Wicked!" I hissed.

She shrugged, unrepentant, and turned to Samuel. "Don't pet her dog. It's a demon." And with that, she left.

The emotional ride I'd been forced onto came to a screeching halt, and I tried to take stock as the bar lifted, freeing me to exit. Queasy? Check. Wobbly legs? Check. Disorientation? Check. At least I had on makeup and my hair was fixed. That was one good thing from the potential client meeting this morning. Although I wished I'd kept my cute dress on instead of changing into yoga pants and a loose tank top.

Chewie interrupted the silence, sniffing and grumbling at Samuel's steel-toed boots. My stare glided up his long, muscular legs. He carried a small notepad and tape measure in his large hands. And he had a pencil perched behind his ear. I placed the card from Conner and Mason on the entranceway table.

Samuel nodded toward my dog. "Your boyfriend?"

"Chewie."

"I see your love of *Star Wars* hasn't faded."

I crossed my arms. "My boys named him."

"So you brainwashed them into sci-fi?"

I narrowed my eyes. "What would you have named him? Elmer?" I held my glower and was rewarded with witnessing the realization dawn on his face.

"As in Elmer Fudd." Now it was his turn to narrow his eye. "You never complained about my hunting weekends."

True. If I had, would he have done them less often?

He squatted, holding out his hand palm-down to Chewie. *Oh no.* "I wouldn't do that."

"How old is he?"

"Ten or eleven. He was a rescue, so we're not sure."

"So you got him when . . ."

"I thought a dog would be a lift for the boys. Turns out it was what I needed too."

Chewie gave one sniff, then snarled and snapped. Samuel pulled his fingers back just in time.

I snickered. "We warned you."

He straightened, scowling at my dog.

Having made his intentions known, Chewie trotted to my side and sat next to my bare feet.

Samuel shifted his frown to our surroundings, taking in the open space that functioned as the den and dining room.

Shoot. I'd only expected Kate and hadn't cleaned up. I grabbed the empty laundry basket next to the coffee table and scanned the piles of clothes I'd folded. Thankfully no underwear or bras. And most thankfully, no granny panties.

"According to the volunteer schedule, you were supposed to help this morning. You didn't show."

My grip on the basket waned. "Your observation skills are astounding."

He moved to the entertainment center, surveying the distressed wood shelves encircling the TV. Framed pictures of the boys filled them, a mixture of school portraits and candids. His attention paused on the last one. The final family photo we'd had with Mark. A slight wince followed, and he turned from the picture, his perusal relocating to where the sofa, love seat, and coffee table sectioned off the living room. "You lined up that Saturday client?"

"Not that it's any of your business, but no. Not yet." I took in my house with renewed eyes, wondering what Samuel thought. This place had been a labor of love and a form of therapy. I'd purchased it not long after Mark's death. The inside had been a mess, but it had good bones. Sort of like me at the time. My obsession with HGTV and being a nuisance at Home Depot DIY workshops saved us oodles and gave me something to fixate on. A distraction from having to give up our old house and the millions of precious memories contained within its walls.

A sparkle lit Samuel's eye, his lips pulling up at both corners.

I followed his line of sight to the Green Beret book resting on the end of the couch. A searing heat flushed my neck, face, and ears. *Oh, Lord. How about the Rapture happening right now?*

With an unhurried stride, he crossed the space and reached for the book, reading the back cover. His pleased gaze ascended, colliding with mine, one brow lifting.

I set the basket on the floor and began methodically cracking my knuckles. "I was curious. Now, if you've finished taking inventory of my house . . ." I walked through the dining area, closed my laptop, and gestured to the back door.

He trailed, pausing at the kitchen tucked away to the right. Crisp white cabinets and a square island painted in coastal blue made up the space. A glass pendant light that had taken some haggling in the French Market hung above it.

"This way, nosy." I opened the back door and stepped onto

the covered patio and into the suffocating humidity. Chewie joined us. A wooden fence enclosed the green lawn and single oak tree. A metal lawn mower shed rested at the back corner, reminding me I had grass to cut this evening.

"This is really nice." Samuel stood beside me, taking in the deep yard.

Chewie growled at him.

"Good boy." Leaning over, I patted Chewie's head. "It's why I purchased the house. I wanted outside room for the boys and this sweet baby."

"How long have you been here?"

"Almost ten years." I walked to the edge of the concrete pad, the sun slanting under the roofline, hitting the only two things out there. A plastic chair and a pot of shriveled snapdragons. I gathered my hair up, holding it against my head, bringing a temporary reprieve to the sweat gathering along my neck and shoulders. "I couldn't afford our old house on my own." Plus, it'd been closer to Mama's, and I'd needed all the help I could get with Mark's parents out of state. I prodded the planter with my toe and glanced over my shoulder.

Samuel's gaze lingered up my body, and what appeared to be appreciation swept across his features.

Fighting a smile, I turned to the rotting plant, and let my hair fall back into place. All these years of eating right and exercising to stay healthy for my boys was paying off in spades for a reason I'd never anticipated. My grin melted. Except for my soft middle. I tugged the hem of my shirt, grateful for its flowy fit. "If you want a dry place to keep your supplies for the job, you can use the garage."

I moved off the patio, vibrant grass prickling my toes, and led the way to the back of the garage. Opening the door, I flipped on the light and took several steps in, the concrete cool and smooth beneath my feet. The scent of vinegar and dust tickled my nose as my attention landed on Princess Tipsy's portrait, suspended from a random nail stuck in one of the exposed studs. At least if Hayley ever questioned where the artwork was, I'd know.

Samuel examined the demented alpaca with clear amusement. "Please tell me you didn't actually spend money on this."

"No. I made it at a painting party."

"What kind of party was it? Were you on drugs?"

I pressed my lips in a tight line. "Is this enough room for you?"

"Plenty." He moved to the folding-table setup against one wall. Gallon jugs of distilled vinegar and club soda sat atop them. Boxes of baking soda and cornstarch too. He nudged one of the glass measuring cups. "You should be proud of what you've done."

I snorted. "It's not hard to make."

"I'm talking about everything." He inclined his chin to the house. "Raising two boys, running your own business."

I began cracking my knuckles again, staring intently at the orange extension cord hanging from the pegboard on the wall. This unexpected side of Samuel would take some getting used to—and would possibly lead to arthritis in my hands.

"But you did fail on that dog."

On cue, Chewie scampered through the open door, and I smiled, but it dimmed. "If you're doing this so I'll go out with you, it's not going to work."

"I'm doing this because I have the extra time right now and like to stay busy."

Invisible fingers pinched my ego.

A flirtatious grin eclipsed his face. "*And* I think it'll get me brownie points with you."

I rolled my eyes. "Come on, I'll give you a key to the garage. That way you can come and go as you please."

"See, my plan's working already. Although I thought we would take things slow this time."

I glared at him. "It's a key to the garage, not my house."

"It's progress."

"Samuel, you don't want to date me. I'm not the same person I used to be."

For a long moment, he regarded me. His stare piercing, his teasing expression shifting to a look of determination. "Neither am I."

11

SUNDAY MORNING I PUT ON MY BIG GIRL UNDIES and attended my regular service. Kate had texted that Hayley wasn't feeling well, so they were skipping.

Sean Crawford, one of the men Kate had mentioned at the painting party, moved into the row before me. "Good morning, Julia." His smile displayed a perfect set of teeth, set in a kind face. What was he? Early forties? Wasn't he widowed too? He veered on the scrawny side but not in a malnourished way. He probably just had a high metabolism or ran a marathon every day.

"Morning," I said, noting not the least bit of zing. Not even the hint of a tingle.

Sean continued on to take a seat diagonally from me. If he had been interested, wouldn't he have tried harder? Or maybe he had before, I'd never noticed, and he'd given up. He turned, and at finding me watching him, he brightened, flashing his perfect smile again.

I whipped my bulletin open, not returning the gesture. If Kate had been right—and it seemed she had—I wasn't going to encourage the guy.

Samuel quietly slipped into the open seat next to me. Poor Sean Crawford noticed, his spine hunching a fraction. Well, at least Samuel had been good for one thing today.

At Mama's house, she and I had come to an unvoiced truce not to talk about Samuel. She'd read her bulletin, and I'd sipped a cup of burned coffee. One she'd no doubt purposefully prepared that way. She'd also added Samuel's name to her enemies list. Right between Benedict Arnold and the neighbor stealing her newspaper.

That evening, sitting on my sofa with Chewie tucked against my legs, I composed an email to Robert Breaux with the quote for cleaning his offices. Maybe along with my professionally worded estimate, I could tack on an addendum: sign here if you agree to both the pricing and not to break my best friend's heart if she decides to date you. Penalty for violating either of these contractual terms would result in termination of cleaning services, and the unleashing of my inner need for vengeance for hurting Kate, including but not limited to stuffing the rims of your Mercedes with shrimp shells.

I pitched my head back, resting it against the soft microsuede fabric of my couch. How would I relay my opinion of this man to Kate? Was her self-professed noninterest in him genuine? Frugality wasn't a bad thing. Shoot, I was thrifty. One look in my refrigerator mimicked a bizarre, minute-to-win-it game—locating the real butter among the two dozen butter tubs I'd repurposed as Tupperware. But Robert Breaux's kind of cheapness rubbed me the wrong way. Would he make Kate pay for her meal if they went out? Have her chip in for gas? I was still ticked at her for bringing Samuel to my home but not mad enough to subject her to having to haul her own garbage if she became Mrs. Breaux.

My phone pinged with a new text.

SAMUEL
I made too much dinner. Can I bring you some tomorrow when I start on the patio?

I tensed. Then again, maybe Kate hauling her trash until-death-do-they-part would be a suitable punishment for what she was currently putting me through.

My teeth sunk into my bottom lip. How much trouble would it be to change my number? I lacked a broad circle of family and friends, so letting them know wouldn't take much. But it'd be an inconvenience to my clients and necessitate ordering new business cards. And what about all the forms listing me with that number as the emergency contact for the boys? Plus, a new number would probably lead to numerous calls and texts from the people the owner of the old number hadn't informed. Would I be acquiring someone else's Samuel?

My attention drifted to the Green Beret book on the coffee table. The cover displayed a soldier's camouflaged face, complete with moss draping his helmet. The only thing marking him as a person were his open eyes. Eyes filled with determination . . . like Samuel. I ran my fingers along Chewie's back. "He'd just get my new number anyway, wouldn't he?"

Blocking Samuel seemed the only logical answer. But what if he needed to reach me for something about the patio? A haggard sigh pushed from deep within. Once the patio was finished, I'd block his number. Until then, I had to be as curt as possible. I typed a one-word response.

ME
No.

SAMUEL
You sound crabby, which used to mean you're hungry.

I scowled at my phone for a good three Mississippis, then put it down, refusing to respond. It dinged with another message.

SAMUEL
I'll be over tomorrow around one.

ME
The side gate will be unlocked. Be careful with
it. It's a little rickety.

———⚬———

Late Monday afternoon, I pulled into my driveway to the
sight of Samuel's ridiculous black truck parked at the curb. The
thing looked like it ran on testosterone instead of gasoline. Having known all day that he would most likely be here when I got
home had been an odd mixture of nervous energy and dread.

I sat in my SUV, eyeing the front door. If it hadn't been for
Chewie being stuck inside with his bladder about to rupture, I
would have gone to Kate's or my mom's. I could swoop in and
take Chewie. But the thought of Samuel knowing he affected
me that much? Unbearable.

With only working on the patio in his spare time, he'd said
this project could take a few weeks. Especially with replacing
a rotting post that held up a portion of the roof and doing
everything solo. I couldn't avoid him that long. Plus, if I visited
Mama every day, she'd know something was up. And there was
no way I'd tell her Samuel was working at my house. I'd never
hear the end of it, and she'd probably sneak over and leave
roofing nails under his truck tires.

I entered, Chewie a frantic blur of fur clamoring at my feet.
He hightailed it to the back door, barking up a storm, alerting
me to the danger lurking in the backyard. If he only knew how
dangerous Samuel was.

I dropped my keys and purse on the entryway table and
moved hesitantly through the living room, my sights on the
windows stretching the rear wall from the dining room and
through the kitchen. Natural light streamed in as though all the
switches had been flipped. Another perk of this house, along
with the modest utility costs.

Samuel came into view through the window over the kitchen sink. He wore a baseball hat, his profile strikingly rugged.

My belly quivered. Quivered! *Buck up, girl. This is only day one.* I unlocked the door, the click garnering Samuel's attention. Through the glass, his gaze met mine, an easy smile spreading across his face. *No, no, no. Think of that gray eyebrow hair. Take control of your hormones rationally. Pluck them away.* I opened the door, bestowing the wrath of Chewie. The poodle mix charged right up to Samuel, barking at his work boots, which probably weighed more than the dog himself.

Samuel narrowed his eye at Chewie. "Hello, Cujo."

Having sufficiently made his intentions clear, Chewie scampered to the grass. For the sake of my unsteady stomach and the hormones I was plucking, I avoided looking directly at Samuel. He, on the other hand? Oh, I could feel his stare on me as though it were a physical touch. Purposeful, wandering. I crossed my arms, surreptitiously wiping my clammy palms on the sleeves of my scrubs.

"Hello, Julia."

"Hello." Chewie ran along the base of the oak tree, sniffing and tipping his head up, surveying the limbs for squirrels.

"How was your day?"

"Fine." A warm, paltry breeze ambled through, stirring several blades of grass that remained on the patio from when I'd cut the lawn yesterday. Like pumping gas, I hated cutting the grass. But with the boys gone, so was my cheap labor.

"My day was good too."

"Great." I said the word as though describing my enthusiasm for a Pap smear.

A low chuckle flowed from Samuel's direction, followed by the scuffing of shoes on concrete.

I glimpsed out the corner of my eye and found him turned away, studying the post at the far end of the patio that connected to the roof. He raised an arm, extending a tape measure to the top of the post and working it down the length of the pole. A line of sweat dotted his spine. His T-shirt lifted, revealing a glimpse of smooth, tan skin. I leaned closer. Was that a ripple of muscles on his lower back? I hadn't realized muscles grew there. Quick as a wink, he peeked at me and pressed the release button on the measure, the metal tape retracting with a harsh zip.

I startled. *Busted.*

My ears, no doubt, matched the shade of Kate's hair. "I wasn't looking at you."

He straightened to his full height, amusement clear on his face. "No?"

"No. There was a . . . a ladybug." I cracked my pinky knuckle.

"A ladybug?"

"Yes. It flew over and was crawling." I fluttered my fingers, reenacting the imaginary insect's flight, adding to my fib.

"On my backside?" His brows rose, his smile barely contained.

"Come on, Chewie." I clapped my hands. Ever loyal, he came running. "If you want something to drink or need to use the bathroom"—I motioned to the house—"help yourself."

"Thank you."

I moved my cleaning supplies from my SUV to the garage and found the space full of proof of Samuel's efforts today. Stacks of cedarwood in different sizes, workhorses with a sheet of plywood over them to create a table, big rolls of screening, several types of drills, and a saw. He'd been tidy, which was not the Samuel I'd known, whose apartment had always been in disarray. Clothes and dirty dishes everywhere, fishing and hunting gear piled in the corners. But here, he'd placed his materials to one side of the garage, as if to show he was giving me space. Not a single tool lay on the table I used to create my cleaning products.

I changed into shorts and a T-shirt and continued my over-analyzing on the elliptical machine set up in a spare bedroom. Today called for working out my stress on the dreaded Rolling Hills program, concentrating on my butt muscles since nothing could be done about the stretch marks and extra skin on my middle. After thirty minutes, I was a sweaty mess with jelly legs and convinced Samuel was trying to wage psychological warfare on me.

Entering the kitchen, I found Chewie sitting at the back door like a soldier guarding his assigned station. The screaming of a drill penetrated from outside, sending Chewie running to me. "It's okay." I picked him up and peered through the window above the sink. Samuel knelt, attaching boards to the outer edges of the concrete floor to make a frame. Unlike my earlier mistake, I did not linger. I set Chewie down and got to work rehydrating and heating up leftovers.

One thing I still hadn't adjusted to was making less food. The appetite of teenage boys was something to behold. And cooking for them all summer had brought me back to making enough for an army. I paused and grudgingly glanced through the window at Samuel. Or enough food for a Green Beret.

The microwave beeped, and I pulled my plate of spaghetti and meatballs from the appliance, setting it on the island behind me. The scent of marinara sauce and basil coated the air.

Chewie growled, retreating from the door as Samuel stepped in. The fur ball barked all the way to the love seat that acted as a divider between the living and dining room. He popped up on the back of the couch as though gaining height would increase his ferociousness.

"Chewie," I called. "That's enough."

He yapped once more, maintaining his watch on Samuel.

"That dog has the beadiest, evilest eyes I've ever seen."

"He does not." I opened the utensil drawer, retrieving a knife.

"Have you checked him for horns?"

I shut the drawer with more force than necessary and turned to him, my ponytail flipping off my shoulder. "Are you done for today?"

"I am." He removed his hat, wiping perspiration from his face with his forearm.

At least I wasn't the only one sweating.

"Can I take you up on that offer of a drink?"

"Can you say one nice thing about my dog?"

A smile flickered, the corner of his good eye creasing. I assumed his bad eye did the same, but I couldn't tell with the patch shielding it. He stared at Chewie, assessing. "Despite his puny size, he's a good guard dog."

My gaze flicked to the ceiling. "Drinks are in the fridge."

He moved to the sink, turning on the faucet and washing his hands.

I skirted the island, adamantly keeping it between us.

Using the towel hanging on the dishwasher's handle, he dried his hands, watching me. "That looks good."

"It sure does." I set the knife on my dinner plate and grabbed the fork resting in the open Tupperware holding the angel-hair pasta.

He surveyed the large bowl of meatballs. "And it looks like you have plenty."

"I do." I snapped the lid to the meatball container, covering them.

He snickered and moved for the refrigerator, grabbing a bottled water.

A smidgen of guilt nipped me. I imagined Jesus standing in my kitchen, tsking and throwing me some side-eye. Battling a sigh, I pulled the lid off the dish. "If you're hungry, you can have some."

Samuel heated his food, and I pulled together a spring salad mix. Dinner with the enemy. How had my evening turned into the title of a Lifetime movie? Or maybe it was more of a low-budget knockoff of that Julia Roberts film. Only I did not boast amazing hair and a million-dollar smile. What I did have was six-dollar home-dyed locks, and I would probably end up with basil in my teeth at some point during this dreaded meal.

We sat at the dining table, and *Wheel of Fortune* played on the TV, lessening the burden of making conversation. Samuel's hat lay next to the floral centerpiece, his hair askew in a very distracting way. Chewie still perched on the back of the love seat, like an ornery mockingbird, ready to swoop down and attack.

Samuel scooted his chair closer. "Do you mind if I say grace?"

Somewhere in a medical waste dump, my long-ago removed uterus pulsated. There was nothing more attractive than a hot man praying. Something I hadn't appreciated until returning to the Lord and meeting Mark. As quietly as possible, I cleared my throat. "Go ahead."

Samuel reached toward me, resting his hand on the table, palm up.

Chewie growled.

Nice try. I clasped my hands in my lap and bowed my head.

"Father, thank You for this meal and Your love. Please bless this food, and the hands that prepared it. Amen."

"Amen."

We dug in, eating to the sound of utensils scraping our plates and the charming wit of Pat Sajak. The contestants on the game show introduced themselves, listing their occupations, fabulous spouses, adorable children, precious grandkids, and their exciting hobbies. *Gag.* Was anyone ever honest in their intros?

Hi, Pat. I'm Julia. I'm a widow from New Orleans and have two teenage boys who moved eight hundred forty-nine miles away. I clean houses for a living and had to scrub a toilet today that would've made Vanna toss her tofu cookies.

I lifted my glass of sweet tea, taking a sip of cold, sugary bliss. My gaze slid to Samuel. What would he rattle off to Pat Sajak? I knew the major things, like he was a veteran, had a daughter and carpentry skills, but what else? Was he doing construction work during the day? He'd earned a college degree in business, so that could go in any direction. If this was some other person sitting across from me, I'd be asking questions, getting to know them. Was my effort to be terse only showing my hand at how much he still affected me?

I set my glass down, the ice clinking. "I guess Wyatt and your dad were thrilled when you joined the army." His younger brother and father had badgered him to enlist the entire time we'd dated. Wyatt had just become a Green Beret, and his father had been one too.

Samuel paused in slicing through his last meatball. "They were." His throat bobbed, going along with the uneasy tone in his words.

"How long did you serve?"

He chewed another bite and swallowed. "Eighteen years."

This was all so different from my typical, quiet nights. Kate rarely came for supper since she had Hayley and their routine. Mama couldn't make it through a meal without a cigarette, so she never ate here. Usually, I dined while watching *Gilmore Girls*. But as delightful as dinner with Lorelai and Rory was, it wasn't human interaction.

I could sullenly admit this was nice. "And when did you get out of the military?"

"Three years ago, when I turned forty. That's when the accident happened." He motioned to his patch.

"So you enlisted in the army right after graduating from college?"

"I did." Again with the tense timbre. He tilted his bottled water to his lips, taking long, slow pulls.

Hmm. At that point, he'd been twenty-two and fresh out of college with a degree. I twirled a forkful of pasta until it wrapped all the way around the tines and brought it to my mouth, savoring the taste of tomatoes, oregano, and garlic.

Why would he have surrendered to the influence of his family then? From what I'd read in the library book on Green Berets, a degree wasn't necessary to join the Special Forces.

He set his fork down and wiped his mouth. Only a few strands of spaghetti remained on his dish.

I shook my head. "You still inhale your food."

"And you still take forever to eat yours."

Our eyes locked, too much flirtation reflecting in his. I broke the connection, straightening the salt and pepper shakers on the table between us. "Can I ask what happened to your eye?"

He leaned back in his chair, resting a hand on his stomach. "It's not some glamorous war story. I was tapped to return to North Carolina to help train a new round of Special Forces candidates."

"Oh." I straightened. "I read about that. How they use current Green Berets to train and help select soldiers, and how some of those who make it may end up on their teams for future missions."

He gave a nod, his head tilting slightly to the side, as though pleased with my knowledge. "My specialty was engineering. The student construction team I was in charge of had a kid who'd never handled a saw or driven a nail. Their task was to construct a building from the dirt up. While setting joists on the roof, the kid lost his grip on a board. And that was it."

My heartbeat slowed, an overall heavy feeling weighing on me. "I'm sorry."

He shrugged and studied his hands, running a finger over the callus on one of his palms. "Would it sound crazy if I said I'm not sorry it happened?"

"You wanted to get out of the army?"

"No. I loved it. I was actually going to reenlist for another five years."

Bewilderment expanded through me, question marks duplicating in my mind.

"Throughout my life, there had been this . . . emptiness inside me." He edged forward, elbows straddling his dish, his fingers propped over his plate. "Like something was missing. I tried filling it with different things. Sports and girlfriends in high school. Hunting, fishing . . . you." His gaze ascended to mine, then fell away.

I rasped in a breath. "Why didn't you ever talk to me about it?"

"I don't know." He sighed. "But from the day I entered the army, that sensation increased. I thought it was guilt over everything that happened with us." A smear of dirt stained his cheek, below his brown leather patch. What could only be deep regret emanated from his hazel eye, fastened on my face.

This was so not where I thought this conversation would go. I looked to Chewie. His guarded stance had relaxed, and his face rested on his front paws.

"All these years, that hollowness flared time and again." Samuel kneaded his forehead. "When I was on a mission, it quieted. But as soon as the job was done, it'd return. And intensify. I'd chalked it up to stress. The increased strain with the deployments." His hand returned to the table. "I know now it was God trying to show me an easier way to Him. To peace."

I sat, enraptured. I'd known Samuel was a Christian now, but hearing him actually talk about God was something else. When we'd been dating, religion rarely came up, except when I'd invited him to Easter or Christmas Eve services. But not once had we attended church together or prayed. It hadn't been a priority. What if he'd been *this way* back then? If I'd married Samuel, I wouldn't have met Mark. Wouldn't have my boys. Which felt indubitably wrong. The realm of what-if was a dangerously confusing place.

"That whole week before the accident, tension had built steadily within me each day." He stared out the front window overlooking the street. "It was like this one time I'd been caught out on Bayou des Allemands in a duck blind with a storm approaching. I'd known it was coming but was arrogant enough to think I could sit it out. Each minute that had passed, the atmospheric pressure had built, pressing in all around me. Relentless."

A rueful expression arced his lips. "The day of the accident, I hadn't been able to focus on anything. I'd been going through the motions. When that board came falling, my mind blanked. It wasn't a scary feeling either. It was serene. In the commotion of everything that followed, I had no fear. What felt like a calm, steady hand rested on my shoulder." He placed his palm to the shoulder on the same side as his injured eye. "In that moment, I knew it was Jesus, and I gave my life to Him." A sheen covered his eye, and he blinked it away. "I came to in the hospital after surgery. They'd removed my eye, and God had removed that emptiness plaguing me for so long."

I sank back in my seat, unshed tears blurring my vision, awe warming my chest.

"After meeting Jesus, He began lighting up my life." A tender smile grew, softening the hard lines of his face. "It was like I'd been living with a tinted lens. So even though I was down an eye, everything was much clearer."

A gaggle of goose bumps erupted over my arms, and I rubbed them.

"A lot of other good came from what happened. Soon after, Brooke, my daughter, hit a bit of a rebellious streak." He pulled his phone from his pocket, his fingers moving across the screen. He held up his device, showing a picture of a striking young lady.

My breath halted. She was beautiful, and the spitting image of Samuel. From the shade of her hair to her eyes and nose. Except for the roundness to her face, she looked like a female clone of him. It was a relief to know seeing her didn't hurt as much as I'd feared.

"She needed help with staying on track with school. Had I reenlisted, I wouldn't have been there for her."

"Is she okay now?"

"She is." Pride unfolded in his countenance. He stood, picking up his dishes. "She's aiming for a nursing degree. And now that she's squared away, I'm focusing on my business."

I turned in my chair, watching him. "In construction?"

Shaking his head, he scraped his plate into the garbage can. "I'm starting an outdoor adventure company with hunting and fishing charters as team-building events for corporations and personal excursions for tourists and locals."

My stars. It was the perfect occupation for him. What a sweet gift from God.

He placed his dish in the sink and reached into his back pocket, retrieving a business card, and handed it to me. The thick, smooth cardstock was a manly gray. One side held his contact info, and the other a list of excursions he provided. He gauged me, as if wondering what I thought. "It's one of the reasons I attended the business crawl."

My ego tweaked a hair. So he hadn't been there just for me. *Hmpf.* I set the card on the table. *Well . . . good.*

"I've saved up from the military, taking advantage of extra training to make the most money, signing bonuses from re-ups. And I invested wisely." He rinsed his plate and utensils, and loaded them into the dishwasher.

I took up my own tableware, following suit. Based on the truck he drove, I hadn't thought he'd been hurting for money.

He resumed his seat at the table, as though getting comfortable.

I put my dishes in the sink. "Good night, Samuel."

Lightly shaking his head, he grabbed his hat. "Good night, Julia." Crossing the living room, he threw me a flirty grin.

Another growl rumbled from Chewie.

Samuel glanced toward the dog. "Good night, Cujo." He shut the door with a chuckle.

Later that night, I lay in bed, my mind brimming with wonder over Samuel's testimony. My phone dinged with a text. Unlike last time, I did not go into frantic mode.

SAMUEL
I'm not convinced there was a ladybug on me earlier. Thought you'd like to know I'm vacuuming shirtless, if you'd like to come see.

ME
I'm not coming over. And you're not shirtless.

SAMUEL
I am. I'm thinking of forgetting the outdoor business and going a different route.

ME
Shirtless cleaning services?

SAMUEL
Yes. I'll also clean toilets, do laundry.

Oh, if he only knew he was talking my love language.

ME
I'll be sure to let the church know you can handle the cleaning side of the ministry too. Miss Marlene will be ecstatic.

12

THE FOLLOWING SUNDAY USHERED IN the slightly cooler weather of October. The time of year when the people of southeast Louisiana exhaled a sigh of relief that the peak of hurricane season had ended. Ironically, a long and blustery squall of thunderstorms had blown through the past week, keeping Samuel from working on the patio.

That hadn't stopped him from intruding on my life through my thoughts, though. Waking up this morning, I'd had to fight the anticipation of getting to see him. I was in trouble. It had only been six days since he'd stayed for dinner.

Six days!

As penance, I skipped attending church in person and streamed the service online. My earlier text to Kate that I wasn't coming had resulted in her blowing up my phone with cocker spaniel and chicken GIFs. She too had been amazed by Samuel's testimony when I'd shared it with her. And she had again encouraged me to tell him about my miscarriage. I'd rationalized if the Holy Spirit moved me beyond a shadow of a doubt to tell him, I would. So far the only thing I'd felt the need to do was put some distance between us.

Standing in my kitchen, I held my phone to my ear, the call ringing to Mama's landline.

"Yeah," she said by way of greeting.

"I didn't go to church today, so I won't be stopping by with a bulletin." I stared out the back window, eyeing the lawn needing mowing. All this rain had been like God sprinkling Miracle-Gro.

"You sick?"

"No."

"Okay." *Click.*

With a roll of my eyes, I walked to my bedroom, Chewie shadowing me. I changed from pajamas to running shorts, a T-shirt, and my grass-cutting tennis shoes with permanent green stains marking the soles. The sun had been out for hours, drying the lawn, and I wasn't going to miss the opportunity to get this task done in case another storm rolled through later.

A round of knocking at the front door set Chewie on a tirade. I knew from the machine-gun rapping method who it was. Glancing out the window, I spied Mama's enormous Buick parked behind my SUV in the driveway. I opened the door, struck by how much she mirrored the cartoon character Maxine.

Her gray hair was smooshed at an angle, as though she'd slept on one side all night, and she still sported her bathrobe. "I need ground coffee." She hadn't even taken the TV remote out of her pocket.

I stepped aside, allowing her and her scent of eau de Marlboro in. Mama rarely visited since she wasn't allowed to smoke in my house. And usually if she ran out of something, she asked me to bring it to her instead of wasting her own gas driving all of six blocks over here.

She shuffled her slippered feet through the living room, past the dining table, and into the kitchen. Her steely glare swept the area. Pausing, she lifted her ear to the ceiling. "Do you hear something?" She headed through the opening at the back of the kitchen that led to the hallway, bathrooms, and bedrooms.

My eyes widened. Had she expected to find a man here? A man whose name rhymed with *spaniel*? I bit my tongue. What a booger! "No one else is here," I called out.

She returned and eyed Chewie, who stood next to me. He stared back at her, seesawing his head, as if asking, *"What's up, lady?"* Mama's pursed lips relaxed, seemingly satisfied that if Chewie wasn't in an uproar, then there wasn't a stranger—or a spaniel—here.

Stuffing my aggravation down, I opened the pantry door, seized my extra bag of coffee, and whipped it out to her.

She took the offering and left.

An hour later, I had the front lawn cut and was almost done with the back. Several long, straight stretches of grass in the center of the yard were all that remained. The sun beat down on me, and sweat dripped from every nook and cranny. Flecks of dirt and grass coated my legs and arms. The roar of the old push mower drowned out everything but my thoughts.

They drifted like a plastic grocery bag tossing in the wind, changing direction on a dime. Mama's visit—thank goodness she hadn't noticed the work done so far on the back patio— the boys, Samuel, the cleaning ministry's schedule. I calculated which elderly person had gone the longest without a visit. Maybe I could slip in a quick stop after work one day this week.

Someone touched my shoulder from behind.

I jolted with a scream, turning and raising my arms into a defensive position. The lawn mower killed with my release of the safety lever. It seemed my childhood obsession with Ralph Macchio had stuck with me. My hands had poised, ready to karate chop my attacker into submission.

Samuel held up his own hands, taking a step back, amusement on his face. "Clearly, I need to teach you some self-defense moves."

My chest rose and fell, and I leaned over, bracing my hands on my knees. "What's wrong with you?"

"I tried calling your name. You didn't hear me."

"Obviously."

Chewie's muffled barks carried across the yard. He jumped and pawed at the full-length window of the back door.

"You weren't at church."

"So?" Straightening, I swiped the perspiration from my face with my sleeves. With my complexion and the heat, I knew my face had to resemble a creole tomato.

He scratched the back of his neck. "And you didn't answer your phone."

"I've been busy." I motioned to the lawn mower.

He glanced around. "You skipped church to cut the grass?"

"Yes." *No, I skipped church to avoid you.* I guess God had shown me.

"I had lunch with my daughter before she headed back to school, and I thought I'd swing by. Get some work done."

"Wonderful," I deadpanned.

He inclined his head to the remaining lawn that needed trimming. "Do you want me to finish for you?"

I pulled in a deep breath of exhaust fumes and fresh-cut grass, and stared at the lawn mower. "No. And even if I did, it's not going to start up now. The engine has to cool off."

He surveyed the ancient mower, then reached and pulled the starter cord. The muscles in his shoulders and upper back flexed. Much like my heart, the motor sputtered but didn't turn over.

I raised my brows at him and walked off.

"Julia?"

I turned.

One corner of his mouth hitched north. "It's good to know I still take your breath away." He winked.

I shot him the fiercest glare I could manage and turned back toward the house. At the door, I shucked off my grass-laden Adidas and slipped inside, Chewie greeting me. I grabbed a Gatorade from the fridge and caught my reflection on the wall oven. *Ugh*. My head tipped back in frustration. No makeup, flushed cheeks, sweaty hair wrangled in a topknot. And the cherry on top? Large sweat rings rounding my armpits and grandma beads dotting my neck.

I washed my hands in the sink and ripped a paper towel from the roll. Wiping my face and neck, I checked my phone resting on the counter. Sure enough, Samuel had called.

Chewie trotted to the back door, peering at Samuel through the window. A growl rumbled from him.

"Good boy." I went to him, leaning over and rubbing his ears, trying not to notice Samuel's toned legs.

During the deluge last week, he'd texted, asking me to search the internet and send him pictures of what I envisioned the patio looking like. Since this was a custom job, he'd pressed me to be specific about the design of the railings.

Mason's personal ringtone trilled through the air. Heart soaring, I lunged for the counter, grasping my cell. My baby was FaceTiming me! I accepted the call, his sweet face filling the screen.

Mason's eyes, crystal blue like his dad's, peered through his shaggy blond hair. "Hey, Mom." He needed a trim. Badly.

"Hi." All of my mama-nerves fired at once, creating an emotional overload. *Be cool. Be cool.* The last thing I needed was either of the boys knowing how much I missed them. I wouldn't use guilt like the weapon Mama wielded.

Behind him hung the posters we'd taped to his dorm room walls. He tossed his head, shaking his bangs from his eyes. "You look a mess, what are you doing?"

Sheesh. The brutal honesty of kids. "Cutting the grass. What are you doing?"

"Conner and I wanted to see what's going on with the patio."

He shifted his phone, bringing Conner into view, who was sitting at the foot of Mason's bed, his head bent over his cell.

Conner looked up and waved. "Hey, Mom." Conner, like Mason, was the spitting image of Mark. Pin-straight, dirty-blond hair, blue eyes, slim build. Though Conner kept his hair trimmed short.

"Hi, sweetie." Complete joy gathered in my heart. Since last week, I'd already spoken to my in-laws, and each of the boys, gushing over their generous gift, trying to make up for the elliptical debacle.

Mason moved, taking a seat next to Conner. "So bring us outside. We want to see what's been done."

My gaze flew to the back windows, landing on Samuel.

Oh, tub funk.

13

MY FACE, WHICH I COULD SEE in the upper corner of the phone's screen, drained of all color. "Um, the guy who's building it is here. I don't want to disturb him."

Conner perked up. "He's there? That's even better. We can meet him."

No, no, no. Samuel had already invaded every other piece of my life. Charmed my best friend, poked his head into the cleaning ministry, practically had his own parking spot at church. The man even had a key to my house! Well, my garage. But my kids had been the only area that had been Samuel-proofed. They were like an electrical socket, and I was the plastic plug covering them. And now that shield was being peeled off.

"O-okay." Where had my voice gone? "Hold on." With my heart galloping and my mind racing to catch up, I enfolded my phone in the hem of my shirt and held it to my belly button. I opened the door, Chewie charging up to Samuel. After making his hatred known, he scampered off to circle the tree.

Samuel's attention slid to me, his forehead creasing. He held a power drill in one hand and a two-by-six board in the other. The image of him could have easily graced any month in one of those hunky-construction-men calendars. "Everything okay?"

I pitched my voice low. "My boys are FaceTiming me." I pointed to my stomach and immediately regretted the gesture.

Samuel's gaze drifted to my phone-paunched abdomen.

I wrangled my nausea, squeezing my eyes shut. "They want to meet you—I mean, they don't want to *meet you*, meet you. They want to see the progress on the patio." Move over Hayley, there was a new queen of tween in town. And all the awkwardness for the position had magically been bestowed on me within the last five seconds.

He lifted his hand with the drill, pointing it to where I'd mummified the phone with the edge of my top. "You have them wrapped in your shirt?"

"So they won't hear or see me warning you."

He grew still, his Adam's apple bobbing. "Do you not want me to meet them?"

Was that concern in his features? "No," I whispered. "I'm fine with it." A half fib.

An audible breath released from him, the lines across his forehead smoothing. "Good."

"Just don't mention anything about . . ." I gestured back and forth between us.

He nodded.

I unwrapped the phone, realizing in my haste that Samuel could have glimpsed my middle. And possibly a stretch mark. Fabulous. I held the device up, Conner and Mason still on the screen, their expressions perplexed. Had they heard my exchange with Samuel?

"Here we are." My voice sounded too high and breathy. *Lord, a little help here, please.* I pressed a button on the screen and flipped the view the boys would see, taking it off me and putting it onto Samuel. "This is Samuel Reed. Samuel, these are my boys, Conner and Mason."

Samuel set his drill on the makeshift workbench he'd created out of two sawhorses and a sheet of plywood. He gave a half wave that came across as almost sheepish. If I wasn't bent on squashing all attraction for the man, I'd even say it was adorable.

"Mom," Conner said. "He can't see us. You need to flip the view again *and* turn the phone around."

Mason chuckled. "She's worse than Mawmaw."

I scoffed. "I am not worse than Mawmaw."

Samuel snickered, hefting the board to the worktable.

I flung a glare at Samuel and followed Conner's instructions, bringing us all on the screen to see each other. In the realm of surreal moments, this one topped them all. My shameful past colliding with my precious present. Technology proved a scary and powerful thing.

Samuel shifted closer behind me, ducking his chin to the boys. "It's nice to meet you both."

"You too," Mason said.

Conner straightened his forever-hunched posture. "We wanted to thank you for donating your time."

"What?" My shocked expression was clear to everyone, including me since I could see my face on the phone.

"We're paying for the supplies," Mason piped up. "Well, us and Grandma and Grandpa. But Mr. Samuel is volunteering his time."

I turned to Samuel. "You can't do that."

"Why not?"

"Mom," Mason called. "The phone."

"Oh." I'd dropped my hand. Hoisting it back up, I returned us all to view. "Samuel can't do this for free."

Samuel scratched the skin above his patch. "Yes, I can."

"We can still pay you." Mason shook the hair from his eyes. "Like we wanted to do from the start."

Samuel held up a hand. "Not necessary."

My pulse quickened, resulting from a combination of irritation and how Samuel's hand had barely brushed my back with his motion. "It is."

Mr. October angled, looking directly at me. "You volunteer your time for the cleaning ministry."

I glanced at him through the screen, blocking a direct connection. Technology wasn't so bad after all. "That's completely different."

Mason adjusted his hold on his phone, switching it to his other hand. "How?"

"Yeah, how?" Conner crossed his arms.

Because I can't be indebted to the man who shattered my heart. Because I don't want to think of him as capable of doing unselfish things. I pulled in a breath, my cheeks puffing, and expelled it in a huff. "It just is." Goodness. I had reverted back to middle school. Long live Queen Tween.

"Okay, guys," Samuel said. "You can pay me." He shook his head with a slicing gesture at his neck.

Mason and Conner chuckled.

I looked heavenward. *Lord, I don't want this comradery between them!*

"Y'all want to see what I've done so far?"

Yes, sirs all around.

I slipped on my shoes next to the back door and readjusted the view on my phone, keeping the lens on Samuel, and following him as he pointed out different things. The ground framework he'd completed, the supplies he'd compiled in the garage. The boys asked questions, and Samuel answered with ease. It was like I played the cameraman on a bizarre reality TV home improvement show. *Fixer-Upper with My Mom.* But at least I was seeing my boys. That they were happy.

With the tour complete and their stomachs grumbling for lunch, we disconnected, my arm falling limp at my side. The urge to jump in my SUV and drive to them, hug them, and make them eat vegetables expanded through me, pushing painfully against my ribs.

Samuel stepped toward me and paused, rapping his knuckles on his temporary workbench. "You miss them."

"I do." I pinched the neck of my shirt, lifting it to wipe my eyes. "But they're coming home for Thanksgiving." Too achingly long away.

⊰——⊱

One thing that hadn't changed with adulthood was looking forward to Fridays. But not even the promise of tonight's fresh beignets from Kate's café had eased the parasite of discouragement that had latched on to my heart this morning and sucked at my hope all day.

Robert Breaux had replied to my email with the estimate of cleaning his offices. As though my services were a hand-woven purse for sale in the French Market, he'd made a counteroffer. Of half the price of my quote. Half! Those shrimp shells were calling my name. I'd refrained from forwarding his email straight to Kate. Instead, I'd disclose everything, *everything* to her in person this evening.

Adding insult to injury, I'd fallen back to square one with acquiring Saturday work. What would I do now? Start cold-calling businesses from the phone book? Did phone books exist anymore?

I turned the corner of my street, knowing Samuel wouldn't be at my house. He had headed to Florida for the weekend with his daughter to go boat shopping at some big marina there. This past week, he'd worked on the patio three times in the evening and had dinner with me, Chewie, Pat Sajak, and Vanna White. He'd talked about the types of boats he planned to purchase for his business. A duck-hunting boat and a fishing boat. Apparently, a plethora of differences separated them. But based on the pictures he showed me on his phone, I could only see two: the size and camouflage.

My home came into view, and I fought the pinch of disappointment at not seeing the Testosterone Truck parked at the curb. What I did see, though, was that my grass had been freshly cut. I laid a hand against my breastbone, emotion sweeping over me.

Samuel Reed was not playing fair.

I parked and rounded my vehicle, taking note of how he'd even edged the driveway and sidewalk. And swept. Not a blade of grass littered the concrete. If I had thought cleaning the inside of my house was my love language, this was like slapping on a sizzling, melt-into-a-puddle foreign accent to it. Had he used my lawn equipment or brought his own? The spare key to the shed was affixed on the same ring as the key to the garage I'd given him.

Nearing the front door, the propped lid to my mailbox caught my attention. I reached inside and discovered a small yellow envelope with my name in neat print on the front. I removed the card and found the picture of a white alpaca licking a rainbow. I snorted and opened it. The same penmanship from the front continued.

Julia,
 I'm hoping this card will give me extra brownie points. Believe me, I got some strange looks from the guy working the register at Walgreens. See you at church on Sunday.

      Samuel

14

THE FOLLOWING TUESDAY MORNING I pulled up to the Holdens', the client with the creepy neighbor. It was ten o'clock, everyone off to work and school, the neighborhood quiet. Although I hadn't spied Sir Spamalot for weeks, life had taught me to never let my guard down. Taking chances couldn't be afforded. Especially not after Pete had breached my personal space last time. Instead of packing everything in the trunk like I did for the rest of my clients, I'd stored it on the floor behind the driver's seat. This gave me the advantage of staying on one side of the SUV and using it as a shield.

My pulse stammered, a cold sweat prickling my skin. Was this job really worth it? To be this anxious each week? *Ugh.* If only Robert Breaux hadn't been such a cheapskate. I needed this income. Plus, my lawn mower wouldn't last much longer. It was already older than Methuselah. *Suck it up, buttercup. We need all the work we can get right now.*

I gave one more glance in every direction, confirming the all-clear.

It was time to make like Flo-Jo.

I killed the engine, shoved my keys into my purse, and in one fluid motion, ejected from the SUV, closed my door—gently so as to not make any unnecessary noise—and opened the back car door.

I'd often considered getting one of those magnet decals to stick on my vehicle advertising my services. Now I was glad I hadn't. The last thing I needed was this jerk having my real name and number.

Once inside the house, I locked the door and pulled in a steadying breath. *See, everything's fine. It's not like he was outside waiting for you. You're probably making more of this than you should.* But to be safe, I checked the lock on the back door too.

An hour later, I was moving a set of sheets and pillowcases from the washer to the dryer, when the doorbell rang. That in itself wasn't completely out of the ordinary. Sometimes the mailman or UPS required a signature for a delivery. And in both cases, I ignored them, unless the client had given me permission to accept packages on their behalf. The Holdens had not.

I continued stuffing wet sheets into the dryer. The doorbell sounded again, accompanied by a round of knocking. I frowned, and a slight chill rippled over my skin, despite the sheen of perspiration I'd already worked up from hauling myself up and down stairs. Never was the mailman or UPS that determined.

I stopped wrestling with the damp bedding and slid my hand to the exercise band holding my phone to my upper arm. Through the speaker, TobyMac sang for me to "feel it." And although T-Mac meant for me to be feeling the Lord, the only thing coursing through me was a sense of trepidation. I paused the music.

Ding-dong.

Maybe it was some super-amped Jehovah's Witnesses. Blood thumping louder in my ears with each step, I moved from the laundry room, down the hallway, and through the living room. The doorbell rang again, reverberating through me as though the chimes were stitched to the lining of my stomach.

The narrow foyer lay ahead. Thankfully the front door held no windows. With slow, wobbly steps, I approached. Holding my breath, I poised on my toes, aiming for the peephole without touching the door, in case the wood creaked against my weight and gave my presence away. I balanced and squinched my left eye, looking with my right.

Pervy Pete stood on the other side, holding what looked like a beer.

Sink whiskers. I jolted back.

Pound-pound-pound. "Hello?" he called. "Juanita, it's me." I pictured his meaty fists beating the door, inches away. The doorknob twisted and wiggled.

What in the—a wave of dread surged from my brain, rolling heavy and thick, spreading down my neck, out to my arms, past my gut, and through my feet. I imagined myself as the scarecrow from *The Wizard of Oz*, except instead of straw, sand filled me. Dense and weighted.

The knob rattled again. My body trembled with such force, I stared at my hands in wonder. How was I still standing if I couldn't feel my legs?

Pound-pound-pound. "Juanita, I wanna talk . . . I mean, uh . . . see if I can borrow a cup of sugar."

I placed my hand to my mouth and backed away to the living room. The drapes on the front picture window were drawn, but an ogre-sized, Spam-shaped silhouette moved across them. *Gracious!* Was he going around the side of the house? Retreating the way I'd come, I breathed the Lord's name on each exhale squeezing from my lungs. I stopped in the hallway outside the laundry room. *What to do? What to do?* This didn't exactly warrant calling the police. It wasn't like the guy had broken the door down or hurled threats and insults. I forced a swallow past my dry throat. Maybe he did just want to borrow a cup of sugar.

Ding-dong. Pound-pound-pound.

Or steal some of *my* sugar. My belly lurched. I unpeeled my armband—the sound of Velcro ripping making me wince—and pulled my phone free. I dialed Mrs. Holden and went straight to her voice mail. *Ugh!* I disconnected without leaving a message. What about Kate? Or Mama? No, I couldn't bring either of them into this. I tapped my fist to my forehead, Winnie-the-Pooh style.

Pound-pound-pound.

My vision blurred. I'd always fancied myself as independent and capable. I'd had to be since Mark's death. Like it or not, I'd had to be the pants and the skirt in our family. And I'd done well. Stranded on the road with a flat tire? I'd changed it. Roachzilla? Defeated with a Nerf gun and flyswatter. I hadn't needed a man to come to my rescue or had one who could.

Until now.

With shaky fingers, I dialed Samuel's number. A first since we'd only been texting.

"Well, hello," he answered, surprise clear in his tone.

The relief at hearing him was palpable, my shoulders edging down from my ears. "Um, am I interrupting anything?" The trembling of my body had transferred to my voice.

"What's going on?" His surprise faded to concern.

"I know you're working to get your business up and running, and I'm already using a lot of your time with the patio."

"What's wrong?" His tone dropped to dead serious.

"I'm alone at a client's house." A fat tear plopped down my cheek, landing in a perfect circle on the tiled floor. "And their creepy neighbor is banging at the door. I think he's been drinking."

Ding-dong. Pound-pound-pound.

"Julia, I want you to get on their landline, if they have one, and call 911." His voice emanated calm and steadiness, and I could see how amazing he must've been as a Green Beret, organizing his team for a mission. "Then you need to text me the address of where you are." Keys jingled on his end.

"I can't call 911. It's not like he's trying to break in. I mean, he did rattle the doorknob. But it's locked. The back door too. So this isn't a true emergency." I sniffled, and thoughts of Mark's tragic accident surfaced. "What if someone's dying, and my call goes through before theirs?"

"Julia, please." Composure ruled his speech. A vehicle door slammed in his background. The Testosterone Truck? An engine roared to life.

"I'll text you the address." I swiped another tear. "If I feel really threatened, I'll call the police."

"Stay on the line while you message me."

I copied the client's info from the contact listing in my phone and texted it to Samuel.

"Got it," he said. The sound of a motor accelerating and tires squealing carried over the line. "Do they have a house alarm?"

"No."

"Do you have a weapon on you?"

"I have Mace in my purse."

"Good. Go get it. Do they have a fireplace?"

"Yes."

"I want you to grab the poker, move to the room farthest from the front door, and lock yourself in. Extra points if it's a bedroom with a bathroom. That'll give you another locked door." Tires screeched and a horn blared.

Images from *The Fast and the Furious* flashed through my mind. "Oh, Samuel, please be careful."

"That was someone else." Still with the cool and collected tone.

"Liar." With my eyes pinging between the front and back

doors and all the windows in between, I grabbed my purse from the kitchen counter and dashed for the fireplace.

"Do you have your Mace yet?"

"I've got my purse and the fireplace poker." Goodness, I sounded and felt like I'd run a marathon.

"Good. Now get to that room, lock the door, and stay put until I get there. I'm fifteen minutes away."

We remained on the phone, Samuel giving ETAs every five minutes and asking for a description of Pete, and which house he lived in. Thankfully, the doorbell ringing and knocking had stopped. Had Pete gone home for another beer? With each mile Samuel neared, concern over myself diminished and shifted to worry for him. What if he got into an altercation with Pete? What if Pete pulled a crowbar on Samuel? Or a gun?

A ball of nerves clogged my throat. "Do you have a weapon?"

"Of course." He'd said it matter-of-factly. As though I'd asked if he had a valid fishing license.

My stomach twisted. Maybe dialing 911 would have been better than involving Samuel. Or wasn't there a nonemergency number? Like calling the nurse line in lieu of going to the emergency room. *My child's running a high fever, but I'm not sure if it's an ER-visit fever.*

"But I don't plan to use my weapon," he said.

A shiver rocked my body. Would Samuel fight him bare-knuckles? Were guys taught to kick other guys in the privates the way girls were? I hoped so. And I hoped he wore his steel-toed work boots today.

"I'm pulling up to the house now. I want you to stay inside until I call you back."

"But what if you need me for backup?" My words had been spoken to dead air.

With a canister of Pepto-pink Mace in one hand and a fireplace poker in the other, I emerged from the master suite bathroom, and then the bedroom. I took the stairs, stepped lightly down the hallway, and entered the living room. The kitchen lay on the other side. A block of knives sat on the counter, calling to me. If I grabbed a knife or two, maybe I could hurl them like ninja stars. But where would I put them? Tucked against the elastic waistband of my pants? I considered the weapons already in my hands. What would I use first? The Mace?

My phone rang from the pocket in my scrubs. I jumped, dropping the fireplace poker. It thudded to the area rug. Thank goodness it hadn't hit the travertine tiles. "Hello?"

"I'm at the front door. I don't see any signs of him."

I released a huge breath, my knees buckling. *Thank You, Lord.* I pocketed the Mace, clutched the poker, and opened the door.

That cliché moment in movies when the hero bursts into the room to save the heroine and immediately sweeps her into his arms? Yeah, turned out that wasn't the MO for a Green Beret. Or at least not my Green Beret.

Ack! He's not mine!

Samuel brushed past me, his attention scanning the windows, and proceeded to the back door. He let himself out onto the stone patio, surveying one side of the yard, then moving to the other.

I followed, stepping out the door, the humidity coating my skin. My attention arrested on Samuel. His muscles bunched along his shoulders and upper back, stretching the fabric of his black T-shirt. *What a sight!* Faded jeans ran down to his kick-butt steel-toed boots. Everything in his movements and focused attention gave the impression of a cobra ready to strike. A burly and peeved cobra. I stood on the patio at the ready, metal poker poised like a baseball bat.

He tested the lock on the side gate, his tense posture relaxing infinitesimally. Catching a glimpse of me, he shook his head. "Come on, A-Rod." He motioned for me to return inside first and bolted the door behind us. "Have you talked to this guy before?"

"Yes, he moved in a few months ago." I stared at my hands, rubbing my thumb along a groove in the handle of the fireplace poker. "He's been hitting on me since."

"Is that why you're wearing your wedding ring? You normally don't."

I blinked up at him. Wow, he was really good at noticing small things. I crossed the living room, returning the tool to the fireplace. "Yes."

He crossed his arms, his shirt tightening against his biceps. "Has he touched you before or said anything inappropriate?"

"No, um, well, he talked about whipped cream once and winked. And another time he tried to lure me into his house with a busted vacuum." I rubbed the back of my neck, kneading my stiff muscles. Gracious, this wasn't sounding good at all. "The last time I saw him, he got too close. I think he would've touched me, but I darted away."

Samuel's nostrils flared, only adding to his already murderous glare.

Oh boy. I lowered my hand, realizing how nervous I must have looked. "He thinks my name is Juanita."

His expression softened a teeny-tiny bit.

I scrunched one side of my face. "And that I have five pit bulls."

"Well, I think Chewie could rival a pack of pit bulls." Faint smile lines fanned his eye.

Adoration, warm and consuming, bloomed within. This man had abandoned whatever he'd been doing and come to my aid. No questions asked. "Thank you for coming," I whispered. Oh, how I wanted to close the distance between us and hug him. Wanted his strong arms around me. Wanted to round out the feeling of his protection to full completion.

"You're welcome." He cleared his throat. "I'm glad you

called." His gaze broke from mine, taking in the area. "Are you done here?"

"Oh." I glanced about, gathering my bearings. The draining adrenaline and filling appreciation had left me exhausted and a little foggy-brained. "No, I've still got half a day's work to do. It's a big house." I peered at the front door, massaging my temples. What if Pete returned?

"Whatever you decide, I'm not leaving until you do." Undeniable determination infused his countenance.

A tingle ran up my spine. I shut my eyes a moment, fracturing the spell of the courageous man standing mere feet away. A man who wanted to date me. A man who'd broken my heart.

Think, Julia. Think.

If Pete was sleeping off his beer, it'd be best to leave now and avoid a confrontation with Samuel. If I stayed and cleaned the house, and Pete held true to what he'd done in the past, he'd know when I'd be departing and intercept us.

I gave a wistful glance at the check waiting on the kitchen counter. One I wouldn't be taking with me. "We can go. Just let me turn on the dryer so their sheets don't get mildewed." I made my way to the laundry room.

My bodyguard trailed.

"I'll call Mrs. Holden later and explain what happened." Another pile of bedding waited to be washed. I shoved it to where their dirty clothes overflowed from several baskets. Something else that wouldn't be getting done.

Samuel leaned against the doorjamb. "You need to drop these clients and tell them why."

"I know." I shut the door on the open dryer and turned the machine on. Vibrations and rhythmic thudding filled the room. "But I need the money." I chewed the inside of my cheek. Mrs. Holden had made it clear she didn't want me cleaning on Saturdays when they were home, so that wasn't an option.

Samuel leveled me with a scowl. "If you continue coming here, I'm going to come along every time you do."

I raised my brows, unable to help the smirk forming.

He pushed from the wall, his jaw set. "I mean it."

My brows fell. *Goodness.* He really would too. "I'm not coming back. But I can't go without the money for long."

"How much do you charge them?"

"Why?"

He shrugged.

Understanding dawned. "No. You're not paying me to clean your place."

A suggestive tease spread across his face. "You'll do it for free?"

"Before I so much as stick my big toe in your home, it'll be a cold day in—"

He held up his hand, a smile materializing. "It wouldn't be for me."

"Then who?"

"You'll see."

My lids closed on an exhale, my head falling back.

Ding-dong.

My body shot ramrod straight. *Oh, Lord, not again.*

Alert steadiness overtook Samuel, vanquishing our moment of banter. "I want you to stay inside." His dauntless eye contact held on me, and I realized after a moment, he was waiting for my promise that I would.

"I will."

With a nod, he turned, his confident strides echoing down the hallway. I trailed after him. He reached the front door and stepped out, closing it behind him.

I rushed forward and pressed my ear to the crack. Muffled male voices drifted farther away. Gritting my teeth, I carefully turned the knob and cracked the door open. Technically, I wasn't breaking our agreement to remain inside.

Pete stood on the lawn several yards away, another beer in his hand.

Samuel positioned himself between us, his back to me, his stance rigid. Samuel was taller, but Pete was stockier and at least ten years younger.

Pete pointed to my SUV. "So you're her husband?"

I gasped. Pete *had* noticed my wedding ring. And had still continued with his advances. What a slime bucket!

Samuel remained quiet and still, the sun glinting down on him.

"You're a lucky man. She's super hot."

"Watch it." Samuel growled the words.

"Chill, man." Pete's arrogant chuckle matched his sneer. "I wasn't sure you could get a good look at her with only one eye."

Protectiveness surged, my hand slipping to the pepper spray in my pocket. A squirt—or twenty—would suit Pervy Pete just fine.

"She's got that Alicia Silverstone thing going." Pete lifted his nonbeer-holding hand to his chest, like he held a cantaloupe. "Except with a great set of—"

"Hey!" Samuel snapped. The muscles along his neck tensed, as though his hackles were rising.

A myriad of words flipped through my brain as I beheld him. Dangerous. Lethal. Heroic. Loyal. *Wait.* No. *No, no.* Not loyal. *He cheated on you, remember? Didn't answer your calls when you were pregnant with his baby.*

"Pfft." Pete's head reared. "You don't need to be in my space, bossing me. If I want to talk about her or to her, I will." He moved for the front door, trying to step around Samuel.

Samuel blocked him. "You get your jollies from harassing women?"

Pete's face flashed red. He scoffed and thumbed his nose. "It ain't harassing if they like it."

Lord, please intervene.

"Trust me." Samuel altered his position. "She doesn't like it."

"She would." Pete leered at the door and trudged to one side to move around Samuel again, shoving Samuel's shoulder in the process. "If I got my hands on her and that plump—"

Quick as a snake strike, Samuel swung.

And down Pete went like a dropped slab of meat.

15

HAD THIS HAPPENED ANY OTHER WEEKDAY, I would've gone to my next client. Mondays and Wednesdays through Fridays, I had two customers back-to-back. Their maintenance cleans were a breeze and only took about three hours per house. But the Holdens' home was enormous compared to the others and had five people living there, dirtying four bedrooms and four and a half bathrooms. And they never prepped their space for me, leaving dirty clothes, shoes, and toys on the floor. Plus, Mrs. Holden wasn't a neat cook. Therefore, I'd never scheduled anyone else on Tuesdays. Therefore, I had nothing else to do today.

And apparently neither did Samuel.

He tailed me back to my house, the Testosterone Truck in my rearview mirror the entire drive, as well as his devastating scowl. Was he in pain? His hand injured? I parked in my driveway, and he pulled to the curb. I slipped from my SUV, expecting him to do the same, but he remained in his vehicle, the engine idling.

My stomach twisted. Maybe he needed to go to the ER. I approached the passenger side of his truck, and the window lowered. The aviator sunglasses he wore set off a domino effect of tingles from my brain to my wee little piggies. "How's your hand?"

"Fine."

"It can't be fine. You knocked a man out."

He held up his right hand. Wiggled his fingers.

"But . . . How's that possible? No cuts or swollen knuckles? No bruises?"

"Nope." Tension shadowed the word. His attention slid from me to the windshield.

A cloud of worry hovered over me. He'd been fine at the Holdens' house. Well, up until he'd met Pete. After he'd struck him, he'd told me to get my things, which I had. Pete had come to and hobbled off, rubbing his jaw and cursing threats all the way to his house. Scratch that. His mama's house.

I took in the stiffness of Samuel's profile. Pressure swelled beneath my rib cage, the need to get him to stay a tremendous sensation. All he had to do was throw his transmission into gear and leave, and the thought of him departing with this strain between us felt all sorts of wrong. The man had just slayed a dragon for me. I owed him . . . something. A thank-you at the very least. But if I thanked him now, I was afraid he'd nod and pull off.

I glimpsed the clock on his dashboard. Eleven thirty. "Are you . . . hungry? I can make us lunch."

He clenched the steering wheel, his exhale filling the cab of the truck. "Do you promise never to go back to that house again?"

"Yes, I promise." *Goodness.* Was that his problem? He was worried I'd return? Had I truly given the impression I cared more about making money than my safety? I leaned the front of my body against the door and stuck my hand through the window, holding out my pinky. His vehicle smelled like leather and mint. "I pinky swear I won't go back to that house. Or any house within a twenty-block radius."

The concern on his face cracked, transforming to a hesitant smile.

The relief of his apprehension caused mine to evaporate too.

He reached out his pinky, which had just helped flatten a man, and tenderly shook mine.

The connection, so small and gentle, sent a force through me bigger than I could even try to rationalize.

He removed his sunglasses with his other hand, his hazel gaze connecting with mine.

The current traveling between our pinkies intensified. I was convinced that if I looked, sparks would be flying. I tried to speak and failed. Throat parched, I tried again. "Thank you . . . for today." I withdrew my finger, certain it would be charred from the electricity teeming between us.

His stare roamed my face for a long, drawn-out moment. "You're welcome."

───────

"I still can't believe your hand isn't busted." I opened the door to my refrigerator, scanning our options. What did you make a man who'd possibly saved your life? Steak and potatoes? A pot roast? BBQ ribs? I had none of those items. My sight fell on a pack of deli meat, causing a frown. Serving him a wimpy turkey sandwich didn't seem appropriate. Maybe grilling the turkey would man it up. And adding creole mustard.

"Well, believe it. It's not the first time I've punched someone and come away unscathed." He angled against the counter.

I shut the fridge and looked at him. "Green Beret fights?"

"No. College."

My eyebrows rose.

"Before we knew each other."

I pursed my mouth to one side.

With his pointer finger, he drew an invisible X over his heart.

Chewie perched on the back of the love seat, watching our exchange with disdain.

Gathering my thoughts, I opened the pantry, hoping something wonderful to make would jump out. All I found was

Paul Newman, grinning at me from a bottle of Italian salad dressing. *Not helping, Paul.* "So whose house needs cleaning that's not yours?"

"My dad's."

That pulled me up short. Teddy Reed. Though he was nothing like a sweet little bear. He was a grizzly. Fresh out of hibernation. With cubs to protect. I'd only met the man once, and it'd been enough. I wondered if the flagpole that had been shoved up his backside still resided there.

"He had double knee surgery and can't get around very well right now. Wyatt and I have been doing what we can, but"—he rubbed his chin—"we need help keeping up his home."

I pulled a loaf of bread from the pantry. "What about your mom?"

He studied his thumbnail. "She left him a long time ago."

Not surprising.

Samuel's long eyelashes fanned his cheek, lending a vulnerability to him. After what he'd done for me today and volunteering for the boys' gift, how could I refuse his request? Maybe time had softened his father. Or maybe it had hardened him even more, like a clump of playdough left out overnight. Either way, if I could deal with Mama, I could certainly put up with Teddy Reed for a few hours a week. At least until the man was back on his feet.

"It's up to you if you want it to be a temporary job until you find something else to fill the spot, but the offer for it to be permanent stands."

"Okay."

His brows shot north. "Okay?"

"Yes. I can go to his place next Tuesday, if that's all right. I'll have to do a deep clean my first visit, so it'll take longer than normal. After that I can figure out what the weekly upkeep cost will be."

A wide grin lightened his face. "That'd be great. Thank you."

My own smile followed.

He took a step forward and leaned, resting his elbows on the island. "Have you given up on what to fix us? Why don't you let me make you French toast? You've got bread." He indicated the loaf in my hand. "And I spied milk and eggs in the fridge when you had the door open."

My smile faded, along with my hunger. "No." I set the bread down. "I don't want French toast."

"Why not? You used to love it."

I reached for the kitchen towel bunched on the counter near the sink. Folded it in half. And then another half. "Mark used to make me French toast every Sunday morning." Breakfast in bed had been a tradition Mark had started after Conner's birth. A way for him to grant me alone time after caring for everyone else all week. He'd place the tray on my lap, full of French toast sprinkled with powdered sugar, and close the bedroom door. It was the only uninterrupted meal I'd have all week, and the only food I hadn't been able to manage since he'd been gone.

Samuel straightened, pulling in and releasing a weighted breath. "Sounds like he was a good man."

"He was." I touched the simple gold wedding band still on my finger. We'd married so young and fast that Mark hadn't had enough money for an engagement ring. I stared at the neatly folded towel under my hand. The blue and green stripes matched the coastal ambiance I'd aimed for when decorating this house. Trying for calm in a life that had seemed anything but.

"I'm glad you found someone who treated you right."

My gaze ascended, meeting his, and I found nothing but sincerity on his face. My heart ached in a good way. Mark had been such an amazing husband and father. He didn't deserve petty animosity from anyone, least of all an ex-boyfriend.

Samuel shifted, leaving the space of the sink between us. "I hope you know I want to treat you right too."

A puff of air escaped at his abrupt declaration. I minutely shook my head and folded the towel a third time. "It's not that easy."

"It can be."

I tried ignoring the nerves fluttering up from my belly. "We can be friends, but that's it."

The edge of his mouth quirked, flirtatiousness spreading across his features. "Friends who make out?"

I scoffed a laugh. "No."

He lifted a shoulder, undeterred.

"Samuel." My chastising tone only made him smile wider. The flutters in my gut dissolved, giving way to a notion swelling within, pushing. Just like earlier when I'd been afraid he'd leave. The intensity grew into a relentless nudging. And I realized what it was. *Oh, Lord, right now? Really?* This was the moment the Holy Spirit wanted to tap me to share about the miscarriage?

Slowly, Samuel's smile dimmed and rolled into a somber expression.

I glanced at the window, working up my fortitude. "I need to tell you something." Of all the things I thought I'd never do, this topped the list. Right below skydiving and running with the bulls.

Samuel ran his hand over his mouth. "There's something I need to talk to you about too."

I nodded, wringing the folded dish towel, the stripes twisting like my insides. *Please help me here, Lord.* I released the towel, smoothing an unsteady hand over the material. "Shortly after you broke up with me, I discovered I was pregnant."

Samuel flinched, his mouth parting.

"I didn't know what to do, so I told my mom . . . everything." Oh, what a moment that had been. Mama had hurled *I told you so*'s and glares as though they were Mardi Gras beads and she was riding in a parade. "She hauled me to the doctor to get checked for STDs and to confirm what the over-the-counter pregnancy test had told me."

I'd been so naïve that I hadn't considered contracting an STD from Samuel. It had only added to the humiliation of the situation. I could still hear Mama's smoker's voice in that exam room, directed at the nurse and doctor. *"Make sure you check her for every disease there is. I knew that boy was no good."* Thankfully, those tests had come back clear.

All color had drained from Samuel's face, and he braced a hand against the counter's edge. Would the seriousness of this truth prove too much for him? Would the old Samuel reemerge, and he'd run away? Go into avoidance mode?

"The doctor confirmed I was pregnant and about a month along. I called you every day for two weeks."

His free hand coiled into a fist and covered his mouth.

"I was terrified but happy." I'd been nineteen and had no idea how to raise a baby. I'd never changed a diaper or even held an infant. "I wanted that baby with everything in me." The thought of Samuel and I getting back together and raising our child lessened the sting of his betrayal. Then one night, I'd started bleeding. The claws of grief clutched, reaching out from the past. I severed the intensity of Samuel's stare, glancing at Chewie, who'd fallen asleep. "I planned to come see you when I was further along, but . . ."

"You miscarried."

Tears welled, and I nodded.

"How far along were you?" The words scraped from his throat, sounding like it cost him to ask.

I pulled in a shaky breath. "Eleven weeks."

A vein at his temple throbbed, and he took two steps, engulfing me in a hug. "I'm so sorry I didn't answer your calls." His body trembled on an exhale. "So, so sorry."

Affection and strength and his clean scent surrounded me. I melted into him, folding my arms against his firm torso, my hands beneath my quavering chin. My quiet tears cascaded, bringing with them more than the release of waterworks. It was like crying the weight out of me I'd carried for twenty years.

Time stretched, his steady breath fanning through my hair, the beat of his heart against my ear easing my shudders. Minute by minute, the burden of keeping that secret from Samuel lifted, and a satisfying peace eased in. *Thank You, God.* I pulled up the neck of my shirt, drying the dampness from my cheeks.

"I'm truly sorry you went through that alone." His words vibrated our little cocoon.

I shifted, needing to reposition but not wanting to move this wall of protection around me. I slipped my arms around him like I'd done a million times before. "I had my mom." Though I wasn't sure she had been better than no one.

He burrowed his face deeper into my hair.

Standing like that felt familiar and yet different. Physically, this Samuel was stronger than the man I'd known. From the brawn in his arms banding around me, to his back underneath my fingertips. But the position of his hands, looped around my lower back, was the same. The way his chin sat atop my head? The same as well. But a tenderness existed now. His jaw eased to one side, as though he'd positioned better to breathe me in. This felt . . . right. Like pulling into my driveway after being gone on a long trip.

Closing my eyes, I gave in to the sensation. My body, so much smaller than his, pressed against him. My feet were planted between his, and the warmth of his skin emanated through his T-shirt. Those muscles I'd spied his first day working came to mind. Curiosity took over, and I glided my fingers the tiniest bit.

His rhythmic breathing through the crown of my hair stopped.

The air altered, moving from one filled with emotional exhaustion to one charged with awareness. *Oh my.* You couldn't wedge a popsicle stick between us. One of his thumbs moved, caressing my back. I sucked in a breath, the electric air crackling down my lungs.

Mayday. Mayday.

I extricated myself. "Why don't I make you the best turkey sandwich you've ever had?"

"Why don't you let me take you out for lunch?"

"Nice try." I managed a half smirk. "But, no, I'm still not going out with you."

16

THE NEXT TWO DAYS FOLLOWED THE SAME PATTERN as the last two weeks. I stepped through the front door, Chewie anxious to greet me as though I'd been gone for a year. I let him out the back, and he charged Samuel, same as every other time.

Samuel stood on the other side of his makeshift workbench, his hand on the portable saw, his heavy gaze on me. Attraction zinged my nerves to full alert, and my heart couldn't help but add its two cents, reminding me of Samuel's sincere reaction to my miscarriage. *Hello, emotional whiplash.* I closed my eyes and rubbed the ache above my brow. Maybe I needed another hug. That sure had worked wonders on Tuesday.

Whoa. My eyes popped open. Where had that come from? First roaming fingers and now this? Clearly being friends with the man was not something easily navigated.

Samuel sidled around the workbench, flecks of sawdust falling from his hunter-green T-shirt. "You feeling okay?"

"Just a headache." A Spaniel-ache. Nothing two Tylenol and a thorough kissing wouldn't knock out. *Stop that!* I winced, massaging harder.

"What if I cook dinner while you relax?"

"Okay."

143

His eye lit with surprise. "Being friends certainly has made you more agreeable toward me."

"Or maybe you're wearing me down. Is this some sort of Green Beret psychological warfare?"

He winked. "I plead the fifth."

One hot shower later, I felt better. The sight of Samuel cooking in my kitchen had bestowed wonderful healing powers on my headache, but not my hormones. After making a grocery run, he'd returned with everything to prepare guacamole and chicken fajitas. He'd remembered my soft spot for Mexican food.

The booger.

I sat at the kitchen table, dipping tortilla chip after tortilla chip into the guacamole. Salty bliss with a dash of coolness and heat. I sure hoped heaven had guacamole.

"What do you think?" He nodded to the bowl of avocado ecstasy before me.

"Horrible." I shoveled in another bite, talking around my full mouth. "You won't want to eat any of it."

He chuckled and turned to the stove, poking at chicken, peppers, and onions sizzling in a pan. His ability to cook wasn't a revelation. He'd made simple meals for us back in the day. I hadn't appreciated that trait then, but now? It occupied a slot on my love language list, right under cutting the grass.

I took in the strong planes of his shoulders, the way the cotton fabric of his shirt pulled and relaxed with his movements. A blob of guacamole plopped on my thigh, jolting me, and Chewie, who sat at my bare feet. *Shoot.* I reached for a napkin on the table, wiping the spoils of my ogling, grateful it hadn't hit my shorts. My attention moved from Samuel to safer views of the back windows.

The setting sun's weakened rays streamed through the tree branches, hitting patches of lawn here and there. Like Mason's hair, the grass needed trimming again. Forget death and taxes. Mowing grass in the South was inevitable. I inhaled another mouthful of chips and guac, soothing away the qualms of homeownership.

The patio was coming along. Samuel had replaced all of the posts holding up the roof with cedar columns to keep the look uniform. Some of the supports had been partially rotted anyway, so it wasn't a total waste to remove them. From the sawdust on the concrete floor below the workbench and the smaller boards piled to one side, it seemed he was working on the custom railing.

A hard and brisk knock rapped at the front door. As though an angry woodpecker had descended.

I froze.

What felt like cold, nicotine-stained fingers trailed up the back of my neck.

Chewie ran to the door, barking.

No, no, no. I whipped my attention to the picture window and found Mama's Buick parked behind my SUV. All that guacamole I'd devoured rolled in my stomach. That's what I got for being a glutton.

I glanced at Samuel, who'd turned from the stove, a set of tongs in his hands. Whatever he saw in my expression caused his face to cloud with concern.

"It's my mom." I whisper-strained the words over Chewie's yapping, feeling like a teenager hiding her boyfriend in her bedroom when her parents came home early from work.

If I didn't answer the door soon, she'd poke her nosy head in the front window. If I snuck under the table, the couch would hide me from her snooping. And from where Samuel stood in the kitchen, Mama wouldn't see him. She had a key, but if she saw no one through the window, she could think I wasn't here and wouldn't need to let herself in. For all she knew, I was off with Kate and Samuel's truck belonged to a neighbor. Although, I wouldn't have left without shutting my TV off.

I stared at Lorelai Gilmore, beseeching. *Come on, Lorelai, we're both single moms with complicated mothers. Help a sister out!* A commercial break took over. My molars ached from grinding. Time was running out! If I crawled under the table to the other side, I could reach up to the back of the love seat where the remote lay.

I motioned for Samuel to stay where he was and began my descent, sliding down my chair. My chest cleared the tabletop, my shoulders approaching next.

Mama's gray-haired head appeared in the window, her beady eyes meeting mine.

Busted.

She moved to the door, using her key to let herself in.

I picked up Chewie, shushing his unfriendly welcome, and deposited him on the couch. With sweaty hands, I reached for the remote and muted the television.

My ex, my mom, and my overprotective dog. All in one room. This had the makings of a Jerry Springer show.

Mama wore a pair of baby-pink pants older than me. A soft yellow, no-frills top tucked into the pants' elastic band at her middle. The corner of a handkerchief poked out from the waistband, as if waving for help, hoping to be rescued from the polyester prison it was jailed within.

A storm of tension swirled, thick and heavy, and unnervingly quiet. Like being in the eye of a hurricane.

Samuel stood on the other side of the island, next to the stove, the tongs still in his hand. There was a tightness in his appearance I hadn't seen since that first day we'd talked at church. One side of his bottom lip rolled inward, and he tipped his head in acknowledgment. "Mrs. Anne."

Standing next to the dining room table, Mama stared him down. Clad in all pink and yellow, she looked like a ticked-off Easter egg.

I hovered between them, my focus on Mama. "Conner and

146

Mason gifted me with screening in the patio for my birthday."
I motioned to the windows and the work Samuel had done.
And by motioned, I'd flapped my hand chaotically. "Well, along
with Mark's parents. So they asked Kate to find someone to do
the job. She'd planned to hire Earl Taylor, but his gallbladder
went rogue, and so that's when Samuel came into the picture."

Mama's shrewd glare examined the kitchen, Samuel, then
turned to me. I winced, imagining what we looked like through
her eyes. Samuel, with a dish towel slung over his shoulder and
cooking. Me, in comfy clothes with wet hair from my shower.
Thank goodness her sight wasn't what it used to be, or she
would've noticed I had freshly shaven legs. And that I'd even
moisturized them.

Samuel turned the range off and slid the frying pan from the
hot burner. "Mrs. Anne, I want to apologize for how I treated
Julia in the past. I was young and stupid—"

"And selfish." Mama crossed her arms.

"Mama," I warned, finding a piece of my backbone.

Samuel held up a hand. "She's right. I was. But I've changed."

Mama snorted.

"I've learned some lessons the hard way, and I know I can't
fix the mistakes I've made." His words and timbre grieved with
remorse. "I'm sorry I wasn't there for Julia during her miscarriage, but I'm thankful she had you."

My eyes stung at his sincerity.

Mama's relentless glower at him continued.

Samuel cast his attention to me.

I knew I should do or say something, but too many things
to process whirled through me.

Something similar to disappointment reflected in his features, stabbing at my heart. He gestured to the stove. "Dinner's
ready. And there's plenty for you both." His thudding footsteps
echoed against the walls. Several paces from the door, Chewie
lunged, biting the heel of one of Samuel's boots.

"Chewie!" I darted for the dog, picking him up and swatting his nose with two fingers. "No! Bad dog."

Samuel kept moving, out the door and down the brick steps.

"I'm sorry," I called from the threshold. Hopefully he realized my apology covered more than the dog's attack.

Without turning, he lifted his hand and gave one of those man-waves. He climbed into his truck, started the engine, and eased from the curb.

A dull ache thrummed within, Chewie now feeling like he weighed fifty pounds instead of twelve. I closed the door and admonished Chewie again, setting him down. He retreated to his perch on the back of the sofa.

"Well." Haughtiness coated Mama's words. "He's still good at leaving." She dropped her keys on the table.

My shoulders slumped, and I dragged in a breath. She was right about Samuel's past tendency of abandonment. But in this case, it had been warranted.

"That evil dog is looking better and better." She stepped toward Chewie. "Good boy."

Chewie growled at Mama, baring his canines.

She shook her head at him and moved to the windows, sizing up the patio. A tsk here, a grunt there. Mama's very essence grated on my nerves, my annoyance growing with each of her disdainful noises.

I headed for the stove and took in the beautiful meal Samuel had prepared. Had thoughtfully shopped at the grocery for and come back to make. And he wouldn't enjoy a single bite.

"I knew this was coming," Mama said.

Twitchy irritation set in. I seized a plate from a cabinet, banging the cupboard shut. "You knew the boys wanted to screen in my patio?" My chafing sarcasm was impossible to miss.

"They'd mentioned something about it a while back, but I'd told them it wasn't a good idea."

I turned, my spine stiffening. "Why would you do that?"

148

"It was a waste of money and not necessary." She shot me a look. "Like when they got you that exercise machine. Why pay all that money when you can walk outside for free?" She patted her pockets, no doubt searching for a smoke. "I suggested they buy you new tires for your car the next time you needed them."

A memory from when I'd been sixteen sprung to mind. I'd bought Mama a gorgeous bouquet of flowers for Mother's Day from a real florist. *These will be dead in a week,* she'd said. *"Buying groceries would've been useful. Or a shirt. That would last forever."*

Oh. My. Word. Was I the apple, and Mama the tree? *No, no, no.* I grabbed a tortilla and slapped it on my dish. We weren't the same. Using the tongs, I plopped strips of chicken and red bell peppers onto the flatbread, the scent of cumin and lime wafting.

I'd had to be practical about finances, but I never put that burden on the boys. My fajita-making motions slowed. At least, I didn't think I had. I'd never discussed money issues in front of them like Mama had with me. And I'd always accepted their gifts with joy . . . well, except for the elliptical. But that was because it was *so* expensive for them.

"I had a feeling they'd go to Kate for help," Mama groused.

I pointed the tongs at her and snapped them. "Don't you grumble about Kate. They came to you first, and you shut them down."

Her gaze shifted to the floor, her mouth pursing.

At times like this, I yearned for a sibling. Someone who understood what it was like to be Anne Walker's kid. Was I earning extra points in heaven for being an only child to this woman? I turned back to my plate, resting the tongs on the trivet and collecting myself as best as possible. "Samuel's just doing a job."

"Pfft. If it's just a job, why was he in your kitchen, cooking dinner like he lives here?"

I needed Mickey's ghost from *Rocky* to appear and toss a

pep talk at me. *"You're no twelve-year-old kid needing to be reprimanded. You're an adult. You take multivitamins, drive responsibly, and have life insurance. Now stop acting like a chump and face your mama."* I placed my fajita on the island. "We're . . ." *Lord, please give me strength.* "We're friends now."

She moved to the edge of the counter and smacked it with her palm, her head rearing with a scathing laugh. "With friends like that . . ." Her half-spoken cliché lingered in the edgy air.

"He's different now."

"People don't change."

I used to think the same thing. But in the past month, that belief had slowly altered where Samuel was concerned. And the reality of God working in me was evidence as well. "You don't think God changes people?"

Mama's lips flattened to a thin line. "That man brought you nothing but grief and heartache. Two pathetic years of it."

True. He had brought me those things. But looking back, I'd allowed him to treat me that way. And considering the kind of life I was living then, how could I have expected to find success in that relationship when God wasn't at the center of it? "There were some good times too."

She balked, hues of red splotching her neck. "Good times involving you having to go to the doctor to get checked for STDs? Getting knocked up? Going through a miscarriage?"

My chin lowered. Oh, how I wished I'd never spilled my raw guts to Mama back then. But I'd been a mess with no one to turn to. I'd foolishly shrunk my world to revolve around Samuel. I'd had no close friends to confide in. And if I'd known I was going to lose the baby, I never would have told Mama.

"Zebras can't change their stripes."

I lifted my head and pressed a hand to my breastbone. "But God can change their hearts."

She cringed as though she'd downed a spoonful of Robitussin. "I can't believe you're taking up for him. Haven't you learned anything?" Her chest rose and fell with agitated breaths, her gaze bouncing from place to place until it settled once again on me. "That man even being in this house is a disgrace to Mark's memory."

The full force of her declaration exploded through me like a swallowed grenade. I laid my palms flat on the island. My arms trembled, black spots dotting my vision. Upholding the fifth commandment in this moment required supernatural power. I squeezed my eyes tight, the pounding in my ears the only steady sensation I could concentrate on. "Get. Out." My tone bordered on a snarl.

Mama snatched her keys from the table and left, slamming the door behind her.

Sinking to my knees right there in the kitchen, I prayed for wisdom in how to deal with her. Because to my core, I knew I'd done nothing to disrespect Mark. I'd been a faithful and loyal wife, devoted to him and our family.

I knew Mama's beef with Samuel better than anyone, but it ran deeper than his past behavior. She'd never been a proponent of love. *Poor Daddy.* She hadn't even been wild about Mark. When he'd been alive, she'd touted the best thing about our union had been her grandsons. Not my happiness or solid marriage. So for her to throw Mark at me like that now? My back teeth ached from grinding.

I had hurt her by keeping Samuel a secret, and now she had hurt me.

But hers had been the lowest of blows, and one that would not be easily forgiven.

17

THE NEXT EVENING I ARRIVED HOME to find the grass cut again, and Samuel's truck parked at the curb. After Mama's departure last night, I'd reached for my phone too many times, wanting to text him. But her words had been like a wasp, striking hard and fast, over and over. And now I was left with the stings. Not once had I thought my new friendship with Samuel was a slight to Mark. But Mama's words had struck deep. If Conner and Mason discovered my past with Samuel, would they feel the same way? *Ugh*. I rubbed my palms into my eye sockets, took a deep breath, and pulled my keys from the ignition.

From inside, I spied Samuel through the back windows, working on the patio. The custom railing had been installed between three of the four posts. How much longer would he be working here? A few more days? Despite the ache in my chest at the prospect of returning to my lonely evenings, I knew this project wrapping up was a good thing. Samuel and I needed firm boundaries and space.

After a restless night of sleep, I'd decided we could see each other at church on Sundays, and I would clean his dad's house, but that would be the extent of our relationship. Unless he really did need a driver for a colonoscopy. No more long embraces, holding pinkies, or flirtatious texts. Maybe we could side-hug on special occasions, like celebrating Jesus's birthday at church.

I stepped outside to the backyard and into the comforting scent of cedar from the woodwork. Chewie tossed a single woof at Samuel as he darted by.

Samuel kneeled at the last stretch of railing he was installing, a nail gun in hand, safety glasses in place. No traces of grass or dirt coated him. Was he paying someone else to cut the lawn? The descending sun highlighted the lighter shades of brown in his hair, the angles of his face, the lines in his forearms.

He stood, sliding off his glasses. No easy smile greeted me today. Just a penetrating gaze full of questions. His sight roamed my face, pausing on my mouth.

Traitorous tingles erupted within. Scratch those side-hugs. We'd have to resort to fist bumps to accompany our wishes for a merry Christmas. With a slowness that could rival the last drop of honey releasing from a jar, his attention moved from my lips to my eyes. One of those ice bucket challenges would've been great right about now.

I redirected my attention to Chewie, who sniffed a leaf. "Thank you for cutting the grass."

"You're welcome."

"Are you paying someone to do it? If so—"

"I'm not paying anyone."

"Oh. Well, you don't need to keep doing it. I'm sure you have your own lawn to maintain."

"It's no bother."

My neighbor's basset hound howled from their yard. Chewie yapped in response, charging to the wood fence and running the length of it.

Samuel shifted to his workbench, setting down his glasses and the nail gun. Behind him, a new chair sat off to the side, next to my old one. It had a similar design as my dining room chairs, except instead of wood, it was iron. And a cushion, in the same coastal blue as my kitchen island, covered the seat.

"What's that?" I pointed.

He cast a glance at the chair. "Something I came across. Thought it'd be nice to have another place to sit out here." He removed the battery from the nail gun, putting it aside.

My plastic, five-dollar Home Depot chair looked pitiful next to the fashionable piece of furniture. There was no way he'd just happened across a chair matching the style of my décor down to the color. This would have taken a long time to find and cost a pretty penny. My sights drifted from the chair to the progress Samuel had made, and the beautiful craftsmanship he'd put into the railings. How was I supposed to relax here once this was completed? How could I sit on a chair he'd thoughtfully bought me and look out through the screens he'd created without thinking of him?

"Samuel, I appreciate what you've done, but I can't accept it . . . or the grass cutting."

He opened a box containing strips of nails. "Sure you can."

"No, I can't."

Uncertainty and maybe a hint of hurt shaded his face.

An awful yearning to wrap my arms around him pelted me. *Fist bumps only.*

He withdrew a line of nails from the box and loaded them into the gun. "You were fine with me mowing your lawn last week."

I had been more than fine with it. But his continued kindness kept popping the lid off my heart like a Pringles can. And considering all the issues between us . . . well, limits needed to be set. "I thought it was a one-time thing." I bit the inside of my cheek. In the distance, the tune from an ice cream truck played, trying to lure kids of all ages.

"You okay?"

"Yes." I cracked a knuckle on my finger, then another. "I'm heading to Kate's tonight. After I shower and take care of Chewie." Instead of walking away like a normal person, I hovered. The need to stay and keep talking to him pulled, like I was losing a game of tug-of-war. What if I gave myself fifteen more minutes? What if we grabbed an ice cream from that truck rolling through the neighborhood? *No. No. No.* I forced myself to turn and head for the back door.

"She really got to you."

"Who?"

He paused from messing with his nail gun and sized me up. "Your mom."

"She did not." I shoved my hands into the shirt pockets of my scrubs. "I always go to Kate's on Friday nights."

"I'm not talking about you not sticking around this evening. There's a whole new stiffness about you. One we'd gotten past." He slid the nail gun's magazine, locking it into place with a harsh, metal clang.

"Maybe I'm a moody person." That wasn't so far-fetched with my lack of sleep, missing my boys, and failure to land a weekend client. Soon I'd be as snappish as Chewie.

"No, that's not it." A mix between a sigh and scoff puffed from him. "Your mom's never liked me, so it doesn't take a genius to realize she would've ripped me up after I left yesterday, wanting to influence you."

I cracked two more fingers and tried for lightness. "My mom doesn't like anyone. Me included."

"I don't blame her holding a grudge against me." Samuel skillfully sidestepped my diversion tactic. "It's just . . ." He placed one of his hands on his hip and ran the other through his hair. "I want you to form your own opinions. Persuasion's a powerful thing, and dangerous in the hands of biased people."

Interesting. The Samuel-sized dots began connecting in my mind. When we'd been dating, he'd complained about his dad and brother riding him on different things. Mainly joining the military. Was he projecting his own issues on me, or was his advice genuine? "By persuading, do you mean the way your dad and Wyatt always told you what to do? How they influenced you to enlist in the army?"

He tensed for a second. "They didn't make me join. That was completely my decision." Something in his countenance said there was more to that. He scratched his jaw, casting his attention to the ground.

"What is it?"

Shaking his head, he schooled his features.

"Samuel?"

He snapped the battery back on the nail gun's handle. "Nothing." That one word, paired with his expression, spoke millions. He was holding back. Curling up on himself like an unearthed doodlebug.

"Let's talk about it."

He set the tool on the table and grabbed his phone, shoving it in his back pocket. "There's nothing more to say." He moved for the side gate and disappeared, leaving me alone.

A clear sense of déjà vu struck. Or really, history repeating itself. Because those same words had been the last exchange we'd had the day he'd broken up with me. He'd been done with the conversation, done with breaking my heart, and had left me standing next to my car in the parking lot at school.

My pulse slowed, my hands clenching at my sides. Mama's words from last night echoed. *"He's still good at leaving."* I hated that she was right.

18

KATE CLINKED HER TEASPOON AGAINST HER MUG. "How much longer are you going to fester over there?"

We sat in the main section of Beignets & Books, which had closed a half hour ago, Kate's staff cleaning up the smaller rooms around us. And she'd been right. I was festering. Big time.

"Sorry." I was still processing the way Samuel had shut down and hightailed it from my house. As soon as he'd departed, I'd grabbed Chewie and driven to the park, needing a change of scenery and to clear my head. It hadn't worked.

"How's things on the work front? Any leads on a weekend client?"

Ugh. That was right. I had work problems too. "Robert Breaux upped his offer to pay sixty percent of my quote."

A scowl lowered the corners of her mouth. "The next time he comes in here, I'm going to give him sixty percent of the rotten words filling my mind over his behavior. Or sixty percent of a sneeze in his café au lait."

"I know you'd said you didn't want to date him, but I'm still sorry things didn't go in a better direction there."

"I wasn't interested. But nevertheless"—she lightly pounded her chest with a fist—"sisters over misters."

A slight ease broke through with unleashing that part of my worries, encouraging me to dump the rest of my internal garbage on the table. "My mom stopped by my house last night."

"That's unfortunate but not devastating enough to cause the sourpuss look on your face." She reached across the table for my empty plate. "You did willingly choose to live in her neighborhood."

"Samuel was there."

Kate paused, her arm outstretched.

"He was in my kitchen—"

"And y'all were making out?" She hurriedly stacked my dish on hers, clattering the plates.

"No! He was cooking dinner."

Her blue eyes glittered. She placed her elbows on the table, her chin atop her interlaced fingers. "Start at the beginning, and don't leave a thing out."

After another round of beignets, Kate had heard every detail of Mama's visit. The sparkle in her eyes had slowly dimmed to an expression of disbelief.

She leaned back in her chair, arms crossing her white button-down shirt with the embroidered Beignets & Books logo. "Have you talked to your mom since?"

"No." I plopped my napkin on the table and brushed powdered sugar from my jeans. "She needs time to calm down. And I do too."

One of the busboys stepped from the sports room, a towel and spray bottle in hand, and moved to the chefs' room.

"What she said about Mark . . ." Kate opened her mouth. Closed it. Shook her head. "It's not right. You haven't done anything wrong."

That boulder of stress, so heavy and jagged against my heart the past forty-eight hours, lifted slightly at her words. Oh, how I'd needed to hear that. Needed validation from outside of myself. "I know that. And you know that." My voice grew raspy. "But I wouldn't want others thinking I'd carried a torch for Samuel all this time. That Mark was a placeholder or a rebound."

"But he wasn't. You truly loved Mark. You cherished your marriage."

"I know."

She edged forward, resting her hand on mine, her stare direct. "And most important, Conner and Mason know that."

My eyes stung. Move over, Katniss Everdeen. Had Kate been an archer, her arrow couldn't have hit my bull's-eye any better. I nodded, though it didn't dispel my trepidation where the boys were concerned.

She squeezed my hand and retreated. "And deep down, in the teeny-tiny pea shell that serves as your mom's heart, she knows it too."

I gave a shaky laugh and sniffled. "The irony of all this is that if it hadn't been for Samuel, I might not have met Mark. Or if I had, I wouldn't have been open to him. He wasn't my initial type."

"God works in bizarre ways."

"Preach, sister." I raised a hallelujah hand. "It was like going through Samuel first made me appreciate Mark. They were polar opposites."

"How so?"

"Mark was an open book." My smile couldn't be helped, and the leftover tension I'd harbored expelled at the thought of him. "It's why I fell so quickly for him." My left thumb rubbed against my bare finger, where Mark's ring had held a spot. My flesh may not have been indented with his ring any longer, but my heart was forever stamped by his love. "Traits I had thought of as boring, I now appreciated. He had this . . . light." Fond nostalgia poured over me like a welcome caress. "And honesty. From the first time I met him, he drew me in."

Through the front windows, a group of twentysomething women stood beneath an iron lamppost on the neutral ground, waiting for a streetcar. They were dressed for a night out, no doubt heading to the French Quarter.

Kate's countenance turned thoughtful. "If you date Samuel, or anyone for that matter, it doesn't take away from your marriage to Mark, or the family you've built."

I bit the inside of my cheek, contemplating.

The background music transitioned to an Aaron Neville song, the busboy cleaning in the chefs' room singing along to the chorus. He even tried for the high notes. *Tried* being the key word. Kate and I exchanged amused glances.

She took another sip of her decaf and replaced her cup to the saucer with a light clink. "Did you tell your mom how Samuel came to your rescue with Pervy Pete?"

"*No.*" I dragged out the word, sitting up and stretching my arms above my head, grateful for the shift in conversation away from my love life. "She doesn't even know Pete exists. Besides, she'd die if she knew I was going to start cleaning Samuel's dad's house. Even if it's temporary."

"Let's back up a minute." Kate held up a finger, the red polish on her nails catching the light from the antique chandelier above. "I knew Samuel had stayed for dinner the night he shared his testimony with you. I'm guessing that's happened a lot more if he was full-on Bobby Flay in your kitchen last night."

"Umm . . ." The dough and sugar in my gut began a rumba. "It has."

"Like every night?"

"No." My tone swung high enough to reach those Aaron Neville notes. "He doesn't work on the patio every day."

"Then how often?"

"I don't know, Miss Prosecutor." I shoved my napkin to the side, next to our dishes. "It's not like he's punching a time clock. He's at my house maybe three or four times a week."

"So for three weeks now, you've been spending time together, over a meal, three to four times a week?" She brought her cup to her lips, her brows rising.

Hadn't we moved on to a new topic? I stared at the room the busboy occupied, longing for him to bust out with his awful singing again.

"I'm calling bull on your previous declaration that you can't date Samuel."

"I can't."

"But you're already doing it."

"No, dating means going to date places. Restaurants. The movies. Holding hands. Kissing." *Oh, the kissing.* I had fired off my rebuttal like Annie Oakley shooting targets. "We're definitely not dating."

Kate clucked her tongue. "Sounds like dating to me."

"We're just friends. Once this patio is done, I plan to implement strict boundaries. I'll only see him at church. He'll be like Poor Sean Crawford."

Her head tilted skeptically. "So you're looking forward to getting back to your old quiet life? Nights alone with that devil dog?"

My gaze drifted. It was more than our evenings together, but the witty text exchanges throughout the days too. My soul withered at the thought of all of that disappearing. *We'll be fine.* Had anyone ever given their soul a pep talk? *We've done it before, we can do it again!*

"I've seen the way you get all teary-eyed when you see old couples together." Her forehead furrowed. "Before we became friends, I noticed the way you and Mark were at church. Holding hands, laughing. Everyone could see the love between y'all.

You're not some cold biddy like your mom. I'm actually surprised you've been single this long."

And it looked like that length of time would continue. Because the only man in ten years I'd had a notion of dating was off-limits. There were too many issues, from whether or not I could forgive and trust him, to his backsliding behavior with shutting me out and running away. I began cracking my knuckles under the table, methodically working through each one.

Conner's and Mason's faces materialized in my mind, and their history of reacting poorly to the possibility of a new man in my life. The slimmest chance of hurting them that way again or of them thinking anything besides good and wonderful things about my marriage to Mark was too much to endure. They'd been through enough in their short lives.

Later that night, I sat at my dining room table, sifting through the business cards I'd gathered from the networking event at Beignets & Books. I set each card face up, as though playing a backward game of memory. A motley crew of companies spread before me. Clothing boutiques, an art gallery, souvenir shops, restaurants, hair and nail salons, barber shops, attorneys, Robert No-Go-Breaux. I plucked his card and slowly ripped it in half, enjoying the sound of his thick cardstock tearing. I took the two halves and tore them again.

Although none of the remaining businesses had expressed a need for cleaning services, it wouldn't hurt to follow up. The pale green card for Nancy's Naturals caught my eye. She'd been one of the people who'd asked about my products. Would it have been for her personal use or to sell in her store? The shelves in Nancy's establishment featured vitamins, alkaline water, and organic supplements. Pulse picking up, my leg bounced, waking Chewie, who lay at my feet. What if I made Nancy a few bottles of my products and dropped them off?

My attention snagged on a pink envelope on the floor that had been shoved beneath the back door. I hadn't noticed it before since I'd taken Chewie out front to do his business when I'd gotten home. A tingle rippled across my skin, as though my body knew exactly who'd left it.

I removed the card to find an alpaca on the front, chewing straw. Above its head was *Hay Girl*. Had I not been so disappointed in Samuel, and myself, I would have laughed. Instead, I opened it.

> *Julia,*
>
> *I'm sorry for leaving. Some things are difficult for me to talk about, and I'm working on and praying about getting better at that and not running from hard discussions. When you get home, I'd like to finish our conversation. If not, I'll see you tomorrow when we're volunteering.*
>
> *Samuel*

I pressed a palm to my cheek. The old Samuel wouldn't have been this considerate. Especially when the initial agitation between us hadn't been entirely his fault. But . . . pleasure bled out of me as my heartbeats slowed to a dull thump. One alpaca card did not negate the pile of reasons we couldn't be together. Or dismiss his earlier knee-jerk reaction to leave, even though he'd apologized.

Him pursuing me was all for nothing. And the sooner Samuel realized that, the better it was for us both.

Setting the card down, I reached for my phone and pulled up

the number for sweet and single Emily Miller. With each ring, my stomach churned.

"Hey, Julia!" Emily's angelic voice carried over the line. "What's going on?"

Turning away from the alpaca, I held my hand to my belly. "I'm hoping you can cover my volunteering turn tomorrow."

19

I DID NOT HAVE THE "JOY, JOY, JOY, JOY DOWN IN MY HEART."

What I did have this Sunday morning at church was my ex-boyfriend sitting to my left, my best friend to my right, and Emily Miller seated directly in front of us with one of her friends.

Kate had tossed me a questioning glance when Emily had taken up residence before us. Even Poor Sean Crawford had a moment of confusion at finding Emily and her friend where he normally sat, which pushed him farther down his row.

Southern churchgoing folks were creatures of habit. We sat in the same row, same seats. Week after week. Year after year. Decade after decade. It took something monumental for someone to switch locations. Marriage, divorce, death. Heck, Poor Sean Crawford still abided by the unspoken custom, despite the fact it'd gotten him nowhere with me.

But Emily was of a younger generation. The whippersnapper. Throughout the praise and prayer portions of the service, she stood before me in her svelte black pencil skirt and chic top tucked in at the waist. Her slim, non-muffin-topped waist. When the Lord's Supper had been passed, I hadn't partaken. My mind was too preoccupied to eat and drink in a manner worthy of Jesus.

Church concluded, and I weaved my way out into the open welcome center with the rest of the congregation, intent on heading straight for the exit.

"Hold up a second." Samuel touched my elbow from behind.

I moved toward the wall, out of the way of foot traffic. The fire alarm I'd contemplated pulling that first Sunday Samuel had sought me out loomed within reach again. Well, it was always good to have a backup plan.

"You didn't show up yesterday." Edgy concern emitted from him. "Or return my call last night."

I focused away from his gaze and on fake-rummaging through my purse. "I know."

He drew in a breath and huffed it out. "Are you trying to set me up with Emily Miller?"

Putting him in her sights *had* been intentional. But her plopping in front of him today? That was all Emily. And girlfriend hadn't wasted time. Lifting a shoulder, I continued combing through my bag. Wallet, pen, phone. "She's single and looking. You're single and looking." Lipstick, unavoidable past, aching heart.

"I'm not looking. I've found who I want."

My fingers stopped their pointless perusal, my mouth going dry. "It's not going to happen between us." I zipped my purse shut with more force than necessary. If only I could wad all my feelings away and zip them up too.

"Because *you* won't let it"—he scratched the back of his neck, the movement layered in frustration—"or your mom won't?"

"This has nothing to do with her." I glanced at the bulletin in my hand. *Liar, liar, pants on fire.* Mama's dislike of Samuel wasn't a factor like he thought. But the opinion she'd voiced had struck a nerve.

He gripped his Bible. "Then what is it?"

Emily approached, sans the friend who had sat with her.

Kate, with an inquisitive gleam in her eyes, shadowed Emily as though she drifted a frontrunner in the Indy 500.

I mustered a smile for Emily. "Thanks again for covering for me yesterday."

A tiny gasp escaped Kate's lips as she rounded out our little conversation circle.

"Oh, it was my pleasure." Emily sounded like one of the workers at my favorite fast-food restaurant. She turned to Samuel. "I actually had a question about straightening my uneven coffee table. One of the legs is shorter than the others."

Kate blanched, looking like she was going to toss the Lord's Supper right there at the tips of all our toes.

A vision of Emily sitting on the floor of her place with a hacksaw came to mind. Deliberately sabotaging her table, taking the wood shavings and crafting them into mini potpourri satchels to give away as party favors at her and Samuel's wedding.

Hayley popped up at Kate's side. "I need to talk to you." She grabbed Kate's hand and tugged her several steps away, speaking with dramatic gestures, but Kate's attention stayed glued on me, Samuel, and Emily.

Emily's wrinkle-free eyes never strayed from Samuel. "You did such a great job with Mr. Ramsey's chair yesterday, I hoped you could give me some pointers."

Samuel offered a polite smile Emily's way. "Umm."

Sharpness expanded in my throat. "I need to get going." Needed to go home and throw myself a raging pity party. "Have a good day." *Sheesh.* I'd turned into a Walmart greeter.

Kate, still trapped by Hayley's running mouth and flailing hands, gave me a pained expression as I walked past her and headed for the parking lot.

4:00 p.m.

SAMUEL
Can we please talk?

6:00 p.m.

SAMUEL
What if I told you I found an alpaca farm that
would let us feed and pet them?

7:30 p.m.

SAMUEL
If you're still overthinking, and tired of M&Ms
and pretzels, I can make you guacamole.

8:00 p.m.

SAMUEL
I won't be working on the patio tomorrow.
I'm doing a test run of one of the boating
excursions I plan to offer. Working out the
timing. If I don't talk to you before then, I'll
meet you at my dad's Tuesday morning.

Monday morning I woke wishing I could take the day off.
But that was the downside of my job. No sick or vacation days.
And considering I'd forfeited the Holdens' payment last week, I
had to haul my cookies out of bed and get to it. Bills had to be
paid and money saved, which meant tubs needed scrubbing and
floors mopping. On the next round of new dictionary entries,
I'd petition for *adulting* to be added as a curse word.

I made it through the day, counting small blessings like clients with no pets to clean up after or drains needing to be de-
clogged. And at least I knew Samuel wouldn't be home when I
got there. Yet disappointment still pinched my ribs at discover-

ing the Testosterone Truck absent at my house. And no alpaca card. But this was good! And what I'd wanted. *Distance* with a capital *D*.

Still, I couldn't help but wonder. Had Samuel gone to Emily's after church and fixed her table? Had Emily damaged her piece of furniture to have a reason to approach Samuel? For an innocent way to ask him over? To be wearing a drop-dead ensemble when he arrived and have a freshly cooked meal prepared? *"Look how gorgeous I am, Samuel. No varicose veins, no saggy boobs. See how I can cook too?"*

"Argh!" I crammed my key in the lock at the front door, chastising myself. Thinking those things wasn't right. Emily was a sweetheart, and my issues weren't her fault.

Chewie greeted me with his customary vigor, and I released him into the backyard. The path he'd always cut to the lawn was now completely blocked with the railings and screens in place. It'd taken some getting used to the past two days, but he'd figured out to use the opening where the door would go.

Breathing in the scent of cedar, I lingered over Samuel's quality work. All that remained to finish the job was a screen door and some trim work on the outside of the framing. The thought I'd once had of him purposefully dragging this project out vanished. That earlier squeeze of disenchantment struck afresh.

My attention caught beyond Samuel's temporary workbench to the back corner of the patio, where another new chair sat. It was identical to the first one Samuel had "just come across." He must have stopped by today before leaving for his excursion run. The beautiful seats now bookended my plastic one. My meager purchase looked miserable sitting between what he'd bought. Like the Jan Brady of outdoor furniture.

A slight heaviness descended. I pressed my lips together and crossed my arms. *Ridiculous. This is ridiculous. You've been through worse. Way, way worse.* This was nothing.

But it didn't feel like nothing. I pulled in a shaky breath.

It felt like . . . loss. Over the unknown. Over what could have been. Could I have trusted Samuel? Forgiven him? Given this new version of him a second chance?

With my pulse throbbing at the base of my neck, and a sour taste filling my mouth, I stepped around the worktable and sank into my flimsy chair. Chewie watched me from below the tree, his head tilted. He trotted through the open doorway, across the patio, and jumped onto my lap. The sawdust that had attached to the fur on his paws fell to my scrubs. I hugged him to my body, allowing my pity party from yesterday to resume.

Conner's personal ringtone played from my phone. For the first time in my life, I considered ignoring it. I wasn't in the best shape for talking, much less a video chat. But that's not what moms did. Maybe he needed something. I adjusted my hold on Chewie, and fished my phone from my pocket.

Accepting the call brought Conner's face into view. He sat behind the wheel of the car the boys shared. I glimpsed my image in the corner of the phone. *Yowza.* Bloodshot eyes toting body bags, greasy hair. I straightened my arm, retracting my phone as far from my face as possible. "Everything okay?"

"Yeah. Just dropped Mason off at work and thought I'd check in." A line puckered between his dark blond brows. "How are you?"

"Great!" I slapped on a smile that would make Vanna proud. "I'm sitting outside with Chewie." I slanted the phone, bringing Chewie into the shot. At least with this angle, it cut the worst parts of my face from Conner's sight.

"Is the patio done?"

"Almost." My voice nearly fractured. "Here, I'll show you." I readily flipped the view away from me and walked the area, showing Conner everything except the chairs. There was no way I'd explain they'd been gifts from Samuel.

"Mr. Samuel's not there today?"

"No, he had some things to do for the new business he's starting."

"Mom, you need to turn the phone's view again so I can see you."

Ugh. I returned myself to the screen, extending my arm as though trying to take a selfie with the entire Grand Canyon.

"He's starting his own construction business?"

"No, an outdoor adventure company."

Surprise flitted across Conner's face. "Nice. Like hiking and stuff?"

"Um, I don't think so. More like fishing, hunting, boat tours of the bayous." My shoulder ached from holding the phone so far out.

"Cool. He seemed nice when we met him. Miss Kate said he was a Green Beret. Is that how he lost his eye?"

I stiffened. "When did you talk to Kate?" Had she called him to start planting little Samuel seeds after unearthing my concerns about the boys? *No. No.* Kate was a meddler, but even she had boundaries.

He lifted a shoulder. "A while ago, when we asked her for help with the patio."

"Oh."

"You sure everything's okay?"

"Yeah. Now tell me what you did this past weekend." I tried schooling my features into those of a carefree woman and hoped the outward deception would eventually fool the ache inside.

20

THERE WERE SEVERAL REASONS I didn't live in the French Quarter. Lack of parking, privacy, and the ruckus of people partying into the early hours of the morning. Of those issues, my main one on this Tuesday morning was parking. I'd located Teddy Reed's house, a shotgun planted six blocks from Jackson Square. I'd slowed as I'd approached it, my jaw unhinging. Unique home colors were nothing new in this area. Even the houses neighboring Teddy's were oddly, but charmingly, painted in greens, oranges, and yellows.

But Teddy's house was a tribute to the USA. I loved my country and proudly flew my own American flag. But an entire house in those hues? Bold. Very bold. Red shutters flanked the widows, contrasting with the blue siding, and white covered the door and trim for everything else. This section of the French Quarter required approval by the city on the paint schemes for each home. Teddy must've had some connections to allow this palette.

With the national anthem playing in my head, I commenced my hunt. I circled the block like a shark, grateful the narrow one-way streets worked in my favor with this location. Round and round I went, until a space opened several residences from

Teddy's. And praise the Lord, no parking meters loomed on this street.

I paralleled into the spot and studied my destination. It wasn't the same home I'd visited two decades ago when I'd met Samuel's parents. That had been a two-story in Baton Rouge. Maybe his mom had acquired it with the divorce. Good for her.

Being a shotgun, this dwelling was a simple one-story. No lugging equipment up and down a flight of stairs. Good for me. Two flagpoles bookended the façade, one holding Old Glory, and the other an army flag. They both dangled limply, mirroring my enthusiasm. Taking on this job was the opposite of untangling Samuel from my life.

As I did with all first-time client encounters, I'd donned my best pair of scrubs, styled my hair into a sleek ponytail, and applied basic makeup. But not even my trusty under-eye concealer could hide the circles completely.

I pocketed my keys and phone, and made my way down the brick-paved sidewalk. Three concrete steps greeted me at Teddy's entrance, along with an army floor mat. Pulling in a calming breath, I rang the bell and retreated a stair.

After a moment, the door opened, revealing Wyatt Reed on the other side. The man could have been a body double for Samuel. But that was where the similarities between the brothers ended. Wyatt's black hair and dark eyes, set in a pale complexion, had always reminded me of a yin-yang symbol. Or a vampire.

Wyatt stood before me in a tailored steel-gray suit and silk tie. A hesitant smile completed his look. "Julia, thanks for coming." Another difference between the siblings? Where Samuel had been easygoing, Wyatt had been reserved. Quiet. And painfully so. The few times I'd been around him, he'd barely spoken a handful of words. One glance at his left hand conveyed its bareness. Had he ever married?

I remained on the middle step. "You're welcome."

Instead of inviting me in, he eased halfway out the door, leaving it ajar.

Suspicion twinged. What was he concealing, or really, delaying? Was Teddy a hoarder? Would there be a million cats inside, and stacks of junk mail piled to the rafters?

"Samuel's running behind." He shot his wrist out, glancing at his watch. "He asked me to stop by and show you around."

Thank God for small favors. The last thing I wanted was Samuel distracting me while I got my bearings. I edged to the right, trying for a better peek inside, and spied a coatrack holding no less than ten military ball caps. And the jackets hanging from the pegs indicated they were of the same classification. Teddy Reed's love of the armed forces had not waned with the years.

I noted the worn wood flooring, thankful I could actually see the surface. "He said your dad needs help."

"I don't need help." A grizzled voice bellowed from the other side of the door.

Oh, goodness. It sounded like that pole was still shoved up Teddy Reed's backside after all.

Wyatt leaned in with a grimace. "We'll pay you double." He'd softened his voice, a tone of desperation seeping in.

My gut tightened, and I cut my gaze to where Mr. Teddy's ornery holler had emanated. "I haven't even given you a quote."

"I don't care. I can't keep cleaning up after him."

In spite of the terror looming inside, a job was a job. And more than that, I felt honor-bound to help after all Samuel had done for me and the boys. Plus, I couldn't stand owing him. This would make us even. I would get his dad's place in shape and on a regular maintenance schedule. Then I'd line up another customer for myself on Tuesdays and someone else to seamlessly take over here.

Wyatt watched me, his dark eyes measuring . . . and hopeful.

Ugh. This is only temporary. Temporary! I made a grand sweeping gesture for him to lead the way.

"Thank you." The tenseness in his posture lessened.

I followed Wyatt through the threshold and into another dimension. *Mylanta.* My gaze sucked in too many things at once. Like running a vacuum over the beach. I'd anticipated the narrowness to the living and dining room spaces and the sky-high ceilings. But not what filled them.

An enormous wooden American flag with the army seal engraved in it was positioned above a sofa, a metal army emblem suspended next to it. Large enough to be a substitute for Captain America's shield. Another wall held a collection of smaller framed flags. A piece of artwork in red, white, and blue held the well-known saying of *Land of the free because of the brave.*

Another sign imprinted with the army logo had the words *Family with pride and honor.* I half expected Uncle Sam to jump out, pointing his finger. A throw blanket stretched across the love seat. Embroidered onto it was a bald eagle toting two machine guns, its eyes blood red. If Rambo had a pet, that would be it.

This was nothing like the house from when Samuel's parents had been married. I'd known his dad held a passion for the military. The one time we'd met, he'd been decked out in an army hat and shirt. Had talked of nothing but the latest uproar in Afghanistan. But I hadn't thought his zeal ran this deep.

Reining in my focus, I realized Teddy Reed watched me with suspicion. He sat motionless in a recliner situated in the front corner of the den. He'd aged since I'd last seen him, his hair thinning and gray. His once-sturdy physique frailer. The shorts he wore showed his knees, and the vertical scars puckering his skin from his surgery.

Wyatt stepped forward. "This is Julia Monroe."

Teddy squinted, pushing his glasses up from the tip of his

nose. It was a wonder he could see anything through the finger-prints on the lenses. "I remember you." No smile. No hospital-ity in his tone.

"Hello, Mr. Teddy."

"You dating Samuel again?"

"No, sir." My attention dropped to the coffee table, littered with gun magazines and dirty dishes.

"Well, no matter." He sized me up with a hmpf. "I don't need a nurse, so you can be on your way." He gave a dismissive wave and unpaused the television, *Blue Bloods* continuing.

Oh, for the love of— Here sat the male version of Mama. And if anyone knew how to deal with an old grinch, it was me. "I'm not a nurse."

"Then an aide or whatever you call them. I don't need help." He pointed the remote at the TV sitting on a console on the opposing wall and turned the volume up five notches.

So that's how this was going to go? Fine. Bring it on. "With all due respect, sir," I elevated my voice, "I'm not here to help you."

Mr. Teddy's glower zipped from Tom Selleck to me. He lowered the sound, never taking his narrowed stare from my face.

I, in turn, didn't pull my sights from him. In my peripheral, Wyatt shifted closer, as though to safeguard me. The brothers had more in common than I thought. Their mama had done well, instilling a protective streak in them. They certainly hadn't inherited it from General Grumpy.

"I clean homes for a living. And that's what I'm here to do."

Teddy scoffed. "My house doesn't need cleaning."

I arched a brow at the coffee table and the plates dotted with crumbs, the mugs stained with coffee rings. It was my best mom-look. The one successfully used on the boys in the past when they'd dared to give me lip or hadn't replaced the toilet paper.

"That's . . . that's from breakfast." Teddy waved his remote. "I haven't gotten around to them yet."

Hmm. I scanned the room, searching for something that would strike old Teddy where I needed it to. An upright piano, in a beautiful walnut finish, was oriented against the wall next to the television. Atop it rested a triangle glass enclosure, which held a carefully folded American flag. The flag of a fallen soldier. The harshness of reality sobered my thoughts. Was it a comrade's or maybe a sibling's? Mr. Teddy's father's?

I crossed the camo rug. After swiping a finger along the upright's top, near the flag, I held up my dusty findings. "You have too many precious memories here not to give them the reverence they deserve."

Teddy creaked forward in his recliner, turning three shades of red before settling to a faint pink. "Don't think I don't know what you're doing."

"I'm simply here to complete the job Samuel hired me to do." I squared my shoulders. "And as a woman of my word, I intend to do it." I nailed a pointed look at the *Family with pride and honor* artwork.

"Bah!" He jolted back, shaking his head, the loose skin beneath his chops wiggling. "I'm gonna kill that boy."

"Great." I shrugged. "That would make my life easier."

"But not mine," Wyatt muttered.

The front door rattled open, and Samuel appeared. My senseless heart pitter-pattered while I allowed the briefest of moments to take in his track pants and army T-shirt. Was that to appease his dad? Did I need patriotic scrubs to get on Teddy's good side, or for the man to merely tolerate me?

Samuel's gaze swept each of us, lingering on me, as though assessing the situation. "How's it going?"

"We're taking a vote on me killing you." Teddy jabbed the remote toward Samuel. "So far it's two to one."

Samuel patted Wyatt's back. "Thanks for taking up for me."

His attention slid my way, his expression softening. Holding steady eye contact with me, he gave a scarcely perceptible nod in the direction of his father and mouthed *thank you*.

A horrible, double-crossing tenderness for him swelled within. *No. No. No. Think of the boys. Get that guard up, girl. Up. Up. Up.* "If it's okay with you," I turned to Teddy, "I'd like to walk through your house and figure out what supplies I'll need to bring in."

He blinked. "You're gonna walk through my house?"

"Yes, sir."

"But . . . What about . . ." Teddy scooted to the edge of his chair, wincing with the effort.

"Dad," Wyatt said, "I already picked up your clothes from the bathroom."

Oh, that was his concern? "Mr. Teddy, I've had a husband, raised two teenaged boys, and have been professionally cleaning for a decade. I assure you nothing in your house will shock me." I peered past the dining room to a hallway no doubt leading to the kitchen, bathroom, and bedrooms. "Unless you're hiding something back there. Like a dead body or a meth l ab."

A trace of amusement touched Wyatt's dark eyes.

Samuel clamped his lips together, fighting a smile.

Something flickered in Teddy's countenance. A hint of surprise? He readjusted himself to his original sitting position, grunting and cringing with the movement. "The last time I saw you, you hardly spoke two words. Just hung on Samuel's arm like a tick on a coonhound."

"Dad." Samuel moved forward, his voice a low warning.

I lifted a staying hand to Samuel and spoke to Teddy. "Sir, my tick days are over. Now can I please get to work?"

He grumbled a reluctant *yes* and switched the volume back up on his program.

Teddy Reed didn't have dust bunnies. He had dust grizzlies. And if my itchy eyes and sneezes were any indicator, they hibernated all around the house. Granted, the Reed brothers had done a decent job of keeping the home in shape. But over time they would've lost the battle. Especially in the bathroom. A deep cleaning was in order. And since dust fell, I'd used my stepladder and started with the ceiling fans and light fixtures.

After I proved I could hold my own with the La-Z-Boy Grouch, the sons had left—Wyatt to work and Samuel to the grocery to replenish his dad's food. Before the refrigerator would be restocked, I'd cleaned the shelves and bins. After starting the bedding in the wash, I dusted the window blinds and wall decorations, then the actual furniture and knickknacks. I'd saved the dining and living room for last, hoping Teddy would doze off like Miss Marlene always did.

No such luck.

From his recliner, a newspaper blanketed his lap, his leery stare following me through his smudged bifocals.

I butted my shins against the sofa, using my duster on an extension pole to reach the top of the wooden American flag.

"I don't clean that." Teddy may as well have barked the words.

"That's fine. But if it's okay with you, I am."

"No one looks up there."

I paused, lowering the duster. "That layer of dust is one of the first things I noticed when I entered this room."

"You're crazy."

I eyed him and propped a hand on my hip. "Give me your glasses."

"What?"

I set my cleaning tool on the coffee table and stepped toward him, holding my hand out. "Your glasses. Give them to me."

He removed them with a glower, handing them over. "You're bossy."

179

"And you're not?" I made my way past the dining room table and through the small hallway housing one of the bathrooms and the laundry closet. I emptied into the kitchen, where my caddy rested on the tiled floor. The style of the bathrooms and kitchen appeared to be from the 1930s, which was probably when the house had been built. Regardless of their age, they were in good condition. And rather delightful.

I pulled out my homemade glass cleaner and a new microfiber cloth. A squirt and thorough rubbing on each lens cleared the smears. Suppressing a smugness I didn't want to tick Teddy off with, I brought his spectacles back to him.

His nose wrinkled. "They smell like vinegar."

"The scent will go away in a second."

He put them on and fluttered his lids several times, his eyes the same greenish-brown shade as Samuel's. "Hmpf."

I pointed to the wooden flag. "Can you see the dust now?"

He tilted his face up, squinted, and grumbled, returning his attention to the paper.

Pursing my lips, I continued my task, my sinuses tickling from the uncaptured particles. The weekly maintenance on this place would be a cinch. The challenge lay with finding someone to tolerate Teddy Reed. But if the brothers paid an inconvenience fee, that would help with securing my replacement.

Teddy turned the page, his newspaper crinkling. "Earlier you said you had a husband. You're divorced?"

I inwardly groaned. I did not want to talk about Mark with this old crankster. If Teddy insulted him, I wasn't beneath walking out. After changing the channel to Hallmark and hiding the remote. "No, sir. Widowed."

"Was he a veteran?"

Usually at hearing my widow status, people offered condolences. I should've known better from Teddy Reed. And oddly enough, it was refreshing to not get the pitying expression or be handled like I was fragile. "No, sir."

"And you have two teenaged boys?"

"Yes, they're eighteen and nineteen."

"They in the military?"

"No, sir, they're in college."

He grunted. "Do you think they'll end up joining?"

I smothered a moan and moved on to dusting the circular metal army emblem. "They've never shown interest, so I don't think so."

"Sometimes we need to push our children so they *get* interested."

Like how you pushed Samuel? Though, according to Samuel, enlisting in the army had been his decision. That still didn't take away from all the harping Teddy and Wyatt had done. I moved to the arrangement of framed flags on the other wall.

He shifted, as though his back bothered him, and it wasn't any wonder since he hadn't moved from his recliner all morning.

"Aren't you supposed to get up and walk around every so often?" I motioned to his legs and the incisions running in a single line from above his kneecaps to below them.

"You just stick to cleaning. If I need medical advice, I'll call my doctor."

Clamping my teeth on my tongue, I began wiping the piano, starting with a graduation picture of Samuel's daughter. With her aspirations to be a nurse, Brooke had to have some kindness in her. Was her mom kind? Samuel hadn't married, but had he been engaged to her mom? Loved her? *Stop! Not going there!*

I moved on to a figurine of a soldier kneeling in prayer. Was Teddy a believer? Had something happened to harden him? Maybe he was a softy on the inside—like a Rolo—and needed time to open up.

He snapped his paper. "Be careful with that." His tone matched his motion.

My lips pinched. Scratch that. He was a Jolly Rancher, minus the sugar, flavor, and jolly.

The next few hours dragged by in a state of apprehension once Samuel returned with Teddy's groceries. Just being in the same house with him—and the likelihood we'd have to interact—proved too much. Especially in a shotgun without a lot of room. I'd used my earbuds as a deterrent and to block out his voice when he talked to his dad, but it hadn't eliminated the visual of him while he helped Teddy do knee exercises. Or sat at the dining room table helping Teddy pay his bills. Or when he'd made lunch and invited me to join them. I'd declined, eating a protein bar while vacuuming the baseboards.

During that time, I'd begun planning what I'd say to Samuel. *We can't be friends after all. Friends shouldn't be attracted to each other, and you give me major zings. Friends should be happy for each other when they find someone special. And watching you stand next to Emily Miller on Sunday made me want to irrationally punch you both in the throat.*

By the time I'd finished Teddy's house, I'd resigned myself to facing Samuel today just to be done with it. I was exhausted and ready to hole up at home and have a whopper of an ugly cry in the shower. The sun descended in the late afternoon sky as I packed the last of my supplies in the back of my SUV. I hated the thought of going back into Teddy's house and asking Samuel if we could talk.

As I headed up the sidewalk, Teddy's front door opened, and Samuel emerged. The furrow to his brows indicated he'd perceived my aloofness. Combined with my actions this past weekend, it couldn't have been missed. This was not going to be an effortless conversation. But considering nothing had ever been simple about our relationship, then or now, it seemed appropriate. He hesitated on the last stair, weakened sunrays catching on his face and the concern in his eye.

Had feathers sprouted from my pores? Because I sensed myself chickening out. I stopped several feet away, hovering at the edge of Teddy's property, near the wrought-iron door leading to his narrow alley and courtyard. "Um, when I come back next Tuesday, I'll have an invoice for today." Sweat trickled down my spine.

He stepped onto the pavement, his open stare continuing.

A car rumbled past, leaving exhaust fumes in its wake.

I scuffed my tennis shoe against the herringbone brick pavers, scattering loose grit. *Chicken.* "I'll have a quote for the maintenance cleans by then too." *Stop procrastinating. There's no future with him. It's best for everyone. The boys, you, and Samuel.* For the sake of procrastination, I pulled my phone from my scrubs and glanced at the screen. Returned it. Studied my keys in my hand. I'd never broken up with anyone, but that's what this seemed like. Which was preposterous. We weren't even dating.

He loosened a sigh, shoving his hands in the pockets of his track pants. "You're shutting me out."

I risked a glance at him. There and away. *Cluck-cluck.* Jazz music drifted from the tavern on the corner, a harmonica and guitar adding a spark of soul to the air.

"Do you remember the times when we were dating and I pulled away from you?"

My gaze shot to his, my imaginary feathers shedding. That was exactly what I'd needed in this moment, a reality check. "All the times you crushed my heart? Yes." I released a humorless laugh. "I remember them very clearly."

His lips rolled in with a wince. "I wish you could understand how sorry I am for that." He stared at the ground between us. "Back then, I was always up front with you that I wasn't ready for something serious."

That was achingly true. Our relationship had been an unwavering combination of closeness and separation.

"I didn't have the best example of a healthy marriage. My parents were always arguing, splitting up, getting back together."

My stomach hardened, a flush of warmth spreading through me. "But we weren't like them. We never fought. You would just vanish and leave me hanging." The murmur of a breeze traipsed by, barely lifting the flags on Mr. Teddy's poles.

"I thought being with you would wear out, like the other women I'd been with, and it didn't. You made being together easy. Every time I realized how close we were, it scared me. I knew you wanted more than I was ready to give." He massaged his temples, the tips of his fingers nudging the strap on his patch askew, revealing a slight indentation in his skin where the leather had left a mark. "The strain to be something I wasn't ready for would mount. And I'd see how miserable my parents were. So I'd put distance between us."

I gave a slow blink, Samuel's words from last Friday returning. *"Persuasion's a powerful thing, and dangerous in the hands of biased people."* Had he been referring to his parents? I'd always had an inkling they'd had something to do with his behavior. "Then why did you keep getting back together with me?"

"I had this . . . draw to you. I'd get tired of fighting it." He cupped the back of his neck with both hands, his sight slowly rising to meet mine. "And mostly, I didn't want to risk losing you to someone else."

I clutched my keys, the hardware biting into my palm. When we'd been together, I hadn't let myself believe he was stringing me along. After the breakup, though, I'd known. And I'd loathed myself for allowing it. But hearing him actually admit it was nauseating.

"Your mom was right last week when she called me selfish." His arms fell, as though they'd become too heavy to hold up. "I was."

My hardened belly clenched. These two versions of Samuel

were too hard to process. The man who'd hurt and treated me carelessly, and the man I'd come to know the past six weeks.

"With graduation looming, I dreaded becoming an adult. Being trapped in a nine-to-five job."

I drew back, my lips parting. I'd dated a man who'd had Peter Pan syndrome? "You never mentioned it."

"It wasn't something I was proud of." His head dipped, and he tugged at the sleeve of his shirt. "But I knew Wyatt had felt the same way, so I confided in him."

My mouth grew drier by the second. Wouldn't I have noticed if Samuel had been struggling? I mean, he'd been quiet at times. I stared at the ground, as though it held answers. Had I been too absorbed in my own insecurities to notice his issues? I hadn't wanted to broach the topic of why he was disappearing on me. Hadn't wanted him to think me needy, or give him a reason to withdraw more.

"Everything Wyatt pitched about Special Forces seemed like the ideal escape plan from the student loan debt I'd accumulated and being stuck at a desk job. A way to press *pause* on the path I was on and try something else. Something I could be excited about."

I touched my forehead, my baffled mind trying to work through the new information. Trying to look back on our relationship with a different perspective. "I . . . I wouldn't have stopped you from joining the army."

"I know."

I would have waited dutifully for him. Been the perfect military girlfriend. Sent care packages and greeted him at the airport for furloughs.

As quickly as those scenarios had flowered, they wilted. And a question, buried deep in my heart since the day he'd dumped me, arose. I hadn't voiced it then because I hadn't thought he'd be honest with the answer. But now . . . My hands shook, jostling my keys. I gripped them harder and worked past the lump in my throat. "During those years we were together, did you cheat on me, other than at the end?"

"No." Sincerity and truth were written on his face, in his unswerving eye contact.

My legs wobbled, along with my chin. I turned to the street, discovering a mule-drawn carriage carrying only the tour guide. The black-and-red covered wagon turned the corner, the animal's hooves clip-clopping at a steady pace, matching my pulse.

"It only happened once." His voice floated over my shoulder. "At the time, a lot was hitting me. I'd felt like I was inside this . . . pressure cooker. Some friends from high school came to town, and it turned into a foolish weekend of drinking and . . ."

So it was someone from his high school that he'd been unfaithful with? I closed my eyes, willing the tears not to appear. "It was still your choice to make. To lead me on all that time. To cheat on me. Not to answer my calls when I was . . ."

"I know. And I own that." His shadow on the ground approached mine stretching along the sidewalk.

"You owning up to your past behavior doesn't fix the damage that was done. Or the fact that I don't know if I can forgive you. Or trust you not to revert to who you were, like when you left last Friday."

"It was wrong of me to leave, and I'd driven all of seven blocks before I turned around and hightailed it back. But you were gone."

My stars. He'd come right back? *Okay.* That was a good thing, and yet . . . it didn't change how this had to end.

"I'm not the same reckless kid I was back then, and I'll prove it to you if you let me."

I pulled in a trembling breath and straightened. "There's nothing to prove because we can't be together." I turned toward him. "The last time the notion of me dating came up, my boys reacted badly. To the point they almost went back to counseling. And that was with someone I had no history with. What would they think if they found out we dated before I met my husband?"

He blinked, plainly caught by surprise. "We haven't seen or spoken to each other for over twenty years."

"That doesn't matter." I edged backward, needing more space. "I can't chance them thinking I harbored anything for you during my marriage. They already lost their dad." The power in my voice dwindled. "I won't take anything else from them. Including the certainty that my feelings for Mark were loyal and true."

Face pale and posture slumped, Samuel's gaze slunk to the ground, like a man who had been beat.

And I was about to deliver the final blow. "I don't think we can even be friends."

His stricken look left no questions as to what he felt. "I think you've been inside your head since Thursday night when your mom showed up." Thick emotion coated his tone, and he neared. "Let's talk this through." He reached toward me, his strong hand gentle against my face, his calloused thumb caressing my cheek.

Oh, how I wanted to lean into his touch. But it would only make things worse. "No." I retreated another step. "I *have* been in my head, but I keep coming to the same conclusion." I contemplated the lock button on my key fob, wishing I had that option on my heart. "And it's not fair to you. Or me. Being around you is . . . difficult. So I'd appreciate it if you weren't here on Tuesdays when I'm cleaning. And if you could find somewhere else to sit on Sundays too." There. I'd driven the last nail into the coffin, and from the way my chest ached, the nail in my heart too.

Samuel didn't move. And I was too much of a coward to glance any farther north on him than the stripes on the sides of his Adidas pants. An ugly cry was imminent. I wasn't going to make it to the shower. Not wanting an audience or to drag this moment out, I climbed into my vehicle and started the ignition. Mama's bulletin sat on my dashboard, right where I'd tossed it Sunday after church. I pulled in a breath. *Lord, can You carry me a little longer today?* I longed to fall asleep with a clear conscience tonight, and Mama was the blockade from that.

21

THANK GOODNESS FOR RUSH-HOUR TRAFFIC. It had allowed me to wallow safely at a turtle's speed while making my way to Mama's house. I entered through her side door and found her sitting at her kitchen table, glasses perched at the edge of her nose, playing solitaire. A haze of smoke hovered above her. The local evening news droned in the background. Per routine, I left the door open to air out the room and latched the screen door.

With a scowl, she pushed to standing, her chair scraping the floor, and moved to the kitchen peninsula. Maybe those lines around her mouth were from frowning her entire life and not from smoking. She reached for her pills-of-the-week container, the tablets rattling. "It is Tuesday, right?"

And those were the first words to break our five-day silence. I hadn't expected anything less. She wasn't known for affection or empathy, other than where Conner and Mason were concerned. The boys were her one and only soft spot, squishy like a browning banana. Whereas my standing was more of an unripe avocado.

"Yes, it's Tuesday." I pulled out the chair across from hers and sank onto it, dropping my purse to the floor and the church communiqué on the table.

"Just making sure I didn't take the wrong medications. You showing up with a bulletin and all."

And there it was, Mama's not-too-subtle jab at my absence. I'd needed extra time to recover from her harsh words, and after watching Emily's bright eyes zero in on Samuel after church on Sunday, I hadn't had the stamina to face Mama.

She stabbed an air freshener in an electrical socket and re-took her seat, resuming her game. "You're lookin' pretty rough there." She flipped a card from the deck in her hands.

I braced my elbows on the table and made a silent plea to the Lord for help. "I want to talk about what happened last week."

"You mean when you kicked me out of your house?"

Warmth flooded my cheeks. What about her flippancy that night? Brother Buford's voice from Sunday's sermon whispered through me. *"Be slow to speak. Think about what you say."* At the very least, I had come here to apologize. "I'm sorry about that."

Unmoved, she studied the progress of her game.

I stared at her. *And here's where you express your regrets, Mama.*

She turned an ace and placed it on the table, right next to an ashtray stuffed with cigarette butts. No reaction. She should've been playing poker. Or maybe she was already engaged in a mental game with me.

No matter. I wasn't anteing up. "I shouldn't have kept Samuel working on my patio a secret. But I knew it'd tick you off, and I didn't want to be lectured."

With a grunt, Mama grabbed the ashtray and aimed for the garbage.

I slid my hands to my lap and drew in a breath of stale air tinged with faux lemon. "What you said hurt."

She stopped short. "Do you think finding that man in your house felt good to me?"

"No, I don't." I picked at my cuticles, then met her gaze, my mouth going dry. "Did you only say what you did out of spite, or do you really think my friendship with Samuel is disrespectful to Mark?"

"Well . . ." The glower in her eyes lessened, and she dumped the cigarettes, thumping the tray against the inside of the can. "There was some spite."

I knew it! I schooled my features. Maybe I was in this mental poker match after all.

"But any contact with Samuel isn't good."

"Because of how he treated me before?"

"Despite what you think, people don't change. Only suckers believe that."

I bit my lower lip, holding in my retort.

"You've been married and had kids. You're done. Why go ruining a good thing now?"

I scoffed. "I'm only forty, Mama. I've got the next half of my life to go." I straightened one of her rows running off the king of diamonds. "And I don't want to live it by myself." The declaration burst from my lips, unexpected and so un-me. Maybe there really were moments of the heart overruling the head. When the subconscious piped up after being ignored for too long.

"You're crazy." She clattered the empty ashtray to the table and stiffly lowered onto her seat like the Tin Man needing his oil can. "You sound like one of those cheesy romance movies."

I snatched Mama's newspaper and stood at the screen door, flapping in fresh air. What had crawled up her rear and died for her to be such a grump about love? It hadn't started with Samuel's desertion. No, as long as I could remember, she'd been indifferent. Unaffectionate. Unless . . . My pulse slowed to a thud. The streetlamp at the end of the driveway flickered on, even though the sun still hung low in the sky. I moved my attention from outside to her. "Did Daddy cheat on you?"

"What?" Her face scrunched, and she gave me a double take.

"No." She chortled and overturned another card. "Why would you ask that?"

The tension in my arms uncoiled, and I loosened my hold on the paper. "By the way you've always acted, it's like some great wrong happened that you can't get over. Even when Daddy was alive, you were . . ." I fanned in several more strokes of clean air. "It was like y'all were roommates more than a loving married couple." Never holding hands except for mealtime prayers, no *I love you*'s or kisses. Without any siblings, I wondered if they'd only done the deed once, purely to conceive me. *Poor, poor Daddy.*

"All that sappy stuff isn't me." She licked her thumb and turned a seven of spades. "It never was. My parents weren't that way. And I swear, if I hadn't seen you come out of me, I wouldn't think you were my child. Romance and love and feelings. Pah!"

"But Daddy was romantic. At least he tried. I remember him trying." Like the time he'd made her a candlelight dinner. I'd been ten and snooping from the hallway. Mama had come in from work, flicked on the lights, and blown out the candles. The disappointment on Daddy's face had been heartrending. To me, anyway.

"Your father knew from day one I wasn't a . . . *feelings* person." Her face contorted on the word. "I come from a long line of practical people. Or as my mama used to put it, we are wired differently. My aunt Celia even put an onion in her handkerchief at her husband's funeral."

I retook my chair and rubbed my temples. Was there some sort of sensitivity dysfunction gene that had skipped me? And if it had, thank the Lord. But I was left with the truth of my family having a history of pitiful relationships. And I didn't want that repeating. "Mama, I want us to get along."

"We do."

Ha! Debatable. Especially since it had been five days since we'd spoken, and Mama would've let that silence stretch until

Thanksgiving, and only then because the boys would be in town. "I need you to understand that I am a feelings person."

Her dark eyes peered at me from above the rims of her cheaters. "Believe me. I know." She dealt a deuce and laid it on her ace.

"And we're different. You thrive on being solitary." I motioned to the game. Irony at its best. "I don't. Since the boys have gone off to college, I've hated how quiet my house is."

"You've got that yappy dog."

"It's not the same. Having the boys far away has been hard. Tougher than I've let on." Only Chewie and God knew how hard. I'd even put on a brave front for Kate. Had tried to convince myself too. My throat burned, my vision blurring. Sheesh, I really was a feelings person. "There have been times I've considered moving to North Carolina." Voicing these thoughts was a first, making them all the more real and truthful. But Mama needed to hear it. Even if she didn't understand my stance, at least I could rest knowing I'd tried to explain.

The deck slipped from Mama's hand, cards scattering across the tabletop. "But your job is here."

"You don't think people need their homes cleaned there?"

"But . . . I'm here too." Face growing pale, she regathered the cards, fumbling several of them. "And you know I can't move." Her eyes blinked in rapid succession. "This is my home." She gave up and began patting her pockets, retrieving a lighter. "It's paid off. I'm comfortable here." What she didn't say was that she probably had a mild case of undiagnosed agoraphobia.

"I know. And that's why it's never been more than a thought."

Her fidgeting slacked. "You've just got that empty nest syndrome, that's all."

"This has been going on longer than the past few months. The older the boys have gotten, the more I've been left alone. I've tried to make myself believe I'm fine with it, but I'm not. And I'm tired of the burden of carrying everything on my

shoulders all these years. Not having a partner to lean on."
Samuel's reentry into my life had only shoved those longings
into the spotlight.

"You can lean on me."

"Oh, Mama, it's not the same."

She eased back in her chair, crossing her arms. "So this big
speech is to say you're gonna start dating Samuel?"

"No." I glanced at my hands, discovering ink on several
fingers from the newspaper. I wiped them against my scrubs.
"Once he's done with the patio, that's it."

Her stare sharpened. "Then why's that man cutting your
grass?"

Great googly moogly. A cold sweat broke across my skin.

"I saw him last Friday." She bent forward. "On your front
lawn. Cutting. Your. Grass."

My leg jittered beneath the table, visions flashing of Mama
with binoculars, doing a stakeout from her boat of a Buick.
"You're spying on my house?"

"And when did you get a new lawn mower?"

"I haven't." My leg bopping halted, breath catching in my
lungs. Had he bought me a new mower? *Don't jump to conclu-
sions.* He could've brought his own machine.

She moved the obituary section of the paper, uncovering a
pack of smokes. "I saw him cut the grass with a new mower
and leave without it."

Oh no. I'd already researched how much a new mower would
cost. Samuel could have easily dropped several hundred on one.
Could he return it? Knowing him, he wouldn't, that stubborn
man. I'd have to sneak it to his place. Maybe the church would
give me his address.

But how in the world would I lug it there?

Finding her cigarette pack empty, Mama headed for the
kitchen. "Then I followed him to his place."

Leaky trash bags. I covered my face and sunk into my chair.

Apparently, an expiration date on mothers embarrassing their children didn't exist.

"He lives in a new condo in Metairie by Lake Ponchartrain." She opened a bottom cabinet. "From what I could tell, he went in and showered, changed clothes, and returned to your place."

Unbelievable. Instead of *Magnum P.I.*, I had Mama P.I. "Mama, you were trailing a Green Beret." I folded my arms over my middle. Had Samuel known? He hadn't mentioned anything about her spying on him. *Sakes alive.* Had Mama outmaneuvered a Green Beret? The very thought was terrifying.

"I also watched him fix your side gate." She tossed a new box of death sticks on the counter and shut the cupboard. "Have you given him a list?"

Nausea swirled. "No. And none of that matters now. I'm not dating him."

"Hmpf."

"I'm not. And you need to stop stalking him."

A hint of mischief touched her face.

"I mean it, Mama. It's an invasion of privacy. And you're wasting your time. I have no future with Samuel. It's too big a risk."

Her brow quirked.

I finished gathering the cards into a stack. "Among other things, what you said the other night, though wrong, got me considering the boys—"

"And how upset they got about that teacher?"

"Yes. And more so, I don't want them thinking I still cared for Samuel while I was with Mark." I leveled her with a death glare. "Which I didn't."

Her hands shot up. "I wasn't gonna say you did." She smacked one end of the new cigarette pack against her palm several times. "Goodness knows you were a schmuck for Mark." She unwrapped the cellophane from her smokes. "So you're what? Signing up for one of those dating websites? And not telling the boys? Aren't they filled with serial killers?" She stuck a cigarette between her lips. "Talk about risk."

"No. No dating sites. I'm just going to have an open mindset from now on when I'm out in the world. Maybe God will drop the right man in my life for me and the boys. Like He did with Chewie."

Mama rolled her eyes, a sound of disgust radiating from her throat. Or maybe her smoker's cough was about to erupt.

My attention drifted to the TV and the meteorologist. Ignoring what he said about the weather here, I focused on North Carolina, and the cool front graphic moving in that direction.

"I'm sorry about what I said last week . . . about Mark." Mama nudged her glasses up her nose.

"Thank you." Maybe her Grinch heart had grown tonight, and she'd start looking at things through my eyes, considering my feelings.

"You promise you're not gonna move away and leave me?"

Or maybe not.

I sighed. "No, Mama. I won't leave you."

22

CONNER'S PULSING DOT HAD NOT BEEN in his dorm room all night long. I knew this because I'd been up at all hours monitoring it. He'd been at a new location I'd never tracked him to.

Zooming in on satellite images, I'd learned it was an apartment complex about thirty miles from campus in a run-down area. Using the street view via an online map, I'd found the name of the place: Shady Lane Apartments.

Not comforting.

The façade hadn't helped with giving me warm fuzzies either. The dwelling needed major TLC—or a wrecking ball. The exterior had missing siding and graffiti. Dirt covered a narrow stretch of lawn where a garden and grass should've been. Tipped-over garbage cans were the crowning beauty, with trash and red Solo cups littering the ground.

I rubbed my forehead, a headache having long taken root last night as each hour had ticked by. This was the first night that he hadn't spent in his dorm. Mustering all of my restraint, I'd waited until seven thirty this morning to call and text Conner. I'd reasoned he had a class at eight he never missed, and I was helping him keep that perfect attendance streak. But my attempts to reach him had gone unanswered. Not wanting to draw suspicion that I was invading his privacy, my text had been vague: *Call me when you can.*

Next, I'd dialed Mason to see if he knew anything about Conner's whereabouts. I had ended up in his voice mail too. Not surprising. His blinking dot had showed him already in his first class, which meant he'd probably had his phone off, studying before the exam he had this morning.

It was now nine. My attention, unfocused and hazy, latched on to the work pants I'd laid on my bed. I needed to go. I was already running late for my first client. And yet, I couldn't make myself pull those bottoms on. Couldn't leave the house. Conner's pinpoint still pulsed in that questionable apartment. Or in the apartment's dumpster. *Stop! Don't stumble down that rabbit hole.*

Ugh! Just wait until Conner had kids. That's when he'd find out how horrific parenting was. Especially teenagers. I'd been so stressed at the prospect of raising babies. But those were the easy years, when they couldn't get away from you. You knew where they were every second of the day. You knew if they were eating and pooping right. You could pick who they played with.

Having teens out on their own was a whole other heaping of ulcers. Having teens living several states away was a cardiac arrest waiting to happen.

A knock sounded at the front door, and Chewie rushed to it, barking, setting my nerves further on edge. Glancing out the window, I spied Mama's Buick in my driveway. I opened the door.

"You're still home." Her keys dangled from her hands.

My molars ground together. Would she ever greet me properly? "Please tell me you're not spying on my house again."

"No. I was on my way to the grocery and saw your car's still here." Her blue blouse was tucked into the elastic band of her red capris. Or as Mama called them, pedal pushers. If she spun in place, she'd resemble a barbershop pole. "You're still not looking good."

"That's because I'm freaking out." With my teeth clenched, it came out like a growl.

Her eyes widened, and she peered behind me, nosy as ever. "Why?"

I brought her up to speed, pacing from the kitchen to the living room, the top half of me dressed for work, my bottom half still in sleep shorts, uncommitted to what my day was going to turn into. Concern edged deeper in Mama's expression with each lap I made. For all her coldness, Conner and Mason were her Achilles' heel. She'd been there for everything for them from birth to first baths and haircuts, sicknesses, school events, ball games, and all the holidays in between.

"Conner called me last night." Mama's thin eyebrows slanted into a V. "Before heading to a basketball game on campus."

I paused on my millionth pass past the sofa. "What did he call you about?"

She shrugged, glancing at her white Velcro tennis shoes. "He calls every now and then."

"Mama." My hand coiled into a fist. "This is not the time to be coy."

"The boys are worried about you."

The muscles in my shoulders constricted. Apparently, I needed to take acting classes before my next video call with them. But I couldn't worry about that now. I waved a hand and that thought trailed away. "Did Conner say who he was going to the game with?"

"No."

"What about parties afterward? Did he mention anything?"

Mama scoffed. "Conner is *not* a partying kid."

"I know, which is why I'm stressing." I braced my hands around my neck and squeezed. "What should I do? Is this something I can call the police about?"

"On *Blue Bloods* they make people wait twenty-four hours before reporting a missing person."

"This isn't a TV show!" I flung my arms wide. "And we don't know if he's missing . . . not really."

She perked. "What about Mark's parents?"

"They're in Ohio."

She muttered a curse. "How can they be out of town? They're on grandchild duty. I never once left town when the boys lived here." Forget the fact she never left town anyway. Not even for a category four hurricane. "Where's Mason?"

"In class for the next hour taking a test. I thought of sending him after Conner, but that place looks shifty. And there are at least forty or fifty units in that complex. How would we know which one Conner's in?"

Another knock rapped at the front door. Chewie tore off on tantrum number two.

My chest seized. "What if it's the police, notifying me Conner's injured, or dead, or found in a tub filled with ice with one of his kidneys removed?"

"This fast?" Mama shook her head, retrieving her smokes from her waistband. "The police never move that quick."

Was she speaking of real police or TV police? Heck, at this point, maybe I'd have a cigarette too. I opened the door and found Samuel. Every molecule within me froze.

He ignored Chewie yapping at his boots, his gaze sweeping my face, his brows pulling together in a negative assessment. "I stopped by to get some work done but saw you're still here. And your mom's car. I didn't want to just let myself in the back." He glimpsed the space behind me. "Everything okay?"

My last thread of composure unraveled. The sob I'd held in all night and morning burst. Just him being here, another capable adult who didn't rely on television knowledge for moments of crisis, was a relief. I gestured him in.

While I composed myself, Mama grabbed two wooden

spoons from the kitchen and shepherded a still snarling Chewie to my bedroom, closing off his raucous yelping. She handed me a box of tissues and relayed everything to Samuel. I resumed pacing and watching Conner's spot on my phone through blurry eyes and hiccuping breaths.

Samuel listened to Mama and watched me. The stillness in his posture contrasted with Mama flapping her hands and my frantic movements. In a T-shirt and jeans, with his arms crossed, he radiated steadiness. Something I desperately needed.

With her contribution to the situation fulfilled, Mama disappeared to the back patio, simultaneously leaving the door cracked and lighting her cigarette.

"I know you're upset," Samuel said. "But most likely, there was a party at this place after the game, and that's just where he spent the night."

I clung to his rational reasoning. This man had fought in wars. Had seen the worst of things and people. Had faced terrors I couldn't imagine. If he wasn't concerned, I'd take confidence in that.

He shifted. "Or his phone was stolen, and he did return to his dorm last night."

"He would've let me know if his phone was taken."

"Okay." He scratched his jaw. "I think everything's fine, but I also think it wouldn't hurt to call the local police there."

My knees buckled, nausea rearing. I threw a glance at Mama through the glass door. Having heard Samuel, her face had paled, and she took a drag long enough to turn half of her cigarette to ash.

Samuel stepped toward me. "I don't know how long it would take the police to follow up on your request. But if it's okay, I have friends in that area. I can make some calls."

"Make the calls!" Mama hollered, a trace of smoke slinking inside.

I nodded and shuffled on wobbly legs to the dining room

table. It looked like a command center with its current setup. Last night, I'd cleared my centerpiece, making room for my laptop, phone, and both chargers. Multicolored sticky notes, with info about the apartment building, numbers for local law enforcement, and flight schedules in case I hopped a plane created an eerie rainbow around three drained coffee mugs.

A small travel bag also sat atop the table, with essentials I'd started packing. I rummaged through my notes, looking for the police station's number, tears pinging my hands and dotting the papers.

Samuel pulled his phone from his pocket. "Have you tried calling the superintendent for the building?"

"Yes, no one answered. They're probably passed out with a needle stuck in their arm." I sank into the chair I'd occupied all night.

Taking the seat next to me, he pressed his phone to his ear. "Hey, Tank. How are you?" A pause. "I need some help. Do you know anyone on the Chapel Hill PD?"

My sight sharpened on him. Tank? Was it a military buddy? Another Green Beret? The churning in my stomach lessened.

"Perfect," Samuel said. "Thanks, man. I'll call him." He disconnected and met my stare. "An old friend from Special Forces is on Chapel Hill's PD."

I pinned a shaky hand to my mouth, a spark of hope igniting.

"Call him!" Mama shouted from outside.

He skimmed through the contacts on his phone and held the device to his ear. "Barberi? It's Reed." A beat of silence followed. "Good and you?" Another pause. "Yeah, I need some help. My friend's got a tracking app on her nineteen-year-old, and he's been in a strange location in Chapel Hill since last night. Not answering his phone. He's a good kid, so this isn't his usual MO." Samuel scanned the papers in front of me. "Shady Lane Apartments." A flicker of relief appeared. "That's what I was hoping you'd say."

Another round of tears gathered, spilling over my lashes.

Samuel reached over, placing his hand on mine, and gave a light squeeze.

My heart felt the gesture more than my fingers.

"Yeah." He spoke into his phone, withdrawing his touch. "I'll send it to you now." He hung up. "Can you text me a recent picture of Conner, his height and weight, and a screenshot of where he is on that tracking app?"

Praise the Lord! I had someone from Special Forces on the case! My very own mini A-Team. I quickly texted Samuel the information, and he forwarded them to whoever Barberi was. I imagined him as Mr. T. minus the layers of gold necklaces.

Several minutes later, Samuel's phone rang, and he answered, pushing up from the table and walking toward the kitchen. "Yeah." He leaned forward, resting an elbow on the counter. "Thanks, man." He turned, his gaze skipping to me, and nodded.

The kind of nod that made the next breath into my lungs a little easier to handle.

"I owe y'all." Hanging up, he straightened.

Mama entered through the door with an air of readiness, her attention on Samuel.

"Barberi and his partner are going to the apartments now."

A quiver traveled from my bare feet to my lopsided ponytail, a few more tears falling. "Just like that?"

Crease lines fanned from the corner of his eye. "Just like that."

In that moment, I was ready to pledge a life of servitude to the man. I'd clean Teddy's house forever. Let Samuel sit wherever he darned well pleased at church. Even right in front of me with Emily Miller.

Samuel's regard trailed from me to Mama and back. "I'd like to pray, if that's okay."

I stood on tingling legs and moved toward him, reaching for

his hand, which enclosed mine in a secure clasp. I extended my other hand to Mama.

After a slight hesitation and pinch to her lips, she completed the circle, bringing the scent of smoke but leaving her animosity for Samuel behind. At least temporarily.

Once the prayer was over, I resumed checking the tracking app, and Mama resumed her distance from Samuel. She rummaged my cabinets for a disposable cup, added water to it, and took up position on the back patio with her makeshift ashtray.

I glanced up at Samuel, the usual zings of attraction replaced with pangs of gratitude, the sensation expanding through my body. "I don't know how to thank you for this."

"I'd say you could let me take you on a date, but I think I know the answer to that." Although he'd posed it as a tease—no doubt to lighten the moment—it had been spoken on a foundation of sincerity, tinged with sadness.

My heart thudded. Would one date really hurt? Everything inside me stretched and pulled to give in. Photos of Conner and Mason on the entertainment center captured my attention. Next to them sat the last family photo we'd taken with Mark.

That thud turned into a clench. One date really could hurt because I had a feeling I'd want another. And I also didn't want to give Samuel false hope. Or for the boys to find out. Or to invest in someone I hadn't truly forgiven.

"In case you haven't noticed," Mama yelled, her voice charging through the crevice in the door, "the screen door's missing out here."

One corner of Samuel's mouth twitched. "I know, Mrs. Anne. I'm not finished." His phone dinged with a text, and he read it, his voice pitched to reach Mama's ears. "It's Barberi. They're there. The first guy I called, Tank, is on his way too."

Mama ambled the patio perimeter, inspecting Samuel's work and puffing on a cigarette.

"Is Tank in law enforcement?"

He shook his head. "Special Forces. He's on furlough in Raleigh."

Samuel must be well-liked by these men for them to drop everything and help him.

"What is this?" Mama hollered. "Cedar? It smells."

I shot a glare in Mama's direction. Unbelievable.

Another whisper of amusement colored Samuel's face.

"How can she smell anything except smoke?" I angled toward the door and raised my voice. "If you want to talk to us, come inside like a normal person."

Samuel snickered. "Have you had breakfast?"

"Does Pepto-Bismol count?"

"Not up for eating?"

"No." I refreshed the tracking app. Conner's dot remained unmoved.

Samuel drifted to the table and motioned to my travel bag. "Were you planning on flying out there?"

"Or driving if I couldn't get a flight." I laid my phone on the kitchen island and rubbed my eyes.

"By yourself?"

"Yes." A weary sigh pushed from the depths of my lungs. It wasn't like I could ask Kate to go. Or Mama. In moments like this, with the weight of the world crashing on my shoulders, I longed for someone to bear some of the burden.

He shifted, muttering something under his breath.

"What is it?"

Crossing his arms, he took in my bare feet. "I would've gone with you."

I knew he would have. The thought had crossed my mind with each item I'd packed. How much I'd wanted to call him. And how unfair to him it would've been to ask. Plus, what would it have looked like to the boys, showing up with Samuel? "Thanks. I appreciate that."

The space had grown quiet. Too quiet. As in Mama not bel-
lyaching. I whipped my attention to the back door and found
her standing there, ear hovering near the crack. A geriatric
James Bond. My body temperature rose by several degrees. I
tiptoed over, and thrust the door shut with a satisfying thwack.

She startled.

A mournful wail erupted from my bedroom. Chewie.

"Time to unleash the kraken." Samuel hooked his thumbs
on his front pockets.

"Would you like a wooden spoon for self-defense?"

"I'm good."

I opened my bedroom door, and Chewie bounded out, a
white blur of fur and teeth. He stopped short at Samuel, releasing a bark at his work boots, and hustled for the back door.
Mama opened it for him, using the opportunity to leave the
door ajar again. The snooper.

Samuel pulled the handle on my refrigerator and surveyed
the contents. "How about an omelet? Can you stomach that?"

"I don't think so."

He removed an egg carton and a bag of shredded cheese.
"I'll make a small one then."

I sank onto a chair at the table, my leg jittering and head
pounding. The torturous game of what-if played through my
mind. Conner could be dead in an alley or lying in a ditch or
passed out. Though he wasn't a partier. Not that I knew of anyway. What if he'd been slipped something? Or gotten caught up
with the wrong kids? "What if they don't find him?" I kneaded
my breastbone with the heel of my hand.

"They will." Samuel dropped a pat of butter into a frying
pan he'd already placed on the stove. He moved through my
kitchen with familiarity. Taking care of me again.

And this would be the last time.

The only reason he was here now was because he'd come
to work on the patio, and that was nearly done. Would he fin-

ish it today? I swallowed past the tightness in my throat and redirected my sights from him to the backyard.

Mama slid on her glasses, scowling at a section of railing. Chewie dashed around the tree and moseyed to the shed, sniffing a corner and lifting his hindquarter, which reminded me. "Do you know why there's a brand-new lawn mower in my shed?"

"I do." With one hand, he cracked an egg into a bowl, then another. "It's mine."

From what Mama P.I. had uncovered, he lived in a condo. Which meant he wouldn't need a mower. Maybe that smoke I smelled wasn't Mama's cigarettes but Samuel's pants.

"I don't need it right now because I live in a townhouse with an HOA." He whisked the eggs with a fork, the tines scraping the dish. "But once I buy a house, I will. And when I came across a sale on that mower, it was too good to pass up. I figured I could keep it here, and you could use it in the meantime." He poured the beaten eggs into the skillet, eliciting a sizzle. "I should've asked if it was okay, but . . ." He set the bowl into the sink.

I moved to the kitchen, rinsing the dishes he'd dirtied and placing them in the dishwasher. "You assumed I'd say no?"

He shrugged, taking a spatula to the food.

"I'm happy to store your lawn mower, but you can't keep cutting my grass."

"Think of it as a barter." He tilted the pan and nudged the eggs.

"Absolutely not."

Mama tapped on the window above the kitchen sink. "Are these new chairs out here?"

"Samuel, promise me you'll stop mowing my lawn."

He brushed past me to the window, tilting the skillet to Mama. "You want some?"

Forty minutes later, after we'd each had a helping of omelet, Samuel's phone rang. The air crackled, electrifying with apprehension. Like last time, he moved away as he answered, heading for the living room. Was it to hide his reaction to whatever news he was hearing? Adrenaline lit through my veins, sending my pulse on a wild sprint.

After a brief pause, he turned and gave a thumbs-up, along with a full smile.

I cheered and hugged Mama, my eyes watering with relief. "Thank You, Lord," I whispered, wiping my cheeks. Chewie yapped with the commotion, hopping onto the sofa, and I swooped him up, hugging him to my side.

"Tell everyone thanks, and I owe them." Samuel disconnected and faced us. "They found Conner. Well, I should say, they woke him and five other kids. Said it looked like the aftermath of a party."

Mama wrung her hands over her middle. "They're sure it was him?"

"Yes, ma'am. They checked the IDs on everyone present."

Thank You, sweet Jesus. "What did they tell them?"

"That they were searching for a possible missing person." Samuel pocketed his phone.

I pinched the bridge of my nose. "Conner's going to kill me."

"He doesn't know it was him they were looking for. They made it appear like they were continuing with their pursuit."

Mama lowered to the arm of the love seat. Her hands trembled in her lap, and her lips parted with a murmur of appreciation to God.

I met Samuel's gaze, wishing it was him in my arms and not Chewie. Wishing he could peek inside my heart and see how grateful I was. Saying *thank you* seemed grossly inadequate. "I . . ." My voice constricted.

He held up his hand. "You're welcome."

Mama stood from her perch. "Thank you, Samuel."

"I was happy to help." He tipped a nod to her.

"And just so you know," Mama said. "I found a spot on that railing you need to sand."

A chuckle radiated from him. "Then you better show me." He gestured for her to lead the way.

⚘

That evening I arrived home later than usual. Despite the delayed start to my day, I'd cleaned both of my clients' houses, departing the second dwelling as the homeowner had shown up.

There was no ignoring the disappointment at not finding the Testosterone Truck parked at my curb. I plopped my keys and purse on the entryway table, walked through my house, and released Chewie into the backyard.

My heart shriveled at the sight before me. The patio was complete. A thick rubber band of loneliness squeezed around my ribs. I numbly took the step down from the door. Chewie paced at the new screened entrance, looking from me to this strange barrier in his way. Set in the bottom of the screen door was a doggie door, tailor-made to Chewie's size. A mixture of emotions festered, steadily working north and clenching at the base of my neck. I didn't have the energy to show Chewie how to use it, so I held the door open instead. He darted to the grass.

The concrete had been swept clean of the sawdust that had taken residence the past several weeks. And two more chairs had appeared, along with a rectangular coffee table. Samuel had arranged the chairs to form a semicircle on one side of the table, allowing each to view the yard. The mental and physical exhaustion of the day overtook me, and I shuffled to the closest seat, sinking into the plush cushion.

The lowering sun leaked through the oak tree's branches and graced the top of the shed. I took in the remaining three chairs. Conner and Mason would fill two of them when they were here, and the fourth . . . That band circling my ribs tightened, and I wiped my nose. A purple envelope lay atop the coffee table, answering exactly who I wanted to occupy that last chair. I leaned forward and grasped it, surprised by the weight.

The envelope held another alpaca card, and the spare keys to the garage and shed. They may as well have been stabbed into my heart.

Julia,
  If you ever need anything, please call.

                        Samuel

An undertone of finality encompassed his words and this finished project. I filed away the last shreds of hope I'd harbored that this would all last a little longer. With a cleansing breath of cedar, I straightened. "It's time to stop being a mopey wimp. This is not who you are."

Conner's ringtone trilled from my pocket. Once he'd been found this morning, I'd sent a follow-up text, playing off my message and call to him as accidents. He'd simply replied with an *okay*. The extreme lengths we'd gone through to locate him would remain a secret Mama, Samuel, and I would carry to our graves.

Glancing at my phone, it notified me Conner was asking to FaceTime. Good. With the party-aftermath findings from the A-Team, I'd planned to video call him. To check if his eyes were bloodshot. Discuss greasy foods in detail to see if they elicited a green face and gagging. Blare a foghorn unexpectedly into the phone's speaker.

I accepted the video call.

Both boys appeared on the screen. Conner's bright eyes and rosy cheeks contradicted a night of heavy partying.

My mama-heart eased. "Hey, guys."

They sat on the trunk of their shared car, one of their dorm halls situated behind them.

"You feeling okay?" Conner's dark blond brows pulled together. He wore a long-sleeve LSU shirt, despite being a UNC student.

Mama's conversation popped into my mind. Conner had told her he was concerned about me, and my current appearance wouldn't improve his worries. The incident from this morning had left me with cried-off mascara I hadn't bothered fixing. Had I even combed my hair? The boys were used to seeing me pulled together. Right now *I* resembled a person who'd been partying wildly all night. If only Hayley were here. She could put one of those animal filters on my face. "Yes." I yawned, deep and lengthy. It couldn't have been timed better. "It's been a long day."

Mason tossed his hair from his eyes. "You haven't been looking good for longer than that."

"Thanks." I nailed him with a dramatized glare. "But I'm fine. I just haven't been sleeping well. Maybe it's a hormonal thing with me getting older. You know, menopause and all that is around the corner." They cringed. Ha! Talk about a subject-changer. "The patio's done. Do y'all want to see it?" I flipped the view on my phone and walked the perimeter. "The best part is this." I neared the screen door. "Chewie has his own personal entrance." On cue, Chewie bounded over. I squatted, holding the flap open. He stepped through.

The boys laughed, my favorite sound in the world.

"Looks like Mr. Samuel did a good job." Mason fidgeted with his hair. Again.

I rubbed Chewie's ear. How much longer would Mason go without a cut? There was even a Supercuts in the strip mall where he worked. *Pick your battles.* "He did a great job." I retook my chair, grateful for the thick cushion, and propped my feet on the coffee table.

Conner readjusted his hold on the phone. "He seems like a nice guy."

My gut tightened, my gaze sliding between them. What was up with all the Samuel man-crushing? "He is."

"And he goes to our church?" Mason bent forward, placing his elbows on his knees.

Perspiration gathered along my spine. "What is this, twenty questions?"

Beneath that shaggy hair, Mason's eyes widened. "No." He glanced at Conner. "It's just . . ."

Conner came to his rescue. "It seemed like y'all were familiar with each other when we met him."

My feet slipped off the table, smacking the ground. *Heavens above.* They never noticed dirty laundry piling underneath their noses or the toothpaste buildup in their bathroom sink, but they'd picked up on *that*? Regardless of the warm air, a chill broke across my skin. Had they heard what I'd whispered to Samuel that day? Warning him not to talk about our past? My mind reeled, trying to remember what they could have eavesdropped.

Oh, snap! Had Mama told Conner about Samuel when he'd called her last night worried about me? Surely she wouldn't have crossed that line. My fingers tingled, and I wound my free hand into a fist, cracking my thumb knuckle.

I was stuck.

Lord, please guide me. "I actually knew him in college."

Conner stiffened. "Why didn't you say so?"

Sakes alive! I cracked my pointer finger. This was all going to come out for nothing. "It's . . . kind of awkward. We . . . dated. But it was before I knew your dad."

Chewie hopped onto a chair, sniffing the new cushion.

"You could have told us," Mason said. "It's not a big deal."

But it was a big deal! Wasn't it? Even if I had forgotten their visceral reactions in junior high to my dating life, the horns and

212

blacked-out teeth of Mr. Buras in their yearbook were admissible evidence. I fought the urge to rub my throbbing temples and faked a blasé shrug.

The concern on Conner's face was endearing. "Was it weird being around him?"

Extremely. "It was a little at first. But he's a nice guy, so it was fine." I gave another shrug. *Goodness.* I really did need acting classes, and a transition to a safer topic. "Have y'all decided what day you're flying down for Thanksgiving?"

23

SATURDAY MORNING KATE AND I SAT on an iron bench in Jackson Square, catching up on our week and sipping café au lait in to-go cups from Café Du Monde.

Last night I'd bailed on our standing date. When I'd rolled up to my home, the grass had been cut, leaving me with a heaping of guilt over all Samuel had done—and was still doing—for me. Had this been a normal situation, I would've baked him a dessert as a thank-you. But that wouldn't be ending our relationship. It would be nurturing it. *Ugh*. I'd have to beat him to cutting my lawn next week. *Ridiculous*. At least the warm weather would be winding down, slowing the frequency of mowing.

Kate tucked her hair behind her ear. "I'm glad tracking apps didn't exist when we were teenagers, but I sure am happy to have them now. That's the first thing I'm putting on Hayley's phone when she gets one."

Several yards away, and out of earshot from our discussion, Hayley sat on a stool across from a local artist, having a caricature done. Other artwork for sale by the artist hung along a section of the cast-iron railings encircling the garden, fountain, and famous statue of Andrew Jackson on his horse. Behind us, and opposite the enclosed park, the St. Louis Cathedral stood in its regal glory, flanked by the Cabildo and the Presbytere museums. But other than those historic, architectural beauties, surrounding us was rare silence. We'd arrived early enough to avoid the throngs of tourists and street performers, but that wouldn't last.

A cool front had traipsed through, ushering in cloudless skies and easing the temps. Not cold enough for sweaters and boots, but perfect for sitting outside without sweating or mosquitos. With weather like this, I'd plan to be outdoors as much as possible. Because in a few days the heat would return. October was such a tease.

Kate rested her elbow on one of the armrests sectioning our bench into seating for three. "Who's volunteering today for cleaning?" An inquisitive gleam sparked in her eyes.

My own wanted to shoot daggers back at her. Part of coming here was to keep my mind occupied and away from who may or may not be working together today. "Why don't you ask what you want to know?"

"And what's that?" False innocence coated her tone.

My lips pinched, and I set my coffee on the bench space between us. "I'm not sure who's on the schedule today."

"You really don't know?"

"No, I don't." I leaned back into the curve of the seat. "And I don't care."

A man with dreadlocks pushed a closed wooden cart past us, angling for an open spot on the square's railings. He locked his cart's wheels in place and began removing artwork, setting them up for display. His pieces included a mixture of jazz musicians playing brass horns and fleurs-de-lis in various sizes and colors.

Kate angled sideways, folding one lean leg on the bench. "Do you *want* to know who's volunteering today?"

I whipped my head toward her. "How would you know?"

"I happened to talk to Sydney Dupré yesterday." Her brows rose with a know-it-all flair, and she plucked a piece of nonexistent fuzz from her sock.

Sydney Dupré. The church secretary who now organized the ministry. I wasn't biting. *Nope. Nope. Nope.*

"It's Emily."

My heart wilted. Right down to my tennis shoes.

"But not Samuel."

My heart perked.

"Earl's completely recovered from his gallbladder surgery."

"That's great." I checked my enthusiasm. "For Earl, I mean."

"Yes." Her expression turned indulgent. "For Earl."

A breeze flowed, coming from the direction of the Mississippi River two blocks away. The leaves on the live oaks and crepe myrtles awoke, flitting and turning, as though dancing. Such a contrast to the sharp iron railings fencing them within the garden space.

Kate, still with the smug look on her face, tipped her cup to her lips and took a long sip.

"The boys know I dated Samuel."

She sputtered, spewing coffee, her hand covering her mouth.

Hayley shot a glare our way, her tween-embarrassment radar going off.

Cockiness filled me at my superb timing. "Take that, you busybody."

"When did they find out?" Kate asked. "And why are you just now telling me?"

I lifted a shoulder.

She wiped her mouth with the back of her hand, and then her hand on the thigh of her black leggings. "What was their reaction?"

"It didn't seem to bother them."

Behind Kate's growing smile lurked a barely contained shriek.

I held up a hand. "Their response was based on Samuel being a guy who'd done some work on my house that was now finished. That's way different from it being a man I was considering dating again."

Her smile dimmed. "I thought we were past that concern."

"You were." I pointed between us. "Not me."

A teenager carrying five-gallon buckets took up residence at the corner of Pirate's Alley. He turned two of them over and removed a pair of drumsticks from his backpack. Taking a seat on one bucket, he began tapping on the other as though it were a drum. A third pail served as a tip collector.

Kate's posture deflated. "You're really calling it quits on Samuel?"

I nodded, reaching for my to-go cup.

The drummer's slow beat was unusual for the fast-paced, grab-your-attention rhythm typically found with street performers. The teen's hat perched low over his face. Maybe he was nursing a broken heart. Or a hangover.

"I can tell there's more to this you're not saying," Kate said, "because those circles under your eyes are a-talk-talk-talking."

I picked at the paper sleeve on my cup, contemplating the unease I hadn't been able to shake since the blowup with Mama. "Normally, when I've made a decision, things get easier. I adjust and move on. Like with the boys going to college out-of-state. But this time, with severing ties to Samuel . . . it's only gotten harder. Each day has been progressively worse to get through."

Kate's empathetic gaze shifted from me to her coffee. Pondering. "With those decisions where the outcomes were easier to handle, had you prayed over them?"

"You know I did."

"Did you pray over this circumstance with Samuel?"

The drummer's pace increased, kicking into second gear. Just like my pulse. "Well . . . no. It seemed like a simple choice to make."

Her lips pursed in consideration. She glanced at Hayley and back to me. "Don't you think God wants us to come to Him for everything?"

I scoffed. "I think it's pretty clear God wouldn't want me around the guy I'd been sinful with."

Kate's mouth opened, but no words came. Instead, she chewed her pinky nail.

"I'm looking at Samuel's reentry into my life as a way of opening my eyes to dating and easing the boys in *if* it comes to that. I'm realizing I want someone to spend time with. Someone who'll have my back."

"The way Samuel's had your back?"

I narrowed my eyes at her. "Are you getting a relationship commission if we get together?"

Tiny smile lines fanned the corners of her eyes. "I know it seems that way. But ever since he showed up, I've felt pressed"— she laid a hand to her breastbone—"about the two of you."

"Maybe what you're feeling is angina."

Kate ignored my attempt to lighten the mood. "Why don't you ask God what He thinks Samuel's return into your life is for?"

My stomach bottomed out. I hadn't asked God because I didn't want His answer. What if it was too scary? Or made me too vulnerable? Because other than my boys' thoughts on the matter, I was afraid to let go, to truly risk my heart again. I turned my attention to my lap, frowning. "Let's tackle another question instead."

She shook her head with a fond smile, letting me off the hook. "Okay."

"Of all the men in the world, why am I only attracted to the one I shouldn't be? Why can no one else give me the zings?"

Brisk air gusted through, fluttering the edges of the beach umbrellas the street vendors had positioned to shade themselves. Kate stood, roping her purse strap over her neck to cross her torso. "Maybe you're attracted to the only man you should be."

Ugh. What a depressing thought. I glimpsed Hayley's way, finding her standing and stretching. Her session had ended, her caricature complete and as adorable as she was. When she wasn't tweening.

Kate threw her cup in the garbage several feet away. "I think if you're honest with yourself, it's more than Samuel's zing-ability that has you struggling with your decision."

She was right. It was more than the zings Samuel generated. I liked this version of him. A lot. Too much. And that was the problem.

24

TUESDAY MORNING I ARRIVED AT TEDDY REED'S HOUSE ready for
battle. As a Christian, I had been taught to put on the armor
of God. Today, I included patriotic scrubs I'd scored at Wally
World. With my caddy and dust mop in hand, I climbed the
three concrete stairs of his stoop and rang the doorbell. I'd
make another trip to my SUV for the rest of my things after
assessing.

Deep in my uneasy gut, I knew Samuel wouldn't be here.
I hadn't spoken to, texted, or seen him in days. Not even at
church on Sunday. Though Emily Miller had still sat in front
of me, to Poor Sean Crawford's great delight.

Samuel was honoring the requests I'd made. This was a good
thing. *Do you hear that, heart? A good thing.* My heart replied
with a skeptical sigh.

One moment bled into two. A refrigerated delivery truck
advertising fresh oysters rumbled by, its brakes shrieking for
mercy when it neared the stop sign at the corner. Was Teddy
still asleep? I hadn't been given a key to the place since he would
be here. Last week he'd been smudgy-eyed and prickly-tailed.
Most likely he was awake.

And probably ignoring me. I shifted my mop to my other

arm, lifted a fist to the wooden door, and gave six hard knocks. *Good grief.* I was turning into Mama.

"Yeah, yeah." Teddy's griping floated through the door. A second later came his square-shaped face, complete with smeared glasses. "You're back."

My smile was already in place. Catching flies with honey and all that. "I am."

He shuffled a turn, wincing with the maneuvers, and made his way to his recliner. *Law & Order* played on the TV.

I closed the door. "How are you today?"

"Peachy."

Referencing a lemon would've been more appropriate, because that looked like what he'd been sucking. I made my way through the living room, past the dining table, beyond the hallway to the kitchen, and set my supplies on the tiled floor. A cursory glance showed dishes in the sink but nothing alarming. I glanced in the direction leading back to the front of the house. Having the owner at home upped the awkwardness and the feeling of having to tiptoe around them. Having your ex-boyfriend's cranky-pants father as that person kicked it up another level.

I grabbed my window cleaner, a fresh microfiber towel, and braced myself for the grizzly's den.

The throw blanket with the machine-gun-toting eagle draped Teddy's lap. On the television, one of the detectives slammed a perp up against a wall.

"If it's okay with you, I'll start in the back of your house."

A cross between a snarl and a grunt emanated from him. Between his buzz cut and square face, he resembled a bulldog.

"It's a miracle you can see anything through your glasses."

His glare flashed to mine. An angry bulldog.

I motioned for his spectacles. "May I clean those for you?"

His lips puckered, as though he held in a choice word. He removed his glasses—by touching the lenses—and passed them to me. No wonder they were always so smudged.

Once spotless, I handed them back. His hazel eyes, so much like Samuel's, came full force through the clear lenses. He took me in, finally noticing my scrubs. His expression eased on the sourpuss scale from sucking a lemon to an orange.

I retreated to his bedroom for his hamper of dirty clothes. Maybe for my next visit, I'd find him a mini spray bottle to leave behind, along with a small microfiber cloth. That way he could clean his cheaters every day. Or several times a day the way he pawed them.

Around noon, I was in the kitchen, going toe to toe with what appeared to be burned chili on the stove top. A male voice, not belonging to Teddy or the TV, arose from the front room. I halted scrubbing, held my breath with anticipation, and tipped my ear.

"I brought your favorite," the voice said.

Wyatt. My shoulders slumped, and I used my forearm to brush a strand of hair from my face. I continued scouring, putting more pressure on the stubborn stain. I was glad it was Wyatt.

Liar, my heart murmured.

He paused in the opening to the kitchen, his appearance similar to last time. Clean-shaven, gray slacks, navy button-down. "Hi, Julia."

"Hello."

"Are the floors wet?" His black hair had a curl at the edges today. Probably from the humidity that had returned with a vengeance.

"No, they're dry."

He placed a bag from Central Grocery on the eat-in kitchen table, and I knew without a doubt what resided inside. Sure enough, after washing his hands, he retrieved a bundle shaped like a UFO and wrapped in butcher paper. "I thought you may still be here, so I ordered extra." He unwrapped the most delicious sandwich in the world. A muffuletta.

The scent of olive salad and salami woke my appetite, reminding me I'd skipped breakfast again this morning. "That's nice of you, but I can't."

"Do you have another client you need to get to?" His dark brows edged together.

"No." That reminder of my working predicament stung. My search for a house big enough to completely fill my Tuesdays, or a smaller one for the afternoon slot, had been unsuccessful, and it had pushed the hunt for weekend work to the back burner.

"Then you have time to eat." He opened an upper cabinet, retrieving three plates. After moving half of a muffuletta onto one, which took up most of the dish, he carried it to the front room.

Like a creeper, I peered down the hall. Instead of making his father get up and sit at the table like Samuel had, Wyatt positioned a TV tray before Teddy in his recliner. I moved back to the stove, staring at the sponge in my hand, contemplating my options.

Wyatt reappeared, grabbed a Diet Coke from the fridge, and made his way back to Teddy.

I eyed the food on the table, so much more appealing than another chalky protein bar. I dropped the scrubber, washed my hands, and moved a quarter of a muffuletta to a plate. The melted provolone and mozzarella cheeses stretched, and my stomach rejoiced at what was coming.

Wyatt reentered, heading for the refrigerator. "What can I get you to drink?"

"Water's fine. Thank you."

He deposited two bottles on the round table and took a seat. I did a double take. "Um, you can have lunch with your dad."

"I know." He gave a small, wry smile, claiming the remaining section of muffuletta. His eyes slid shut, and he bowed his head.

I outright stared. How had I landed into this bizarre meal? I'd thought Wyatt would join his dad, and I'd scarf my food and be on my way. And when had Wyatt become this comfortable with me?

He opened his eyes and took a napkin from the holder on the table, placing it next to his plate, ensuring it was evenly parallel. He turned his dish clockwise, then moved his water a few inches to the left.

Were these new habits? Or ones I hadn't noticed the few times we'd been around each other when Samuel and I had dated?

I said my own prayer and began eating. My first taste was bliss. Crispy Italian bread gave way to the olive salad, cheeses, and salty meats. *Perfection.* I snagged a napkin, wiping my mouth. "Do you work nearby?"

He nodded, finishing his bite. "Downtown. Across from the Superdome." He opened his water and drank, returning it to precisely where it had been. "Samuel and I take turns looking in on Dad every day. Once he's steadier on his feet, we'll slack off."

Reaching for my water, my motion slowed. How had Samuel found the time to care for his dad, start a new business, and work on my patio? Plus, he'd been mowing my lawn and volunteering on Saturdays for the cleaning ministry.

I unscrewed the lid from my drink. Had he been here, checking on his dad, the day I'd called him to rescue me from Pervy Pete? My gaze drifted around the mint-green vintage kitchen, where, thankfully, Teddy's décor had not encroached. Maybe I'd clean his house longer than I'd planned. Especially if Samuel wasn't going to be here. I held the rim of the bottle to my lips, the cold water trailing down my throat. An idea formed. A way I could be helpful to Samuel like he'd been to me. "I came across some papers while dusting, showing at-home exercises for people after knee replacements."

Wyatt nearly snorted. "It's a pain getting my dad to do them. Those workouts are our last resort since he won't go to physical therapy."

"Would it be okay if I tried?"

"Of course. But I don't think he'll cooperate."

As if to punctuate Teddy's attitude, the volume on the television increased. Had he heard us talking about him?

"I might try next week." I repositioned my hold on the sandwich. "I think he's still too leery of me to attempt it today." It'd also give me time to research. Surely YouTube would have something useful. The website had shown me how to tile and grout my bathroom backsplash. Find studs in the walls to hang shelves. There had to be something on physical therapy for grouches. "But I'd appreciate it if you didn't mention it to Samuel."

Wyatt's countenance softened, and he wiped his mouth. "You're a good person. And for the record, I always thought Samuel treated you wrong."

The striking of a judge's gavel came from the TV in the front room. A new episode of *Law & Order* had started, as well as a conversation I hadn't seen coming. I released my muffuletta and leaned away from the table, unsure how to respond.

"When y'all were dating, and I'd check in with Samuel during my training, he was always . . . blasé about your relationship. Sometimes y'all would still be together, sometimes not." He nudged a slice of green olive that had fallen to his plate. "After meeting you, it was clear how you felt about him." A hesitant vulnerability touched his features. "I went through a similar situation that didn't end well."

Goodness. This was the most he'd talked to me. Ever. I glimpsed his bare ring finger. Maybe Samuel and I weren't the only people with unresolved issues from decades ago. Based on the sorrow in Wyatt's eyes, it seemed safe to assume he'd been me in his own messy circumstance. I pulled in a low breath. "I'm sorry you had to go through that."

He nodded, a slight, thoughtful smile following. "Samuel

was a real screw-up back then, but that's not who he is now. Or who he's been for a long time."

Curiosity piqued, my mouth speaking before my brain could stop it. "How long?"

"Since Brooke was born." A deep adoration swelled in his eyes. "Since the moment she was placed in his arms."

My mama-heart squeezed. I could understand that being Samuel's game-changing moment. Because I knew how having a baby altered everything. *Everything.*

Wyatt departed for work, and I finished the last of my tasks. Our chat wrestled through my mind, stirring up questions I shouldn't want answered. Like wondering how involved Samuel had been in Brooke's life, and why his relationship with her mother hadn't worked. Had he handled her horribly too? I cast a final glance around the kitchen and gathered my things. In the end, the answers changed nothing. They wouldn't erase my fears about the boys and their perception of Samuel, or the cold reality that he'd shredded my trust in him.

"You've been quiet since Wyatt left."

I startled, dropping my plastic carrier with a clatter.

Teddy stood in the kitchen entryway, one hand on a wall for balance. "And you're jumpy."

"I'm jumpy because you snuck up on me. Was stealth your specialty in the Green Berets?"

He drew himself up. "All Green Berets are stealthy. But my specialty was weapons. Wyatt's was communications, and Samuel's was engineering."

I fetched the caddy, straightening a few items within it, and grasped my mop propped against the wall. "You must be proud of your boys for serving."

"I am. But they could be doing more." Teddy maneuvered a turn for the front, his steps resembling Frankenstein's rigid walk.

I followed. "More?"

226

"Wyatt should still be in service, not tinkering with computers." His large hand grasped the top of one of the chairs at the dining room table. "At least Samuel will be back at Fort Bragg soon enough, teaching the candidates for Special Forces."

My supplies nearly slipped from my hands again. "What?"

Teddy's thick neck twisted, his gaze roaming my face, as if to question my outburst.

I schooled my features. "I mean . . . Samuel's starting a business here." I knew from what I'd read so far in the Green Beret book that Fort Bragg resided in North Carolina, an hour south of Conner and Mason's college.

That portion of muffuletta I'd eaten began revolting in my belly.

"A business?" Teddy scoffed, continuing his stiff trek to his recliner. "Planning hunting and fishing parties for strangers. What kind of business is that?"

"So Samuel could be training soldiers?" Was that an option for him with his disability?

"As a civilian employee with Northrop Grumman. They're always looking to hire retired Green Berets, who are then contracted to assist the military. And they want Samuel." Teddy eased ungracefully into his chair, wincing. "They've been after him like a fly on a pile of—" His stare reached mine. "Well, they've been after him. This *business*"—Teddy air quoted the word with his fingers—"is a hobby. A shot in the dark, which Samuel knows, which is why he met with them."

Oh, man. Oh, man. He'd interviewed with Northrop Grumman?

This was good. This. Was. Good.

My heart shook its head, not buying what my mind was selling.

"And I don't see how giving outdoor tours will pay for Brooke's education." He gestured to his granddaughter's picture on the piano. "Especially with the price of nursing school."

I cleared the plethora of emotions clogging my throat. "That's a valid worry." And one I had daily. College was expensive. Even with scholarships, there were additional costs that quickly added up.

Teddy's mouth opened and closed. His expression revealed one of unexpectedness, and maybe a little disappointment at not having to continue his tirade. "Yes, it is. And that's what I keep telling him."

In a daze, I surveyed the room, ensuring everything was where it should be and that nothing would cause Teddy to fall. "Is there anything you need before I go?"

"No. So . . . next Tuesday, you'll be back?"

"Yes, sir."

He nodded and reached for his newspaper on the end table.

I let myself out, feeling oddly stunned. Between Wyatt and Teddy, it was like I'd been walloped with a combo punch from Mike Tyson. Teddy obviously had his own views about what his kids should be doing. But he'd spewed a lot of specific facts about Samuel's situation. Was Samuel not committed to staying in New Orleans after all? Was returning to Fort Bragg his real plan?

An ache of betrayal swelled within. I loaded my gear into the back of my SUV, lowered the hatch, and leaned against it. The warmth of the metal seeped through my scrubs. Rubbing my forehead, I tried to think rationally. Samuel's future was none of my concern. And good riddance to him if he did leave. That would be best for everyone. For him to move to a galaxy far, far away.

25

THE NEXT WEEK FOUND MAMA STOPPING BY almost every evening. And yet that rubber band of loneliness relentlessly tightened around my rib cage. I'd lie awake at night, Chewie's hot breath panting on my arm, staring at my bedroom ceiling and imagining a boa constrictor squeezing my heart.

Thursday evening, I'd gotten home from work and immediately set out to cut the grass. Against my initial intentions, I'd used Samuel's new mower. There may have been a few tears that blended with my sweat. But it was better that way. Had I come home the next day and Samuel had not cut my lawn, it would've been too crushing.

Friday night I met with Kate at Beignets & Books, but not even Harry and carbohydrates could loosen that band.

The next evening, Mama and I had handed out Halloween candy to trick-or-treaters. Several times I'd caught her gawking at me as though I had crawfish crawling out of my ears. *"Maybe you have the flu,"* she'd said. *"Or encephalitis. You know how mosquitos are the ticks of the sky."* I'd assured her I was fine. And had even allowed her to check my temperature when she'd persisted.

I had not seen Samuel at church or at Teddy's the following Tuesday.

On the work front, I'd set up an account with a home maintenance website open to the public. It only took one day for the creepers to come out. I'd had a message from a guy looking for services, but he only wanted me to clean on Saturday nights, when he was home. Another man had asked if I wore a French maid uniform while cleaning. *Seriously?* I'd promptly deleted my account. And showered. And moved my gun from the safe to my nightstand drawer. This was why my current clients had come from recommendations. From a connection to someone I'd already known. Robert Breaux had also emailed, offering to pay seventy-five percent of my quote, which I'd politely declined.

Thursday arrived again. I pulled into my driveway that evening, exhausted to my bones. My second client of the day had adopted a dog and cat without giving me a heads-up. All that had been left was a note to clean the kitty's litter box. And although the terrier mixed breed was sweet, she wasn't housebroken. And she'd left presents for me everywhere. Even on the bedding I had just changed.

I gazed through the windshield at the sky above my roofline, the sun's waning light painting a cotton-candy effect on the clouds. A sigh, deep and heavy, loosened from me. I had to push through and cut the grass before the sun descended and the flying ticks emerged full force. I pressed the garage door opener, exited my vehicle, and rounded to the trunk. My attention skimmed over my lawn and reversed.

The grass had already been mowed.

I sucked in a ragged breath, and relief rushed through me like a tidal wave. I was weary enough not to fight the reason for my reaction. Not to blow off my response as just being thankful the task had already been done. Nope. It was because Samuel had been the one to do it. He had come here and cut my lawn. He had thought about me.

Time and distance and sticking to this decision had not improved my circumstances. It had only drained me more and more each day. I carried my supplies into the garage, hit the button to lower the door, and sank to my butt on the concrete floor. Hanging from the wall, Princess Tipsy gave me a consoling wink. My fingers brushed against a piece of sawdust on the floor. A remnant from when Samuel had used the space.

"Lord"—I clasped my hands around the cedar shaving—"this is hard. I thought I was doing the right thing, but I'm so confused. And tired."

Bleary-eyed, I took in the table and containers where I concocted my cleaning mixtures. Another part of my life that, like Samuel, felt unfinished. And another part of my life I'd neglected to bring to God because it had felt like too great a risk. One I was ill-equipped to handle. But even though I hadn't talked to God about my loneliness and dreams, He still knew about them. Still cared.

I was a fool.

My eyes slid shut. "Oh, Lord," I exhaled. "We both know I've avoided bringing these items to You because they seem too scary in their own ways. But I know You want what's right for me." I sniffled and rubbed my nose with the back of my hand. "I'm officially turning Samuel, and these products, over to You. Please show me the way and give me the courage to abide by Your will."

⚜

The next evening, I sat at my dining room table, finishing my dinner with Pat and Vanna. After talking with God last night and spending extra time in His Word, my appetite had returned, and I'd made a huge batch of chicken-and-sausage gumbo. Thank goodness I had a lot of Tupperware. I'd bring some to Kate tonight and freeze the rest.

Movement outside the front window hooked my attention. Mama's Buick parking behind my SUV. Groaning, I pushed from the table with my empty dish and headed for the sink. *Lord, if I'm coming to You with everything now, is there something that can be done about Mama?*

The front door creaked. Chewie barked. Mama hissed at him. Just like every night the past week.

I flipped on the faucet. "I'm leaving for Kate's soon."

"Great! Can we come?"

I whirled with a gasp.

There stood Conner and Mason, wide smiles on their precious faces.

My mama-heart ballooned as I enveloped them in a hug, latching an arm around each boy, taking turns pressing my head against their shoulders. I hadn't realized how much I'd missed them until that moment. Or how much they'd grown. I released them, dabbing the corners of my eyes. "What are y'all doing here?"

"Mawmaw offered to fly us in," Conner said.

Mama stood next to their luggage in the living room. She waved a dismissive hand. "There was a sale on plane tickets. It would've been a waste not to bring them home." She pulled a pack of smokes from her pocket and aimed for the backyard. "And don't worry. They're still coming for Thanksgiving." The door clicked shut behind her.

"Do I smell gumbo?" Mason scanned the kitchen. "I'm starving."

"Yes." I laughed, shaking my head. "In the fridge."

Conner huffed. "Good. Because Mawmaw wouldn't stop to pick anything up."

The boys rummaged the refrigerator, cabinets, and drawers. Such a comforting sight.

I poked my head out the back door.

Mama stood at the opposite end of the patio, a trail of smoke lazing around her.

"There wasn't a deal on flights." I would know. I'd been looking for one myself.

"You needed a lift. You've been in the dumps for three weeks now." She took a drag from her cigarette. "Even Jesus rose after three days."

Gracious. It had to be bad if Mama was throwing Jesus in my face. I smiled so wide, my cheeks hurt. "Thank you."

She shooed me. "Close the door before the smoke gets in."

The microwave beeped, and Conner pulled a steaming bowl from it, unleashing a mixture of Cajun spices into the air. Mason heated his dish next. I reached for my phone, thrilled to share the news with Kate that they were coming with me.

She answered after a few rings. "Hey."

"I'm bringing two guys with me."

"Hmm . . . Are they both tall, blond, and have blue eyes?"

"You know!"

She laughed. "I do. Did they tell you what we're all doing tomorrow? For the record, I had nothing, absolutely nothing, to do with it."

Conner sat at the table, propping his phone against the centerpiece so he could watch his screen while eating. Mason tapped a spoon against the island, waiting for his food to heat.

I glanced between them. "What are we doing tomorrow?"

"Oh." Conner looked up from his phone. "We're going on a swamp tour with Mr. Samuel."

My legs wobbled, and I lowered onto the chair across from Conner.

"I looked up his website and thought it'd be fun." He shoved an enormous spoonful of gumbo into his mouth and resumed looking at his device.

Noooo. It had never occurred to me one of the boys would look up Samuel's website. I, on the other hand, had become extremely familiar with it ever since the night he'd given me his business card.

"Breathe," Kate said through the phone.

I followed her instructions.

"I would have told you," Kate said, "but Conner made me promise not to ruin their surprise visit."

Mason pointed to the counter and the package of empty travel spray bottles I'd found and intended to use for Teddy and a few other seniors who wore glasses. "What are these for?"

"Um, they're for . . ." A snippet of what Kate had first said echoed through my mind. About what we were *all* doing tomorrow. "Wait, who's going tomorrow?"

"Breathe," Kate said again.

Not a good sign.

Mason retrieved his dish from the microwave. "Us, Miss Kate, Hayley."

Okay. It wasn't ideal, but—

"And Mawmaw."

Cat litter clumps.

⟡────⟡

I lay in bed that night, elated the boys were home, peace unfurling that they'd be under this roof the next two nights. And yet, sleep evaded me. Because tomorrow was going to be a headache of a day. According to Kate, Conner had also made Mama and Samuel vow not to mention their trip to me.

My phone pinged with a text. Chewie startled from his slumber with a woof. I reached for my cell from the nightstand, squinting against the brightness of the screen.

SAMUEL
Can you talk?

The alarm clock read ten fifteen. I shifted from under my sheet, padded to my door, and peeked into the hallway. The doors to both of the boys' bedrooms were shut, though that

234

didn't mean they were asleep. I carefully closed my own door, crossed the room to my closet, and slipped inside. Flipping on the light, I called Samuel.

"Hi." He picked up after the first ring.

My insides clenched at hearing his deep timbre. "Hi."

"I wanted to tell you about tomorrow, but Conner was adamant their visit be a surprise." Concern edged his tone. "I even talked to Kate about it."

"I know. She told me." My gaze drifted around the small space with clothes on hangers and shelves holding folded jeans. Like a teenager preparing for the first day of school, I'd already planned what I'd wear.

"He contacted me through my website last week. I didn't want to raise any suspicions, so I agreed to the tour. But I don't want to put you in an awkward spot, so I can call him after we hang up and cancel it."

Tempting, but . . . "No, don't do that. The boys are really excited. It's all they've spoken about since getting here. Well, when they weren't busy stuffing their faces with food."

Chewie scratched on the other side of the closet door. I opened it, and he stepped through, looking up at me as though I'd lost my marbles. I gave him a shrug and closed us in.

"You know, your mom's coming too."

"Yes," I sighed. "This isn't a hunting excursion, right? I don't want a gun in her hands when you're within sight."

He chuckled. "No, it's a tour of the Honey Island Swamp. Plus lunch." A muffled rustling sounded on his side of the line. Was he in bed under the covers? Pulling a shirt over his head? *Sakes alive!* Had he been talking bare-chested? Based on the way his clothes fit him, and that slice of skin I'd spied when he'd been working on the patio, I'd bet he still had that six-pack.

I nibbled on my thumbnail. "They know we dated."

Chewie's hefty panting filled the silence.

"Samuel?"

"I'm here." A pause. "When—I mean—how? I mean . . . When and how did they find out?"

"It came out naturally a few weeks ago." The tiny space began to warm and reek from Chewie's breathing. I cracked the door, letting in fresh air. Chewie fled his own stench.

"How did they react?"

I fanned the door several times and shut it. "Like it was no big deal."

Samuel exhaled, long and even.

A smile touched my lips. It was endearing to imagine him, a big bad Green Beret, nervous about the boys' response. "So I'll see you tomorrow?"

"Yeah. See you in the morning."

26

"**THAT ALLIGATOR CAN'T GET IN THE BOAT, RIGHT?**" I shifted beneath my life jacket, eyeing the ten-footer sunning itself on a log above the murky swamp water. Just a stone's throw away from us. Okay, maybe three stones' throws.

"No, it can't." Samuel spoke from the captain's chair of the pontoon boat, the engine idling as he maneuvered us closer to the wild creature. It had been the umpteenth time he'd answered that question from me for the past two hours, never losing patience.

The vessel lurched on a wake. "That's close enough!" I shrieked, my heart in my throat.

Snickers erupted from Conner and Mason, who flanked me on one of the cushioned benches on the front of the vessel. I kept a hand on both of their arms, as though they were toddlers who might slip overboard to their watery graves.

Across from us, on an identical bench, Hayley gave a shy giggle. Although we'd seen alligators, raccoons, feral pigs, and a plethora of birds, she'd only had eyes for Mason. She also was the only other person wearing a life preserver. Not by choice, though. It was a requirement for kids under sixteen.

Despite my protests, the boys had refused flotation devices, thus my death grips on their forearms from time to time.

Kate, sporting a sun hat we could all huddle under if a downpour struck, sat next to Hayley. Mama stewed at the back of the boat, no doubt counting the seconds until she could smoke again. She'd not said one word to Samuel but had given him a slight nod hello and had allowed him to help her onto the party barge.

Another cool front had rolled through, leaving the skies clear and the temps in the high sixties. A gift from above. Practicality had won out with my wardrobe selection of tennis shoes, skinny jeans, a long-sleeved tee, and a zippered hoodie to ward off the chill when we were running on the open river. Everyone else had dressed in light layers too. Except Samuel. He'd been alarmingly distracting in his aviator sunglasses, jeans, and simple T-shirt. His arm muscles flexed as he steered the vessel, quiet control in every movement.

I breathed in damp, earthy air, and continued averting my gaze from Samuel for fear I'd be caught lusting by one of the boys. Samuel had been extremely knowledgeable about each animal we'd encountered, the Pearl River, and the homes along its shoreline. The swamps themselves seemed like old friends to him with the handful of stories he'd relayed of funny and scary memories from his teen through adult years fishing here.

He was confident but not cocky, and he'd taken our safety seriously. It was reassuring . . . and sexy. You knew you were a woman of a certain age when a man became alluring because he'd made the well-being of your family and dearest friend a priority.

"Y'all ready to head back for lunch?" Samuel asked.

"Yes!" I eyeballed one of the cypress trees surrounding us, and the clump of grayish moss hanging from its branches. The perfect hiding spot for a snake. "Get me back on land!"

Conner shook his head with a smile and turned to Samuel, speaking across me. "Is it safe to say you never got my mom out here when y'all were dating?"

Crikey! Where was one of the Irwins jumping on a gator as a distraction when you needed them? It was impossible to see Kate's eyes underneath her sunglasses and that umbrella of a hat, but I *knew* her sights were locked on mine. Our minds tapped Morse codes of *Oh my word* and *What do I do?* across the three-foot walkway between us.

"No." Samuel's tone held a natural ease with a hint of amusement. "Your mom never went along on my trips."

"Figures." Mason flipped his hair from his eyes and snuck Conner a knowing look.

"Hey!" I elbowed Mason. "I've done plenty of outdoorsy stuff with y'all."

Mason snorted. "Camping in the backyard doesn't count."

My lips pursed. Well, that was probably true. At least I'd had Mark's dad to take them on hikes when they'd visited their home in North Carolina during the summer months. And thankfully we moved past the Samuel-and-I-having-dated topic.

Samuel eased the boat next to the pier where our journey had begun, asking Conner to steady the wheel, and Mason to help him tie off the vessel. The dock stretched a bank of land about the width of my home. Trees and brush bordered the shoreline on either side. A lawn slightly inclined to a leveled area devoid of trees. Resting there was one of those movable tiny houses like I'd seen on HGTV. Cedar planked the exterior, and a peaked black metal roof topped the structure. *Rustic chic* came to mind when I'd first laid eyes on it when we'd arrived.

This morning, we'd packed into my SUV and made the hour-long trek north. Regardless of the detailed directions Samuel had provided, the deeper we'd driven into the woods, the more unsure I'd become. Mercifully, there'd been a yard sign at an unmarked turnoff, like he'd said there'd be. It held the same logo as his business card, with an arrow pointing the way. The long dirt drive and trees pressing in hadn't been encouraging.

But then the land had cleared, unveiling the charming house on wheels, and the Testosterone Truck.

With the boat secure, I unbuckled my life preserver, and we emptied onto the wharf, everyone stretching after being seated for so long. Mama trudged off for the path leading to a fire pit. Cut tree logs served as the seating around it.

Samuel checked his watch. "Lunch should be ready in a few minutes."

Next to the house sat a long picnic table beneath a canopy tent fully enclosed by mosquito netting. So far, everything had been well thought out, demonstrating Samuel's seriousness in treating this like a real business and not a hobby. *Take that, Teddy!*

Samuel motioned toward the house that, though small, featured a full bathroom, kitchen, living room, and sleeping quarters. "Feel free to wash up inside."

"Do you need help with the food?" I asked.

The door to the home opened, and a woman emerged.

I stood frozen.

Descending the three steps, the mystery lady carried a platter of food. She was in her early thirties and beautiful in a girl-next-door way. She definitely had not been here before we'd left for the tour.

"That's Miranda," Samuel said. "She's a potential caterer for when I do these kinds of excursions." He took off up the pathway toward her. The boys and Hayley followed.

Kate sidled beside me. "There's no wedding ring on Miranda."

My heart slid to the pier, squeezed between the boards, and belly-flopped into the river.

The kids moved past Samuel and disappeared inside. Miranda made her way through the canopy's netting and placed the dish on the table. She reemerged and exchanged a few words with Samuel. He'd slipped off his aviators and easily spoke to her. She smiled. He smiled. She laughed, lightly touching his arm for a second. My teeth clenched. Maybe Miranda was vying to be his potential girlfriend as well.

Kate removed her hat, revealing a head full of flattened auburn hair. "I'm sure there's nothing going on between them."

"Then why did you point out the absence of her ring?"

She shrugged. "It's a habit."

Conner and Mason reappeared, making their way to the food, of course. Samuel accompanied Miranda inside the little dwelling. At least Hayley was still in there. Maybe she'd overhear something. And maybe she'd spill what she'd heard for a seat next to Mason on the ride home.

A minute later, all three exited. Miranda hooked her purse strap on her shoulder and made her way to the other side of the house, where we had parked. A car engine echoed against the forest, petering out with distance.

"Breathe, sister." Kate grinned and headed up the trail.

Unfortunately, the food was delicious. Fried chicken bites, an assortment of po' boys from warm roast beef to cold chicken salad, potato salad, and peach cobbler presented in mini glass jars. It seemed Miranda would be a keeper. *Grumble, grumble.*

Samuel and the boys stood on the dock, where he was teaching them to fish. Mama, having had enough of nature, had retreated inside the house, probably snooping. Hayley remained at the picnic table, whispering to a friend on Kate's phone. Undoubtably about Mason and how he'd handed her a jar of peach cobbler during their meal.

Kate and I sat at the fire pit, where a few small flames burned. With the cooler weather, it was the ideal amount of heat to keep us comfortable in the shade.

Conner clumsily cast his line into the water and said something. Samuel responded. Mason focused on his cork floating on the surface. The sight of them all together stirred confusing feelings within me. An ache of tenderness mixed with a dash of regret. I'd always worried about the dad-hole that had been left in the boys with Mark's death. And today had proven that concern as valid.

"How are you holding up?" Kate asked.

"I'm not sure."

"He's great with them."

I nudged a stick with the toe of my shoe.

"And they seem to like him."

"They may like him, but I'm sure they wouldn't like him dating me." I reached for the twig, using it to poke at a pinecone.

Kate lifted her shades, making direct eye contact. "Conner set all this up knowing you used to date Samuel."

"I made light of our past relationship when I talked to the boys about it. Trust me, Conner was more interested in doing this swamp tour than anything else."

"Mom," Mason called. "Can you take my pole for a sec?"

I made my way over, and at the pier he passed me his pole, saying he'd be right back. Staring at the cork bobbing atop the water, I hoped a fish wouldn't bite. Or something bigger, like a gator.

Conner took several paces down the dock and cast his line in a smooth arc. It hadn't taken him long to catch on. Samuel's gaze lingered on Conner, creases fanning at the corner of his eye, as though he were proud.

Tender affection flourished. *No! Don't soften to him.*

Conner reeled his line in and handed it to Samuel. "I'm gonna get something to drink."

What? And leave us alone? I glanced back and found Mason sitting at the fire pit with Kate. Why hadn't he returned? Was it on purpose? My pulse pounded in my ears.

Samuel propped Conner's pole against an ice chest on the pier. "Your boys are great."

They were *great* when they weren't putting me in awkward situations. Like this one. Like this entire day. "Thank you." The water shimmered, and I wished I hadn't left my sunglasses on the picnic table. They would have made a good barrier from the water's glare—and from Samuel.

He reeled his line in and fiddled with a lure resembling a worm, except for the neon color and spiral tail. His gaze flickered back to the group. "Since Conner arranged all this after finding out we'd dated, I'm guessing they don't know why we broke up."

"They don't. And I'd rather keep it that way."

His fingers stilled. "Thank you." Sunlight reflected from the river, projecting a soft glow in his eye, bringing out the darker green hues. "I don't deserve that kindness from you. I'm grateful for it." His attention returned to the decoy bait. "Do you think they left us alone on purpose?"

I curbed a sigh. "I don't know. This is all new territory to me." The view across the river from us lay untouched by man. Bald cypress trees stretched tall, their small, fern-like leaves drooping. Brush and cattails filled the lower spaces. I wiggled the pole, bobbing the cork. *Bleh*. Fishing was boring.

"You really haven't dated anyone since your husband's passing?"

"No." Mark's death had been a shock. Unexpected. It seemed both our hearts had stopped beating the day of the accident. The grief, the sole responsibility for the boys, the care of the finances all crowded my life, granting no room for romance. Or any desire for it. And even if there had been, the fallout from the English teacher had been too great a chance for history to possibly repeat itself.

In one fluid sweep, Samuel cast his line, the lure hitting the water with a *thunk*. After a second, he reeled in at a slow rhythm, until the whirling of his spool stopped.

I cautioned a sideways peek and found him staring at me, a crease between his brows. My mouth went dry. "What?"

He continued reeling, until the bait positioned a few inches from the end of his pole. "Nothing."

"It's not nothing." A cricket chirped, growing louder before dwindling.

"It's just . . . now don't go taking this the wrong way—"

"Are you sure it's wise to finish that sentence?" I cocked an eyebrow.

A smile tugged the corners of his lips and faded. "You look tired."

I bristled. Was my lack of sleep that obvious? I'd need to invest in a better under-eye concealer. Maybe it wasn't Maybelline. "You're not looking so hot either." A dragonfly flitted, circling the cork and landing on it, sending out a ripple.

"So you're saying normally you *do* find me hot?"

Something between a laugh and a scoff escaped, and it felt good. Natural.

His flirtatious grin dimmed. "It's been a rough few weeks." The dark circle under his eye confirmed his statement.

Two weeks and four days. Perhaps I wasn't the only member of the Heartbreak Club. Or possibly, he'd been losing sleep for another reason. "How many Mirandas have you had out here—I mean, considered for catering?"

A pained expression shadowed his face. He pulled in a measured breath and released it. "Zero women have been out here until today. Y'all are my first family outing, and my first time employing Miranda. I'm considering today a test run. And I'd like you to let me know if there are any ways I can improve this experience."

A mosquito buzzed my ear, and I swatted it. The only improvement I'd suggest was hiring a male caterer. *Hold up.* "Test run? You better not be doing today's excursion for free."

He turned away, casting his line again.

I gripped my pole tighter. "I may not be an outdoorsy person, but I know it takes gas to run the boat, plus your time. This setup had to cost a lot of money." I motioned to the new wharf, the tiny house. "And I'm sure Miranda's not offering her services for free." At least I sure hoped she wasn't. Or that she wasn't bartering her chicken bites for a date with him. I cranked the handle on the reel. Once. Twice. Three times.

"What did you say?" Mirth layered his tone.

Oh, crud. Had I said that last part aloud? "Nothing!"

"Didn't sound like nothing."

I rolled my lips inward.

He smirked, mischief gleaming in his eye. "Something about bartering."

If I hadn't had witnesses behind me, I would have knocked his butt into the river.

A shallow chuckle rumbled from him. "I think I've made it clear where my interest lies. Now, if *you'd* like to work out a barter system with me, I'd be all for it."

Tingles erupted across my skin, and my cheeks warmed.

"In exchange for today's tour"—he rubbed his jaw—"you could give me several hours of your time."

"A date? Not happening."

"I have renewed hope that it will." He inclined his head to the boys.

Conner added another log to the fire. Mason prodded the embers with a stick. Was today a matchmaking scheme? Or them simply desiring to do something different on their visit?

I shook my head. "You're getting off topic." At the end of the dock, a white egret landed on a post, warbling a squawk.

"And what's the topic?"

"Money."

"I'm not worried about it."

He had a daughter in college. How could he not be concerned about finances? Teddy's insinuations about Samuel's career choices intruded in my mind. I repositioned my grip on the pole, the movement waking the dragonfly to flight. "So this new business is steady?"

"I've got some bookings over the next month. Two for fishing, one for duck hunting."

"Hmm." Was that stable work for this type of business? I studied his masculine profile. The way he squinted against the reflecting sun. The way his neck and shoulder muscles contracted with his movements. He cast his line again, his bicep and forearm flexing. Maybe fishing wasn't so bad after all.

An old man on a flatboat puttered past, his scraggly white beard blowing in the wind. He waved. Samuel and I returned the gesture. The boat's wake reached us, lapping against the shore beneath the pier.

"What was that 'hmm'?" Samuel stepped closer. "What's really eating you?"

I hesitated. The old Julia wouldn't push at a tender subject, but then again, the old Samuel wouldn't have pushed and wanted to figure out my thoughts. He would've walked off, going into avoidance mode. I tipped my chin up, meeting his stare. "Your dad said you're going to end up working for Northrop Grumman in North Carolina."

His eye slid shut, and he exhaled, sharp and low.

A million questions perched at the tip of my tongue. Like what was the point of him pursuing me if he wasn't staying? To string me along again? Was it that old selfish nature of his he'd admitted to?

Shaking his head, he muttered something about his dad. "I'm not moving to North Carolina."

"Did you interview with Northrop Grumman?"

"Yes. Six months ago." He cupped the back of his neck. "At one point, that was my plan."

"What happened?"

His arm dropped, and he angled toward me. "I saw you again."

My breath caught. That may have been the most romantic thing ever spoken in all time. At least to me, anyway. A breeze whispered through, rustling the leaves on the trees, and stirring the wisps of hair that had escaped my ponytail. The clean scent of his soap drifted over my senses. Somehow, we'd edged near each other, blips of electricity charging the air and heightening with intensity.

"Julia!" Mama hollered. "I'm ready to head home."

I startled, jerking my pole, tangling my line with Samuel's. Our translucent nylons twisted into a mess, the symbolism not lost on me. Nothing between Samuel and me had ever been, or would ever be, anything short of problematic.

27

SUNDAY AFTERNOON MY SUV'S TIRES thumped across the interstate, devouring the distance to the airport and hastening the
departure of the boys. Conner sat in the passenger seat. Mason
in the back. We'd attended church that morning, which, unfortunately, was not uneventful. They had spotted Samuel sitting
solo two sections over and invited him to join us. Everyone
else had gleefully shifted a seat to make room. Emily Miller
had also given Samuel a hearty welcome, as well as Poor Sean
Crawford. Sean had even made a bold play during his greeting,
moving over and leaving only two open seats between himself
and Emily.

Conner cleared his throat. "I don't know how to say this
without weirding you out."

My heartbeat faltered, then jumpstarted. "Okay." *Please give
me strength, Lord.* Had Conner been up to no good? Last night
on the drive to eat at Port of Call, I'd squeezed in a conversation
about college parties, which had garnered a mild eye roll from
him and a snicker from Mason. *Be cool. Be cool.*

Conner scratched his cheek. "It's about Mr. Samuel."

My gut clenched, along with every other muscle in my body.

Don't overreact. It could be that they just wanted to set up another excursion with Samuel when they visited during the Thanksgiving break.

"When he was working on the patio," Conner said, "we noticed a change in you."

"A good change," Mason chimed in from behind me.

It took every ounce of strength not to swerve from my lane. A semi and a moving truck pulled alongside us, sandwiching me in. Which seemed appropriate for my current state of mind. How could I squeeze myself out of this conversation?

"And then once the patio was finished, well . . ."

"You slipped into a funk," Mason said.

Sweat gathered between my shoulder blades. *Gracious*. I flipped the A/C on. "It's not . . . I mean . . ." I didn't want to lie, but I also didn't want the truth out there, hovering between us and gaining traction, hurting them.

"We want you to know that if you want to date him, we're fine with it."

"Yeah, he's cool."

Conner fidgeted with the sunglasses in his hands. "And we realize we didn't react well when Mr. Buras asked you out. It was just . . . hard back then. You know? But we're good with it now."

Talk about an unexpected turn of events. My armpits began perspiring. We zipped past pieces of a blown-out tire littering the emergency lane, and I imagined that was what my brain looked like in this moment. If only I could remember the breathing technique my counselor from all those years ago had taught me. I opted for several slow and steady four-counts, causing the longest awkward pause in the history of the world. "I'm not sure what to say." I resumed my hold to the proper ten-and-two positions on the steering wheel. "But I appreciate your concern, and your intentions with looking out for me. You boys are very sweet."

"There's one more thing." Conner angled to face me.

I stiffened. "Don't make me take back my last sentence."

They chuckled, the sound easing the tension in my body. And really, what else could they throw at me that would be worse than discussing an ex-boyfriend?

Conner rubbed his palm against his kneecap. "We think you should be selling your cleaning products."

My mind blanked. *Really, Lord?* Using my kids? Talk about a blindside. We approached another overpass, the airport appearing on the horizon.

"We've watched you make them all our lives," Mason said. "What's the harm of trying to sell them?"

I scoffed. "It's not as easy as you think. I looked into it once."

"When?" Conner's voice was direct.

"I don't know . . . five years ago?" I took the exit for the airport.

"So much has changed since then." Conner's excitement was palpable. "There's all sorts of resources now for start-ups."

Mason leaned forward. "Yeah, public funding websites, *Shark Tank*."

"*Shark Tank*?" I shook my head, braking for the red light. "I'm not going on a TV show. And I'm not asking strangers for money." My pulse pounded in my head. They were tag-teaming me! I may as well be in a WWE wrestling ring. Was the Junkyard Dog still around? Could I tag out of this conversation?

Conner glanced at his phone. "You could have a whole line of products."

"What line of products? I have two mixtures. One for surfaces, the other for windows and mirrors."

"What about those eyeglass cleaner kits you made?" Mason asked.

"Those aren't kits! Those are mini spray bottles with a cutting of cloth stuffed inside a Ziploc bag."

"It can be tweaked to look more professional." Conner drummed his fingers against the armrest on his door.

"There are free design programs where we can create labels," Mason said. "And your brand."

"A brand?" *Mylanta*. "Where's all this coming from?"

"I've been taking a marketing class," Conner said. "One of our projects is to put together a marketing plan for a product. So, naturally, I've been thinking about your cleaning stuff."

Sakes alive. When God started moving, He really started moving. When I got home, I'd return to the garage and pray for firmer skin and elevated boobs.

A sparkle lit in Conner's blue eyes. "I'd like to call your product line Green Girl or Green Grannie."

A bit of bile rose in my throat. "Green Grannie better not be your way of telling me something else."

He laughed. "It's not. It's just most people trust grandmas, so it has a built-in reliability factor."

My head spun. "Y'all have had all weekend to bring this up, and you've waited until now?"

"We learned that strategy from you." Mason grinned in the rearview mirror.

I narrowed my stare. Maybe we had time to make a pit stop at a barbershop. That would surely wipe his smug expression. "I don't have strategies." The red light turned green, and realization dawned. My head tipped back against the seat. They'd waited until I was in the car, trapped, and unable to avoid the conversation. They'd done what I had done to them their entire lives. *The turkeys.*

❦

With the fall weather in full effect, Kate and I had decided to enjoy our Friday night carb-fest in the courtyard of Beignets & Books. Beneath the white lights strung along the branches of the live oak, we caught up on our week, and packed our faces with warm beignets and decaf café au lait. Even Hayley had deigned to momentarily grace us with her presence before retreating to their upstairs dwelling.

Kate relaxed against her cast-iron chair, her pale, slender arms draping the side rests. She'd arrived straight from a business mixer, dressed in a sleek dark brown skirt and a copper, sleeveless top that matched the cardigan she'd draped on the back of her chair. "Have you talked to Samuel since Sunday?"

"No."

"He stayed away from his dad's when you were there on Tuesday?"

"Of course." I fussed with the strings on my gray cotton joggers. "Nothing's changed."

Her forehead creased. "I'd say a lot has changed based on last weekend."

"As far as he knows, nothing has." I averted my gaze from her questioning one to the three-tiered fountain in the middle of the courtyard, and the water glistening as it trickled. "I don't want him knowing about Conner and Mason's approval." As a result, culpability had nipped at my heels all week.

"Why not?"

I pulled a face. "It'd be like waving a red cape before a bull."

"Exactly! What's the problem with that?"

"What's *not* the problem?"

"Not Conner and Mason, which has been your chief worry."

I clasped my upper arms, fighting a chill. "What about our past, and what he did to me?"

She winced, remorse tinging her features. "Oh, Julia, you're right. I tend to forget about the old Samuel since I never saw that side of him." She smoothed her napkin over her lap. "Do you think you can forgive him?" A dog's bark echoed from one of the closer residences, eliciting another canine with a deeper timbre to chime in.

"I don't know." I pinched a clump of powdered sugar from my plate and squeezed, pulverizing it.

A long silence ensued. "When y'all were hanging out when he was working on your patio, how was that?" Kate's pointer finger traced the handle on her mug. "Was it hard to be around him because of what he'd done?"

I shrugged, wiping the sticky residue from my skin onto my napkin. "I guess it didn't bother me so much. But I was operating under the guideline that we were friends. There was a firm roadblock in place. Going down a path of opening my heart to him . . ." I shook my head and reached for my lightweight hoodie behind me. The air had cooled considerably over the past hour. "It's a whole other level of trust I don't know that I can give."

She pondered the half of beignet left on her dish. "Other than being able to forgive him, is there anything else bothering you?"

"Plenty."

"Like?" She lifted her cardigan from the back of her chair and slid her arms through.

"What if his business doesn't succeed, and he ends up taking a job in North Carolina?" My foot tapped under the bistro table. "Where does that put me? You know I can't leave my mom."

"What if his business is a wild success?"

"It's such a big unknown. And then there's this new version of him. He seems too good to be true. I keep wondering if Samuel 2.0 is going to reboot to his original factory settings."

"So you're waiting for him to fail?" Her auburn brows edged together.

"Yes." I cringed. "No. It's just . . ." The moon peeked through the tree limbs above as though eavesdropping.

Kate folded her napkin and draped it on her plate. "From what we've seen, Samuel's changes seem genuine. The love of God compels, alters, marks us." The sincerity in her face, the sway in her tone. I swore she belonged in a pulpit instead of running a café. "He's a grown man now, with adult responsibilities. His commitment to the military goes against his old habit of bailing, right? And didn't his brother tell you Samuel's daughter was a turning point for him?"

"He did."

"You could ask Samuel about her and their relationship. Get a feel for how strong or flimsy it is."

I held my napkin to the side and snapped it like a matador. "Hello, waving the red cape again."

She pursed her lips. "If only there was a sneaky way you could get her alone."

"Like kidnapping?"

She snickered. "Yeah, that didn't sound right." Her sights roamed the back of the mansion, the first- and second-floor wraparound porches. "What about the family day at church for gathering Christmas toy donations? Samuel mentioned he's volunteering. Maybe she'll attend, and you could meet her then. That wouldn't be waving a red cape."

I chewed my thumbnail. "Maybe." A vehicle with thumping bass drove down the side street, the vibrations waning as they kept rolling along.

"Any other Spaniel concerns?"

"What if he wants more children?"

"Has he said that?" Her voice pitched.

"No."

"Does he know about your partial hysterectomy?"

I shook my head. "It hasn't seemed important enough to mention."

"Well, I'm sure he knows having babies is unlikely based on your age." Kate sipped her coffee and set her cup on the saucer.

"There is one thing you haven't brought up that I'd love to talk about." A gleam struck her bright blue eyes.

Wariness slanted mine.

"Last Saturday, Conner mentioned his marketing project to me."

No. No-no-no.

"For the record, my vote is Green Girl."

28

SUNDAY AFTERNOON I NESTLED under a throw blanket on my sofa, TV remote in hand. A bowl of pretzels mixed with M&Ms sat on one side, Chewie snuggled in on the other. A *Star Wars* marathon in chronological order was about to start. Hours of young Ewan McGregor followed by hours of young Harrison Ford? Yes, please!

My house phone trilled, which meant it was Mama. Even though I called her from my cell, she still only rang me on my landline. She was the only reason I'd kept it this long. Would I be a horrible daughter if I didn't answer? Just this once? The theme song to *Star Wars* began playing, and I longingly stared at the scrolling words. If I didn't answer, she'd probably come over.

I unearthed from my cocoon and padded to the phone on the kitchen counter, taking my snack with me.

"What took you so long?" Mama groused.

"I had to get up and get to the phone. If you'd called my cell, I would have answered faster." *Maybe.* I popped an M&M into my mouth.

A sigh carried over the line. Or it could have been her exhaling a cloud of smoke. "I've got a busted pipe under the kitchen sink. Can you call Samuel?"

I coughed, nearly choking on the candy. "What about a plumber?"

"The guy I normally use is out of town." The irritation in her voice grew. "And no other plumbers are answering."

"But . . ." I set the bowl down and pushed up the sleeves on my long-sleeved tee. "Samuel's not a plumber."

"He knows more than I do. He offered to look at a leaky faucet for Kate."

"When?"

"On the swamp tour," she said, exasperated. "Now call him! And call me back when you're on the way."

Click.

I shook my head, grinding my molars. This was such a crummy thing to do. What was I going to say? *Hi, Samuel. I know I've made it clear I want nothing to do with you, and it seems like I just take-take-take, but can you drop whatever you're doing—again—and help my mom? You know, the woman who has you on her enemies list?*

Forcing my teeth to unclench, I reached for my phone and dialed his number. After several rings, I landed in his voice mail. *Hallelujah.* I disconnected. At least I could truthfully tell Mama I'd tried. I returned to the kitchen and opened the junk drawer, rummaging past Scotch tape, rubber bands, and chip clips. I was certain I'd tossed a plumber's business card in here at some point. Hopefully it hadn't been someone Mama had already attempted. My mobile jingled, Samuel's name filling the screen.

Shoot.

"Hi," I answered.

"Hey."

"I'm sorry if I'm interrupting anything."

"You're not. I'm about to leave my dad's."

"Is he okay?"

"Yeah, I was just checking on him."

My ribs squeezed. There he was, helping his dad, when I'd

contemplated not answering a phone call from my mom. "I feel like a total rat fink for doing this, but my mom called. She has a leaking pipe under her kitchen sink. And she can't get ahold of a plumber. She has some wild notion you can help."

"I can. I'll swing by my house and pick up my tools, then come get you."

I touched my fingertips to my forehead. He hadn't even hesitated. Mama had been griping at Samuel at every opportunity, and the man was willingly stepping into her smoky domain. Without a second thought. "Are you sure? I'll gladly tell her I couldn't reach you."

"I'm sure. I'll see you in a few."

After calling Mama to tell her help was on the way and switching my sweatpants for jeans, Chewie and I waited out front to save time. Samuel's truck pulled to the curb, and I opened the passenger door before he could get out to do it for me.

His left arm casually draped the steering wheel. Wearing aviators, a camo army baseball cap, and a long-sleeved black Henley, he had no right to look that hot. "You feel the need for a chaperone?" He nodded to Chewie, who slightly trembled at the strange vehicle, unsure of what was happening.

"No." *Yes.* I deposited Chewie on the bucket seat and climbed in, adjusting him to my lap. There was no way any glints of romance would occur with the dog's snarls between us. I closed the door. "Thank you, again."

"You're welcome."

I inclined my chin straight ahead and clicked my seat belt into place. "She lives six blocks down."

"That close?" Had I been able to see his brows, no doubt they would've disappeared into his hairline.

"Yeah," I grumbled. "When I bought my house, it seemed like a good decision at the time."

He checked the street, then accelerated. "You volunteered yesterday?"

"I did." Lightness bubbled within. A tangible goal had been achieved that impacted the physical and mental health of someone. But . . . my smile dimmed. I'd lose that happiness once I found a weekend client. At least the ministry would continue. "Miss Marlene wasn't pleased to find Earl on her doorstep instead of you."

"Well, I was very pleased not to find myself filling in for Earl."

We passed a neighbor cutting their grass. Thankfully with the cooler weather, my lawn hadn't needed mowing this week. I stroked Chewie's ear, trying to alleviate his anxiety and some of my own. "I should warn you. My mom has an enemies list on her fridge."

"And I'm on it?" Laugh lines creased at his good eye.

"Right between Benedict Arnold and the guy who's supposedly stealing her newspapers."

He shook his head with a chuckle.

"I'm glad you find it humorous. Most people would get peeved." To our right, a group of girls played hopscotch on the sidewalk, trying to make the most of the daylight before the sun vanished.

"I can now better appreciate her stance in wanting to protect her daughter. If someone were to hurt Brooke . . ."

Like you did to me?

He rubbed his jaw, the stubble bristling against his fingers. "It wouldn't be pretty."

Was this change in him only for his daughter, or could I trust him to extend it to me if I gave him another chance? A breathless moment of hope expanded, pushing and pressing, trying to make its way out.

Conner and Mason gave their approval.

I clamped my tongue and pulled in a lungful of air. It was too much of a risk to find out.

Samuel was positioned on his back, his upper body stuffed into the cabinet beneath Mama's kitchen sink. Everything that had been housed in the cupboard littered the floor to one side of him. Dishwasher detergent, a box of garbage bags, cleaning products that weren't my concoctions. *Sigh*.

I kneeled on Samuel's other side, holding a flashlight so he could see better. When we'd arrived, I'd expected to find a disaster site and water everywhere. Not so. There *was* water in the cabinet, but Mama had a towel soaking it up and had situated a pot to catch the dribbling leak.

Samuel shifted his awkward position, a grunt escaping. I winced at the way the ledge bit into his side.

His cargo shorts were not aiding in curbing his appeal. He'd always had amazing calf muscles. I once again imagined Marie Kondo on my shoulder. *Yes, Marie. This sight does spark joy.* Mama lurked behind me, grumbling from time to time.

Chewie sniffed the floor around Samuel's feet, which were clad in tennis shoes. Samuel moved again. A low growl emanated from Chewie.

"Chewie," I warned, reaching for him. Before I could grab his little body, he snapped, biting Samuel's ankle.

Samuel flinched, a muffled oath emanating from the cupboard.

"Chewie!" I dropped the flashlight and held him, swatting his nose. "Bad dog!"

Mama snickered.

I shot her a glare and turned to Samuel. "I'm so sorry! Are you okay?" I eyed his ankle where a red mark now appeared, but no broken skin.

"Yes, but I'd be grateful if you held that demon while I'm defenseless."

I handed Chewie to Mama, who held him at arm's length, and resumed my job of pointing the flashlight.

"This looks like a simple valve leak." Samuel reached, grasping something and twisting. "That should do it." He maneuvered out from the cabinet to sit on the floor and assess the dog bite.

"Sorry." I leaned back on my heels, turning off the flashlight.

"It's fine." He stood, his gaze moving to Mama. "I'd keep the pan under there for a day or two, just in case. But it looks like the valve only needed to be tightened." The back of his shirt was dotted with dampness from the water not soaked by the towel.

"Thank you," Mama mumbled. She let Chewie loose, and he scampered off. The little vampire.

"You're welcome." He offered me his hand.

I grasped it, letting him pull me up. Electricity glinted at the touch, the feel of his rough skin on mine. Our hold lingered. I envisioned Marie Kondo sliding on sunglasses to shield her eyes from the plethora of sparks. "Um, the back of your shirt is wet."

He took the flashlight from me and placed it in his toolbox. "That's okay." In one fluid motion, he shut the lid and grabbed the handle. "I can drop you back home."

"Thanks." I led the way out, Chewie dashing past the screen door and to the patch of grass between Mama and her neighbor's house. Like he always did, he inspected the line of azalea bushes there. I took in a cleansing breath of nicotine-free air and brushed my arms to ward off a chill. It was only five thirty, but because of Daylight Saving Time ending, darkness already encroached. The streetlights turned on, and we were serenaded by crickets and Mama's flicking cigarette lighter.

Samuel and I headed for his truck, parked behind Mama's Buick in her driveway. He hefted his toolbox over the side and into the truck's bed.

A nearby car backfired, and Chewie startled, darting past us.

He kept running, right to the middle of the street. An SUV barreled our way. Chewie froze in its headlights. My heart plummeted. My scream stuck in my throat.

In a blur of movement, Samuel ran after Chewie, swooping him up like a fumbled football. The car's brakes squealed. The sickening smack of Samuel's body making contact filled my ears. His hat went flying through the air.

29

"**THE SUV ONLY GRAZED ME.**" Samuel ground out the words, his face contorted in pain. He sat inclined on a gurney in the back of an ambulance, shirtless, his right arm in a sling. A nasty scarlet bruise progressively developed across his chest.

One first responder took his vitals, while another asked him questions. They'd arrived in record time, the police closely behind them. Red and blue lights flashed against the dark sky and the faces of those who'd gathered to lookie-loo. After getting our statements, the police had turned their attention to the driver of the SUV.

The paramedic checked the sling they'd carefully slipped Samuel's arm into after receiving permission to cut his shirt off. "No doubt you have a dislocated or separated shoulder, and probably a concussion."

My stomach twisted, the tightness in my chest refusing to loosen.

The EMT scribbled on his chart. "We'll take you to the hospital for a thorough screening, and they'll get you fixed up."

"Can you check her?" Samuel pointed with his good arm. "I think she's in shock."

It took a second to register that he was talking about me. My mind had been stuck in slow motion. I'd heard of adrenaline slowing the senses but had never experienced it.

Samuel had bounced off the SUV, his shoulder taking the brunt of the hit, and rolled to the curb. The entire time he'd never let go of Chewie, even when the dog had been biting his hand like the dickens. Unable to escape, my scream had imploded within me, unlocking jagged agony from the past I thought I'd been freed from. I'd crumpled to the driveway and crawled to where Samuel had lain.

Although I hadn't been there when Mark had died, his face had flashed repeatedly before me, along with the regret of all the things I'd never told him before he'd passed.

"Ma'am?" One of the paramedics stepped down from the ambulance, eyeing me.

I blinked. "I'm good." I refused to give in to the remorse from the past trying to devour me. Falling apart would not be helpful to Samuel.

Mama stood behind me, holding Samuel's hat, worry deepening her wrinkles. She'd put Chewie inside her house after calling 911 and had kept up a continuous mumble of prayers since.

The pinch of metal in my hand drew my attention. I held Samuel's keys. My brows pulled together. When had he given them to me? I glanced back at him. Pale faced and bruised and obviously in pain. My vision swam.

Samuel attempted a smile, but his agony was clear. "Julia, I'm fine."

There sat a man who had been so, so good to me and my family the past two months. I tried to swallow, my throat feeling like it had been stuffed with cotton balls. Against all odds and my better judgment, my heart terrifyingly softened. My lips parted. *Conner and Mason gave their approval.*

"We're taking him to East Jefferson General." The EMT turned to shut the doors on the ambulance.

"Wait." I neared, my gaze locked on Samuel. If there was

one lesson I'd learned from Mark being ripped from my life, it was not leaving things unsaid. "I forgive you."

A blend of emotions played across his face. Surprise, relief . . . hope. Samuel hadn't shed a single tear after being pummeled by a car or chewed on like a dog bone. But now, his eye glossed.

Easing backward, my chin trembled. "I'll see you at the hospital."

⸎ ⸎

I couldn't stop staring at Samuel's bare torso. Or I should say, the delicious tattoo on his left pectoral. Old English font spelled out *De Oppresso Liber.* The first time he'd caught me peeking at the hospital, he'd explained it was the Special Forces motto. *To free the oppressed.*

Lying there on the emergency room bed, he'd reached for my hand. I had eyed his fingers with suspicion. "It'll make me feel better," he'd said. Despite the mischievousness in his expression, I'd granted his request, his massive hand enveloping mine. Had a heart-rate monitor been attached to me, it would have exploded.

In between being dragged off for an X-ray and a CT scan, he held my hand. He didn't stroke my fingers or try to make anything more of it. It was just steady contact. A reassurance. And it was . . . nice. Extremely nice. Even as several female nurses fawned over him—and thoroughly appreciated his tattoo—he never let go.

The X-ray revealed his shoulder had in fact been dislocated. I'd waited outside the exam room while the physician popped it back in place. The distance hadn't prevented me from hearing Samuel's slight howl during the process. For the next three days, he'd need to apply an ice pack at regular intervals. He'd also have to put up with a sling until he followed up with an orthopedist.

The CT scan resulted in the diagnosis of a mild concussion. Because of the brain injury, he'd need constant looking after for the next forty-eight hours. An unspoken understanding had passed between us that I would be the one caring for him. When I called Wyatt to let him know what had happened, he'd volunteered to step in. But I'd immediately declined his assistance. I wanted to be the one looking after Samuel. The mere thought of leaving his side opened a cavernous hole in my heart.

Earlier, when he'd ridden off in the ambulance, I'd driven his monster truck to my place, thrown together some essentials in case I'd be staying the night at the hospital, and sped my vehicle to the ER. All the while streaming a litany of prayers.

Now we were in my SUV, heading to his place. At every red light, I looked over, ensuring he was awake, and there was the tattoo. One of the nurses in the emergency room had offered Samuel an undershirt to wear home, but he'd refused, saying it'd be too painful to maneuver on and off. Hence the bare-chested man in my front passenger seat.

Any assumptions I'd had of him still retaining his six-pack had been validated. *It's like we're at the beach or a swimming pool. His upper body is not a big deal.* Hopefully he had a robe at home, otherwise the next two days were going to be very interesting.

I drove like a grandma transporting an atomic bomb, cringing over every bump and dip, terrified to cause him any more discomfort or damage. Samuel never complained. He gave simple directions to his place, and we arrived in no time thanks to the lack of traffic at eight thirty on a Sunday night.

I pulled up to a row of well-lit, modern townhouses. The rear of the structure backed up to the levee that helped contain Lake Ponchartrain, which I had expected due to Mama's previous surveillance. Landscape lighting highlighted the angles of the architecture of each of the five dwellings. Three stories of black-trimmed windows stood out against the stone-and-wood façade.

"It's the last unit," Samuel said.

I pulled in the farthest driveway and parked before a garage door. From the backseat, I grabbed Samuel's discharge instructions and my overnight bag. I made my way to his side and found he'd already exited the vehicle. A shiver rocked his body from the cold night air. And no wonder. All he wore were cargo shorts. I shut his door as gently as possible for the sake of his headache. "Let me get your keys." I fished them from my purse and handed them to him, hovering at his side in case he lost his footing.

The front door opened into a hallway with oak floors that ran parallel to the garage. Straight ahead metal stairs waited. I followed Samuel up and cringed at the red bruising marring the back of his arm and shoulder. His movements were slow, and he held the rail.

At the landing, he reached for a panel on the wall, light illuminating the open area. He winced and blinked several times. To the right, I found a pristine, contemporary kitchen. To the left, the living room. A glass-and-iron chandelier was suspended between the two spaces, above where a dining table should be. The walls were stark white and barren. A caramel leather sectional sofa sat before a matching ottoman. A large flat screen TV hung above the empty fireplace mantel.

At the very least, he'd been living here three months. And yet there was no sense of permanence or attachment to this place. My scalp prickled. Teddy's hopes of Samuel returning to North Carolina to train Special Forces candidates crept into my mind.

Samuel paused at the marble kitchen counter acting as a separator between the kitchen and what would have been the dining room. He braced his hand there for balance. "Can you help me up to my bed?" No trace of flirtation coated his tone. He had to be in serious pain.

My stomach churned. "Of course." I stowed my bag and

purse on the floor next to the wall and placed his discharge papers on them.

He shuffled past me to the staircase, gripping the railing with his first stride up. I positioned my hands on his lower back for stability. On the third floor, we reached his bedroom, which consisted of a queen-sized bed covered by a navy comforter, a dresser, and two nightstands.

He lowered, sitting on the side of the bed, the mattress dipping beneath his weight. His good hand pressed against the bed, as if steadying himself.

I knelt at his feet and removed his tennis shoes. "Don't lay back until I get some pillows behind you. The ER nurse said propping you at a forty-five-degree angle would reduce the stress on your shoulder." I crimped his body pillow in half and situated it against his headboard, adding his regular pillow in front of it.

Samuel maneuvered atop the duvet and toward the pillows, grimacing, until he'd settled as best he could. "Can you turn off the light?"

"Yes, and I'll make an ice pack." I flipped the switch on my way out, casting his room to darkness. The open stairwell allowed the downstairs lights to flood my path. I quickly rummaged his kitchen, locating a box of gallon-sized ziplock bags. After filling one with crushed ice, I wrapped it with a damp dish towel and dashed up the stairs.

Back in his room, I turned the light on in his en suite bathroom and cracked the door so that it wasn't too bright for his headache but enough for me to see to take care of him. "Brace yourself." I carefully laid the ice against his shoulder.

He sucked in a breath.

"Sorry," I whispered.

"It's okay." Little by little, his body relaxed, his breathing slowing to a balanced rhythm.

Towing the blanket from the other side of the bed, I folded it over his body. After several long moments, his good arm went limp, sleep arriving. I pulled my phone from my back pocket and scheduled a timer to go off in twenty minutes to remove the ice, then programmed an alarm to notify me in three hours to wake him.

In the hallway, I called Mama, giving her a hushed rundown on Samuel, and thanking her for keeping Chewie. I returned to his room and texted my Monday clients that I'd be unable to clean their houses tomorrow. God willing, they'd understand, especially since I'd never bailed on them before. Missing their income would hurt, particularly since I had already been taking a hit each week since losing the Holdens.

My attention floated to Samuel. Sorrow and regret twisted, knotting in my core. This was all my fault. One hundred percent. And the end result could have been so much worse. Regardless of how my clients reacted, caring for Samuel was my priority. I was right where I needed to be.

In the dim light, I surveyed the room. No TV, no decorations. A belt, some change, and a gas receipt rested on his dresser. The rear wall held sliding glass doors, probably leading to a balcony overlooking the lake. For now, the view was pitch-black, the glass reflecting the room and my slumped posture.

I shifted around the bed to the sliding doors, leaning the side of my face against the cool glass. *How did I end up here, Lord? These past two months . . . Is this Your doing?* My eyes lifted to the full moon. *Is this really Your will? That I end up with Samuel?*

My exhale fogged the window. All I could do was keep my eyes on Him, believing He would make a way. I didn't have to understand His plans, or even like them at times, but I knew He'd be faithful to show me the good at some point in the journey. He always had.

Glancing at my phone, the timer gave Samuel fifteen more minutes with the ice pack. I slipped off my sneakers, padded downstairs, snagged my things, along with Samuel's release forms, then returned to his bedroom. I glided into the bathroom, shutting the door and changing from my jeans into the pajama pants I'd packed. This space was modern, like the rest of the townhouse. Large walk-in shower, freestanding tub, double vanity. An electric toothbrush, razor, and shaving cream occupied the counter.

I opened the door and stared at him. The continual rise and fall of his breathing. The bruising that seemed to have finally stopped growing. Itching to be productive, I grasped his discharge instructions and stood in the threshold where I could keep an eye on him and have enough light to read.

The sling was advised to be worn until he could be reevaluated by an orthopedist. *Okay. We knew that. Not too bad.* He'd be able to resume most activities in two weeks. *Rats.* We'd need clarification on that description. Did "most activities" mean driving? Cooking and cleaning I could handle. But Samuel would not be happy about being stuck at home.

I fumbled over the next section. *Avoid heavy lifting for six weeks. Complete recovery in twelve to sixteen weeks.* My hand holding the pages dropped to my side, my heart sinking. He had excursions planned for the next month that, if they were anything like our swamp tour, would involve heavy lifting.

Oh, Samuel.

❦————❦

Throughout the night, my phone alarm went off every three hours, and I'd dutifully woken Samuel long enough to ascertain he wasn't showing any deteriorating symptoms. Every four hours, I'd given him Tylenol. At three o'clock this morning, I'd applied a fresh ice pack for twenty minutes. In between tending to Samuel, I'd settled on the other side of his bed, worrying about his health and his business, and taking fitful catnaps.

Since waking him at his last symptom check, even the fitful catnaps had eluded me. I had lain on my side, facing the glass doors, the accident running through my brain, a tsunami of what-if scenarios crashing through me.

The sun's ascent slowly chased the darkness, revealing a balcony with glass railings and a beautiful prospect of Lake Ponchartrain. I was not in the mood for beautiful things. I rolled onto my back and rubbed my eyes. Checked my phone. Samuel had another thirty minutes before I woke him again.

I turned my head toward him and found his gaze on me, smile lines creasing at the corner of his eye. Like his hair, his patch was slightly askew. My heart pitter-pattered. Maybe I *was* in the mood for beautiful things. "How do you feel?"

"Pretty good, waking up with you in my bed."

The tension that had built within me the past ninety minutes lessened. If he was flirting, he really was feeling better. "Samuel." I spoke his name with a light chastisement.

He pressed his fingers into the side of his neck, working his way to his injury. "My head and shoulder hurt, but I think the dizziness is gone."

Thank You, Lord.

"Can I ask why my nightstand has been moved?"

"I was afraid with your equilibrium off, you'd roll out of bed and smack your head on it."

Using his good arm, he navigated himself to a sitting position, wincing with the movements. He slid his legs over the side of the mattress.

"Careful." I rounded the bed to him.

"Are those my sofa cushions on the floor?"

"Yes." I'd filched two seat cushions from his sectional. Grabbing them now, I propped them against the wall, out of the way. "Again, I was worried you'd roll out of bed."

271

He set his socked feet on the floor. "You must like me a lot to have done all that." After the seriousness of last night, his teasing tone was a blessing to my nerves.

"I don't."

"No?" His eye rose, connecting with mine.

I crossed my arms. "Not even a little."

"Then why did you hold my hand last night?"

Poker face. Poker face. "You must have been having a delusion. That's common with concussions."

He stared me down, calling my bluff.

"Fine." I fidgeted with the sleeve of my shirt. "I did hold your hand. But only to ensure you didn't get out of bed without me. I didn't want you attempting those stairs. Or sleepwalking. Or doing anything without me knowing."

A roguish glint lit his face. "How long can we keep this me-not-doing-anything-without-you situation going?"

I ignored his question. "Are you hungry?"

"Yes, but I'm going to shower first."

"Wait." My hands shot out. "What if you fall in the shower?" He hadn't been wholly steady on his feet last night and had yet to stand on his own this morning.

His brows peaked. "Are you offering to assist me?"

In spite of the blush heating my cheeks, I nailed him with a glare.

"You sure are sexy when you're sassy." He eased to his feet, scowling with the effort.

I darted forward.

"I'm fine, Julia. Really." His battered appearance and the painful squint to his eye called him a liar. And the ER tests agreed.

"But you're not." Pressure squeezed my throat. "You could have been . . ." My hands clenched into fists at my sides. The despair from Mark's death I'd worked through so long ago clawed, scratching with jagged nails at the edge of reason.

Be still.

The words, not of my own volition, were gentle and pure, and settled me. They offered the sensation to pause. To turn my thoughts to God.

And that's what I did.

Thank You, Lord, for Your presence. Please replace my fears with Your truth. Like an emery board, swiftly scuffing back and forth against a sharp point, my anxiety receded. Sweet clarity, and a little shakiness, remained.

Samuel appraised me during this quiet moment, and I could tell when comprehension dawned. He exhaled, his forehead furrowing. "I'm sorry I scared you." He moved toward me.

I inched back, my calves butting the couch cushions leaning against the wall.

"Going after Chewie was a knee-jerk reaction."

"You could have been seriously injured. What if you'd lost your other eye?"

"But I didn't."

"But what if you had? It's not like we could train Chewie to be a seeing eye dog."

Tenderness softened the planes of his face. "I love the way you used *we*."

Oh, gracious. A deep longing to erase the gap between us and wrap my arms around him seeped into me. The urge to blurt out Conner and Mason's approval pressed for escape. This was not good. I needed time alone to sort through my feelings and insecurities. Time away from Samuel and the haze his very being cast over me. But that wasn't coming anytime soon. We had a full day and another long night ahead of us.

Lord, give me strength.

30

I WAS ON THE VERGE OF BECOMING A BIG FAT SNOOPER.

The shower from Samuel's en suite had been running for a good five minutes, so the odds of him having made it in without my assistance, versus falling and splitting his head open without me hearing, had to be good.

After brushing my teeth in the guest bathroom and changing into the joggers and sweatshirt I'd brought, I stood in the hallway outside Samuel's bedroom, eyeing two closed doors. My lips pursed. Why were they shut? What secrets did they hold? *It's none of your business.*

Or was it?

One could argue it would be smart to know what lurked behind the walls of Samuel Reed's home. Especially given our history. And especially given the fact he hadn't had time to hide anything since he hadn't expected me to end up at his place.

The irony of this situation wasn't lost on me. Two decades ago, this scenario had played out in Samuel's apartment. He'd been in the shower and mistrust had been eating at my gut like a snared animal gnawing its way free. He'd stopped answering phone calls in front of me. And he'd been vague about making future plans. In an effort to ease my concerns, I'd gone snooping and had discovered the bikini tramp picture.

Remnants of suspicion sifted through me. What if those rooms contained questionable things? What if Samuel hadn't truly changed? *God, what do I do here?* There was no question what Black Widow would do. But invading Samuel's privacy didn't sit right. Would I want him nosing through my things? *Ugh.* The Golden Rule really bit sometimes.

I retreated to the main floor and stood in the silent open space, feeling like a trespasser. A wall of windows along the back framed a view of green space leading to the levee. Although the lake itself wasn't visible from this vantage point, the triangular tip of a sailboat coasted by. My stomach rumbled, as though remembering I hadn't had dinner last night.

Coffee. That was my first priority. Then food. I set my phone on the kitchen counter, my attention halting on a stack of papers. A real estate agent's business card sat atop them. Curiosity buzzed beneath my skin. Was it prying if the items lay in plain sight? The theme song to *Mission: Impossible* began playing in my head. I nibbled my lip and crept closer. The flyer on top showcased a home in New Orleans.

"Oh." My audible declaration caught my own ears by surprise. I covered my mouth with my hand while my heart danced a jig. *Stop that*, I scolded, and resumed scanning the home's info. My mouth squeaked open again. It was an expensive home. I skimmed through the leaflets of house after house. *Sakes alive!* They were all in the same dollar range. He must not have been lying about not being worried about money. Then again, maybe he was living beyond his means. I tidied the pile to its pre-rummaged condition.

Cracking a knuckle, I surveyed the rest of the space now that I'd slunk into reconnaissance mode. Samuel's Bible lay on the coffee table, next to a photo album. My palms began to sweat. I tossed a glance at the stairs and hurried toward the den, ducking the fabulous chandelier with no purpose. The leather from one of the remaining cushions I hadn't repurposed in Samuel's bedroom greeted my bottom.

I studied the album, my socked feet bouncing against the wood floors. The nondescript thick burgundy cover gave no indication of what prowled within. A warning Mama had gifted me with as a teenager echoed through my mind. *"Once you see something, you can't un-see it."* Truer advice had never been given. But something inside me nudged, encouraged. I pinched the corner of the cover and slowly peeled it back.

Oh, heavens. A newborn picture of who had to be Samuel's daughter, Brooke, peered up at me underneath the clear overlay film. She rested in her hospital bassinet. Her rosy face and fuzzy-haired head topped her little body, wrapped snugly in the same blue-and-pink-striped swaddling my boys had been enfolded in. I straightened. Had she been born at the same hospital? The one I'd just driven Samuel home from?

Samuel had mentioned that Brooke was a sophomore, which put her around Conner's age of nineteen. I hadn't given much thought to the woman Samuel had conceived Brooke with, other than assuming she'd been in the military too, since that's where he'd been all this time. But then again, he would have come home on furloughs and could have met someone local. And Brooke attending LSU jibed with that.

Beneath that initial shot came a picture of Samuel awkwardly holding her. He appeared to be in uniform. Simple khaki T-shirt, camouflaged pants. With a shaved head and wide eyes, he radiated being overwhelmed. It was probably the first time he'd held a baby. The photo next in line featured Teddy and Samuel's mom, Patricia. With the precious baby cradled in Patricia's arms, tension lingered on their faces. If they hadn't already divorced by the time of Brooke's arrival, it seemed imminent.

I turned the page, expecting additional birth snapshots, and found myself deposited into Easter pictures and Brooke now several months old. I flipped back to the previous sheet, certain I must have missed Brooke's mom. *Huh.* I hadn't. Had Samuel removed the ones with her? Or perhaps there had been difficulties with the delivery, and she was still in recovery when these photos had been taken?

I moved through the memory book, entranced with watching Samuel's child grow, and him captured at every moment right along with her. With each cataloged milestone, Samuel's face matured, as well as his body. His once lean physique packed on muscle and strength with the years.

Each of Brooke's birthdays was documented. The themes of her parties morphed from unfussy yellow balloons and streamers to full-on *My Little Pony*, complete with a live pony ride. Images of holidays were interspersed, along with vacations. Amusement parks, the Grand Canyon, beaches, white-water rafting. As though timed perfectly, the last page held shots of Brooke's high school graduation. Again, Samuel was there. As well as Patricia and Teddy. No other grandparents rounded out the photos. The only other relative to have made an appearance in the book had been Wyatt. The entire album was void of Brooke's mom.

I pulled in a breath and blinked, gathering my bearings. Like being in a dark movie theater as the show ended, I'd been sucked into another world and needed to readjust to mine.

At least two truths and one mystery had unfolded from my foray with espionage. Samuel was committed to staying in New Orleans, and he loved his daughter. But what had happened to Brooke's mom? Had he cheated on her, too, and she'd cut him out of her life? Did she have her own album of Brooke's life with just her family and no reference to Samuel?

"You seem absorbed there." Samuel's voice came from behind.

I startled. At some point, the book had grown legs and crawled onto my lap.

Samuel moved farther into the room. Shirtless and wearing pajama bottoms, he held his sling with the hand of his injured arm. A thin, navy robe hung from his other forearm. The bruising across his chest and shoulder had darkened.

Embarrassment at being busted had shifted my pulse from neutral into third gear. But his appearance kicked my heartbeat up to fifth. A bead of water dropped from his hair, pinging his good shoulder and rolling south over his tattoo. *De Oppresso Liber*, indeed. His bare feet continued the silence of his steps, and he held his wounded arm close to his body at a ninety-degree angle.

"I didn't hear you coming."

"Clearly." One corner of his mouth lifted.

My eyes narrowed. "You Green Bereted me."

He grinned. The rascal.

"Well . . ." I cleared my throat and returned the album to the coffee table. "I didn't find any pictures of women in bikinis." As soon as the words were out, I regretted them, how juvenile I sounded.

His smile fell away, his forehead furrowing. "I wish you could know how sorry I am for that." His attention drifted to the rear windows. "My only excuse is I was a red-blooded twenty-two-year-old male. And stupid." He draped his robe along the sofa's back.

I stood and took the sling from him, gently maneuvering it around his elbow, like the ER nurse had shown me. "I shouldn't have made that comment." Warmth and the clean scent of soap exuded from his damp skin. *Focus. Focus.* I moved behind him, bringing the sling's straps behind his back. *Gracious.* He was a wall of flesh and muscle. I folded the top strap over his good shoulder, circling to the front of his bruised and battered body. Carefully, I pulled the band through a ring on the harness, folding the tie back up and securing it to the Velcro.

"I've gotten a lot wrong in my life. But I've gotten some

things right too." His breath stirred the hair at the crown of my head.

My knees weakened, my brain turning to mush. *Think. Think.* What was I supposed to do next? An untethered strap dangled. At his side, I pulled the second line across his upper back, then under his good arm. Standing in front of him again, I clipped that band onto another section, my fingers grazing his skin below his tattoo in the process. A burning zing tingled through to my core.

His chest expanded and deflated at an increasing tempo.

I slid my hands to my sides. If I looked up, I'd be a goner. How many times in the past had I fallen asleep with my cheek pressed against the spot now holding the tattoo? I cautioned a peek at his face and licked my lips.

His stare zeroed in on my movement, his Adam's apple bobbing.

We were the Wooly Willy toy all over again, the nerve endings under my skin craving and reaching for him, drawing me to him.

He raised his unbound hand toward my face and paused, the moment stretching, a battle raging in his gaze. He closed his eye and withdrew a step.

The electricity humming between us fizzled, leaving me cold and with a crushing sensation of disappointment.

"There are some things I want to explain." He rubbed his jaw, the auburn-and-brown stubble on his chin scratching against his fingers.

"Dad?" A feminine voice called from the direction of the staircase that led to the entranceway on the first floor.

Skid marks! I didn't want to meet his daughter yet! And most definitely not with him being half-naked and looking like we'd been up to something. Like we'd been up to something all night and had just woken up. I cupped my palms to my warm cheeks. I could not appear flushed! I waved my hands in front of my face.

A smug glint lit Samuel's expression, replacing the seriousness from a second ago. "In here," he called. A grimace followed, and he massaged his temples.

Footsteps and jangling keys neared. "Whose SUV is that in the driveway?"

I darted sideways from Samuel, smoothed my hair, and adjusted my shirt. Hopefully I didn't look like a woman who wanted to kiss her dad senseless.

Samuel seemed to be enjoying my rattled state more than he should. "It's Julia's," he answered, as though his daughter would know who I was.

Wait. Would she? I panic-whispered to Samuel, "You told her about me?"

He winked at me. Winked!

Coming up the stairway, Brooke's face emerged first. Similar to her graduation pictures, she wore understated makeup, her long honey-brown hair cascading in waves. Her resemblance to Samuel was undeniable. She carried a phone in her hand and had a backpack slung over her shoulder. Her vivid, rounding eyes instantly latched on to me.

"This isn't what it looks like." I held up my hands as though Brooke was a police officer with her weapon drawn.

A snicker emanated from Samuel. "Brooke, Julia. Julia, Brooke." He motioned between us.

I lowered my hands. "Hi." This was not improving my flushed-cheek situation.

"Hi." Brooke's soft voice matched her face. She paused at the landing, her attention captivated by the wood floors under her ankle boots. A tentative smile grew, her cheeks tinging pink. She flicked her gaze up the stairwell to the third floor, as though planning her escape. But then her sight finally landed on Samuel. Her shyness instantly gave way to concern. "What happened?" She stepped forward, her backpack thudding to the floor.

"I'm fine." Samuel reached for his robe on the sofa. "It's just a dislocated shoulder."

280

I moved to his side, helping him slip his good arm through the sleeve and draping the other side over his shoulder. "And a mild concussion."

Samuel shot me a perturbed look. *Oops!*

Brooke's lips parted, a flash of wounded bewilderment in her eyes. I hadn't thought to call her last night, only Wyatt.

Samuel sighed. "I knew it wasn't serious. I didn't want to upset you."

"Just like when you were serving," she mumbled, the corners of her mouth edging down.

My face slid into a mirror image of hers. How many times had he been injured in the military? There was so much I didn't know about that side of his life. "Last night he rescued my dog and was rewarded with getting hit by a car."

"Grazed. I was only grazed." Samuel adjusted his harness beneath the robe. "I was also bit by your dog—repeatedly."

"He's a little poodle mix," I explained to Brooke. "A speck. Not some monster animal your dad is making him out to be." I turned to Samuel. "He didn't even break your skin."

"He's the devil incarnate."

"That is sort of true."

"It's exactly true."

Brooke's attention hung on our exchange. The wrinkle between her dark brows disappeared, her facial countenance lifting, as though she were pleased.

Samuel embraced her in a careful side-hug and kissed the top of her head.

My heart melted like peanut butter on hot toast. *Stop that! Stay firm!* All of this softening toward him would only lead to worse things. Like love. *Gah! Don't even think the L-word!* I'd only just forgiven him yesterday. That was a big enough step for a long time. For eternity.

"I hadn't expected to see you until next weekend." He nudged her farther into the room. "This is a nice surprise."

Brooke tucked her hair behind her ears, revealing silver dangling earrings. "I'm attending a luncheon and tour of the LSU nursing school downtown today. My morning class was canceled, so I figured I'd drive in early and stop by."

The alarm on my phone sounded from the kitchen counter. "Sorry." I reached for it, turning it off. "That's for your dad. It's time for his medicine and an ice pack."

"That's fine," Brooke said. "I've got homework I can catch up on, so I'll get out of y'all's way and head to my bedroom." She pointed upstairs, retreating a smidge.

"You can stay." My voice pitched. I cleared my throat. "I mean, it's not like anything's going to happen that you can't . . . you know . . . stay." My face and neck felt impossibly hot.

Samuel chuckled.

Brooke watched him closely, a blend of disbelief and adoration flitting across her features.

"Have you had breakfast?" I reached for the Tylenol next to where my phone had been on the counter. Popped the top and shook out two pills. "Maybe you can help me find something to make?" I handed the medicine to Samuel and faced Brooke again. "Your dad's pretty useless," I teased.

A smile tipped her lips. "I'd love to help."

With his stomach full of scrambled eggs, drop biscuits, and bacon, Samuel snoozed on the couch, his feet propped on the coffee table. Brooke had stuffed several folded towels behind his elbow to keep his arm forward and stabilized. Smart girl.

The TV played an old episode of *Friends*. Originally, Samuel had turned on a recorded UFC fight he'd missed over the weekend. But after groans from Brooke and me, he'd changed it. She now sat on a barstool at the kitchen counter, finishing her meal.

I scraped the crumbs from Samuel's plate into the garbage, the fork dragging against the ceramic. "How do you like LSU?"

"It's nice." She poked the last of the eggs on her dish into a pile. "The campus is huge."

"Are you living on campus?"

"No, I live with my grandma in Baton Rouge." Her tone indicated the annoyance of a teenager craving independence and being denied. "Once prerequisites are done, I'll move here to be closer to the nursing school."

I deposited Samuel's dishes in the sink and returned for mine. "Is that your mom's mom or your dad's that you're staying with?"

"My dad's mom." She set her fork down. "I've only met my mom's parents a few times."

"Oh, do they live out of town?"

"No, they're here in Metairie. At least . . . they used to live here. I guess they could have moved. We've never been close."

My steps toward the sink slowed. Had they not approved of Samuel? Of the way Brooke had been conceived outside of marriage? Those two factors weren't Brooke's fault. What grandparents wouldn't want to be near their grandchild? I opened the dishwasher and rolled out the top rack. Not even distance had kept Mark's parents from Conner and Mason. They'd driven in regularly to see them. Plus holidays and birthdays. Up until Mark's death, we'd spent our summers in North Carolina, staying at their house. After Mark's death, his dad would fly down and fly the boys back to keep them for most of the summer while I stayed home to work.

I peered out the window above the sink, the view of the street and Samuel's driveway before me. Behind my SUV sat a newer-model Toyota Corolla. No doubt Brooke's vehicle. What must it be like for her? To know she had grandparents here who didn't want to make an effort? My boys had been fortunate to have two sets of grandparents most of their lives. Additional adults to look up to as role models. Even my mom had her good qualities. I turned, giving Brooke my full attention. "I'm sorry they aren't close with you."

Her gaze drooped from me to her coffee mug. "It's okay." She gathered her plate and utensils and made her way over. "My dad told me y'all used to date."

"A long time ago." I turned on the faucet, the water cascading into a bowl we'd mixed the biscuits in.

She put her dishes next to the sink. "Before I was born."

"Yes."

"And he told me you have two boys."

"I do." I rinsed a measuring cup and added it to the dishwasher. "They're both at college in North Carolina."

"My dad said they were just in town." She made another trip, retrieving her mug. "That y'all did his swamp tour."

"They were, and we did. I was a nervous wreck thinking they'd lose a limb to an alligator."

She stacked her cup atop her dish and lingered. "That's nice. I mean, not that you were worried, but . . ." Brooke fidgeted with her earring, her slender hip angled against the lower cabinets. "My mom . . . she's never really been a mom. I guess it's not in her nature."

My mama-heart clenched, an unanticipated fondness for this girl blooming within. The photo album was starting to make sense. Again, I turned my full attention to her, taking in her sweet face. "I'm sorry to hear that."

She glanced over her shoulder at Samuel, as though ensuring he still slept. Pitching forward, her voice lowered. "My dad has a lot of guilt about my relationship with her, and I guess with my other grandparents too."

"But you're close with your dad's parents?"

"Oh yeah." She lifted the frying pan from the stove and positioned it next in line for washing. "Meemaw is who took care of me while my dad was in service."

Not her mom? I resumed my task, moving on to the skillet,

the water growing hot against my skin. Was the woman an addict? A top-secret government spy?

"And I'm close to my Peepaw too." She grabbed a dish towel and shifted to the other side of the dishwasher. "I'm sorry I kind of weirded out earlier. It's just . . . I've never seen my dad with another woman. I mean, well, you know what I mean."

My grip on the pan slipped, my belly fluttering. Either Samuel hadn't dated, which seemed unlikely, or he'd hidden it from Brooke. If it were the latter option, I couldn't help but respect him for sparing Brooke from the sensitive confusion it would have caused her.

"Your dad and I are just friends." I slanted the now clean skillet onto the drying rack.

She reached for it, working the towel over the surface, eyeing me with what appeared to be open curiosity. "Either way, I'm glad you're here."

Something in the way she said it expressed her gratitude for more than my caring for her dad in this situation. My fondness skyrocketed to affection.

31

I WAS IN A LOSING GAME OF PEEKABOO WITH SAMUEL'S TATTOO.
For the sake of my sanity, we'd relocated to my home, so I wouldn't fret about him tumbling down the stairs at his townhouse. After Brooke had left for her luncheon, we'd packed his necessities for him to spend the night. For the sake of car safety and eliminating distractions like chiseled pectorals and six-pack abs, we had traded Samuel's bathrobe for a zippered hoodie.

He now sat at my dining room table, his jacket hanging open. He was on the phone with an orthopedist, scheduling a follow-up consultation. I was cleaning up from lunch, waiting for Mama to drop Chewie off.

He leaned forward, aiming for a pen on the table. When he straightened, his hoodie slipped.

Peekaboo!

I redirected my sights, flicking off the faucet and drying my hands on a dish towel. I'd purposely packed a button-up flannel I'd found in his closet. Hopefully by tomorrow his shoulder would be a little better, and he'd be up for wearing it.

Samuel disconnected from his call, placing his phone on the table. "I have an appointment Wednesday morning."

Shoot. What would I do about my client? I opened the pantry, reaching for a new roll of paper towels. Forfeiting additional income this week would be a huge hit. Maybe I could ask Mama to take Samuel. Her vendetta against him had to have subsided—or at least eased.

"If I need a ride—"

"If?" I shut the pantry and sent him a pointed look. "Your arm's in a sling."

He smiled. The scoundrel. "And it's feeling better."

Then why are you still shirtless?

"If I need to, I can take the sling off to drive." He slanted against the chair's wooden back, as if testing his shoulder's mobility.

I opened my mouth to disagree.

He held up his good hand. "Wyatt texted earlier, checking in. Said he could help if needed."

I had no doubt about Wyatt's offer. But whether or not Samuel would take him up on it was something else. I ripped the plastic covering from the paper towels. "I have his number now, too, you know. I'll ensure he's the one taking you to that appointment."

His lips pulled to the side, annoyed delight filling his features. "I don't remember you being this bossy."

I rolled my eyes and slid the new paper towel roll onto the holder. Wyatt may be able to take him to a doctor appointment, but he had a full-time job. It wasn't like he could step in and run Samuel's business. The grilled cheese sandwich I'd had for lunch twisted in my stomach. "Did you read your discharge papers? You're probably going to have to cancel those excursions you have booked. Your recovery could take up to sixteen weeks."

"I'm not going to be out of commission that long."

"How do you know?"

He stood, all calm composure, and grabbed his glass of water. "This isn't the first time I've dislocated a shoulder."

"Oh." That pulled me up short. But given Brooke's grumblings this morning, I shouldn't have been surprised. I tossed the plastic wrapping into the trash. How much worrying over Samuel's well-being during his Green Beret days had fallen on Brooke's young shoulders? Maybe that was why she seemed so mature for her age.

"I already did two of those outings last week. If I need help with the third one that's scheduled, I can ask Wyatt." He neared, setting his glass down.

"And if Wyatt can't help?"

"It's a deacons' outing Brother Buford arranged. I know he'll be fine with postponing it if we need to." He tucked his hand into the pocket of his jacket.

Peekaboo!

Who knew font could be sexy? I swallowed, casting my attention out the window above the sink. "Okay." When Chewie arrived, I planned on spending a lot of time with him in the backyard and giving myself space from Samuel. I turned for the refrigerator, opening the freezer and pulling out a Tupperware container of gumbo to defrost for dinner. At least Samuel wasn't being bullheaded about rescheduling that last excursion.

Questions about Brooke and her upbringing resurfaced in my thoughts, momentarily pushing away concerns over his business. "Brooke is really great."

"She is."

Not wanting my expression to give away my scheming objective, I returned to the pantry, coming face-to-face with Paul Newman again. This time on the label of a jar of spaghetti sauce. His smile seemed skeptical of my espionage skills. *Shut up, Paul. I need answers.* I turned the bottle, hiding his smirk. "I couldn't help but notice the photo album at your place didn't have any pictures of her mom."

A beat of quiet passed. "That's what I was going to talk to you about. But then Brooke showed up."

I grasped a bag of rice I would cook later and closed the door.

He stood, motionless, the heaviness of the coming conversation weighing down the air. "There's no easy way to say or sugarcoat this." One side of his bottom lip reeled inward.

Oh, gracious. Not his lip roll. I steeled myself, my breathing shallowing.

"Brooke was the result of a one-night stand."

My grip on the rice tightened, the grains shifting beneath the pressure. I couldn't look him in the eye and instead stared at my hands, disappointment whirling through me. Samuel and I hadn't been together during that time, but still. I'd assumed he'd had a long-term relationship with Brooke's mom similar to what ours had been. Had his life been a string of hookups? My heart thumped at a sluggish tempo.

"Her mom . . ." His exhale conveyed regret. "She wanted to get an abortion."

My eyes flew to his, a chill expanding through my core.

"I talked her out of it." His stare pleaded with mine, as though imploring me to understand the truth. "That's one thing I got right."

I released my hold on the rice, pressing my fingertips to my lips.

The coloring in Samuel's cheeks paled. "During that short period of time, I realized two things." He cupped the back of his neck. "She was motivated by money, and she wasn't going to be a good mother. I told her if the baby was mine, I'd cover the medical bills for her pregnancy. I'd also pay her a lump sum to sign full custody to me." His arm dropped to his side. "She was adamant I was the father. After Brooke was born, we did a cheek swab. The rest is history."

I forced myself to take a measured breath. This all resulted in a plethora of angst and warning flares. He'd only become a Christian three years ago. He'd lived the majority of his life doing what he pleased. Taking pleasure wherever he wanted. He was still sort of new to the faith, and the sinful nature wasn't easily avoided.

And being a Christian didn't mean Jesus controlled our minds like robots. We were free to make choices. Good and bad. I was proof of that. I'd been saved as a child, drifted away from the Lord, and had sunk into temptation. Had willingly given in to sin with Samuel and suffered the consequences. I shifted to the window, gazing past the patio and to the heavens. I had also been overwhelmingly embraced by God when I returned to Him and had reaped the rewards of His love. The pure cleansing of my past.

A past I would never fall back into.

I gripped the edge of the sink, my chin dipping. "The physical relationship we had before . . . was a mistake. One I learned from." Turning my head, I glanced his way. "One I won't be repeating."

His attention slunk to his socked feet, and what appeared to be opposing emotions played across his face. After several seconds, he rubbed his hand through his hair. "Despite what you now know, I haven't led a tawdry life of sleeping around."

The dark musings over Samuel's promiscuity gave way to relief . . . and guilt. I had presumed the worst of him. And if the worst had been true, it hadn't been my place to decree judgment. Who was I to pick up a stone against Samuel? Closing my eyes, I pinched the bridge of my nose, sifting through this new information. Had the repercussions of Brooke's birth scarred Samuel from becoming deeply involved with other women?

"I don't plan on crossing that line again until I'm married." His direct gaze made his future intentions clear. His declaration assuring me we were on the same page.

My knees buckled a hair. *Conner and Mason gave their approval.*

A hard and fast knock rapped at the front door. Repeatedly.

I exhaled. Rescued by the angry woodpecker.

Glancing out the front picture window, sure enough, I spied Mama's car. I opened the door to find her holding the hat that had been knocked from Samuel's head the previous evening. Her other hand held the end of a leash I had not brought to her house. Which meant she had come into my home at some point to retrieve it. Which also meant she had probably snooped through my things in the process.

Chewie whined and clamored at my feet. I picked him up, soothing him. "Thank you for bringing him home."

Mama followed me into the living room, her attention landing on Samuel. "I hear you're going to live."

"I am." He stood next to the table. Thankfully he'd zipped his hoodie, sparing us a lecture from Mama on the depravity of tattoos.

Mama handed Samuel his hat. "Well . . . I'm glad to hear it. And thanks again for fixing my pipe."

"You're welcome," he said. "Have you noticed any other leaks?" A slight trace of amusement dusted his tone.

"No." Mama's brows lifted. "Everything seems fine now." Her attention bounced to me and back to him again.

Had I missed something? I unhooked Chewie and set him down. Not one to discriminate, he growled equally at Mama and Samuel before heading for his water bowl in the kitchen.

Mama retreated for the front door.

"Would you like to stay for coffee?" I moved past Samuel, putting the leash on the edge of the kitchen counter. "I was about to make some."

"No, I've got things to do." Her eagerness and the glint of mischief in her eyes were not comforting.

I narrowed my stare at her. "Like?"

A slow and wicked grinch-smile unfurled from her lips. "That buzzard down the street's in for a surprise when he takes my paper in the morning."

"Mama," I warned. Images of all sorts of unruly tactics

entered my mind. Nets dropping from trees, the use of fireworks.

She waved me off. "Mama, nothing."

"I'm not bailing you out of jail."

Samuel snickered.

I shot him a look.

"Psh, you won't have to," Mama said. "All I'm doing is
switching out my paper after it's delivered for an old one."

"Oh. Well, that's not—"

"An old newspaper with dog poop smeared between the
pages."

32

FOR THE REST OF THE DAY, Chewie maintained a disdainful eye on Samuel. After an early dinner we'd settled in the living room. Samuel on the sofa with towels stuffed beneath his wounded arm, and Chewie and I on the love seat out of biting distance. Pat and Vanna had just bid us good night, and I was ready to turn my sights on the Green Beret book. I was on my third and final checkout period with the library, so time was ticking. And since Samuel had seen the book long ago, there was no point in hiding it.

Samuel moved, adjusting the ice pack on his shoulder.

Chewie growled.

"Chewie." I tapped his nose with my fingertip. "This is all your fault to begin with."

"I'd say the fault mostly falls to your mom."

"You mean her busted pipe."

"I'm ninety-five percent certain she rigged it to leak."

"What?" My disbelief punctured the air. Chewie startled, jumping to the floor with a yelp. "Is that why y'all exchanged that look before?"

"It is, and I'd appreciate it if you didn't say anything to her. It's taken over twenty years to win her somewhat-approval."

293

First Conner and Mason, and now Mama. *Lord, I don't know if I'm ready for this.*

Samuel's phone rang. He pulled it from his jacket pocket and glanced at the screen. A tiny smile sprouted. He silenced the call and set his phone on the couch, facedown.

A knot looped in my gut. If it was a call that brought him happiness, why hadn't he answered? Chewie hopped up on the far edge of the sofa, opposite from Samuel. He circled twice and curled into a furry ball.

Samuel stood, moving around the coffee table and heading for the kitchen. "Do you mind flipping on the game?"

Ugh. It was Monday night in America, which meant one sport in particular. "I do mind."

The opening and closing of the refrigerator filled the silence. He returned without the ice pack and eased back to sitting.

Peekaboo!

Regardless if he was ready for a shirt tomorrow, he was wearing one.

"Why do you mind?" He adjusted his sling, allowing a glimpse of his bruising. Blues and purples had begun replacing the reds. "You love football."

"I pretended to love football."

His head pulled back with a blink.

I gave one full, haughty nod.

"What else did you pretend to like back then?"

"Boxing, Adam Sandler movies, *The Sopranos.*"

His lips parted farther and farther with the list. "You sure spit those out fast."

I shrugged, unrepentant. "But since you're injured and everything, I'll make an exception." I reached for the remote and found the game's channel. I opened the book to the Post-it marking my place and tuned the television out.

"You reading that book is about the hottest thing I've ever seen."

A tingle ran along the back of my neck. "I think we need to institute a no-flirting rule during your convalescence here."

"What about a pro-flirting rule? Or a pro-kissing rule?"

Gnawing my lower lip, I shot him a glare and swerved my attention to the book. I finished a chapter on part of the training Green Berets go through and glanced at Samuel.

His heated gaze was already on me. Or perhaps it had never left. The greens and browns of his eye revealed quiet intelligence. Intensity. Desire.

Gracious. The tingle graduated to a full-blown zing and blazed a path to my middle. *Distraction! We need a distraction!* I peered at the open pages. "Can you tell me how you did on the STAR navigation course?" The course required candidates to navigate solo through woods and streams. In the dead of night, with no illumination. They had to carry seventy pounds of gear and reach predetermined points using basic tools like a paper map and compass, and all under a time constraint.

"Four for four on the initial course."

"Impressive." And it was. In the military world, that was considered acing it.

"I'd like to impress you in other ways."

Heat flushed my skin, and I tugged the neck of my top. Instead of a hot flash, I was having a zing flash. Or really, a Samuel flash. *Pull it together! Look unaffected!* "I . . . I've read in here that Special Forces soldiers earn extra money for each language they learn. How many do you know?"

"Four. Spanish, Pashto, Arabic."

"And . . ."

Mischief creased the corner of his eye. "I can read lips."

My brain flipped back to the conversations I'd had with others when Samuel had been in lip-reading sight. Church, the business crawl. *Gasp!* Had I been within view when I'd made the comment about a scorned woman forking him in the eye?

"I did everything I could to make the most money for Brooke; my mom, who was caring for her; the future. Each language added to my pay, as did earning additional qualifications, like airborne and scuba. And then there were reenlistment bonuses, which increased over the years as I became a senior SF soldier with specialized skills."

Speaking military lingo should be counted as its own language. And probably the sexiest. "What was the hardest part of your career with the army?"

He fidgeted with the zipper at the hem of his jacket. "Missing special occasions with Brooke."

"That photo album at your place proves otherwise."

"Most of those parties were done after the fact. I've missed being there for her actual birthdays and holidays more times than I was there. We just celebrated them when I got back from deployment. Or before I left." He frowned at the zipper. "Once I had to leave during her piano recital."

The heaviness he projected permeated me. My eyes dipped to the book in my lap, then resettled on him. "Do you think Brooke ever worried you wouldn't come back?"

He allowed a tight nod.

"I'm grateful she didn't have to experience losing you." That she hadn't had to go through what Conner and Mason had. I hugged my arms to my body, the earlier warmth quickly seeping away. Anguish, thick and prickly, pierced my core.

"Losing their father had to be extremely difficult for Conner and Mason." Samuel leaned closer, compassion in his features. "How old were they?"

"Nine and eight," I rasped. I cleared my throat, only to have it clog again. "The night of Mark's funeral, both boys were in bed with me. Conner had cried himself to sleep on one side, but Mason was still awake." I'd been smoothing the hair across his forehead. Mason's tears had soundlessly streamed, and I had been struggling to withhold my own. To be strong for him.

His soft and clammy little-boy hand had reached, touching my cheek. "He whispered to me, 'Don't die.'"

My vision swam, but I could make out Samuel's hand on my knee. Feel the pressure of his reassuring touch. I rubbed my eyes. "I've never told anyone that."

"Thank you for trusting me with it."

Taking a cleansing breath, I pushed to my feet and headed for the dining table. The last twenty-four hours were catching up to me. The stress, the lack of sleep. I took a long sip of water, collecting myself.

Samuel had picked up my book and was reading the back cover. The pregame show had started its highlights on the teams about to play.

I resumed my spot, tucking my legs under me. "So if you hadn't gone into the army, do you think you would have started this outdoor adventure business?"

"I don't know. Maybe eventually." He balanced the book on his thigh. "What about you? If you hadn't had to start cleaning houses for a living, do you think you would have tried selling your products?"

"Possibly." I cracked my pinky knuckle and continued on with each finger. With Mark's help, it probably would have seemed more achievable. And with his income, I wouldn't have had the financial pressures I'd had all these years. The necessity to avoid risk.

"You have the perfect opportunity to pursue it now. Especially with people clamoring for them."

"Clamoring?" I scoffed.

"People at the business crawl, church. I can read lips, remember?" One of his brows quirked, lifting his patch a smidge. "And I'm guessing you've had people ask about buying them when I wasn't around."

I burrowed into the couch, hugging a throw pillow to my

stomach. "I can't do something big like that on my own. I can work and do what I know and save and be—"

"Comfortable and unhappy?"

My molars clenched like a vise.

"Between Kate and I, we have the know-how and means to help. Even your boys want to be a part of it."

I squeezed the pillow. "How do you know that?"

"They told me when we were fishing." A slight grin escaped, as though he knew Conner and Mason were his trump cards.

Grumble, grumble.

"Everyone wants to help you."

"Why do *you* want to help? Because you feel beholden? You don't owe me anything."

"I want to help because I think it'll make you happy."

I gave an empty laugh. "So if I start selling my cleaning products, that's going to make me happy?"

"If you start selling your products and dating me."

I flicked my eyes heavenward.

He studied his hand, all joking fleeing his expression. "Somehow, I'm going to earn Conner and Mason's approval. Show my respect for their dad. Ensure they know my intentions are honorable." He met my gaze, and it was more than a look. A pledge. "I know it'll take time. Even more so with them living out of state, but I'm determined."

The moment stretched, the TV noise fading, my apprehensions dissolving too. Something shifted between us. Or maybe it was my heart moving, opening.

33

THE NEXT DAY ROLLED BY like a quintessential Mardi Gras parade. Slow moments mixed in with spurts of frenzy.

Samuel had stayed the previous night in Conner's bedroom, and I'd woken him every three hours for his symptom check. I slept in my own bed for those in-between hours, and it was a deep, sweet sleep. Even with Samuel injured, it had been the safest I'd felt in my house. Not that I lived in a crime-rampant area, but still. It had been nice.

We spent the first part of the day at his dad's house, where I'd cleaned like usual and ensured an ice pack appeared on Samuel's shoulder at regular intervals. Teddy hadn't seemed the least bit fazed by the accident, or the two of us arriving together. He'd simply handed me his smudged glasses for their cleaning.

Samuel coerced Teddy into doing his physical therapy exercises, and I made a simple lunch for the three of us, using the groceries Wyatt had dropped off the day before. With Teddy taken care of, Samuel and I went to his place. Against his objections, I laundered his bedding and dirty clothes, and dusted and vacuumed his townhouse. The two mystery rooms on the third floor turned out to be an office and Brooke's room. Unlike the rest of the dwelling, the latter had been decorated in loving detail.

We ate an early dinner and washed the dishes, Samuel help-ing as best he could. With the forty-eight-hour concussion watch over, it was no longer a necessity to stick to his side. And what a nice side it'd been. Hiding my reluctance, I'd left him and retreated home to see to Chewie, shower, and obsess about the predicament I now found myself in. I had fallen for my cheater ex. *Good grief.* I was the walking title for a *Dr. Phil* episode.

Wearing dog-printed pajama pants and a matching tank top, I sat on the sofa with my phone, my finger hovering over the tracking app on Conner and Mason. I hadn't checked their puls-ing dots or spoken to them since before the mishap on Sunday. Instead of finding their locations, I switched to texting, sending a "checking in" group message. "See," I said to Chewie. "I'm getting better with this."

Chewie cast an unconvinced look as if to say, *"You're not fooling anyone, lady. If they don't respond in two minutes, you'll be on that app."*

They both replied before paranoia propelled me into stalker-mode. Which meant they'd responded in ten minutes. Conner was at work, and Mason was at the campus cafeteria eating. My phone rang, Samuel's name appearing on the screen.

Giddiness twirled within. I composed myself for a neutral greeting, putting him on speaker. "Hello."

"I miss you."

My heart swooned. "It's only been a few hours."

"Seems longer."

Chewie rolled his eyes and headed for one of the throw pil-lows on the couch, sticking his head behind the cushion and retrieving a Milk-Bone he'd buried there. I took the phone off speaker, held it to my ear, and stood, too antsy to be still. I glanced out the windows along the back of the house. The sun had long set, darkness shadowing the yard.

"I know things between us need to go back to how they were

before the accident, but going cold turkey after being together the past two days . . . well, it's kind of harsh."

I huffed a laugh, straightening the centerpiece on the dining table. "You want to negotiate a detox plan?"

"Yes. Since I'm used to a twenty-four-hour-a-day dose of you, I think I should be gently weaned from your presence."

My reflection in the decorative mirror hanging on the wall revealed a woman with a huge goofy grin. My smile faded, a nervous gurgle bubbling in my stomach. "Conner and Mason gave their approval . . . for us to date."

Silence.

"Samuel?"

"I'm here." Astonishment infused his tone. "When did they tell you?"

"On the drive to the airport after their weekend visit."

A beat ticked by. "So you've had time to process their consent." It wasn't a question but a statement. As though he were talking to himself. A gust of his breath carried over the line. "I . . . um, I need a minute, okay?"

"Sure."

Beep-beep.

I looked at the phone. *Seriously?* He'd hung up on me? The earlier gurgle in my gut hardened, my ribs growing tight. That was not the response I'd expected. I'd waved the red cape and . . . nothing? Had Samuel 1.0 reemerged that fast?

A light knock struck at the front door. Chewie leapt from the sofa, yapping. "Fabulous," I sighed. If it was a Girl Scout, she'd be in for a record-breaking sale because I was in need of a cookie-therapy session. I flipped on the front porch light and peered through the peephole. My breath halted.

Samuel.

I opened the door. Chewie surged forward, sniffed Samuel's tennis shoes, and returned to the couch, gobbling the crumbs from his treat.

There Samuel stood, in the red flannel shirt I'd helped him into that morning. No words passed between us, but a very different dynamic did. An understanding that seemed to have its own silent language.

The space around us thickened with awareness. With possibility.

He gestured toward the street. "I'd already taken an Uber here when I called."

"You must think highly of your negotiation skills." I crossed my arms, warding off a chill from the night's temperature drop.

"I do."

I had been imagining revealing the boys' approval akin to waving a red cape at a bull. But the expression on his face, the energy charging the air. It was like a river that had been held back for ages by a dam, and that dam had just been blown to smithereens. The barrier removed for the waters to surge, unhindered.

Never taking his searing gaze off mine, he pocketed his phone.

The backs of my knees tingled, and I held on to the door's frame for balance.

He edged forward. "Will you let me take you out tomorrow night?"

I nodded.

Briefly, one edge of his mouth pulled up. He shifted again, pausing inches away. "And tonight, will you let me kiss you senseless?"

The knee-tingles flared to zinging. Again, I nodded.

He angled down, closing the distance.

The scent of pine and soap and the potential of a new future swirled around me. And then an irrational thought burst through, blurting free before I could stop it. "I don't have a uterus."

A crease formed between his brows, and he eased back. "What?"

I covered my face, my voice gushing through my fingers. "The

302

last time you kissed me, I had a uterus. But since then, I had to have a partial hysterectomy. So no more babies are coming out of me."

He laughed softly. "I hadn't planned on having more kids. And if we're disclosing things, you should know I'm missing an eye. The last time you kissed me, I had both eyes."

Stars above. I could feel my budding smile.

His hand lifted, cupping the side of my face, his thumb brushing my cheek. And then his lips were on mine, warm and gentle and unhurried. A slight trace of familiarity flowed in our rhythm, but there was something more. A maturity in his touch. Everything within me yielded to him. My mouth, my breaths, my thoughts . . . my heart. I swayed. He slid his hand from my face, down my neck, trailing across my shoulder, steadying me. I rose on tiptoe, gliding my hands behind his neck, mindful of his injury. His good arm wrapped around me, the heat of his palm pressing my lower back.

For a second, we ever so slightly broke away. I sucked in a faint breath and closed the gap, angling into his side to avoid his wound, and becoming lost in him, the security of his hold. How could I feel so weightless and yet so anchored? Like I was a balloon on a string, tied to him.

My fingers flexed against his upper back, grabbing fistfuls of flannel, my body bending to his. Long-buried cravings resurfaced, and I found myself both grateful for and loathing the obstacle of his sling between us. He held me tighter, his arm banding across my back and curving around my side, the warmth from his skin burning through the thin cotton of my top, his fingers splaying across my ribs.

He ended the kiss, resting his forehead against mine, our chests rising and falling in sync. "I don't want to leave, but I know I need to."

My heart swooned for a whole other reason. Twentysomething Samuel wouldn't have abandoned this opportunity. But the man standing before me, who looked at me like I was a massive chunk of his world, was exhibiting his faith by showing his respect for me. For us. For God.

I loosened my grasp on his shirt, clarity making its way through the hormone-haze. *Sakes alive.* What if Mama had driven by and witnessed me looking like a human sling on his other arm? I took a half step back. "How's your shoulder?"

He rubbed the two-day growth on his jaw, a roguish smile spreading. "I guarantee I feel no pain."

"Do you want a ride home?"

His stare roamed from my eyes to my bare feet.

My cheeks flushed, realization shooting through me that I was dressed for bed. I grabbed a sweater from the coatrack by the front door, slipping it on. "I'll change clothes first."

His Adam's apple bobbed, and he withdrew a step. "And maybe bring Chewie."

34

I WAS ON A HUMDINGER OF A DATE with a Green Beret. It was the next night, and I donned the same red dress from the business crawl. My only other feasible option had been my funeral dress, and since it had witnessed people mourning, it didn't have that fun, first-date vibe. I was beginning to realize I needed to loosen the purse strings and invest in another nice frock. And possibly a new pair of heels.

Samuel had arrived at my house promptly at seven. He'd held a bouquet of crimson calla lilies and wore a dark navy suit with a white button-down shirt. No tie and no arm sling. At my objection to the sling, he promised the doctor he'd seen that morning had deemed his shoulder injury on the minor side. The sling would be worn for sleeping but was optional for low-activity daytime use. He'd also been given permission to drive again. I'd placed the flowers in water, while Chewie had growled at Samuel's shoes.

We'd dined at the Palace Café, our table on the second floor, overlooking Canal Street. We people-watched and admired the red streetcars that ran a separate line from the one that passed before Beignets & Books. He held my hand across the table between courses of fried crab cakes, rich seafood gumbo, and tender filet mignon with roasted shiitake mushrooms. We effortlessly talked about our day, our kids, and our parents, and I discovered we had more in common now than when we were younger. The finale to our decadent meal featured our waiter making the restaurant's famous flaming bananas Foster tableside.

The dining part of our date I had known about so I could dress accordingly, but now I found myself in the Testosterone Truck headed to an undisclosed location. I held my clutch on my lap. "We better not be going to your tiny house in the swamp."

He chuckled, never taking his attention from the road. "I promise your heels won't hit any dirt." Shadows and light splayed across his masculine profile, his freshly shaven jaw. "*Tiny house* doesn't sound very manly. I think of it as more of a camping house."

"Did you say *doll house*? That does sound more like it."

Delight crinkled the lines at the corner of his eye. "Is my camping house really that bad?"

I unfastened and fastened the magnetic clasp on my purse. *Click, clack.* "No." The reluctance in my tone made him smile. And what a fabulous smile he had. I stopped torturing my clutch. "Your *teeny-tiny* house is actually nice."

"Nice enough that at some point in the future, and under the right circumstances, you wouldn't mind staying there for a weekend, every once in a while?"

I veered my gaze to him, flutters erupting within, and fidgeted with the clasp again. *Click, clack.* Surely he hadn't bought that little dwelling with me in mind. He'd purchased it for his business. But thinking back, his camping house did have the same color palette as my home's interior. As well as similar plumbing and light fixtures. *Ridiculous!* It was all coincidence.

One of the entrances to City Park came into view. Brick columns flanked the road, their tops connected by an arched, iron sign. He flipped on the blinker and turned, bringing us into the thirteen-hundred-acre sanctuary and land of majestic live oaks. Lampposts lit the way, highlighting the trees closest to the street, their massive branches dripping with thick moss.

"But that reminds me," he said. "Would it be okay if I asked Conner and Mason to go fishing one morning when they're visiting next week?"

We crossed a small bridge over Bayou Metairie.

I scraped my bottom lip between my teeth. Samuel alone with the boys. I trusted him with their safety, but . . . was that too big a step? *Click, clack.* Was I overthinking? No doubt the boys would love to go. "What about your arm?"

"If there's any heavy lifting I can't handle, they can do it."

"Won't they need fishing licenses? And extra-strong life jackets?"

His grin revived. "I'll take care of it. I just wanted to check with you first." He braked for a stop sign. Before us lay the entrance for Carousel Gardens, an amusement park nestled among the trees. "What do you think?"

Unexpected excitement pushed my overanalyzing to the background. "I think this has been one of the best nights I've had in a long time."

He winked and pulled into a parking slot. "And I haven't even kissed you at the top of the Ferris wheel yet."

I mock scoffed. "I said nothing about kissing tonight. I only agreed to a date."

"You forget my amazing negotiation skills."

Hand in hand, we walked underneath the oaks, my stilettos clipping over brick pavers. Lights from the Ladybug Roller Coaster and bumper cars added a festive ambiance, along with the laughter of children and adults. Samuel's thumb dipped, rubbing mine.

I hadn't realized how much I'd missed this. This connection with someone. This open show of closeness. The old Samuel had rarely shown affection in public. When he'd held my hand during dinner tonight, it had been a lovely surprise. Another thing I hadn't liked about him before had changed. I couldn't help but smile.

Our steps slackened as we approached the enclosed, historic carousel anchoring the park. Golden light poured from the wraparound windows of its protective structure, illuminating the stained-glass transoms. Inside, ancient wooden horses, giraffes, and camels passed, mirrors sparkling at the carousel's core. Several sets of forest-green French doors had been propped open, tinkling music floating out.

Despite the numerous hurricanes that had pummeled this area the past hundred years, this carousel had withstood them. She'd been bruised and battered, but she'd returned with the help of others and still stood triumphant. Maybe God had held her up during the worst storms, provided her with the support she'd needed to thrive again . . . like He had with me.

A cool breeze rustled through, as though God were nodding. *Thank You, Lord.* I breathed in His goodness and rubbed my arms against the chill.

Samuel shrugged out of his coat, the effort not seeming to hurt his arm, and draped it over my shoulders, feathering a kiss to the side of my head.

"Thank you." His jacket engulfed me, and I pinched the front closed to keep it from slipping off.

His hand soothed up and down my back. "You're welcome."

Beyond the carousel sat our destination: the Ferris wheel. A rainbow of lights ran along its frame. Being an uneventful Wednesday night, we walked right onto the ride and took our seats on the hard bench, the cab rocking as the conductor secured the bar over us.

I threw a nervous glance at Samuel's shoulder.

"I'm fine." He wrapped his good arm around me, drawing me near.

I crossed my legs and snuggled against him. In light of his healing injury, and the fact that we were dressed up, we'd decided to stick to the Ferris wheel and one of the sleighs on the carousel.

Up we went, our passenger car slightly swinging as it rose above the canopy of the trees. The land devoted to City Park stretched before us. At the pinnacle of the wheel, in the far distance, downtown New Orleans shone, the white roof of the Superdome unmissable.

Samuel's large hand slid across my bare knee.

Zing-a-ling-a-ding-dong!

The warmth from his touch chased away the coolness in the air and the need for his jacket. His fingers traced my kneecap in measured, lazy sweeps. Every nerve ending beneath my skin sat at attention, as though my knee were a telegraph machine, and his stroke transmitted electrical messages through my body, awakening every inch.

I needed clarity. I needed to know more about Samuel before I got carried away into this relationship any further. *Think! Think!*

The ride swept us down and around again, our car swaying, knocking us closer. I grabbed the safety bar and strove to recall one of the questions I'd thought of before. "I have something to ask that may seem out of the blue."

His fingers ceased weaving their enchantment. "Okay."

"The other day, you said you hadn't been involved with anyone since Brooke's birth." The wheel continued its rotation, squeals pealing from the occupants above us as they purposely rocked their car.

"I didn't want anyone else taking away attention from Brooke. My time with her was limited as it was."

That was a long span without companionship. Had he craved someone to share the burdens of life with like I had? Especially considering the stressful duties he'd had as a soldier? I released my hold on the bar, returning my arm to the shelter of his jacket.

"What about you?" His fingers tapped my leg. "Other than worrying about your boys' reaction, why haven't you dated?"

"I guess for the same reasons as you. But other than that, I never met anyone I was interested in."

He nuzzled my neck. "Until me."

I laughed, straightening from his hold and facing him with brows raised. "You may not know this because you're still sort of new to Christianity, but the Lord loves a humble heart."

"He also loves a thankful heart." He tucked a strand of hair behind my ear, his caress lingering. "And I've definitely got a lot to be thankful for." The tenderness in his expression overwhelmed me.

Hope, terrifying hope of a true future with him, swelled. I drew in a breath, past my dry throat. "We need to take this slow."

"How slow?" His eye narrowed, flirtation edging up one corner of his mouth. "Do I need to call Brother Buford and tell him we won't be getting married tonight?"

I suppressed a laugh. "You're impossible." The wheel ground to a halt, our position suspended on the top, the world extending before us.

His teasing glint fell away. "I'm impossibly in love with you."

Mylanta. "That's . . . not taking things slow."

"I think you know I'm not a slow kind of guy."

The air thinned, the dark skies pressing in, faint stars twinkling above.

"But I'll try for you." His fingers dipped against my skin, skimming from my earlobe to the side of my neck. "I just wanted to be clear first on how I felt."

And then, true to his word, his lips met mine, reverently, as though asserting his profession of love and his intentions.

35

SAMUEL NOT ONLY HAD AMAZING GUACAMOLE SKILLS, but he also possessed the power of killer corn-and-crab bisque. The next night, he'd cooked dinner at my place, wowing me with his culinary talents yet again.

The evening after that, I kept my standing date with Kate at Beignets & Books, starting our conversation with *"I spent Sunday night at Samuel's, and he spent the next night at mine."* Oh, the reaction that had garnered! Once I had explained, and her eyes had reattached to their sockets, we'd caught up on each other's week. And although it was nice spending time with Kate, I couldn't help but miss Samuel.

Absurd! We'd seen each other every day that week. And hadn't I told him we needed to take things slowly? Plus, I would see him tomorrow. We had plans for a picnic lunch at the lakefront with Brooke and possibly Chewie.

When I got home from Kate's, I found a small teal envelope taped to my front door. Happiness fluttered through me. The note card was similar to the others from Samuel. The alpaca on the front was brown with a daisy tucked behind one ear. I opened the card to Samuel's neat handwriting.

Text YES if you want to see me tonight. Text NO if you want to crush my ego.

I sigh-smiled and unlocked the door.

Chewie danced at my feet, nails clicking frantically across the floor. I set my keys and purse down and fawned over him. "I've only been gone a few hours." After a thorough greeting, he ran to the back door. I turned on the patio lights and followed him out. He darted through his doggie door and onto the grass. A light trace of smoke fragranced the air. Someone's BBQ or fire pit. Though it wasn't cold enough for the latter. I lowered onto one of the chairs and read Samuel's note again.

Every day he was proving he wasn't the man of my past. Case in point, the card in my hand. He'd been making a way to see me. Daily. In our old relationship, I had always felt like I was the one reaching out to him to spend time together.

The old Samuel had never made future plans and had the propensity to disappear on me. Samuel 2.0 was all about arranging dates. For tomorrow, the next week. He'd even lined up an outing months from now, securing us tickets for the Sky Lantern Festival.

Old Samuel had been undependable and disappointing. New Samuel had been steadfast. Dropping everything—several times—to come to my aid. This Samuel paid attention to details about me, like the alpaca cards (though misguided, they still counted), and the outdoor furniture he'd searched for.

Chewie nosed open the screen door Samuel had made for him. *See?* Another detail Samuel had paid attention to.

All of this equaled one frightening truth that kept popping up on me like that gray eyebrow hair. I fell back into the chair's cushion. Chewie jumped onto my lap, sniffing the card. "Oh, Chewie." I ran my fingers through his soft fur. "I think I might be in love with Samuel again."

Chewie looked at me, head cocked, as if to say, *"Might be? Who do you think you're fooling, lady?"*

"This isn't smart." I switched from rubbing Chewie's ear to the back of my neck. "But I don't think I have a choice."

I pulled out my phone and texted *yes*.

⊷——⊷

The next day, my picnic lunch with Samuel, Brooke, and Chewie at the lakefront had gone well. Extremely well. My second impression of Brooke solidified the first. She was kind, observant, and mature compared to other college-aged girls I'd been around. Heck, she held more maturity than Mama.

Conner and Mason flew in that evening, and we had dinner with Mama, who regaled them with Chewie's contribution to the latest battle in her newspaper war.

Sunday, with the boys and Brooke in town, our row at church had expanded. The three teenagers had achieved awkward introductions before taking their seats. Which brought another concern to ponder. Blending our families—*if* it came to that. Emily Miller already sat before us, and Poor Sean Crawford had appeared, narrowing their gap by leaving only one space between him and Emily. *Attaboy, Sean!*

Monday, while I'd been working, Samuel had spent the day with Conner and Mason, making preparations for their fishing trip the next morning. One would have thought it was Christmas Eve with how excited the boys had been that night, even going to bed early.

Tuesday, they'd returned triumphant, and I'd prepared their catch, making blackened redfish for everyone, including Samuel. Despite Conner and Mason having promised to do all the heavy lifting on their excursion, I'd watched Samuel like a hawk for any tells to his shoulder hurting and was relieved to find he did seem fine. We'd sat on the patio, them telling me about their

313

day. All four of the chairs Samuel had gifted were filled, along with my heart.

Thanksgiving Day rolled around. Samuel celebrated the holiday in Baton Rouge at his mom's house with Brooke. The boys and I had hosted Kate, Hayley, and Mama. Samuel and I had texted like two lovestruck teens throughout the day.

Before I could blink, Sunday morning arrived, and I was taking Conner and Mason to the airport. My mama-heart ached the entire drive there, the sensation escalating with hugs goodbye and the inevitable watching them walk away. I managed not to cry, though. A total victory in my book.

I drove home in a brain fog, reasoning they'd return at winter break. They'd be home for a longer stretch of time then too. Regardless of that reassurance, the ache in my heart wouldn't ease. Even though they'd be back, they were getting older, gaining independence. My apron strings stretched farther and farther.

During their visit, they'd mentioned that when home for the semester break, they'd be working at their old jobs and hanging out with friends from high school who'd also be in town. *Ugh.* They'd been preparing me. Slowly snip-snip-snipping those strings. *This is good. How it should be.* This was the circle of life. I squeezed the steering wheel. *Darn you, Simba.*

Pulling up to my house, my spirits lifted at the sight of the Testosterone Truck. It had been five days since I'd seen Samuel. Not that I was counting. Before I could kill the engine, he approached my door, opening it. He wore athletic pants and a plain white cotton tee, and was clean-shaven. The pullover shirt spoke volumes about the recovery of his shoulder.

I moved straight into his embrace, breathing in the scent of his soap and relishing his strong hold around me. The ache that had plagued me this morning dulled. Or at least, lessened to a bearable degree. I slid my arms around his solid frame, pressing the side of my face against him. "Brother Buford would disapprove, but I'm glad you're playing hooky from church."

"I figured you might be a little down with the boys leaving. I'm going to make guacamole and watch a *Star Wars* movie with you."

I straightened with a chuckle. "You must really love me." The words escaped, and I instantly wished them unsaid. My strategy to avoid the *L*-word had gone awry. Though my heart was there, waving a Team Samuel banner, my brain had been keeping a lock on making the declaration.

His hand soothed up my back. "I do."

The earnestness in his gaze was too much to endure, the pressure to verbally return his feelings building. I used the best distraction I could think of. I leaned up on tiptoe and kissed him. "We don't have to watch *Star Wars*, but you do have to make guacamole."

36

THE NEXT SATURDAY, our church held its annual Christmas toy
drive. The sprawling lawn beside the worship center had been
covered in varying jump houses, a petting zoo, a face-painting
station, and food lines serving some of the best jambalaya and
BBQ in town. The entrance fee for the festivities was a toy
donation.

I'd showed up after filling in for Norma with the cleaning
ministry that morning. Norma's mother, who lived in Florida,
had fallen and fractured her hip, the poor thing. After arriving
at church, I'd found Samuel and Brooke—who'd driven down
for the weekend—at the edge of the event, under a pop-up
tent. I'd joined in with helping sort the donations into bins
according to age.

With the function winding down, our duties had shifted to
merely keeping an eye on the toys until they could be stored
inside. Brooke had been noticeably quiet and had excused herself to the bathroom a few minutes ago.

Samuel and I sat on folding chairs, people-watching. Christmas music piped in through speakers, and a cool breeze carried
the scent of grilling burgers. Children with painted butterfly
and tiger faces ran wild, their harried parents trailing.

"I've been thinking," Samuel said.

I adjusted the thin red sweater over my scrubs. "Famous last words."

He gave a soft chuckle.

Nearby, the dinosaur-themed bounce house had been handed over to a group of teenage boys who'd waited patiently for a kid-free go at it. They slammed into the net walls and each other, laughing. I fidgeted with a button on my sweater. The mom in me yearned to move closer and urge caution.

"I'd like to take you to North Carolina in the spring. That way you could see Conner and Mason midsemester."

I slowly turned toward him.

"I've got a ton of frequent flier miles I need to use before they expire. I figured we could straddle it over a weekend so the boys don't miss their classes, and you don't miss as many workdays."

Samuel 2.0 had struck again. So many times, I'd wanted to do a quick trip to see the boys. But there had been blockades. The cost of flight tickets had been hard to look past. And the thought of driving that far alone hadn't sat right either. Appreciation expanded through my chest, curling around my heart. "Thank you. That sounds amazing."

One side of his mouth pulled up. "I'd like to show them some of my favorite hiking trails and waterfalls I discovered when I was stationed there." He stared at his clasped hands in his lap. "And I thought you might like to visit Mark's parents."

Gracious. Would Samuel want to meet them? I hadn't considered that whole dynamic. How would Mark's parents feel about me moving on?

A bleating goat garnered my attention. A little girl was trying to hug the animal. On the other side of the temporary fencing, I caught sight of Emily Miller. And holding her hand was Poor Sean Crawford. I gasped and reached across Brooke's empty seat to tap Samuel's forearm.

He followed my line of vision. "Ah, Sean finally made a move."

"Or maybe she did." I couldn't help but smile.

Samuel's phone rang. He fished it from his jeans and checked the screen. A shadow fell over his face.

"Everything okay?"

He silenced the call and returned the device to his pocket. "Yeah."

Muscles knotted across my shoulders. Everything was most definitely not okay. "Are you sure?" My mind flashed back to a few weeks ago when he'd received that mystery call at my house. Though that one had elicited a smile.

His hazel gaze met mine, along with a guardedness that the old Samuel had used too often.

My throat thickened. Would I ever be free of the past?

He glanced at a container holding footballs and soccer balls, and rubbed his palms down his thighs, as though gearing himself up.

Brooke approached, retaking her seat between us. "I'm not feeling well."

Samuel extended the back of his hand to her forehead.

She dodged him like a true teenager in public. "It's not that kind of sickness. It's cramps." She hugged her purse to her middle. "Can you take me home?"

"Oh." Samuel winced. "I'm supposed to help pack up once this ends. But that won't be for another thirty minutes or so."

Brooke slouched in her chair.

I nudged a bin containing arts-and-crafts kits with the toe of my tennis shoe. "What about your shoulder?"

"It's fine," he said. "And if I need to lift anything heavy, I'll use my good arm."

Part of me wanted to stick around to ensure he didn't hurt himself. But one glance at Brooke's miserable appearance trumped that. "I'll take you home," I said to her.

A smile of relief smoothed her worry lines. "Thank you."

The drive to Samuel's consisted of a conversation focused on the evil perils of menstruation. I'd shared my streetcar–white jeans tragedy. Brooke revealed a similar story, involving being in the midst of a final exam. I'd advised her of the remedies I'd used for the worst days of my periods. The Advil she'd known about but not the heating pad. I couldn't help but feel fortunate for this time with her. That I finally had someone to impart some womanly wisdom to.

I pulled to the curb at Samuel's townhouse and found an old, unfamiliar Ford Taurus parked behind Brooke's car in the driveway. The dark tint on the rear windshield peeled from one corner.

"Oh no," Brooke muttered. Her lips flattened into a white slash.

I scanned the area. "Do you know that car?"

"Yes," she sighed. "It's my mom's."

My stomach tightened.

She reached for the door handle and hesitated.

"If you don't feel safe with her, you can come to my place." I did not want to meet Samuel's ex today. Or ever. But especially not in my scrubs after I'd been cleaning all morning. And especially not after indulging in jambalaya and corn bread.

"Thanks, but it's okay. She's not dangerous, just . . ." Brooke's chin dipped. "She's not here for me. She breezes in and out, and Dad just gives in to her. Never tells her no."

Never tells her no to what? Seeking comfort? Money? Needing a guacamole fix?

The driver's door on the Taurus opened, and a woman unfolded.

The bikini tramp.

An icy fist of dread punched through my core.

I blinked. And blinked again, my brain refusing to register the reality before me. Had Samuel hooked up with his old coffeehouse coworker years after we'd broken up? It was a logical scenario. But one that seemed too endurable to be true. "How . . ." I struggled to breathe. "How old are you?"

"Twenty-one. Why?"

The other shoe finally dropped with an echoing thud. Time slowed, my thoughts twisting in a haze, my future shifting. "I thought . . . you were nineteen." My feet trembled, the sensation moving to my calves. "You're a sophomore."

"I started college late." She cracked open her door. "Thanks again for the ride. And the talk. It was nice, you know, having a real mom to talk to. My Meemaw . . . well, she's a grandma. It's not the same." She exited, purse hanging from her hand, nearly skimming the lawn.

Oh, how I wanted to soak in her sentiment. The genuine foundation we'd built in a brief span of time. But it had all been for nothing. The trembling seized my knees and escalated to full shaking.

Brooke's mom lifted her hand in greeting. Her pink-and-white striped shirt raised with the movement, revealing a flat tummy. Of course. Did she still own that bikini from the photo? If so, she could probably fit in it.

The shaking overtook my upper legs. This was the woman Samuel had cheated on me with. And regretfully, I could see why. She was beautiful. Her long legs stretched from beneath a short, flirty skirt. Judging by the perfect waves in her light brown hair, she'd taken her time in fixing it. Her makeup too.

Brooke trudged to the front door of Samuel's townhome, but her mom proceeded toward me. *No. No, no, no.* Nausea twisted in my gut. Would she remember me from the few times I'd visited Samuel at work way back then? I eased my foot off the brake pedal, rolling forward. The woman hurried her pace, waving harder and bending to peer through the window. *Crud.* I stopped the SUV from advancing.

She tapped the glass.

Sweat broke across my skin. *Lord, please help me hold it together.* I pressed the switch on my door panel, lowering the passenger-side window.

"I'm Chloe. Brooke's mom." The fragrance of cotton candy floated in with her words. Her manicured nails grasped onto the doorframe like talons. No wedding band on her ring finger.

I swallowed against my lunch threatening to reappear. "Hi."

"Are you a friend of Samuel's?" The delivery of her question held immature jealousy. Did she harbor hope for a relationship with Samuel? Had I been in her shoes, I would have asked, *"How do you know my daughter?"*

All I could manage was a nod.

She scrutinized me for half a beat.

Pulse thrashing in my ears, I swallowed again, tasting bile with a hint of baked beans. "I have to go." My voice wobbled. I rolled forward, and Chloe removed her hold. With great effort, I maintained the speed limit until I reached the stop sign at the corner. I glanced in the rearview mirror just in time to witness Chloe walking through Samuel's door without hesitation. I hit the gas.

Several blocks from Samuel's place, the trembling overtook my arms and hands. I pulled to the curb between a span of houses. Chloe's perfume lingered. Strangling. My clammy fingers fumbled at the window switch, finally managing to roll the glass down. Cool air swept in. Never again could I eat cotton candy. Or smell it without thinking of this moment. Of the blindsided betrayal tumbling through me.

When Samuel got home in a little while, Chloe, no doubt, would be there. How many times since he'd reentered my life had they seen each other? Had been alone in his home? *"He never tells her no."* Intimate imaginings of them flashed in my mind. Even if nothing had happened recently, they *had* been together. My stomach lurched. How could I possibly trust him now?

Lunch jolted its way up. I shoved my door open and heaved, grateful I'd parked over a storm drain. I wiped my mouth on my sleeve and straightened.

Why hadn't he told me? He had to have known I'd find out. What felt like a honed blade pressed against my heart. A precise cut. Long and deep. Everything I'd held inside, the fears, insecurities, the future I'd dared to hope for. They all gushed out, leaving me exposed and vulnerable.

I closed my eyes against the pounding in my head. Samuel had a baby with Chloe. When I'd been having a miscarriage and mourning the loss of my baby, Chloe had wanted to abort hers. *How is that fair, God?* Resting my head against the steering wheel, I blubbered a prayer to Jesus. Poured out incoherent words of anguish and disappointment until I just sat there. Exhausted and numb.

⟨⟩

A couple of hours later found me at home, hair still wet from my shower, and on the sofa with Chewie. I lay on my side, Chewie's body curled against mine. The quietness surrounding me was a parallel opposite to the tornado revolving through my mind. Thoughts whipping like shrapnel. I should have known better. Should have trusted my original instincts to distance from him.

My phone rang from the coffee table. I tensed. I wasn't ready to talk to Samuel. Wasn't sure I'd ever be. Glancing at the screen, my weary muscles relaxed. It was Sydney Dupré, the church secretary. I sat up and answered, forcing normality.

"Hi," Sydney said. "I'm sorry to bother you."

"It's no bother."

"I'd hoped to catch you at the toy drive, but . . . well, Norma's moving to Florida to care for her mom. Permanently."

"Oh." *Just when this day couldn't get rottener.*

"Apparently, she'd been contemplating the move, and this accident decided it for her." Concern edged Sydney's voice.

I pulled in a breath and released it. "So that leaves three volunteers for the cleaning ministry."

"Yes."

This did not bode well. The cleaning ministry had a history of lacking volunteers. For years now, the need had been broadcasted in the weekly church bulletin to no avail. "I'll fill in for her on the schedule." It wasn't like I'd landed a Saturday client yet. And I wouldn't be spending my weekends with Samuel anymore. A dull ache throbbed in my chest.

We ended our call as a knock rapped on the front door. Chewie leapt from the couch, barking. My ribs squeezed. I knew it was Samuel. Mama was at an all-day bingo binge, and Kate was covering the hostess shift at Beignets & Books.

I'd anticipated his appearance. Especially since I'd ignored his calls and texts. The first thing I'd done when I'd arrived home was close the curtains on the front picture window and ensure the side gate was locked.

Knock-knock-knock. "Julia," he called.

My vision blurred at hearing his voice, my disposition vacillating between hurt and anger. I remained anchored to the sofa. Chewie must have recognized Samuel's voice. He quieted, staring at me, his head tipping left and right, as though trying to understand my unusual response.

"Please let me in." Samuel's voice carried through the door's crack. "Let me explain." Desperation radiated in his tone.

I sucked in my cheeks and bit down on them, focusing on the discomfort.

"I tried to tell you about Chloe several times."

Pain speared me at her name arising from his lips. That long-ago afternoon of Samuel's confession of unfaithfulness resurrected with agonizing clarity. The humiliation. The shame. The heart-wrenching sorrow. Everything I'd strived so hard to avoid for two decades had returned. Except this time, it was my fault. I'd finally taken a risk. *Foolish, foolish girl.*

I pushed to standing and approached the door on shaky legs, pausing a few inches away. Chewie, ever faithful, stood next to me. "I can't look at you. This is . . ." A tear fell. "This is bringing back the past. But it's worse because you knew better this time. You're not some careless guy in his twenties. You're a grown man."

"You're right. And I'm sorry. My plan was to ease you in. Wait for the right time. I'd planned to tell you the day of that run-in with your client's neighbor, but then you shared about miscarrying our baby."

Our baby. There was such a tenderness in the way he said it.

"After that, it seemed too insensitive."

My mind drifted back, my lips parting. He *had* mentioned needing to talk about something.

"I wanted to tell you a few days later, but your mom showed up. The night she walked in on me cooking. The next day, you started pulling away, and I bolted like a jerk. I returned, determined to tell you, but you were gone."

I flattened my palms against the door, covering the peephole with one hand. Hadn't I detected a hesitation on his part that evening? That he was holding something back? It was why I'd pushed him. The note he'd written that night made even more sense now.

"The morning after rescuing Chewie, I was going to tell you, but Brooke showed up. And then when you told me about Conner and Mason's approval, I . . ." The door creaked, as though his weight leaned against it. Longing softened his voice. "I just wanted to be with you."

I rested my forehead against the door, another tear slipping free.

He cleared his throat. "I know this'll sound like a lie, but I had decided to tell you today. I almost did it at the toy drive."

And then Brooke had interrupted. Again. I slid my eyes shut, bracing myself. "Who called you earlier during the church event?"

A beat passed. "Chloe."

Bitterness bristled. Sharp and relentless. Like I'd guzzled a bucket of demon balls from a sweet gum tree. "And what about the other times when we were together these past few weeks? A call would come through, and you wouldn't answer."

Another beat. "Conner."

"Conner?" I stiffened.

A sigh muffled. "He's been asking for advice about starting a business for your products. He wanted to keep it a secret."

Heat charged through my veins. Conner and his secrets. I was going to lay one into him.

"Julia, this doesn't have to change anything."

I scoffed, swiping the cascading tears. "It changes everything."

37

LIKE AN ANNOYING CUCKOO CLOCK, at the top of every hour, Samuel had reappeared. I hadn't spoken to him since the first time he'd shown up on my doorstep. But after his third re-emergence, I needed a break. Even if it was from the chance of his return. I'd packed clothes and essentials for tonight and tomorrow, and sought refuge at Kate's, picking up dinner for us along the way.

Hayley had been thrilled. Of all the humans in the world, other than the boys and me, Chewie adored her the most. Of course, Hayley had been sneaking him treats for years. Smart girl. As soon as I'd arrived, Chewie had cut a path to her. Hayley had done her best to hide what appeared to be a sliver of deli meat in her hand.

Kate and I sat on the front balcony of her residence on the second floor of Beignets & Books. Late evening had descended, shading the skies a dusky blue. The weather had taken a notice-ably cooler dip, making the Christmas decorations Kate had put up even more charming. Green garland adorned with white twinkle lights draped at precise intervals along the railing. Huge red bows added a festive feel. The same garland, lights, and ribbon motif swooped along the three-foot iron fence running the perimeter of the property.

Swathed in throw blankets, we nestled into our chairs, a small table between us, and dessert in our hands. Hot chocolate made from scratch, complete with mini marshmallows.

I'd mostly held my mug for warmth, my desire for sugar having fled as I recounted everything to Kate once we were alone. She'd taken the news as I'd expected. Quietly and carefully absorbing it, surprise and concern layering her delicate features.

Below us, a couple holding hands strolled up the walkway to the café. They disappeared from view, and the faint ding of the bell on the front door sounded.

Kate lowered her cup to the table. "Do you think Samuel will come here?"

"No, that would be too stalkerish. And he wouldn't put you or Hayley in an awkward position."

"When's the last time he called?"

"I don't know. I blocked his number."

She stilled. "So it's . . . over?"

My stomach churned, and I hoped to keep my supper down. "He lied to me." I placed my still-full cup on the table and hugged my arms to myself.

She nodded. "He definitely lied by omission."

A streetcar neared, its lone headlight shining. Its whirring and clanking increasing and fading as it passed.

Kate tucked a strand of auburn hair behind her ear. "Didn't he tell you before that Brooke's mom was motivated by money? That was how he'd gotten custody? I bet that's what Brooke meant today when she said Samuel never tells Chloe no. She probably hits him up for money every now and then."

"That was one possibility that crossed my mind."

Two women, chatting excitedly, walked along the sidewalk on the other side of the fence. They turned in at the gate and made their way up the steps to the café.

"I can understand why he didn't tell you after you'd revealed the miscarriage. That would've been cruel." She rubbed the worry-crease between her brows. "Did he really try to tell you other times after that?"

The headache that had subsided returned, tightening a band around my skull. I rested my elbow on the table, my cheek in my hand. "Yes. Which is what makes this such a sticky mess. But in the end the fact remains that he could have and didn't." Which stirred other doubts about what else he could be hiding.

Kate eyed me, gnawing her lip, her expression altering from reflective to pensive. "I think we should look at this . . . rationally."

"Oh my word," I sighed, straightening. "It's not like this is something we can put on a spreadsheet."

"Everything can be analyzed on a spreadsheet." Resolve and a pinch of challenge sparkled in her eyes.

I hooked a brow. "Prove it."

She darted inside, her blanket billowing behind her like a cape. *It's a bird! It's a plane! It's Super Spreadsheet Woman!* Returning with her laptop, she positioned it on the table. After powering her computer on, she considered it. Closed her eyes.

"Are you conjuring the Yoda of Excel?"

"No." She shot me a pointed look. "I'm praying to the Jesus of Christ." Interlacing her fingers, she cracked her knuckles, as though she were a pianist about to perform. She began typing.

And typing.

And typing.

Gracious. Was she writing a book? Turning my life story into a sordid romance novel? Would Fabio grace the cover, donning a Green Beret uniform? Vehicles rumbled past on the street. My attention drifted to the two live oaks between the sidewalk and St. Charles Avenue. Their height cascaded well past our spots on the balcony. Their thick branches reaching toward each other, as though trying to embrace.

"Didn't Samuel tell you the truth about Brooke's mom when you asked? As far as it being a fling?"

"He did."

Tippity-tap-tap. "How many times did he try to tell you she was the woman he'd cheated on you with?"

I scoffed. "You want a specific number?"

She motioned to her laptop. "This is a math program."

Readjusting my throw, I smothered a sigh and burrowed against the chair's cushion. The streetlights flickered on, illuminating the neutral ground. Other than the exact instances Samuel had mentioned earlier, there had been other times when it had seemed like he wanted to tell me something but was struggling with it. "Six, maybe seven."

"We'll be conservative and go with six." She made one keystroke.

Goodness. Maybe she really was creating some sort of mathematical formula to spit out the answers I needed. Like the spreadsheet she'd generated for me to easily calculate cleaning quotes. I leaned, peeking at her work. "You're making a glorified pro-con list!"

"It's still extremely helpful to see things in this type of format."

The heading of the spreadsheet read *Samuel 2.0.* The pro column was twenty-five items deep—and missing little things Kate didn't know about. Like Samuel's guacamole. The con side was woefully empty. I gestured to it. "You need to list all the rotten things he did to me in the past."

Eyebrows arcing, she tilted her head. "Is that how you want God to look at you?"

I flinched. Talk about a sucker punch to the gut.

She held her arm out to the side and mimed dropping a microphone.

"You fight dirty." I gathered the blanket high around my neck, resisting the urge to pull it over my face.

She gave an unapologetic shrug. "What are the wrongs he's done since stepping back into your life?"

"Other than crushing my heart again?"

"Obviously."

"He didn't reveal the entire truth about Brooke's conception."

She nodded and tip-tapped.

"He still has a relationship with Chloe."

"You already knew he'd still have a connection to the mother of his child."

True. My molars clenched. But I hadn't known it was the woman he'd cheated on me with.

Kate spun the pearl earring in her lobe. "If Samuel were to do a list on you, you'd have a whopper of a con in your column."

I glanced up.

"You kept a secret from him for over two decades. One that directly involved him and his baby."

My leg jittered beneath the table.

"It seems you both harbored a secret all that time." Her thoughtful stare leveled on me. "It's just that he held on to his a little longer."

I stared at the table, my mug, the car trying to parallel park across the street. My eye twitched at the irritation chafing. I was not in the mood to see things rationally. Or to slip into Samuel's shoes and walk a mile.

"What other cons do you have to add?" Kate waited, fingers hovering over her keyboard.

Nothing else came to mind. I glared at the computer. *Curse you, Excel.*

The gray eyebrow hair was back. And it had brought a friend.

Talk about a bad omen. This was what I got for peering into my compact magnifying mirror. Too much worrying and overanalyzing about Samuel last night had to be the culprit.

I'd tried to pray but had found my focus shifting bitterly to Chloe. To the past.

My heart stammered a weak beat. *Enough. This is the last time Samuel Reed will hurt you.* I needed to create a playlist of female power ballads and keep that baby on shuffle. Tina Turner, Alanis Morrissette, Carrie Underwood. Yup. If I accomplished one thing today, that would be it.

I plucked each follicle of evilness, snapped the compact shut with a decided click, and carried on. Moisturizer with SPF, no makeup since I was still in martyr mode, and hair in a ponytail. Sweatpants and an old, hard-earned Crescent City Classic T-shirt completed my homebody look.

I left the guest bedroom and found Kate and Hayley in the kitchen, along with Chewie, who had spent the night with Hayley. The streak of losing the men in my life to other women continued. See? Spoken like a true martyr.

"I took Chewie for a walk this morning," Hayley said.

"Thank you." I slid onto a barstool at the island.

Chewie dashed to me for a quick sniff and lick, and promptly returned to Hayley. *Traitor.* Hayley scooped fruit salad onto a plate, next to a biscuit and a pile of bacon, no doubt for Chewie. She headed for the living room, my dog hot on her heels.

"Coffee?" Kate asked. Even though we'd agreed to lay low today, she still appeared ready to face the world. Makeup, hair styled, skinny jeans, violet blouse with a matching cardigan.

"What time did you wake up?" I glimpsed the clock on the wall. *9:00 a.m.*

"I had some things to do." She rested a steaming cup before me, the nutty scent of her breakfast blend wafting.

My Spidey-senses tingled. "What kind of things?"

"Things." She wouldn't meet my gaze. Pulled the creamer from the stainless-steel fridge and set it before me. Nudged the sugar bowl my way too.

"Kate," I warned.

"I had some restaurant stuff to take care of."

"But you're closed on Sundays."

"Just because the café's closed doesn't mean things still don't pop up."

I doctored my coffee and took the first sip, relishing the smooth richness. Phone in hand, I checked Conner's and Mason's pulsing dots and my email. Three new messages waited. One from Spanx, as if I needed another blow to my ego. Another from Samuel. Darn him and his Green Beret ways of getting my address. *Delete.* The third was from Robert Breaux. I opened it and read, a haze rolling in like the fog on Lake Pontchartrain. I slowly placed my phone on the white granite counter.

Kate took the stool next to me. "Since you blocked Samuel from calling and texting, I'm guessing he emailed you?"

"Yes, but I'm not reading it." I glided my phone to her.

She took a bite of cantaloupe and read Robert Breaux's message, chewing and scrolling. Then went back up and read it again. "He's agreeing to your original full quote to clean his offices on Saturdays."

I nodded, rubbing where I'd yanked the gray eyebrow hairs, wondering when my excitement would kick in.

"And he wants you to clean his house. On Tuesdays. The day you go to Samuel's dad's place."

"Did you have something to do with this?"

Her lips puckered. She touched one finger to my phone and pushed it back to me, her disapproval clear. "I had nothing to do with this."

"You don't think he'll stick to the price agreement?"

"He's put it in writing, so you've pretty much got him there. But I don't think you'll be happy leaving the ministry short-staffed." She speared another square of melon with her fork. "Or giving up Samuel's dad for that matter."

My shoulders caved forward. She was right on both counts.

With Norma moving to Florida, the ministry would dwindle to two volunteers without me. And this week would mark two months of cleaning Teddy's house. His cranky-pants manners had grown on me, and I'd like to think I'd grown on him too.

But happiness didn't pay the bills. This opportunity was exactly what I had wanted to accomplish all those months ago. It was like a present, wrapped with neat edges and a big shiny bow.

Dropping Teddy also severed my only tie to Samuel. Uncertainty itched under my skin. I enfolded both hands around my coffee, the heat seeping through my fingers. *This is a good thing.* I took a long gulp and traded the mug for my phone. I opened the music app and began compiling that anti-love playlist. *Hello, Tina.*

Next, I would find a replacement for Teddy and be done with every single Reed. My heart ached at cutting out Brooke. She really was a sweet kid.

No.

I set my jaw. It was time to start thinking with my brain, not my heart. I'd find and vet another cleaner for Teddy and get in touch with Wyatt on the change. I could search through that home services website I'd pulled my profile from. Maybe I could feel the person out about helping with the ministry too. Or ask Brother Buford to make a special plea to the congregation.

And if that didn't work . . . My hands wilted to my lap. *Buck up. This is what you've wanted all along.* But if that was true, why didn't it feel as good as I thought it would?

38

SCORNED WOMEN GOT THINGS DONE. After streaming church yesterday from Kate's, I'd hopped on my laptop and finalized my service agreements with Robert Breaux via email. Next, I'd found two possible replacements for Teddy. I'd spoken to one of the women, who had three solid references I'd already contacted. This week, I would meet her in person. The beauty of Teddy was that he would easily slide into any open day or time slot for another cleaner.

Monday morning, I arrived at my first client of the day, Gloria Gaynor pumping through the speakers of my SUV. Gloria insisted I'd survive. *Hey, hey.* That had to count for something. I killed the engine and dialed the church's office. Sydney Dupré answered.

"Hey, it's Julia Monroe."

"Hi, Julia." The secretary's chipper tone in her greeting nosedived. "I was about to ring you."

My courage-via-music-buzz fizzled. "Okay."

"Emily Miller resigned as a volunteer."

"*What?*"

"She called a few minutes ago. Said she needs to keep her

Saturdays open for her boyfriend. It's the only day of the week they can spend together because of their jobs."

My free hand strangled the steering wheel. "Poor Sean Crawford," I muttered.

"I'm sorry, what was that?"

"Nothing." I dragged in a breath. "That only leaves one volunteer."

"Well, two with you."

"I was calling to let you know I wouldn't be able to help anymore. I have a Saturday client now." I kneaded the back of my neck. This did not feel right. Not at all.

"Oh." Rustling papers carried over the line. "I'll let Brother Buford know. We may have to cancel the ministry. At the very least, stop adding names to the waiting list. And rework the schedule."

I knew the schedule better than anyone. With one volunteer working once a month at best, Miss Marlene and the other regulars would be lucky to have their homes cleaned twice a year. Unwarranted anger at Emily Miller flared. I'd finally landed a good, nonpervert Saturday client. The extra earnings I'd been hoping for. And now it came at a hefty price I hadn't anticipated.

By the time I'd reached home from work Monday evening, my mood was beyond sour. I'd just released Chewie into the backyard when my phone pealed Conner's ringtone. I answered, and after ascertaining he and Mason were not dying and the call was merely a check-in, I asked the question that had been burning a canyon in my brain since Saturday.

"Have you been calling Samuel to ask for advice with starting a business for my cleaning products?"

On Conner's side of the line, wind whipped, and then cut to silence with the closing of a door. "Um, yes."

I lowered onto my chair, a coil of tension in my neck unknotting. At least Samuel hadn't lied about those mystery calls.

"Is everything okay? You sound kinda off."

"It's been a long day." *A long three days.*

With his nose down, Chewie sniffed, circling something in the grass. He flopped on his back, rubbing against whatever he'd found. Probably a dead worm. *Ugh.* Now I'd have to bathe him. I shook my head. At least one of us could be happy in this moment.

"Look," I said. "I appreciate your wanting to make something of my products. But you need to focus on college. You have a full class load and a part-time job. And I don't have the time for it. Particularly not now." I gnawed the corner of my thumbnail. Oh, how I hated to reveal this to Conner, who would blabber it to Mason. But this project had to be stopped before it got out of hand. "I signed my first commercial client." I infused fake excitement into my voice. "It's an insurance office I'll be working for on Saturdays."

"What about the cleaning ministry?"

My spine wilted, and what felt like a pit of emptiness opened in my chest. "It'll continue without me." *Maybe.* I winced.

"But you love doing it. I figured you'd start serving more with Mason being up here now."

All four of Chewie's legs stuck straight in the air, delight exuding in every wriggle. Shouldn't I be experiencing the same joy? The income from Robert Breaux would provide the financial cushion I'd long desired. This was huge. Huge! And yet the pit spread from my chest to my stomach. Like a black hole. "This opportunity was too good not to take. And as far as my products go, I think it's great you can use them for your marketing class. But other than that, you need to let it go."

⚜

Tuesday morning I had braced myself for Samuel being at Teddy's house when I arrived. He hadn't been. I had re-braced myself for him to be waiting outside when I left. He hadn't been. A muddle of relief and disappointment had walloped me each time.

I hadn't mentioned to Teddy my plans to hand him off to another cleaner. It seemed unnecessary until I'd completely vetted the woman I had my eye on. What if when we met, I discovered she despised veterans? Or had newly dyed green hair? Teddy wouldn't trust someone with green hair in his home. And if she didn't meet Teddy's standards . . . well, based on the stats Robert Breaux had given me on his home, I would probably have enough time to keep Teddy as a client.

As long as Samuel didn't show up when I was there.

I pointed my vehicle home, replaying our last talk. The tentative hope in Samuel's voice that nothing had to change. "Ha!" I scoffed to no one. Turning into my subdivision, I slowed, realizing I couldn't remember the drive here. "Not a good thing, Julia."

Also not a good thing? The Testosterone Truck parked in front of my house.

I took my time exiting my SUV. It wasn't like I could outrun a former Green Beret to my front door. And really, I didn't want to. We had to have this conversation in order to move on. My heart ached, a slow pulse thudding out from it. *You've been through worse. You can manage a few minutes.*

Samuel stood to the side of the walkway, giving me space to pass. He wore tennis shoes, jeans fraying at one knee, and a wrinkled long-sleeved shirt. Several days of growth shadowed his usually clean-shaven face. His hair haphazardly swooped in multiple directions. Like someone who'd just woken—or had been anxiously jabbing their fingers at their skull.

His ragged appearance should have given me pleasure. It didn't. All I could think about was how strange it felt to not step into his arms. To have my defenses up again in his presence.

I brushed past him. "I expected you to be at your dad's."

"I didn't want to risk you dropping him as a client."

Smart man. I inserted my key in the lock.

"Can we please talk?"

I stepped inside, leaving the door open behind me. Chewie clamored at my feet, hurling several barks in Samuel's direction. I set my purse and keys on the entrance table, then lifted Chewie. His body wiggled against me as I toted him to the back door. I let him out, silently sending up a prayer for strength. Or for a tornado to spawn and whisk me away to the land of Oz.

Samuel hovered in the space between the living and dining rooms. "I need you to know how sorry I am." Regret marred him. The red rim to his eye, the shadows beneath, the heaviness he appeared to carry on his shoulders.

Apart from those physical indicators, there was a genuinely caring side to Samuel I'd come to know these past months. A prickling tightness expanded under my ribs. I believed his remorse. But that didn't alter the crux of my issue. I turned my attention to the yard. To Chewie and the sunlight pouring through the tree.

Samuel edged closer. "I also want to ensure everything between us is clear."

A splinter of unease whittled through my joints. I cracked a knuckle. And another, unable to meet his gaze.

"About two months before I broke up with you, I had a one-night stand with Chloe."

I glanced at the nearest chair, needing to hold something for support, but incapable of moving. *You knew this. It matches the timeline of finding that picture in his apartment.*

"A month later, she came to me, claiming to be pregnant. That's why I ended things with you."

Breathe. Just breathe. "Why didn't you tell me about her being pregnant then?"

He shifted from one foot to the other. "I could see the hurt just ending things was doing to you in that moment. I didn't want to add to that pain. Plus, I wasn't certain at the time the baby was mine. And all of that is why I never answered your calls."

Breathe.

"You said you called every day for two weeks. It was actually sixteen days."

Breathe.

Chewie scratched at the door, snapping me from my paralysis. I let him in. He scampered past us to his water bowl, lapping several gulps.

"From the start Chloe wanted an abortion, but I persuaded her not to." Samuel rubbed his head, his fingers disheveling his hair further. "Then she planned to give the baby up after she found out how much money she could make for an illegal private adoption. That was my deciding factor with joining the army. I gave Chloe my enlistment bonus in exchange for her having the baby and granting me sole custody if it was mine." His hand dropped to his side. "Once Brooke was born and we did a DNA test, the full custody to me went through. From that point on, my mom helped me raise Brooke."

My vision misted, and I reached for that chair, my fingers curling around the top of the smooth wood. "What else haven't you told me? There's no excuse to hold anything back now."

His chest slowly rose and fell, his eye closing for a long moment before reopening and settling on me. "I haven't told you that all these years, I've loved you. That pull I had to you when we dated never disappeared. It faded at times but always returned."

My fingers, still grasping the chair, tingled with exertion.

"The night of the accident," he motioned to his patch, his sight dipping to the floor, "I lay in the hospital, and this . . . notion to find you struck. I thought it was a result of shock, so I ignored it." His body grew still, except for his jaw muscle flexing. "Especially with all the unknowns I was facing with recovery and my military career." His throat bobbed. "A few months later that notion hit again. Insistent." His stare met mine. "I did some searching and found out you'd been widowed."

I tipped forward. "How did you—"

"Your mom's Facebook page is public."

I covered my mouth with my other hand, sliding it to my neck. *Goodness.* Wouldn't Mama love to know she'd unwittingly orchestrated our reunion.

"That nudge to reach you persisted for over a year. And it made no sense. I was in North Carolina. You were here. And then after taking a gap year, Brooke decided to attend LSU." He gave a disbelieving shake of his head. "We relocated to Louisiana and got her and my mom settled in Baton Rouge. I moved here to help with my dad and figure out what I was going to do for a living. During that time, I started attending your church on Saturdays. Back when we'd dated, I remembered you mentioning it once. How much you liked the people there. Soon as I started going, it felt . . . right." He looked away, the creases in his forehead smoothing. "I hadn't had that connection to my church up north. Then I got to know Brother Buford." He gave a simple shrug. "You know the rest."

Sakes alive. I scraped back the chair I'd been clutching and sank onto it, my mind circling through everything he'd revealed, unable to land on any single point. Had God truly nudged him to find me? My head spun. Even if that were true, it could have been for a plethora of reasons, like bringing us closure.

Which made the most sense considering the issue now standing between us. My hands fell limply on the table, resignation shuffling through my body with each lackluster beat of my heart. "It doesn't change that the woman who you cheated on me with is connected to you for the rest of your life."

He eased forward again. "We don't see her that often."

"Last Saturday proves otherwise." I pressed my back into the chair's spindles, conjuring any remaining strength. "Why was she there? Looking for money or was it something more? Is she interested in you?"

His hesitation spoke volumes.

My heart plummeted.

"My only interest in Chloe is as Brooke's mom and doing the right thing for my daughter." Sincerity burned in his tone, in his gaze. "Over the years, Chloe has popped up. Mostly when looking for money."

Mostly was not always. I pulled in a shallow breath. "You once chose her over me. Who's to say that wouldn't happen again?"

He drew back as though he'd been slapped. "I'm a different person now. Besides, she's toxic and selfish and manipulative."

"And you'd bring her into my life? Into Conner and Mason's?"

Slowly, his face registered the realization. His mouth shut, and he studied his hands, a vein pulsating at his temple. The silence of truth weighed heavy in the space surrounding us.

Drawing in another flimsy breath, I cleared my throat. "I don't want to wonder if Chloe's going to show up on a random day, hitting on you or asking for money." I slid my hands into my lap, wringing them. "Or having to be around her for family holidays. Or Brooke's milestones, like graduating and getting married."

He pinched the bridge of his nose, appearing two times as worn as a moment ago. "Chloe's not the type of person to be involved in those things."

"But she could be. If she's still interested in you, who's to say she wouldn't want to start being included now that I'm around? Or go all *Fatal Attraction*?"

"She's not dangerous. She's just . . ." He clasped the back of his neck. "Self-centered. I've set a bad precedent by helping her financially in the past. But that stopped when Brooke turned twenty-one."

"And yet she showed up on Saturday."

He paused, as though his thoughts had finally brought him to the same conclusion I'd arrived at seventy-two hours ago. His features darkened. "There's only so much I can control with Chloe."

"Exactly." Defeat leached into the marrow of my bones. "And I can't live my life with my guard up."

39

WHEN ONE DIDN'T HAVE AN APPETITE for fresh beignets, something was wrong.

Friday night, Kate and I sat alone in the chefs' room of Beignets & Books. Framed pictures of Paul Prudhomme, Justin Wilson, and Leah Chase decorated the walls. Even New Orleans's adopted son, Emeril, held a spot. A single floating shelf running at eye level wrapped the room, interrupted only by the window and cased entrance. Cookbooks lined the shelves, as well as hardbacks on the history and many facets of the cuisines making up the melting pot of New Orleans.

Kate set her phone on the table. She'd been texting with Hayley, who was currently miserable spending the night with Kate's parents. "When do you start at Robert Breaux's offices?"

"Tomorrow." I lifted a beignet, determined not to waste the heavenly dessert, but Miss Marlene came to mind, my gut souring. Had it not been for my new client, I would be at her home tomorrow. I returned the uneaten beignet to my plate. A melancholy mix of instrumental jazz poured through the sound system, weighing my psyche further.

"Have you cleaned his house yet?"

"No, that'll start next week. I'll do his house first, and then go to Teddy's."

"I'm glad you're keeping Teddy."

"Me too." Teddy was my consolation prize. As long as Samuel kept his distance. With a sigh, I pushed my dish aside and tipped my sights to the antique chandelier suspended from a medallion clinging to the center of the ceiling. Despite being the smallest of the themed rooms, this space still had the same ornate moldings.

Kate quirked an eyebrow. "Are we going to talk about the invisible Spaniel in the room?"

I snort-scoffed and leaned back. "Way to be subtle."

"Best friends don't have to be subtle."

True. I'd called Kate after Samuel had left my house three days ago, needing to share his revelations that had latched on to my heart. "Nothing's going to change there. Chloe is . . ." I twisted the cloth napkin on my lap. "She's forever tied to Samuel. A reminder he chose her over me."

"That's understandable." She sunk her teeth into her bottom lip, examining me.

I squirmed in my seat. "I sense a *but* coming."

She raised a shoulder, her nose crinkling. "Once again, you're holding on to the old Samuel. The Samuel Reed of today is choosing you." Kate shot me a no-nonsense look. "The version of him you prefer." She adjusted the cuff on her long-sleeved café button-down. "I'm not trying to push him on you. For all we know, Samuel's coming back was a way for you both to let go of the past so you can each move on."

A reluctant thought I'd already had. A bead of condensation rolled down the side of my water glass. "What if I'm in a relationship with him and can't cope with the Chloe aspect?"

Her expression turned somber. "Maybe you can't. I just want you to take some time and look at this from every angle. What if Chloe's behavior was exactly the same, but she wasn't the woman Samuel had cheated with? Would you still feel this way, or would you be willing to deal with it?"

My stomach churned. "I don't know."

She hesitated, her attention dipping to her empty plate. "I say this out of love . . . but sometimes you make decisions hard and fast."

I pulled in a slow breath and held it for three counts. She wasn't telling me anything I didn't know. When my emotions ran high, it clouded my decisions.

Kate settled the full weight of her soft gaze on me. "Once upon a time you had an idea of selling your products and returning to your ministry full-time."

My throat swelled. That had been five years after Mark's death, and I'd started truly coming out of mourning, wanting to be helpful to others again. The idea had seemed so simple and achievable.

It'd been anything but.

Other than my not having a brain for business, there were laws, federal requirements, and liabilities of every kind with legal consequences. And then came the financial and time components. Both of which I hadn't had. In the end, it had all been too overwhelming and the risk too great.

"Sometimes God opens a door. A door that scares the pants off our enemy. And that's when the enemy bombards us in fear and discouragement." She reached across the table, laying her slender fingers over mine. "Don't let fear cripple you or hinder your life any longer than it already has."

Goodness. Was she talking about my cleaning products or my love life?

"Have you considered that God planted that dream in your heart for a reason? A higher purpose?"

My hand, beneath hers, blazed with heat. As though I were being made to pay attention.

She released her hold, easing back. "The same could be said

for the Lord orchestrating Samuel's return. Maybe it's not a future with him per se, but perhaps God brought him into Conner and Mason's life for a reason. Or to connect you with Brooke. She must need a steady mom figure."

A wave of light-headedness hit. "That's a lot to take in." I rubbed my palms into my eye sockets. "And there's only so much I can handle."

"It's time you stopped looking at what *you* can handle and start looking at what God can."

⚜

The next day, I'd arrived at Robert Breaux's insurance agency. Excitement and relief should have effervesced from my pores. Instead, guilt and unease filled me. So much so that on Sunday morning, I found myself at Miss Marlene's doorstep. Mama would have to suffer without her church bulletin two weeks in a row.

Back home, I unloaded my supplies in the garage, my arm and back muscles aching, fatigue from seven consecutive days of physical labor catching up. I stared at the jugs of ingredients underneath the folding table, waiting to be mixed for the coming week's work. A withered groan escaped. "Six more days to go," I said to Princess Tipsy. "Then I'll have a break."

Her Highness regarded me with no pity.

And she was right to do so. I'd done this to myself. I stretched my neck, the tendons in my shoulders throbbing. Commercial work involved more vacuuming and toilet scrubbing than residential. And windows. Tall and wide and never-ending storefront and private office windows. But more than bodily exhaustion weighed. My gaze drooped to my feet and the hem of my green scrubs.

Over a month ago, I'd sat in this space and prayed God's will. Then I'd gone and made decisions on my own. Hadn't consulted with the Lord before my conversation with Conner about his hopes for the products. Or asked God for direction about the Samuel-Chloe situation.

My heart thudded dully. I'd plowed right ahead with agreeing to clean Robert Breaux's business. Another hard and fast decision made when emotions had been running high. Just like Kate had mentioned.

A crisp December breeze invaded from the open garage door. I pinned my arms against my shame-riddled stomach. *Why do I do that?* I shook my head at how quickly I'd snatched my issues from God's hands. Especially when things weren't going my way. I'd fallen back on what I could do, rather than leaving my problems where they belonged, in God's never-failing presence.

"Oh, Lord. Here I am again." I swallowed past the lump in my throat. "Thank You for not tiring of me. I'm sorry for trying to take control again. Please, help me do what You want. And please grant me patience in the waiting. We both know I need it."

⚬⟶⟵⚬

Upon waking the next day, I discovered a distinct pang of missing Samuel had sprouted. The past week, my feelings toward him had ranged widely from mistrust to anger to disillusionment. I decided to purposefully shove this newfound longing for him aside and direct my thoughts to God. And that's what I did while driving and working. When my mind wandered, I returned my focus. Tried reflecting on the ways God had been leading me before I'd taken over again.

Tuesday morning heralded a silver lining. Robert Breaux's house had been in amazing shape. His previous cleaning lady had been meticulous and retired with short notice, providing the catalyst to him surrendering to my terms.

Later that afternoon, I arrived at Teddy's. He opened the

door, the scent of a fresh Christmas tree a welcoming contradiction to his scowl. At least his grumpiness had lessened considerably each week. White lights adorned the branches, along with red and blue ornaments.

"Very patriotic." I set my caddy on the floor and neared the spruce.

Teddy harrumphed and shuffled to his recliner. "Samuel did it. I told him it's a waste of time and money."

My Samuel-pang grew exponentially. And right along with it, a gentle conviction feathered against my heart. "Oh." I stiffened, my breath wedged in my lungs. Long ago, after struggling through my breakup with Samuel and the miscarriage, I'd been leery about opening myself to Mark. And that was when this same sensation had eased over me.

Teddy scoffed. "You're getting all moony-eyed over something that'll be tossed in the swamps soon enough." He removed his glasses, extending them to me.

With a shaky exhale, I reached for his spectacles. "You don't have to wait for me to clean these." I opened the ziplock bag on his coffee table, removing the mini spray bottle and microfiber cloth I'd left behind weeks ago.

Teddy ignored me, flipping on the TV.

Spritzing and wiping each lens, I directed my attention to God, my mind dithering with uncertainty. *Did I really feel what I think I did? Does it mean the same thing as before?*

The tender conviction washed over me a second time. Again, I stilled.

Teddy shifted, his chair groaning in response. "You okay?"

"Yes," I rasped, returning his glasses. "I'm going to grab the rest of my things." Outside, I paused on the front stoop, gaining my bearings. A truck puttered past, the hum of its engine blending in with the music emanating from the club on the corner. Thick clouds hovered above, blocking the sun.

I lightly pressed my fingertips to my forehead and lowered

to the top step. The cold of the concrete soaked through the thin fabric of my pants. I bent forward, resting my elbows on my knees, clasping my hands. *I'm either going crazy, or You're speaking to me.* I closed my eyes. *This would be so much easier if You just told me what to do.* I shook my head. *But where's the faith in that, right?* A few minutes passed with no other promptings. My legs jittered. *I feel like I need to respond to You, Lord, but I don't want to overstep.* Starting small couldn't hurt, right? *I hope this is the right thing to do. If not, please let me know.*

I reached into the front pocket of my scrubs, pulled out my phone, and unblocked Samuel's number.

40

FOUR DAYS LATER, I STILL HADN'T HEARD from Samuel. The man had supposedly loved me for over two decades, and yet he'd given up just like that? Or was he giving me space? Maybe God hadn't wanted me to unblock his number. Although the Samuel-pang had not weakened, there hadn't been any other featherings of conviction. I continued praying for patience and thanking God for the way He was making.

It was Saturday night, and the boys had arrived home from college for winter break. Mama had joined us for dinner, and then retreated to her place for an evening of cigarettes and an Abraham Lincoln documentary.

I'd purposefully waited for Conner and Mason to be home before hauling out our fake Christmas tree. Not that they really helped decorate. But still, it was tradition. And in keeping with our tradition, *Elf* played on the TV in the living room while Conner and Mason inhaled snacks and added an ornament to the tree every now and then. Just enough to have officially participated.

I removed the lid from a plastic bin, finding the gold star that would top the tree. Discarded wrapping paper from last year enfolded each corner of the star, protecting it. With a wistful smile, I retrieved the decoration and set it on the coffee table.

It was times like this I'd thought how nice it would've been to have a daughter. Or for shopping. Or going to a chick flick. Or commiserating over things like armpit razor burn.

Brooke came to mind. Would she enjoy hanging ornaments and drinking eggnog? Was she staying with Samuel for the school break? During our lakefront picnic last month, she'd confided in me she was anxious about one of her finals. Had she passed?

I unpacked the tree skirt next. Chewie whined. He sat next to Mason on the sofa, poised like a snake ready to strike at any food that went awry.

Mason threw a piece of popcorn his way. "I heard you have a Saturday client now."

My gaze flitted to Conner, who lay on the love seat, his long legs dangling over the armrest. He studied the TV a little too intently. I turned away and kneeled on the floor, draping the red-and-green tree skirt around the base of our faux Fraser fir. "I do." I injected a chipper tone. "It's an insurance agency." The multicolored lights I'd already strung sparkled. Such a contradiction to how I felt.

"You're not doing the cleaning ministry anymore?"

I paused from straightening the fabric. *Keep that cheerful attitude.* "No, I don't think I can." Any hopes I could still assist on Sundays had been squashed last weekend. God wasn't joking about needing a day of rest. I leaned on my haunches, inspecting my work, procrastinating on facing the boys.

"Do you need money?" Mason again. "Is something going on we don't know about?"

"No." I pushed to standing and found his expression concerned. Conner's too. Regret tweaked. "I promise everything's fine. I've been wanting a weekend client for a while now. Extra income is always a good thing."

The boys exchanged dubious looks. In the back of my mind, I seemed to recall Samuel once mentioning money had never been a motivator for me. Had the boys come to that same conclusion as well?

"Just in case," I added. "For vacations, retirement, a new car." *Abrupt death.*

"Wow." Mason's forehead creased. "No more cleaning ministry." He thumbed his ear. "You started it when I was in kindergarten, right?"

I nodded, casting a glance at Conner, who remained quiet.

"I remember how your supplies would rattle in the trunk on the way to school." Mason tossed another piece of popcorn to Chewie.

Conner repositioned to sitting, setting his phone on the cushion next to him. "And after she picked us up, she'd talk about the person she'd helped that day."

My insides twisted. Was this another planned tag-team effort? If so, it wasn't fair. Not with my heart already bruised and frail from Samuel—which they had no clue about. I curbed a sigh. The boys and I had talked more about the ministry and my products in the last month than we had in a decade. I dug through the box, retrieving a bag of red bows, directing my focus to God. *Is this You working through them?*

Conner scooted to the edge of the couch and hesitated, his light blue eyes meeting mine. "I know you told me to let your products go, but I think there's something there. Even my professor agrees." A dimple flashed in his cheek. "I got an A on my marketing plan."

Pride tugged my lips into a warm smile. "That's amazing, Conner." Reaching into the container, I unearthed a ball of white tissue paper, nestling a painted cardinal carved from wood. My heart pinched. The ornament had been a gift from Mark the first year I'd started the ministry. He'd said cardinals were a bright spot of color in winter, a symbol of hope and joy, and that's what I was to the people I helped. My ribs squeezed. I'd gone from chasing a dream to surviving . . . and settling there. Not exactly how I wanted the boys to see me or how I wanted to see myself. Pulse slowing, I rewrapped the bird and returned it to the bin.

A gentle conviction nudged within. I stilled. My attention landed on a reindeer ornament Conner had made as a child. *Oh, Lord, what if I encourage him, and it's all for nothing?* The impression swelled, like a song reaching its crescendo, then ebbed, leaving me with a layer of peace. I ducked my head, giving in to the sensation, humbled by the certain direction. Laying a hand against my breastbone, I quietly cleared the emotion from my throat and settled my attention on Conner. "I'd like to see your marketing plan, if that's okay."

Conner blinked, and Mason's hand stopped midway to his mouth.

Breathe. "I probably won't understand the technical stuff—"

"That's okay!" Conner's countenance brightened. "Um, I mean, I can explain it." He dashed for his bedroom. "I'll grab my laptop and pull it up for you." In two seconds, he'd returned, depositing his computer on the dining room table.

Mason shook his shaggy blond hair from his eyes and devoured a handful of popcorn. "We ran a poll." He spoke around the food in his mouth. "Green Girl won over Green Grannie."

"A poll?" My gaze flipped between them. "Wait." I held up a hand, gawking at my youngest. "You're in on this too?"

He swallowed his bite, his posture puffing. "I created the logo and branding."

I could actually feel my eyes widening.

"He's a genius with design," Conner said.

Mason's brows rose with an air of smugness. Or at least, I thought they had. Some sort of movement had happened in that general area beneath his too-long hair. Maybe as my Christmas present, I'd ask him to get a cut.

Conner's fingers sailed over his keyboard. "Next semester, I'm taking a business class. Part of that course is creating a business plan." His motions slowed, and he slanted his attention my way. "I want to use your products. It wouldn't be distracting from school like you're worried about. It'd be helping."

I glanced at my hands and the reindeer ornament made out of popsicle sticks.

Mason moved to the kitchen island, swapping his bowl of popcorn for a bag of Skittles. "If everything shakes out with the business plan, we want your approval to move forward to create a company. One we can all be a part of, since it's always felt like a family thing."

Heavens above. A stirring, deep and rooted in my core . . . shifted. But not so much a shift as a lift. As though a long-buried load hoisted. Or maybe a long-buried dream resurrected. I peered once again into the box holding our hodgepodge of ornaments. Peering up at me was one Mason had crafted in pre-K. His little face was glued to a felt angel cutout, complete with a golden pipe cleaner halo. I reached for it, now holding a creation from each of them. It seemed incomprehensible to reconcile the children who'd made these mementos to the young men standing before me. Young men with big visions.

Conner swiveled his laptop my way, his leg bouncing. The introduction page to a PowerPoint presentation filled the screen. "Once the business generates enough income, you could receive a salary and be cleaning full-time for the elderly like you used to."

"Or do whatever you want with your time." Mason, Mr. Design Genius, wiped his hands on his shirt.

I shook my head, hooked the ornaments on the tree, and began cracking my knuckles, working my way through each finger. "This all feels wildly impossible."

"It's not, Mom." Conner laughed. "If it's successful enough, we could hire additional staff to make the products. We could dedicate a percentage of sales to grow the cleaning ministry as a legit nonprofit." His words tumbled over each other, his excitement palpable. "Hire people to clean and increase the number of individuals you can help."

Mason stepped next to Conner. "With enough backing, we could build it to be a regional or even a national nonprofit."

A national nonprofit? Sweat gathered along my spine, the idea pinging through my mind. I'd been overwhelmed with only selling the products. And here they were pinning their sights beyond what I could have imagined.

But not beyond what God could do.

Sakes alive. "Let's just look at your marketing plan first." My attention snagged on the bin, the red cardinal's head peeping out from the white paper. Fingers tingling, I lifted the little figurine and hung it on the tree, whispering a prayer.

Christmas came and went, and still no word from Samuel. It had been seventeen days since I'd unblocked his number. Two Sundays of not seeing him at church. Two weeks of dodging questions from Conner and Mason about Samuel's whereabouts. My Samuel-pang had continued growing, like a fireball pressing on my chest.

Making things worse was his Christmas gift, sitting wrapped on my dresser. Each day that had passed since the twenty-fifth, the festive snowmen faces on the paper grew depressed, as though they knew they wouldn't fulfill their Christmas destiny. There was nothing sadder than an unopened Christmas present gathering dust.

On New Year's Eve, I'd woken with either a scorching desire to lay eyes on Samuel or a serious case of heartburn. I'd muddled through my Friday clients, snacking on the last of my Tums and praying. Before heading home, I stopped at Walgreens, needing to restock on antacids for my rocking New Year's Eve party for one.

Conner and Mason would be at an all-night lock-in at church in the newly opened recreational center. Free Ping-Pong, foosball, laser tag, a rock-climbing wall, and a basketball court awaited any teenager with a driver's license. Plus, endless food. Praise the Lord for keeping them and the other teens off the road tonight.

The glass sliding doors whooshed open, the heated air coating my face. The temperatures had dipped harrowingly into the low fifties, calling for a light jacket to protect my thin Southern skin. "Celebration" by Kool & the Gang streamed overhead, and I bypassed displays of champagne and party poppers as I trudged to the back corner of the store, quickly locating the Tums. Not escaping my notice on the same aisle? Supplements for bone strength, six-packs of Ensure, and incontinence undergarments that looked cuter than some of my own underwear.

Grabbing two bottles of my drug of choice, I detoured for the pet section. Maybe I'd buy Chewie a new bone for the new year. Scanning the treats, my gaze halted. Next to the last pack of rawhides sat a lone alpaca chew toy.

A featherlight conviction whispered across my heart. Same as the one I'd had with Mark. Same as the one I'd had seventeen days ago. Fingers trembling, I reached for the plush figure, my vision tunneling on it, the bustle of others around me fading, until it was just me and the Lord.

It would have been easier to stay resolute against a future with Samuel if the same man of twenty years ago had reentered my life. The man who had been selfish and immature with our relationship. Who had made no attempt to get to know my family and friends. Who had handled my heart carelessly. Especially at the end.

Had the roles been reversed, would I want him holding on to who I'd been back then? It seemed unfair, because I knew, to the depths of my soul, that God had forgiven me for how

I'd lived. By God's grace I'd changed. Matured. Had found my way in Jesus.

Just like Samuel had.

I tucked the alpaca beneath my arm, grabbed the last package of dog bones, and made for the checkout line. A verse from Psalms boldly shot through my mind. *"He is a shield to all who trust Him."* I nodded to God and picked up my pace. Being a Christian wasn't easy. But it was worth it, because I wouldn't be alone in whatever came my way. Either with Samuel or Chloe, or whatever else this fallen world flung at me.

After making my purchases, I got in my SUV and headed to Samuel's.

The fire beneath my ribs lessened with each mile, disappearing altogether when I slowed for the stop sign at the corner of his street. I'd heard of God speaking through still, small voices but not heartburn and alpacas.

I zeroed in on his townhouse. The Testosterone Truck was parked in the driveway, Chloe's vehicle behind it. My heart thudded like lead. But the Lord had brought me here for a reason, and I'd see His way through. Samuel and Chloe stood on his front lawn, deep in conversation. I eased to the curb in front of his neighbor's place, using his truck and her car as a screen.

I killed my engine and watched them, undetected.

Samuel appeared tired . . . and peeved. His arms barred his body, his jaw clenched. Chloe's mascara trailed down her pretty face, and she gestured wildly, motioning to her car.

Samuel gave the appearance of a statue. Unmoving. All hard angles. I scanned the street for Brooke's car and came up empty. At least she wasn't here witnessing this event. Or maybe she'd seen worse. My mama-heart ached for her. A gust of wind whipped, pulling at Samuel's track pants and long-sleeved T-shirt. Chloe's caramel hair billowed, her snug jeans and sweater remaining glued to her slim figure. She placed a hand on his shoulder, her eyes beseeching. He shrugged her off in one sharp step back.

A muted whoop escaped from me, along with a mini fist pump.

Samuel said something and nodded to Chloe's car, as though advising her to scram. Her arms dangled at her sides, her posture hunching.

"Thank You for letting me see this," I whispered. Again, that verse came to me. *"He is a shield to all who trust Him."* Before I knew what I was doing, I'd opened my door and was making my way toward them.

Samuel's gaze connected with mine. His stern facial expression went slack, his arms uncrossing.

What felt like an invisible, physical line pulled me toward him. He shifted in my direction, as though he sensed the tug, too, but paused, his neck cording, the color draining from his face.

Chloe rounded the trunk of her car, lips crushed in a severe line. With jerky movements, she yanked open the driver's side door, cranked the ignition, and left.

Samuel's pained stare held on me for a moment, then fell to the grass between us. "She just showed up." He gave a weak shrug, slipping his hands into his pockets. "Asking for money for a new car."

"I believe you." I stepped forward, hating how defeated he looked. How he wouldn't meet my eyes. "And I forgive you for not telling me the full truth about her."

He gave a slight nod, a muscle twitching in his jawbone.

Not the reaction I'd expected. A twang of unease quivered through me.

"You were right." Emotion choked his voice. "I can't stop Chloe from popping into our lives." He motioned to where her car had been. "I had a long talk with her, reinforcing that she's not getting any more money, and that she can't come here again. And if she hits Brooke up for money, we'll file a restraining order for harassment."

Goodness. "Brooke's okay with that?"

He nodded, focus still on the ground. "It was her idea. But none of that removes Chloe's tie. Brooke could change her mind and want a relationship with her mom. I can't control that."

"And you shouldn't. That's Brooke's decision." A chilled breeze burst past, and I wrapped my arms around myself. Why hadn't he asked me inside yet? Why wouldn't he look at me?

He fixed his sight down the street, as though wrestling with his thoughts. His features darkened.

My stomach twisted. "Samuel—"

"All of this leaves a lot of uncertainty." He heaved a full-body sigh, the material of his shirt tightening against his shoulders and upper arms. "These past three weeks, all I've thought about is what you said." He rubbed his hand over his mouth, across his chin, to the back of his neck, where he squeezed. "There *are* going to be more situations with Chloe. Most likely bad ones." His gaze landed at my feet, and he dropped his hand. "Knowing how you feel, I can't put you through that." Brokenness tainted his tone. "It's not fair to you." He began turning away.

"Wait a second." I moved, grabbing his forearm. "Don't you want to know why I'm here?"

"Oh." A crease formed between his brows.

"I want you to forget what I said that evening." Afraid to let go, I slipped my hold to his wrist.

He watched my fingers, clasped around his tan skin.

"I was speaking out of fear and hurt. I don't want to spend another second worrying about old regrets." I swallowed past my dry throat. "I don't want to miss what our future could be because I'm worried about what may or may not even happen."

Gently, he unpeeled my grasp, shuffling backward. "You may say that now," his voice rasped, "but—"

"I love you."

359

He stilled. Purposefully closed his eye.

Was he shutting me out? My legs trembled, my heartbeat racing. "Compared to what I feel and know now, I don't think I really loved you before." The words gushed. "I was too young, too far from Jesus to know what love was. *Real* love. But I had it with Mark, and it's what I feel for you now." My breaths pulled in and out too fast, and I licked my lips. "Whatever comes our way, we have God's promise that He'll be with us. Whether it's Chloe or something else, we'll get through it together."

His eye opened, finally, *finally* meeting my gaze. Red tinted his cheeks, and his chest expanded, as though he hadn't taken a full breath in forever.

The line tethered from me to him pulled taut.

He cut the space between us, wrapping his arms around me with a fierce possession.

"I love you." We spoke the words simultaneously, mine muffled against his chest, his caressing the top of my head. I inhaled his clean scent. Grateful for this moment. For all the moments to come.

He pressed a tender kiss to my hair, my temple, my cheek. His calloused hands framed my face, and his vision tipped to the sky, a muttered "thank you" following.

I smiled, understanding the acknowledgment of appreciation wasn't for me.

His lips met mine, sweet and savoring. My arms glided to his waist, grasping his shirt. With one hand, he cradled the back of my head, and the other moved to my lower back, tugging me closer, as though promising he'd never let go. My heart soared at the thought.

The kiss deepened, the moment stretching long and slow, my body bowing against his, the heat between us vanquishing the crisp air trying to swirl through our space and break us apart.

But nothing would separate us again.

Warm pleasure unfurled at his touch, and right along with it, an undeniable rightness, adoration, and security.

I lowered from my toes, still clamping the fabric at his waist-line, desire searing across my skin. Our chests rose and fell at the same hectic rhythm, and the intensity of his stare, the vulnerability in his countenance, nearly undid me.

He nuzzled my neck, his stubble grazing my skin in the most tantalizing way, setting off a shuddering round of goose bumps.

My eyes slid shut.

His lips reached the sensitive spot below my ear, and he murmured my name. And just like that, I could see the rest of my life. Samuel with me every day and night. Steadfast. Stand-ing with him before God, making vows. Our families blended. Raising grandchildren. Growing old together. It all stretched before me like a precious gift.

EPILOGUE

SiX MONTHS LATER
SAMUEL

IT WAS SATURDAY NiGHT, and I was enjoying my favorite pastime: watching Julia. She stood barefoot at her kitchen sink, washing the dishes after making an impromptu batch of brownies. Red shorts hugged her curves, and even more distracting was her loose top, where the neckline kept sliding off her shoulder.

I sat at the table, redirecting my attention to the daily devotional book that lay open. We'd been reading it together after dinner, each message hitting me square in the chest. Today's had been about God being involved in every moment of our lives. That no matter how haphazard this fallen world was, He was there, making a way, shielding those who took refuge in Him.

It was beyond humbling to look back on my life and see all the ways God had done just that, and to have His promise that He would keep right on doing it. I couldn't help but smile as I moved the attached ribbon bookmark to the next page for tomorrow.

Squeak-squeak. I tossed a glance at Chewie, who sat on the sofa, gnawing the head of his alpaca toy. Thankfully, he hadn't growled at me in months, and neither had Julia's mom. It turned out getting hit by that SUV wasn't such a bad thing. I had lost some business during recovery, but God had provided me with more than enough steady work since.

Even better was the success Julia's products were having at a local all-organic store, Nancy's Naturals. Julia had met Nancy at the business crawl last year, and once Conner and Mason had returned home for the summer and created the product packaging for Green Girl, Julia had been emboldened and decided to test the waters. With income from her products trickling in, and weary of missing the cleaning ministry, she'd given her Saturday client notice to find someone else.

If I hadn't known better, I would've thought Conner and Mason were happier with that decision than Julia. And those boys . . . I shook my head. They'd quickly become a huge part of my life. Earlier this year, I'd flown them down several times for weekend fishing trips and to spend time with Julia and her mom.

My attention veered back to Julia, adoration rendering me spellbound. Man, she loved her kids. She loved Brooke too.

My throat grew thick, and I studied my hands in my lap, working to swallow around the emotion that built too fast every time that realization struck. The guilt I'd carried all these years over my consequences affecting my daughter had been a relentless, smothering weight.

Until Julia.

She'd effortlessly stepped in as the mom Brooke had never had. And in Brooke's own private words to me, the mom she'd always wanted and prayed for.

The days I'd gone fishing with Conner and Mason, Julia had made plans with Brooke. Shopping, brunch, or just hanging out. Brooke had even cajoled Julia into going to several jewelry stores and getting a feel for the type of engagement ring she'd like.

Julia bent sideways, placing a bowl on the bottom rack. Her

shirt slipped, revealing her shoulder yet again. I sucked in a breath, all my nerve endings firing at once. With her hands covered in suds, she tried shrugging the top back in place, unsuccessfully.

I made my way over, clearing my throat. "Need some help?" Unable to resist, I leaned in, brushed her long hair back, and slowly pressed a kiss to the slope of her neck. Goose bumps pebbled her skin beneath my touch, and she turned her face, tipping her chin up, her heated gaze on me.

I lowered, pressing my mouth to hers. Her flawless lips, so warm and soft, completely yielded to mine. *Perfection.* She turned, and I gripped the counter on both sides of her, determined to keep some measure of restraint.

Her lips moved against mine, her soapy hands gliding a trail of heat until she reached my shoulders. All space between us vanished, my breath catching in my lungs, my stomach muscles contracting. Her fingers splayed in the back of my hair and tightened, pulling me closer, almost greedily.

My hands slid to her waist, and a shiver surged through my blood. I held her tighter, feeling her searing warmth and wanting *more, more, more.* A faint caution echoed in my mind, growing stronger. Using all the control I could muster, I loosened my hold, returning my grasp to the counter on each side of her hips. I perched forward, resting my forehead against her shoulder, my heartbeat still pounding. "I think God's getting tired of my prayers for self-control. What do you say to a redeye to Vegas?"

She pulled in a ragged breath. "There's actually a chapel in the French Quarter that does quickie weddings."

I shot straight to full attention, as though back in service and in the presence of a commanding officer.

"But only Monday through Thursday." One corner of her kiss-swollen lips lifted.

I narrowed my eye. "You're messing with me."

"I'm one-hundred-percent serious." Her teasing expression fell away, and she turned back to the sink, where the water still ran. "You're not the only one praying for restraint. But Kate would kill us. Or worse, cut off my beignet supply."

Kate had made us swear that when we got married, it would be in the courtyard of Beignets & Books. Julia and I had talked about all the things we both wanted in that event. Close family and friends only, Brother Buford officiating, and a short reception . . . for us anyway. Everyone else could party as long as they wanted.

We'd also agreed on a short engagement and buying a bigger house with enough room for everyone, especially if Brooke wanted to move in with us while she attended nursing school. And based on what was coming tonight, that meant the rest of the year was going to be busy.

This morning, while fishing on Bayou Sauvage with the boys, I'd asked for permission to marry her, which they'd happily given. And the one ring Julia had gone speechless over when visiting those jewelry stores with Brooke was now tucked in my pocket.

Julia turned off the faucet and grabbed a kitchen towel, drying her hands. "Why are you smiling like you know something I don't?" She quirked a brow, flirtation lacing her tone.

"Maybe because I do."

I pulled the ring box from my pocket and dropped to one knee.

ACKNOWLEDGMENTS

Thank you to my husband, Steve, for being my biggest supporter. I'll never forget that day back in 2010 when, out of the blue, I told you I wanted to write a book. You didn't blink. Just went right out and bought me a laptop to get started. Your steadfast encouragement all this time has been a gift from God.

To my sons, Steve Jr. and Alex, thank you for cheering me on through the hills and valleys of my writing career, and for putting up with my lame social media posts.

Thank you to my mom and sister, for reading my writing despite the fact that it's romance. ☺

To my soul sister and critique partner, Rachel Scott McDaniel, where do I begin? Thank you for making my writing better than it really is. You've enriched my life and taught me what the grace of God looks like on so many levels. I'm blessed to do life with you.

Thank you to my dear friends, who, as a bonus, are also my first readers: Joy Tiffany, Crissy Loughridge, Amy Watson, and Jill Wille. I'm forever grateful for your support and prayers.

Katie Powner, you are the tops! Thank you for helping me catch Raela's eye with that *Powner*ful (see what I did there) one-sheet. And thank you for always lending the best advice.

Bob Hostettler, thank you for being my literary agent and personal Obi-Wan. Your prayers and guidance are treasures.

Raela Schoenherr, thank you for your faith in this book and me, and taking a chance on a Southern gal who wanted to write fortysomething romances.

To my editors, Jessica Sharpe and Kate Deppe, I'm so grateful for your wise suggestions and heartfelt encouragement. Kate, your attention to detail is phenomenal. Thank you.

To the fabulous team at Bethany House Publishers (I wish I could name everyone), thank you for your hard work, for making this process easy and fun, and for your hearts in serving the Lord.

And thank you to the faithful Christian fiction community. Your enthusiasm, support, and comradery have touched my heart more than you could ever know.

If you enjoyed
JULIA MONROE BEGINS AGAIN,
read on
for an excerpt from

THE LOVE
SCRIPT

BY TONI SHILOH

Hollywood hair stylist Neveah loves making those in the spotlight shine. But when a photo of her and Hollywood heartthrob
Lamont goes viral for all the wrong reasons, they suddenly
find themselves in a fake relationship to save their careers. In a
world where nothing seems real, can Neveah be true to herself
. . . and her heart?

Available now
wherever books are sold.

Exiting the elevator, I made a right toward the mother-in-law suite. I rapped my knuckles on the door and heard a voice telling me to "Come in." Only darkness greeted me. Ms. Rosie lay in bed, her form hard to make out since the blackout blinds concealed all sources of natural light.

"Ms. Rosie?" I called softly.

Her face turned toward me, showing a furrowed brow and grimacing lips. "I'm so sorry, Nevaeh. I meant to cancel our appointment."

Her voice sounded thready to my ears. My stomach churned. "Are you okay? Should I go find your son?"

"No, please don't bother him." She tried to raise her arm, but it dropped limply onto her duvet cover.

"Does he know you're sick?" Was it the cancer? Had she relapsed? Did she need to go to the doctor? Get a scan or whatever it was medical professionals did to ensure cancer hadn't returned?

In all my time pampering Ms. Rosie, I'd never seen her look so bad. Then again, she'd canceled appointments before. Maybe moments like this had been the reason why.

"He does. It's just a stomach bug. I don't want you to get sick, too, so go." She turned her head the other way, a low moan filling the room.

I bit my lip. "I can make you some soup if he's not around. Is he on set?"

She nodded, groaning at the movement.

That was it. I couldn't leave her alone. "I'm making you some soup." From my understanding, Lamont Booker didn't have a personal chef. I think Ms. Rosie did most of the cooking, and she was in no position to make any meals today.

"You don't have to. I'll be fine," she murmured weakly.

Yeah, and I was the leading lady in the hottest new romantic comedy. Wait, no, it was Sandra Bullock. I had to give her two thumbs up for proving women in their fifties still had it. #Girlpower

"It'll be no trouble. Promise." I slid a hand on my hip, trying to show my sass instead of the worry snaking through me.

"Thank you, Nevaeh."

"Anything for you, Ms. Rosie." I closed her door quietly, leaving my suitcase outside the entrance.

Ever since I'd first seen Lamont Booker's gorgeous kitchen with its white marble counters and double oven, I'd wanted to create a meal fit for a queen. And since the Sexiest Man Alive was a prince in Hollywood, his mom surely fit the bill.

I slid my hands along the ridiculously large island that could seat five people comfortably before opening the stainless-steel fridge. Organic fresh fruits and vegetables gleamed in their open containers while sparkling water and choice cuts of meat filled the shelves. Of course Mr. A-Lister wouldn't have anything highly processed. After walking through his huge pantry, I had a better idea of what I had to work with. Now to find the perfect recipe.

After perusing BonAPPetit on my phone, I found the perfect chicken-and-noodle soup that called for enough ginger and garlic to evict any germs from one's body. This kitchen had every appliance, but it was the gas range stove I wanted to get my hands on. I washed my hands, then got to laying out the ingredients.

Before long, a fragrant aroma filled the kitchen. While the soup simmered, I brought an herbal tea to Ms. Rosie's room. The thermometer confirmed she was fever-free, but she still looked pitiful in her dark room.

"Do you want me to open the blinds?"

"Please don't."

I wanted to argue, but who was I to dictate her environment when she was obviously under the weather? Back in the kitchen,

I stirred the large pot with a wooden spoon. I reached for the egg noodles and—

"What are you doing?"

I yelped, and noodles flew everywhere.

Lamont Booker folded his arms over his impressive chest, glaring at the pasta scattered across his marble countertops.

"Why are you cooking in my house?" He glowered at the mess, as if the spilled food would have the answers to his questions.

"Ms. Rosie's sick, and she forgot to cancel our appointment. I couldn't just leave her here all alone, so I made soup." My words rushed out as I struggled for air.

His gaze rose to meet mine, and I drew in a ragged breath. Whew, I could see why *People* had dropped the coveted title on him.

"What do you mean she's sick?" Every word was elongated, making the question more pronounced.

I blinked. "You don't know? She told me you knew." She'd hoodwinked me!

"How sick?" he demanded.

I took a half step back. Lamont Booker intimidated me by just being *Lamont Booker*. This brooding, towering version made me want to hide behind the pantry door until he turned back into the swoony version I was used to seeing. But I wasn't one to cower, so I tilted my chin up. "She said it's just a stomach bug, but her blinds are closed, and she's lying in bed, obviously in pain."

He flew out of the kitchen, his footfalls pounding against the steps. I winced, then looked at the messy countertops. I found a dishrag and wiped up the pasta, then found a broom to take care of the pieces that had landed on the hardwood floor.

A few minutes later, he stalked back into the kitchen. I froze midsweep.

He stopped in front of the farmhouse sink and ran a hand over his bald head. "I'm sorry for startling you earlier."

"No problem. I was in my own world anyway." Dreaming of owning a place so luxurious. Wouldn't that show my parents that Nevaeh Richards wasn't *just* a stylist? They thought my career beneath me and the education they'd provided. Newsflash: I loved what I did. Even if it didn't live up to their standards or pay enough to get me a kitchen like Lamont Booker's.

"I appreciate you taking care of her. She said you've been checking in on her since you arrived."

"Of course." I dumped the food into the stainless-steel trash can, then put the broom back in the supply closet I'd rummaged through and rinsed out the rag I'd found to clean with.

"I added the noodles, so the soup will be ready in about five minutes. After that, you can pour her a bowl."

He opened his wallet, but I held up a hand. "I didn't do her hair, so you don't owe me anything."

"But you cooked. Cleaned too." He pointed to the gleaming countertops to emphasize his point.

"I don't charge people for helping them. That's just wrong." I blew out a breath. "Besides, the whole point of helping is doing without expecting something in return." I slid my hands into my pockets, wishing Lamont Booker had come home a little later—so late I could've given Ms. Rosie her soup and left unnoticed.

Other than the day he'd hired me and the time we spoke to discuss my fees, our conversations weren't the lengthy types. A greeting here or there. A nod in passing if he looked busy. We didn't normally just stand in his gorgeous kitchen and chat about his mother's health, unless it was hair-care related.

Now he stood before me in a white tee and gray joggers, and I wanted to swoon. Well, just a little. Okay, maybe enough to have a fangirl moment and ask if he'd sign something. Though what I didn't know. It's not like I carried paper around for such a thing. Although, living near Hollywood certainly afforded me opportunities for star sightings. But if I wanted to be taken seriously in this business, I couldn't go up to a celebrity and act uncouth.

"Then thank you very much for taking time to look after her." He smiled.

"Anytime." I walked out of the kitchen before I lost my composure. Surely, I had some kind of paper in my styling case that had space for a Lamont Booker signature.

"Oh, I saw your case upstairs. Let me grab that for you."

Right. I nodded. As soon as he was out of sight, I internalized a scream and fanned my face. Thank the Lord I didn't have to talk to that man on a regular basis. I was better than this. I saw A-list actors and celebrities all the time. Just the other day, I was behind one at a stop sign. I probably wouldn't have even realized it if it hadn't been for the vanity plate on his BMW.

The sound of pattering steps greeted my ears, and I blew out a breath. "Thanks for grabbing that." Time to exit stage left while my inner fan's mouth remained sealed with duct tape.

"Sure. I'll walk you out."

I barely kept my brow from rising. Since when did he walk me out? Was this when he'd lean in close and tell me never to step foot in his kitchen again? To leave his glorious gas range stove to him?

Instead, we walked in silence until he opened the front door. "Thanks again, Nevaeh."

"Of course. I hope Ms. Rosie feels better." Would it be impertinent for me to ask him to text me an update on her?

"Me too." For a moment, his mouth drew down and deep groves appeared, and my earlier thoughts on cancer returned, flooding my brain.

"She'll be okay, right?" I asked softly.

His gaze met mine, and he nodded. "She will."

I gulped and turned away. My foot slipped off the step that had existed since the house was built, but apparently my brain had forgotten, despite the many times I'd stepped down before.

My mouth opened to let out a panicked squeal, only a strong arm swooped around my stomach and tugged me close.

"You okay?" he murmured.

"Yeah," I breathed, heart hammering against my overalls.

He let me go, and my face heated as he lowered the suitcase. Obviously if I couldn't see a step, I couldn't drag a rolling suitcase behind me. Instead of thanking him for keeping my face from kissing the pavement, I pulled the handle up and walked away in embarrassment.

No wonder he was the Sexiest Man Alive. Even my pulse had reacted on instinct, and my stomach felt branded by his touch. Once again, I thanked God that I didn't have to see him on a daily basis. I'd be an absolute wreck.

Rebekah Millet is a Cascade Award and ACFW First Impressions Award–winning author of contemporary Christian romance novels. A New Orleans native, she grew up on beignets and café au lait, and loves infusing her colorful culture into her stories. Her husband is an answer to prayer, who puts up with her rearranging furniture and being a serial plant killer. Her two sons keep her laughing and share in her love of strawberry Pop-Tarts. You can find Rebekah on all social media platforms and at rebekahmillet.com.

Sign Up for Rebekah's Newsletter

Keep up to date with Rebekah's latest news on book releases and events by signing up for her email list at the link below.

FOLLOW REBEKAH ON SOCIAL MEDIA

Rebekah Millet - Author   @rebekahmillet   @rebekahmillet

RebekahMillet.com